SPY AWAY HOME

Book 10 of the NEVER SAY SPY series

Diane Henders

SPY AWAY HOME

ISBN 978-1-927460-30-6

Copyright © 2015 Diane Henders

PEBKAC Publishing Inc.
P.O. Box 67, Station Main
Qualicum Beach, BC   V9K 1S7
www.pebkacpublishing.com

This book is a work of fiction. Names, characters, places and incidents are either the product of the author's imagination or are used fictitiously, and any resemblance to actual persons, living or dead, business establishments, events or locales is entirely coincidental.

First printed in paperback September 2015 by PEBKAC Publishing Inc.
v.6.1

Books in the NEVER SAY SPY series:

More books coming! For a current list, please visit
www.dianehenders.com
Or sign up for my New Book Notification list at
www.dianehenders.com/books

Since You Asked...

People frequently ask if my protagonist, Aydan Kelly, is really me.

Yeah, you got me. These novels are an autobiography of my secret life as a government agent, working with highly-classified computer technology... Oh, wait, what's that? You want the *truth*? Um, you do realize fiction writers get paid to lie, don't you?

...well, shit, that's not nearly as much fun. It's also a long story.

I swore I'd never write fiction. "Too personal," I said. "People read novels and automatically assume the author is talking about him/herself."

Well, apparently I lied about the fiction-writing part. One day a story sprang into my head and wouldn't leave. The only way to get it out was to write it down. So I did.

But when I wrote that first book, I never intended to show it to anyone, so I created a character that looked like me just to thumb my nose at the stereotype. I've always had a defective sense of humour, and this time it turned around and bit me in the ass.

Because after I'd written the third novel, I realized I actually wanted other people to read my books. And when I went back to change my main character to *not* look like me, my beta readers wouldn't let me. They rose up against me and said, "No! Aydan is a tall woman with long red hair and brown eyes. End of discussion!"

Jeez, no wonder readers get the idea that authors write about themselves. So no, I'm not Aydan Kelly. I just look like her.

Oh, and the town of Silverside and all secret technologies are products of my imagination. If I'm abducted by grim-faced men wearing dark glasses, or if I die in an unexplained fiery car crash, you'll know I accidentally came a little too close to the truth.

I hope you enjoy the book!

For Phill

Thank you for being my technical advisor and the most tolerant husband ever. Much love!

To my beta readers/editors, especially Carol H., Judy B., and Phill B., with gratitude: Many thanks for all your time and effort in catching my spelling and grammar errors, telling me when I screwed up the plot or the characters' motivations, and generally keeping me honest.

To Rick and Sandy H. at Hand Crafted Images: Your talent makes my covers extra-special, and your sense of humour makes photo sessions fun even for a camera-hater like me. Thank you!

To Steve A. and the staff at The Shooting Edge: Thank you for lending us your excellent facilities for our cover photo sessions. You guys rock!

To everyone else, respectfully:
Canadian English is an unholy hybrid of British and American English, so I apologize if spellings in this book look odd to you. But if you find typos, please send an email to errors@dianehenders.com. Mistakes drive me nuts, and I'm sorry if any slipped through. Please let me know what the error is, and on which page (or at which position in e-versions). I'll make sure it gets fixed as soon as possible. Thanks!

CHAPTER 1

I inhaled the pleasant tang of gun oil and smiled at my little Glock 26, disassembled on the kitchen table in front of me. "There you go, baby," I cooed. "All cleaned up after that nasty humidity. Isn't that better?"

My grin widened as I flipped my ponytail over my shoulder and leaned back in my chair to indulge in a lazy stretch, soaking up the comfort of my country home. After living in a canvas tent in the B.C. rainforest for the past four months, I'd almost forgotten how wonderful it was to be warm and dry.

Blue Alberta sky filled the window over the sink, and the morning sunbeams caressed the scuffed hardwood floor. My ancient CD player shuffled its contents before filling the room with the lively notes of Louis Armstrong's trumpet.

Letting out a sigh of pure contentment I bent to the uncomplicated task of reassembling my pistol, belting out 'Mack The Knife' along with Louis despite my complete lack of vocal talent.

The phone rang as I was finishing the assembly and I grunted annoyance. Ignoring the summons, I did a final check of the slide's action and reached for my soft polishing cloth.   Whoever it was, they could damn well leave a message. This peaceful morning was all mine.

A thunderous impact shivered my front door.

I leaped to my feet and slapped the Glock's magazine into place, sucking in an adrenaline-charged breath. Lucky I'd reinforced the lock...

A shotgun blast hammered my ears and the wood around the lock exploded into splinters.

Shit!

Time slowed. Everything sprang into hard-edged focus.

I jacked a bullet into the Glock's chamber as the shattered door swung wide under a second kick. The shooter lunged through the doorway, his shotgun swivelling and rising to find me.

My pistol snapped up. Two shots kicked my hands.

The intruder staggered, his face slackening under a brand-new hole in his forehead. His body thudded to the floor with an impact I felt through my feet but couldn't hear through my gunshot-deafened ears.

He lay still.

A slow crimson puddle oozed from under the sprawled body, creeping over my doormat to dribble into the grout lines of my tiled entry floor.

I stood frozen open-mouthed, my gun still trained on him.

The phone's continued ringing was a tinny thread of sound almost lost in the bulging cottony quiet of my overloaded hearing. Louis Armstrong's gravelly voice sang a macabre accompaniment. My answering machine played its outgoing message, adding to the jumble of sound.

I worked my jaw a couple of times in an attempt to get

my ears functioning again. Prying my left hand loose from the Glock, I kept the body covered one-handed while I tottered over to the CD player and silenced it.

The voice emanating from my answering machine barely overcame the high-pitched buzzing that was replacing my deafness. "Aydan, I've been thinking of you. Pick up if you're there!"

I didn't recognize the tense voice, but the code words made me draw a breath of relief. My surveillance crew checking up on me.

Still left-handed, I picked up the handset and thumbed the Talk button.

"Hi." My voice came out ridiculously calm and level. "I'm here. I'm okay."

"Thank God!" The nameless analyst on the other end let out a whoosh of breath, and I spared him a moment of sympathy. He must have had only seconds to spot the incoming threat on the hidden surveillance cameras that monitored my front porch. "Thank God you're okay," he repeated.

"Yeah, I'm fine. Thanks." I still sounded utterly emotionless. "Send me a clean-up crew ASAP, would you please?"

The analyst drew a deep breath before speaking with clipped efficiency. "Dispatching them now. They should be there in about twenty minutes. Glad you're okay."

"Yeah, I'm fine," I repeated mindlessly. "Thanks. 'Bye."

I clicked off the handset, still staring at the intruder over my pistol sights. He hadn't moved. A puddle of urine spread to meet the blood, feathering swirls of red into the clear liquid.

"I think I got him," I said aloud, and a shrill hysterical giggle leaked from my lips. Smothering it, I eased my trembling gun hand down.

Inhale.

Exhale.

Nice and slow. Just like ocean waves.

I couldn't tear my gaze away from the dead man. The shotgun still lay in his outflung hand. His finger was too damn close to the trigger.

Heart thudding, I took one slow step after another until I was close enough to nudge the shotgun out of his grasp with my foot.

His hand flopped over and I leaped back, my gun jerking up to aim at him again. Panting, I clutched the Glock in a white-knuckled grip.

After a long moment I shook my head and forced out a cracked laugh. "He's dead, for fucksakes," I quavered. "Take a pill, woman."

Lacking any pills to take, I drew another deep breath instead and tucked my gun into the front of my jeans with shaking hands.

The slowly-expanding pool of body fluids jolted me back to reality.

"Shit!" I yelped, and sprang for the rag-bag I kept under the kitchen sink.

A few moments later I rose from my makeshift dam. The shallow gory puddle had turned my boots into islands beside the door, but at least I'd stopped the mess before it got to the hardwood or trickled under the baseboards.

"Asshole," I growled, eyeing the bullet holes and blood spatter on my wall before scowling at the corpse again. "What the hell's your problem, anyway?"

Nothing like shooting first and asking questions afterward. Another hysterical giggle welled up.

I drew a deep breath.

Do something productive.

Keeping my breathing slow and controlled, I willed the tremors out of my hands and went to collect a pair of blue nitrile gloves. I pulled them on with a pang, wistfully recalling the days when my only messy jobs had involved paint or engine grease.

Crouching, I reached across the puddle to rifle through the intruder's pockets. My search yielded a set of car keys, a worn but fat wallet, and a perverse sense of satisfaction at the placement of my second bullet in his chest.

One to the head; one to the heart. Nothing wrong with my snap-shooting reflexes.

I let my shaking legs drop me to the floor outside the dam of rags, and sat cross-legged while I perused the contents of the wallet.

Holy shit, that was a serious wad of cash.

The twenty-five one-hundred-dollar bills were so new they stuck together when I counted them. A twenty, ten, and five looked as though they'd been around the block a few times. I frowned at the body. Who the hell carries over two thousand bucks in cash?

Time to find out.

I extracted a driver's license bearing the name Drake Mallard, and snickered in spite of myself. Either he'd been trying to be funny when he chose his alias or his parents had a twisted sense of humour.

The smile slid off my lips at the sight of the only other item in the wallet. My blue-clad fingers trembled as I raised the photograph to eye level. Brown eyes bracketed by crows-feet looked back at me from under long, mostly-still-red hair.

Shit.

I had really been hoping this was a random home invasion. No such luck.

I turned the photo over to see 'Arlene Widdenback, 47, 5'-10", 160 lbs' scrawled across the back, and I let out a breath I hadn't realized I'd been holding.

At least it didn't say 'Aydan Kelly'. So my cover identity was still intact.

My recovering ears caught the sound of a vehicle slowing on the gravel road and I jerked to my feet to peer out the screen door.

Frantic dismay clutched my throat, driving my voice up half an octave. "Damn-damn-*shitfuckdamn*!"

Dropping the wallet and photo, I jammed my feet into my boots. The treads slid greasily on the blood-slicked tiles as I flung on my jacket and zipped it over my gun. A couple of kicks at the dead man's legs and some more frenzied swearing allowed me to close the remains of the interior door, but that would make its damage even more obvious from the outside.

Shit!

I swung the buckshot-riddled door open again and hurried out onto my porch, letting the screen door slap closed behind me as a familiar 4x4 half-ton rolled to a stop in my driveway.

Bounding down my front steps, I jumped the last stair to land in the soggy April-brown grass beside my walk. My bloody footprints might not be obvious against the rust-coloured paint on the stairs, but the pale concrete sidewalk was a different story.

I waved and summoned a face-cracking smile while I hurried toward the truck, surreptitiously shuffling my feet between strides to clean my boots.

A lean figure topped by a cowboy hat emerged from the truck, his handsome face creasing into a smile that crinkled the weathered lines around his sky-blue eyes.

"Aydan!" His smile widened and he swept me into a hug.

Shit! The Glock was small, but he was sure to feel its hardness pressed between us.

My brain spun its wheels in frantic thought. How could I explain the hard spot? A small but rigid waist pouch? An industrial-strength hernia belt?

My mind went completely blank as he stepped back, still smiling.

His hands slid up my arms to clasp my shoulders warmly, and my relief spilled over into a broad smile of my own. Thank God for my bulky jacket and his big-ass rodeo belt buckle. He mustn't have felt my gun.

"Hi, Tom," I chirped far too brightly. "It's great to see you!"

"It's great to see you, too. Welcome home." He relinquished my shoulders to take one of my blue-gloved hands, turning it over with a grin. "Is this the new fashion out in B.C.?"

"Uh... I was getting ready to do some painting," I stammered, desperately hoping there was no visible blood. Retrieving my hand, I pulled off the gloves and stuffed them in my pockets. "How did you know I was here?" I added. "I just got home last night. I didn't think anybody knew I was back."

He chuckled. "I wasn't actually expecting to find you

here, but while you were away I've been driving up to check your place whenever I'm out. I was just coming home from town, so I popped by. I saw the gate open and a strange car in the drive so I thought I'd better see who it was."

"Oh. Uh, thanks... you're such a good neighbour..."

I shot a wild-eyed glance at the rust-pocked Cavalier parked with its front wheels half off the gravelled drive. Didn't that dipshit know you should hide your car if you were going to shoot somebody? Goddamn amateurs.

I sucked in a breath and blurted the first explanation that came to mind. "Um... that's my nephew's car. He just dropped by..."

My words trailed off as Tom's forehead creased in puzzlement. "I thought you said you didn't have any brothers or sisters," he said. "How could you have a nephew?"

"He's, um, not really my nephew; I just call him that..." I snatched a lame explanation out of my ass and flung it down between us. "He's actually the son of a close friend who, um... died a few years ago..."

Tom's lean features softened in sympathy. Thank God.

"...and I kind of adopted him as my honorary nephew," I finished.

Hell, what if he wanted to meet the fictitious nephew? If he moved even slightly to the side he'd be able to see my wrecked interior door through the screen. And since he owned a shotgun himself, he'd instantly recognize the damage of close-range buckshot.

I glanced involuntarily toward the house and gulped down panic at the sight of the dead man's foot, a dark lump behind the screen.

"Um, he's kind of a... an odd kid," I embellished

frantically as Tom began to speak again. Talking over his words, I continued, "He won't stay long. I was just going to give him a beer and chat with him for a while before he goes. There was no beer in the house so I was going to get one from the fridge in the garage. I mean, not that I'd let him drink and drive or anything..."

Shit, don't over-explain. I bit off my babble and went for a rueful shrug. "He's probably just here to ask me for money. Kids."

"I'm sorry to hear he's having problems," Tom said. His blue gaze searched my face. "Do you feel safe with him? You seem nervous."

I managed a laugh. "Of course I'm not nervous. He's my nephew."

"Would you like me to talk to him?" Tom gave me an understanding smile. "My son Cory went through a messed-up phase quite a few years ago, too. It's pretty common for teens whose mothers have passed away. Maybe I could help."

"Oh, thanks, that's really kind of you," I gabbled. "But I don't want to bother you, and I don't think he'd appreciate it. I'm just going to have a quick visit with him and then he'll be on his way, just like always."

He assessed me, those blue eyes seeing too much. "If you're sure you're okay."

"Fine, thanks!" I gave him another too-perky smile.

He relaxed, rocking back on his heels to hook his thumbs in the front pockets of his jeans. He nodded toward the addition on the end of my garage with a smile. "So how's the garage work going? Have you got your lift in yet?"

Shit. I had been so excited about the addition that would

house my new hydraulic car lift that I'd talked his ear off about it before Christmas. He'd know something was wrong for sure if I brushed off the subject now.

I forced another smile. "Not yet. It's still in the crates. The in-floor heating system is laid out, but the floor's not poured. I thought it would be easiest to do the footings for my lift posts at the same time as the floor, but that was before I knew I was going to be gone for four months. Even if I got it all poured tomorrow, I'd still have to wait for the concrete to cure before I could put the lift on it. It'll probably be June before it's done. That pisses me off, because now I'll have to do my spring oil changes the old-fashioned way with my ramps and jack stands."

Hoping that had been enough chatter to allay his suspicions, I racked my brain for a way to encourage him to leave.

"Well, let me know when you're ready for help getting it set up. You'll likely need a few strong bodies. I can call some of my friends..." He shifted position as if to move toward the garage.

I calculated the sight lines, my pulse rate skyrocketing. From that angle he'd likely notice that the dark lump on my doormat had a leg attached to it.

I sidestepped in an attempt to block his view. "Thanks, but I don't think it'll be too big a job." My voice came out sounding tight, and I cleared my throat and tried again, making a sweeping gesture toward the garage in the hope of distracting him with the movement. "You can see how high the roof is, and I've got anchor points in the joists. I'll get a block and tackle on it so hopefully I won't need an army."

"Oh, good idea." He smiled, looking perfectly comfortable and ready to stand there all day gabbing.

The thump-swish of escalating blood pressure surged rhythmically in my eardrums and I suppressed both the urge to scream and the mental image of my head exploding under the strain.

I dragged my lips into one more smile. "Well, it was great to see you," I said brightly. "I'd better go grab that beer now."

He hesitated, then took the not-too-subtle hint with a nod. "Okay, I won't keep you, then."

I drew a silent breath of relief as he turned toward his truck.

He wheeled suddenly to look back at me and my heart kicked my ribs hard enough to rattle my teeth.

"Aydan..." he began.

"Yes?" I smiled as casually as it was possible to do with my molars grinding.

"Would you like to come over for dinner tonight? It would be nice to have a visit and catch up. It's been a while."

God, anything! Just get the hell out of my yard!

Desperation lent a squeaky note to my voice. "Oh, that sounds lovely! Thanks! What time would you like me to come?"

His slow easy smile made me clamp my teeth on my tongue to prevent myself from shrieking 'spit it out and leave!'

"Why don't you come around five?" he said. "I'll look forward to it."

"Thanks! Me, too." My smile hurt every muscle in my face. "See you then."

He headed back to the truck with his leisurely long-legged stride and I balled my fists in my pockets.

Hurry up, goddammit! Get the hell out of here!

"See you." He tipped his hat and swung into the cab.

I smiled hard and offered a wave that I hoped looked friendly as he drove down my lane and turned onto the road toward his farm.

When his truck vanished behind the trees that lined the creek I threw back my head and screamed at the inoffensive sky.

"*Argh!* Shit, shit, *goddamn SHIT!*"

CHAPTER 2

Finished my temper tantrum, I stomped back to my house and hesitated at the porch steps. Should I try to clean up the bloody footprints before the cleanup crew got here, or would my efforts only make their job harder?

A sudden thought tensed my shoulders. What if the analyst routed this up the chain of command and Stemp overrode my request?

Oh, God, he wouldn't.

Would he?

Surely he'd only made me do it myself last time because he was afraid the bad guys had me under surveillance.

I scowled and kicked at the bottom step. He had probably watched the analysts' camera footage and laughed his ass off at the sight of me labouring to scrape up half-frozen blood in the middle of winter. Bastard.

If he cancelled the cleanup crew this time, I'd drag this damn body over to his house and push it through his mail slot piece by piece.

A growl escaped my throat at the recollection that Stemp had no mail slot. Fine. I'd take it over there and shove it up his...

The crunch of tires on gravel rocketed my heart into my

throat, but the vehicle slowing at my driveway wasn't Tom's truck returning. As a dark blue cube van rolled through my gate, two thoughts occurred in quick succession.

I'd closed and locked the gate behind me last night, so how did Mallard get in?

And what if the van held more assassins?

I sprang up the stairs. Letting the spring hinges smack the screen door shut behind me, I leaped over the body and flung myself into a crouch behind my kitchen counter. Glock in hand, I pressed against the cabinets and waited. This cupboard held my pots and pans. They might deflect bullets.

My heart hammered. Oh shit, there were so many ways this could go wrong.

If they were assassins, I'd know when the first of the bullets ripped through the walls. Or through me.

But what if they were innocent furnace-cleaners or something, lost and looking for one of the neighbours' places? They couldn't have missed seeing me dash in here, and the blood-soaked body was in plain sight through the screen door.

The phone rang.

Over six feet away. I'd have to scuttle unprotected across the open space.

Too afraid to leave the dubious shelter of my cookware, I sent a snarl in the direction of the still-ringing phone. "No shit, you guys! I *know* there's somebody coming up to my house!"

The sound of footsteps on my porch made me hunker lower.

My answering machine picked up and an unfamiliar male voice spoke. "Your cleaners are waiting outside."

I eased out a breath. Smart. Nothing incriminating on

tape, but at least now I knew those weren't assassins in the van.

Well, I was pretty sure.

Almost a hundred percent certain...

I eased my head around the corner of the cabinet, ready to jerk back to relative safety at the first hint of a threat.

The movement caught the eye of a bulky coverall-clad man peeking through my screen with equal caution. The corner of his lips quirked up.

"Agent Kelly? We won't shoot if you don't," he offered.

I let out a breath and rose to totter over. "I'll hold you to that. Come on in." I nodded toward the body. "I guess I don't have to tell you where to look."

"Guess not." He jerked his chin at his silent companion and they donned disposable booties, gloves, and hairnets before stepping over the body. Lowering a bulky backpack to the floor, they extracted a body bag. A few minutes later the remains of Drake Mallard were safely stowed in the back of their van along with Mallard's shotgun, and the cleanup commenced.

Apparently the spokesman for the pair, the first man drawled, "Guess you surprised the hell outta him. Nice shooting." He bent to extract cleaning products from his backpack and continued, "He had two shells in the magazine and a spent one in the chamber. Didn't even have time to pump in a new one."

"Hmph." I shucked off my jacket and sank onto a kitchen chair, frowning. "Yeah, that's a little weird. He blew off the lock and kicked in the door a second later, but pump-actions are quick. He should've had a fresh shell in the chamber by the time he got in."

The man shrugged and turned away to join his mute companion beside the grisly puddle. "Nice when they're dumb."

"Huh. Yeah." I eyed the proceedings curiously. "Do you mind if I watch?"

"Knock yourself out."

I observed them in silence for a while before speaking. "So you're armed?"

"Uh-huh," he replied without looking up.

I pulled my gun-cleaning paraphernalia toward me. "Okay, good. Then I'm going to clean and reload while you're here. 'Cause I'm not going to have my gun out of commission again for a good long time. And I won't be listening to any more music, either."

I rushed through a cursory second cleaning, my still-ringing ears straining for the sound of tires on gravel outside. Or footsteps.

Or God knew what. A paragliding ninja, or, hell, a radio-controlled exploding goose.

Right on cue, a vee of Canada geese winged overhead, their distant honking carrying through the screen door. Usually I enjoyed the wild lonely sound of their spring migration.

"Fuck," I muttered.

The speaking half of the duo glanced up. "Everything okay?"

I blew out a sigh and pushed the reloaded magazine into the Glock. "Yeah." I rose and tucked the gun back into my waistband. Even my ankle holster felt a little too far away at the moment.

"Here, you'll probably want to take these with you, too," I added as I pulled the nitrile gloves out of my pockets and handed them over.

He accepted them with a professional nod and a narrow-eyed look at my jacket. "You rub off any blood inside those pockets?"

"No idea." I passed it to him and watched while he examined it with his special light.

"Clean." He handed it back. "We'll do your boots, too. Anything else?"

"I was wearing the gloves when I searched him, and I don't think I touched anything else."

He grimaced. "Yeah, I already picked one of your long hairs off the corpse. You ever think of wearing a hairnet?"

"Not around my house. But next time I have less than a second to kill a guy I'll try to remember to put one on."

He snorted either amusement or disgust, and I added, "You probably saw the bloody footprints on the porch, but I walked to the right of the sidewalk so there'll be blood in the grass, too." I hesitated. "I don't know if it's worth bothering about, though. There's probably still a bunch of blood there from the last guy."

That was enough to startle words out of the silent partner. "There was another guy?" he demanded.

Okay, now I knew why he'd been keeping his mouth shut. Despite his bulk and stature, he sounded exactly like Elmer Fudd.

I held my face under rigid control. "Yeah. End of December. I did a fast cleanup, but all I could really do was scrape up the half-frozen blood and rinse the porch. There are probably still bullets embedded in the lawn, too."

The spokesman sighed and returned to scrubbing grout. "We'll clean the porch and do the best we can with the rest."

"Thanks, guys." I bestowed my warmest smile on them. "You have no idea how much I appreciate this. How about some fresh chocolate chip cookies?"

They both brightened, and I began to assemble ingredients. The soothing routine of baking and the mouthwatering scent of warm vanilla and chocolate calmed some of my ravelled nerves. A half-dozen cookies still hot from the oven along with a tall glass of milk completed my therapy.

While the cleanup crew worked outside I turned my attention to the damaged door and wall. A few trips to my shed procured some two-by-fours and a piece of plywood big enough to replace the door, as well as the necessary tools and materials for repairing the bullet holes.

Some time later I was mudding my drywall patches when a rap on my new plywood panel made me twitch so violently I dropped the taping knife.

A male voice called, "We're done out here."

"Shit." I eyed the glob of drywall compound on my freshly-cleaned tiles before raising my voice. "Hang on; I'll be right there. I'll have to go around back."

When I rounded the corner of the house, the muscle-bound Elmer Fudd was sliding into the driver's seat of the Cavalier and the spokesman was already behind the wheel of the cube van.

I trotted over to the driver's-side window. "Thanks again. Here are some more cookies for the road." I handed over a bag. "Anything I need to know?"

"Nope. Thanks." He eyed the bag appreciatively before tucking it into the console beside him. "Everything's cleaned up, and we'll file a report once we finish with the car and the body. Oh, and we retrieved six bullets from your lawn. That sound about right?"

I sighed. "No idea. There could've been up to ten, but some probably lodged in the body."

"Jesus." The driver frowned with professional disapproval. "Ever hear of overkill?"

"I wasn't the shooter. Long story," I added as his eyebrows rose.

He cast an appraising glance around my isolated farmyard. "You going to be okay out here?"

I shrugged. "As much as I ever am, I guess. Nothing short of a tank is coming through that plywood tonight. I've got two-by-four crossmembers screwed into the frame behind it. But if anybody really wants in, they'll be through the windows in two seconds or less."

He offered me a sympathetic grimace and a semi-salute. "Good luck, then."

"Thanks."

I watched them drive away before trotting up the lane to lock the gate behind them and change the combination, my usual appreciation of the open country spoiled by a nervous tingle that felt like a target on my back.

By the time I had finished the drywall patches and dragged the shot-up door to my shed, I was almost looking forward to Tom's free meal.

But not quite.

Glancing at my watch, I let out a dismal sigh.

As far as I knew Tom was a good cook. He made great chili, anyway. But the thought of holding onto my cover all evening while avoiding anything that might be construed as an expression of personal interest in him...

I sighed again.

If only Kane and Hellhound were here. A meal with them would be full of easy camaraderie and black humour about the inconvenience of dead bodies. No need to conceal my weapon or my reaction to killing a man.

Hell. I'd killed another man. Two in a week. That was absolutely fucking sick. It had been them or me, but still...

I put that thought away to examine later and resumed my pity party with another sigh.

If Kane and Hellhound were here I'd be able to relax instead of twitching and grabbing for my gun every time the house creaked. But no, dammit; right now they were laughing in the California sun, cruising the highway with their knees in the breeze or relaxing at a roadside restaurant with good food and cold beer.

"Suck it up," I said aloud, and went to put on clean clothes.

Hovering in front of my full-length mirror, I eyed my reflection anxiously and readjusted my waist holster. It didn't matter what I did; if Tom decided to hug me when I wasn't wearing my jacket, there was no way he'd miss my gun even with my sweatshirt pulled over top.

And I couldn't object to a hug after letting him hug me this afternoon. Besides, he was such a nice guy. I'd feel terrible if I hurt his feelings, especially since I'd hurt him so many times before.

"This is a really bad idea," I told my reflection. "I should just call and tell him I've got a headache. Or the stomach flu. Or leprosy or something."

"Well, shit-for-brains," my reflection replied with a scowl, "If you were going to do that, you should've done it earlier. Now it's nearly five and he'll have supper on already. And anyway, he'll know you're lying."

"But it might have come on really fast," I argued feebly.

My reflection fixed me with a skeptical gaze, and I sighed and turned away.

Pacing and muttering, I considered my options. Waist holster, risking almost-certain detection?

Ankle holster? Better concealment but not as accessible. And I'd needed every instant this morning.

Leave my gun behind entirely?

Never in a million years.

My steps slowed as another thought hit me.

Drake Mallard hadn't had a personal vendetta. I'd never seen him before, and if he needed my photo with a description written on the back, he obviously didn't know me. And the crisp two-and-a-half grand in his beat-up wallet told me somebody else was probably pulling his strings.

If that 'somebody' saw my car in Tom's driveway, would they shoot up Tom's place to get to me?

"Okay, that's it. I can't do this," I said to my disapproving reflection.

"You're a secret agent, dipshit," my unsympathetic alter-ego snarled. "Figure something out."

"I'm not an agent, I'm just a bookkeeper..." I trailed off, my spine straightening. That wasn't true anymore.

"Okay, fine!" I snapped, and turned away to make my preparations.

CHAPTER 3

When Tom opened his door to my knock, his smile of welcome faltered.

"I brought dessert," I volunteered, and proffered the last of the chocolate chip cookies.

"Uh... thanks..." His smile came back with a hint of a tease as he accepted the paper plate. "Come in. But you're giving me some mixed messages here." He nodded toward the shotgun cradled in the crook of my arm. "Are you going to shoot me if you don't like my cooking?"

I laughed and followed his welcoming gesture into the warmth of his house. "No, I promise not to shoot you," I assured him. I laid the gun on the floor with its barrel pointed in a safe direction and added, "It was such a nice evening I decided to walk over. I went down by the creek and through the woods, but I wasn't sure if that cougar was still around from last summer so I thought I'd better carry the shotgun just in case."

Not to mention that sneaking through the bush allowed me to arrive at his place unseen. And if we got attacked anyway, I'd have a plausible explanation for being armed. With any luck I wouldn't have to pull my Glock.

"Good thinking. I like that you're comfortable with guns

and know how to use them," he replied with a smile as he took my coat.

I eased out a breath as he turned away to hang it up on the wooden coat pegs behind the door. The shotgun had nicely forestalled the question of a hug, too. Bonus.

Kicking off my boots, I picked up the gun again. "I don't want to leave it here by the door in case somebody drops by. I don't have a shell in the chamber, but there are three in the magazine. Is it okay if I put it around the corner by the table?"

"Sure. Go on in and make yourself comfortable by the fire. I'm just going to put our potatoes in the oven and then I'll join you. Would you like a beer?"

"That sounds great. Thanks." I padded through the open living space to lay the shotgun on the floor within easy reach of the dining table before heading for the brown denim sofa in front of the fireplace. "I like that you don't mind me bringing a gun to dinner," I called in the direction of the kitchen. "Most city boys would faint at the sight of an outfit accessorized with a shotgun."

His laughter carried me to the sofa, where I sank into the soft cushions and curled my feet under me. The tang of woodsmoke in the air made me smile.

"What's the joke?" Tom appeared from the kitchen bearing two frosted beer mugs. He handed me one and sank into the opposite chair, stretching long denim-clad legs toward the fire.

"I was thinking that the smell of woodsmoke isn't quite such a treat as it used to be. I just spent four months visiting my aunt and uncle on a commune where woodstoves were the only source of heat and the only way to cook."

He shook his head and took a deep swallow of his beer. "I can't believe people want to live like that. I grew up in a house with no central heat, and you can bet I love my gas furnace."

I laughed and agreed, and the conversation flowed easily while he brought me up to date on the latest happenings in the small town of Silverside and I regaled him with tales of the commune that didn't involve terrorists and secret agents.

Still talking, we moved to the table to devour melt-in-your-mouth beef ribs and loaded baked potatoes. When he brought out a caramel-chocolate cheesecake for dessert, I groaned.

"Oh, that looks so good! But I'm stuffed."

Tom gave me his attractive crooked smile. "We can have it later if you like, but I won't be hurt if you don't want any. I'm a pretty plain cook. I don't know how to bake, so I bought it."

"Well, your ribs are amazing." The unintentional double entendre popped out before I could stop it, and I couldn't help glancing at his chest. Lean muscle under soft faded denim. Mmm...

I dragged my eyes up to his face again and ignored the warmth in my cheeks. Kane or Hellhound would never let me get away with a line like that, but I was pretty sure Tom was polite enough to let it pass.

He was. He nodded toward the living area, warm and welcoming in the mellow firelight. "Let's go sit somewhere more comfortable. Maybe you'll feel like dessert later."

At least I thought that was politeness. Or maybe he'd just offered a double entendre of his own.

He rose and reached for my empty beer mug with a smile. "Can I get you another?"

I stood, too, and stretched before heading for the sofa. "Thanks, that'd be great. I'm not driving and it's only a short stagger home." And it might help calm my still-jangling nerves.

"I can drive you home later if you'd like," Tom called from the kitchen over the clink of beer bottles.

Okay, that *really* sounded like a double entendre to me. But it was probably just my dirty mind.

"Or I can lend you a flashlight and walk you home," he added as he returned with the fresh beers. "That path can be hard to find after dark."

"Oh, I brought a headlamp, so I should be fine. Thanks, though." I accepted the frosty mug along with a brief but rewarding glimpse of soft denim hugging his grope-worthy posterior as he turned to go back to his chair.

Down, girl.

I firmly ignored the small alcohol-fuelled voice that reminded me how safe and comfortable I could be here in Tom's bed instead of startling awake at the slightest noise in my own.

I gulped a determined swallow of beer. Not an option. There was no way to hide or explain the Glock strapped to my ankle if I took off my clothes, and the longer I stayed the more dangerous it was for Tom. I probably shouldn't even be here.

"Did you have a nice visit with your nephew?" Tom asked.

I dragged my attention back to the conversation. "It was short and sweet, but he didn't ask me for money. It was just a social call."

If a blast of buckshot could be considered social.

"Is there anybody else who might have been trying to visit you?" Tom asked. "I've seen a silver SUV around pretty often the last couple of months."

My attention sharpened with a hard thump of my heart. "Uh, no, not that I can think of."

"Well, it's funny." Tom stretched out his legs. "Nobody takes this road unless they're visiting you or me. There's nothing but the old Wright homestead north of us, and it's been abandoned for years." He swallowed some beer. "Sad to see the old house falling down like that. It's a hazard, too. Kids go out there to drink and party, and someday there'll be a fire."

Spoken like the volunteer firefighter he was. I gently interrupted before the conversation diverged too far. "Um, about the SUV?"

"Oh, yeah." He frowned. "I saw it driving past slowly several times. And once when I was coming home it was nosed into your driveway, but when I headed over to see if I could help it pulled out and left before I got there. I caught sight of it once while I was plowing your lane, too, but by the time I got back to the road it was gone again."

My pulse accelerated. That's how they'd gotten the combination to my gate. Tom would have left the lock hanging by its shackle while he plowed. It would only take a few moments for somebody to pop out of their car and note the combination.

Which meant they'd had my place under surveillance for a while. Long enough to know that Tom unlocked my gate and cleared off my lane whenever it snowed.

I drew a slow breath and kept my tone casual. "Did you notice the make or model? A couple of my friends from Calgary drive silver SUVs, so it might have been one of them.

Could you see the driver? Or any passengers?"

"Only one driver, but I was too far away to see if it was a man or a woman. And I couldn't tell you the make or model. It was one of those crossovers, not really a truck or a car. They all look the same from a distance." Tom shrugged. "Useless things. If you need a truck, get a real truck. Otherwise, get a car."

"Mm." I frowned and sipped my beer.

Tom sat up a bit straighter, his brow furrowing. "I mean, I guess lots of people like them. I didn't mean to be insulting."

"Huh? Oh, that's okay, you weren't," I assured him. "I was just trying to figure out who it might have been."

"Oh. Good." He sat back again, looking relieved. "So do you think it was anybody you know?"

I summoned a carefree shrug. "Oh, probably. They'll catch up with me sooner or later."

God, I hoped not.

I swallowed and changed the subject. "While I'm thinking about it, I need to write you a cheque for keeping my lane clear all winter. Oh, and I changed the combination on the lock." I recited the new one, pleased to see that he memorized it instead of writing it down.

After repeating it back to me, he said, "Don't worry about paying me. You weren't even here for most of the winter."

"No, we had a deal," I insisted. "You plowed it anyway so I need to pay you for your gas and time."

After some good-natured argument we settled on a price and I scribbled out a cheque. I was reluctantly considering leaving when Tom leaned forward, his expression grave.

"There's something I need to warn you about," he said.

A chill touched my backbone and I couldn't prevent a fast glance around the room. "Um, what?"

"Beware... the spring thing!" he intoned ominously.

"The... what...?"

The laugh lines crinkled around his sky-blue eyes and my heart gave an involuntary thump of appreciation for the crooked smile that transformed him from handsome to irresistible.

"The spring thing," he repeated, grinning. "You probably missed it last year because you'd just moved here, but as a business owner and member of the Silverside and Area Chamber of Commerce... you are still a member, aren't you?"

"Uh... yeah," I admitted warily.

Tom laughed. "Then you're doomed for sure. Brace yourself."

I managed a sickly smile. "I've already got all the doom I can handle. Should I run for the hills?"

"It won't help." He assumed a gloomy monotone. "It's already too late. No matter where you hide, they'll find you. And when they do..."

A shudder shook me. "Stop it, already!" I protested with sincerity I hoped I'd hidden in a smile that felt too stiff for my lips. "You're creeping me out! What the hell is this spring thing, and why should I worry about it? And who the hell are '*they*'?"

"It's a long story, and you'll need another beer," Tom teased as he rose. "I'll be right back."

He vanished into the kitchen again, and I leaned down to touch the Glock at my ankle. My insides felt icy even though I knew he was only hamming it up. Jokes like that just didn't seem too funny at the moment.

"Here you go." Tom returned to hand me another frosty

mug, and I sucked down a bracing swallow as he sank into his chair again. He took a drink of his own before saying, "The spring thing is a festival the Chamber sponsors every year on the Thursday before Good Friday. Usually it's over by now, but Easter's late this year. The schools and businesses all close so everybody can go to the parade at noon, and there's a little fair with some rides for the kids. Then everybody gets together at the rec centre for a potluck supper."

"Oh." I took another drink and leaned back, surreptitiously easing the tension out of my muscles. "I guess I must have missed it last year because Easter was earlier and I was still getting settled after my move."

I didn't bother to mention that I had been a little occupied with eluding murderers last year around that time, too. Déjà vu.

"So what's the festival called?" I added.

"The Spring Thing."

I frowned at his mischievous expression. "That's what it's called? The Spring Thing?"

"Yep." He grinned. "That's what you get when you do things by committee. They called it the spring thing while they tried to figure out a proper name. They proposed all kinds of high-falutin' handles, but they never could agree on one so it's been called the Spring Thing for over thirty years. Every few years they argue over new names, but it hasn't changed yet. I don't suppose it ever will."

I relaxed further and flashed him a smile before sucking back another swallow of beer. "Small-town politics are always good for a laugh."

Tom gave me a wry look. "As long as you're not involved

in them. And you will be. All the Chamber members are expected to participate. You came home at the worst possible time. The Thing's next weekend and everybody's running around like chickens with their heads cut off."

"Oh." My smile dissolved. "So, um... what will they expect me to do? Surely all the planning is done by now."

Tom grimaced. "It's a committee. The planning is never done. I know they're going to ask you to drive your Corvette in the parade. And if you don't want to do that, they're always looking for volunteers to help wrangle the kids into their costumes and get them rounded up for the Little Clowns Bicycle Rally..." He trailed off at the sight of my horrified expression.

"I don't wrangle kids," I said, perhaps a little more vehemently than necessary. "I especially don't wrangle hyper-excited kids who are likely to run me over with their bikes. And I can't drive the 'Vette in the parade. The cam's so lumpy and the timing's so advanced it won't idle low enough for parade speed. I'd burn out the clutch in the first two blocks."

"Then you better run for the hills," Tom said seriously.

"Oh, come on," I pleaded. "There has to be something else I can do that doesn't involve other people's children. You joined the Chamber to advertise your custom baling services, didn't you? What are you doing for the Spring Thing?"

"I always drive my team in the parade, pulling a hay wagon for the kids." His face softened into a fond smile. "Cory and Charlene are bringing the grandkids up from Calgary. They're just crazy about the horses and the parade, and I get such a kick out of having them here."

No sympathy for my kid-allergy here.

I tried another tack. "What are the other business owners doing?"

Tom shook himself back from his pleasant reverie. "A lot of them make floats to drive in the parade, but you're probably running out of time to do anything like that." He eyed me with a grin. "Unless you can whip something up in a week."

I squirmed and gulped another mouthful of beer. "Um, no. I'm a little busy with my home renovations."

Thanks to Drake Mallard.

Dammit, I hoped Mallard was roasting slowly in hell. Asshole. I might excuse him for trying to kill me, but forcing me to deal with hordes of screaming children was unforgiveable.

Tom took pity on me. "You're welcome to ride on the wagon with me," he offered.

"Uh... There would be lots of kids on the hayride, right?"

"Oh. Right." He looked disappointed for a moment before suggesting, "Maybe you could ride on a float with one of your clients. You do a lot of work for Sirius Dynamics, don't you? They put a float in the parade every year. And Blue Eddy always does, too."

"Oh, good thinking!" I let out a breath of relief. "I'll do that. Maybe that'll get me off the hook."

"Maybe," Tom agreed, but he didn't sound convinced.

CHAPTER 4

Having absorbed more unsettling news than I wanted to deal with, I gulped the last of my beer and stood, pushing a smile onto my lips. "Well, thanks for dinner," I said. "It was great, but I guess I'd better get home. I have to go to work tomorrow and it'll be a shock to wake up to an alarm clock."

"Oh." Tom rose, too, his brow furrowing. "But tomorrow's Friday. Couldn't you take the day off and start fresh on Monday morning?"

I sighed. "That'd be nice, but I really need to go in tomorrow."

"No rest for the wicked." He gave me a smile and nodded at the wall clock. "But it's only eight o'clock. Would you like some dessert before you go?"

"It looked great but I'm still stuffed, especially after all that beer." I sidled around the end of the sofa. "And I know you have to get out to the barn and do your chores tonight."

"That's no problem, they can wait. Surely you've got time for one more beer."

"Two's usually my limit, and I've already had three." I drifted toward the dining table and my shotgun. "So thanks anyway, but I'd better not."

"Oh."

He looked so disappointed my heart squeezed in spite of the knowledge that leaving was the smart thing to do. The beer spoke before my brain could catch up.

"Well, maybe just a sliver of cheesecake," I said, and was rewarded with a smile like a sunrise.

"Why don't you go back to the couch and we can have dessert by the fire," he suggested as he headed for the kitchen.

Warning bells chimed in my brain, too late.

Stupid, stupid, stupid.

Pick up your shotgun and leave. Right fucking now. Get the hell out before...

Tom hurried back bearing plates, forks, and the cheesecake that looked as sweet as his smile.

Dammit, I had no business sharing cheesecake or anything else with sweet guys. Only a few hours ago I'd killed a man and taken pride in my shots. I didn't deserve to spend time with a sweet normal guy, and he sure as hell didn't deserve the dangers of spending time with me.

As if sensing my inner turmoil, his smile faded. "It's okay if you really want to leave," he said softly. "I don't want you to be uncomfortable."

Oh, God.

Guilt twisted my guts and I forced a smile. "Are you kidding? That cheesecake has been calling to me all evening."

"Well, it's time to surrender." He gave me that captivating crooked smile again. "Come and sit down."

I eased out a silent sigh and plodded over to face my fate.

The last rich creamy morsel had just fallen to my fork when Tom spoke again, leaning back in his chair with elaborate nonchalance.

"So are you seeing anybody these days?"

I choked on my cheesecake.

Coughing and wiping away tears while Tom hovered worriedly, I silently debated the merits of feigning unconsciousness, or possibly death.

Probably not smart. Setting myself up for mouth-to-mouth from a firefighter with EMS training wasn't going to lead anywhere I wanted to go tonight.

Hell, who was I kidding? It would lead exactly where I wanted to go tonight, and that was a bad, bad idea.

Wiping away the last of the tears, I straightened and accepted the glass of water Tom proffered. I sipped slowly, searching for the right words. 'Yes, I was naked in bed with Kane and Hellhound last weekend' probably wasn't the best way to phrase it.

"Thanks," I croaked instead. "Sorry. Cheesecake is a little hard on the airways."

Oh Lord, did I just say 'hard-on'?

Shut up. Just shut up and get out.

Tom sank back into his chair. "I'm glad you're okay. A trip to the ER wasn't how I'd planned to end the evening." He grinned. "I'd never live it down if the guys found out I'd cooked you dinner and then had to rush you to Emergency."

I forced a laugh and hauled myself to my feet. "Don't worry, I'd tell them it was the bought cheesecake that got me." Easing away in the direction of my shotgun, I added, "Well, thanks for the delicious dinner and the lethal cheesecake. I'd really better get going."

"Okay." Tom stood and followed me toward the door. "That was a tactful dodge. So I guess the answer is 'yes, you're seeing somebody'."

"Um, yeah, kinda..." I turned to face him, cursing my social ineptitude.

He smiled. "It's okay, Aydan, I didn't mean for that to be an awkward question. I'm your neighbour and your friend no matter what. I just like to know where I stand."

"Right, sorry," I mumbled, bending to lace my boots and hide my burning cheeks. "Thanks."

"I'll walk you back," he said, reaching for his fleece-lined denim jacket.

"Um, no, it's okay..." I began.

"No strings attached," he said earnestly. "If you're seeing somebody, I'd never overstep the boundaries. I just want to make sure you get home safe."

Yeah, and if he walked me home I'd have to explain why I had a barricade of plywood instead of a front door.

I straightened and tried for a humorous but decisive tone. "Remember, I just got back from living in the wilderness for four months. I'm used to moving around in the woods after dark, and I have my shotgun. Thanks for being concerned, but I'll be fine."

He smiled. "That independence is another thing I admire about you. Just give me a quick call when you get in so I know you got back okay."

"I will. Thanks again." I stepped out into the darkness before I could change my mind.

Only a few yards beyond the reassuring glow of Tom's yardlight, I was already regretting my choice.

Squaring my shoulders, I donned the small LED headlamp I'd brought and strode forward with my best imitation of bravery.

Tom's company wouldn't make me any safer. I was

probably better off without him. At least if I had to react to an attack I wouldn't have to worry about protecting him as well as myself.

That train of thought did nothing to reassure me. The silent wooded darkness brought back the too-recent memory of muzzle flashes blazing in the night and the hellish cries of dying men.

Dammit, this headlamp might as well be a glowing target on my forehead. Why the hell hadn't I brought my night-vision headset?

Because I couldn't risk Tom discovering it when he handled my jacket, that's why.

The snap of a twig and rustle of undergrowth made me jump sideways, pumping a shell into the chamber and landing in a crouch with my shotgun at the ready.

Heart hammering, I glimpsed a deer's hindquarters vanishing at the edge of my headlamp's range. I straightened slowly, panting and trembling.

Down by the creek a lone coyote howled and its fellows answered from somewhere to my right. The eerie cries curled like dark smoke through the cold night air, making me shiver even though I knew they were probably more afraid of me than I was of them. I'd rather face a pack of coyotes than a human predator any day.

Oh, God, what if somebody was stalking me right now? My headlamp was like a beacon.

I clicked the light off and sucked in shaky breaths, straining my eyes and ears against the night.

Okay, breathe. Just breathe. Nobody's there.

My heart pattered like the footfalls of fleeing prey. If they had night vision I didn't stand a chance.

All rational thought vanished and I clicked the headlamp

back on and ran. Feet thudding unevenly on the treacherous path, breath sobbing in my chest, I crashed through the woods. Twigs slashed my face and tore at my hair, and the racket of my own charge through the underbrush spurred me to even more frantic flight.

Heart thundering, lungs labouring, I hesitated for an instant at the edge of the woods just outside the warm glow of my yardlight.

If somebody was waiting with a rifle I'd be an easy mark when I crossed the open space between the woods and my house.

Gulping down a sob, I forced my trembling legs into a final dash for the back door. I nearly dropped my shotgun in my frantic scrabble to get my key into the lock. And dammit, I'd forgotten that the surveillance analysts would see me as soon as I got within ten yards of the house.

I let my hair swing forward to hide my face and exerted all my will to calm my shaking hands enough to unlock the door. But they'd still be able to see my shoulders heaving with my struggle for air.

God, how humiliating.

Maybe they hadn't noticed anything amiss. They'd have seen me bounding up the stairs, but I hadn't paused long enough for them to get a good look at me.

I twisted the key in the lock, pasted a smile on my rigid lips, and saluted the hidden camera with my shotgun before diving through the door and slamming it behind me.

I snapped a hurried glance around the quiet entry, all my senses strained to their limits. Everything seemed undisturbed.

But somebody could be hiding, ready to ambush me...

Fighting to control my ragged breathing, I crouched to draw my Glock from the ankle holster. Shotgun in one hand, Glock in the other, I hesitated. Stupid to try firing the shotgun one-handed, and the Glock was a better close-quarters weapon anyway.

But there was no way I'd risk getting shot with my own shotgun. I fumbled the shells out and dropped them into my pocket before lowering the empty shotgun to the floor. Trembling, I crept forward with my Glock at the ready.

Each blind corner hoisted my heart higher in my chest, nearly incinerating it in the blaze of adrenaline as I pivoted around the corner pistol-first. A few moments to draw a breath. Then repeat the process at the next corner.

And the next.

At last I'd cleared every closet and corner, and I was certain I was alone. I pressed my back to the hall wall and stood still.

Breathe. Slow like ocean waves. In... two, three, four; out... two, three, four...

Idiot. I thumped my head gently against the wall behind me. The analysts would have texted me if anybody had broken into my house. I was fine. I would have been perfectly safe without clearing the house.

My heart lolloped in an uneven rhythm, my tense muscles resisting my efforts to belly breathe. Maybe I was safe now, but any minute the phone could ring. Any minute a fusillade of bullets could rip through my walls.

Okay, stop it. Just breathe...

The phone rang.

I flung myself to the floor, gun in hand. Heart pounding, I belly-crawled with frantic speed to the living room phone and snatched up the handset. My 'hello' came out in a breathless gasp as I wedged my back into the corner beside the sofa. Only some foam and a bit of wood between me and a bullet. No protection at all if somebody fired through the window.

"Aydan?" Tom's concerned voice made me suck in a breath that was half relief, half chagrin. "Is everything okay over there?"

"Fine." The word came out weak and tremulous and I did my best to cover it with a laugh that didn't sound much better. "I'm sorry, Tom, I just got in..." I had to stop and gasp a couple of breaths to supply some oxygen to my still-racing heart. "Sorry, I'm out of breath..."

I racked my brain for some logical reason why I'd be out of breath. Preferably a reason that didn't include being a shit-scared wimp.

"Um... I'm sorry I didn't call you right away," I began. "It was such a nice night that I dawdled on my way back." I crossed my fingers, hoping I wouldn't be struck by lightning for the giant lie. "And when I got home I realized, um..."

I cast a frantic glare around the room, searching for inspiration. Relief filled me at the sight of my fresh drywall patches.

"...I realized I'd left my bucket of drywall compound just inside the door and I nearly tripped on it when I came in. I just finished carrying it downstairs and had to run back up to get the phone."

"Oh, right, I forgot to ask about your renovations earlier. What are you working on?" The warm interest in his voice steadied me like a friendly hand and I hugged the phone closer.

"Nothing much." My voice sounded more like me now. I

kept my tone light. "Just a few touch-ups to the drywall before I paint the entry. And I thought I'd replace my front and back door with those insulated steel ones. I've been meaning to install new weatherstripping on the wooden ones, but they're so old I think it'll be better to just get new ones."

We chatted about renovations for a few more minutes before Tom wished me good night and hung up.

I let out a long breath, the phone sagging to the floor beside me while my shoulders eased down from around my ears.

A creak from the kitchen sent my heart rate into orbit all over again, but a moment later I realized it was the normal sound of the house contracting in the cool night air.

I blew out a shaky breath. This sucked.

There was no way I'd be able to sleep here tonight. Every time the house creaked I'd be leaping out of bed with my gun drawn.

I fought the urge to call Tom back and tell him I'd been fibbing; that I wasn't seeing anybody and I'd like to come over and spend the night.

He'd jump at the chance. And he'd almost certainly be good in bed. He was a considerate guy, and the couple of kisses we'd shared last summer had been decidedly promising...

No.

Just no.

I rose and firmly replaced the telephone handset on its base unit. Then I went to unearth my camping gear.

CHAPTER 5

Making a nest with my air mattress and sleeping bag in the corner of my garage, I sniffed appreciatively. The happy smells of rubber and motor oil mingled with a faint whiff of gasoline to create a blanket of reassurance almost as palpable as the warmth of the heated concrete floor.

No assassin would think to look for me here in the middle of the night. I straightened and drew a few more breaths, easing the tension from my shoulders. Wandering around the garage taking yoga breaths, I trailed my fingertips over the smooth shiny surface of my tool chest and patted the fenders of my automotive friends.

The '66 Corvette, exuding raw power and tempting me to fire it up for its first joyride of the spring. My patient '53 Chevy sedan, its faded rust-pocked paint urging me to finish its restoration. My battered, indomitable half-ton. The dirt bike waiting next to the door like an eager puppy begging to get out and run the fields. My blue Subaru Legacy, serene and confident in its role as the most modern vehicle in the garage.

Drifting over to the edge of the addition, I surveyed the excavation crisscrossed by heating pipes, and imagined a smooth concrete floor with my new hydraulic lift ready and waiting. With a sigh of contentment I turned away, then hesitated and turned back to eye the reinforcing steel poking up from the footing-to-be.

It'd be just my shitty luck to go sleepwalking in the middle of the night and fall off the edge of the slab to impale myself on the damn rebar.

With a shudder, I upended a plastic pail over the spikes. Just in case.

A final tour of my domain left me feeling relaxed enough to turn off the lights and retreat to my sleeping bag. The cool darkness enfolded me and I drew a long breath and let it out slowly.

Safe.

Be calm. Breathe...

I drifted into uneasy dreams wracked by violent nightmares.

The peal of my cell phone's alarm jerked me to wakefulness. I let out a heartfelt groan as I silenced it, then pried myself reluctantly from my warm nest to stand shivering in the chilly air. I'd worn the T-shirt and long johns that served as my winter-camping pajamas, but the garage was the right temperature for working on cars, not standing around in my underwear.

The thought of a hot shower attracted and repelled me in equal measures. The hot water would be glorious, but the thought of being cornered naked in my shower if someone attacked...

Nope.

I sighed and made for the house, where I stayed exactly long enough to throw on clean clothes and grab my gym bag and a couple of granola bars along with my work paraphernalia. Five minutes later I was on the road to Silverside, munching my unsatisfying breakfast and looking forward to a quick workout and the hot showers at the gym.

When I arrived freshly showered in the Sirius Dynamics lobby on the dot of eight o'clock, Leo the security guard offered me a warm greeting. We chatted for a few moments, catching up on the last four months, and I was leaning over to sign for my security fob when a familiar voice made me straighten and turn with a smile.

"Aydan! Welcome back!" Clyde Webb's cheeks were flushed with delight above his broad grin as he hurried across the lobby, his beanpole six-foot-two all awkward angles and bony elbows. He flung his arms around me and exclaimed, "It's so great to see you!"

"Spider! It's great to see you, too!" I replied, and returned the hug before withdrawing to survey him with a grin of my own. "Being engaged seems to agree with you." I reached up to pat his glowing cheek. "Just think, in another four months you'll be an old married man."

I tactfully refrained from voicing the thought that he looked far too young to be getting married. No need to bring up the boyish features that were the bane of his twenty-seven-year-old existence.

"Thanks, Aydan! I can't believe it's only four months away. I can hardly wait! And you look great, too!" His enthusiasm faltered as he took in the dark circles under my eyes. "Um, but you look a little tired. Are you still recovering from your trip?"

"Yeah." I turned away to retrieve my security fob and changed the subject as I stepped aside so Spider could sign in. "So what's new? How's Linda? Are you enjoying your promotion to team leader? How are Brock and Jill and Tammy getting along?"

I was pretty sure I hadn't imagined the stiffening of his shoulders as he bent to sign for his fob. When he straightened the joy had drained from his smile, leaving an anemic replica in its place. With heartiness that sounded forced, he replied, "We've got tons to catch up on! Come on upstairs and I'll update you on everything. The team doesn't start 'til nine, so you'll see them later."

Uh-oh.

Worry nibbled at me while I followed him through the security doors and up the stairs.

"I have a permanent office up here now," Spider said as we strolled down the second-floor hallway. "I'm right next to you, and Brock's a couple of doors down on your other side." His words were delivered in a tone that would have been appropriate for 'I have an office on death row', and his smile looked as though it hurt his face.

We turned into the office next to mine, instantly identifiable as Spider's by the half-assembled electronic gadgets and parts crowding the desk and the large worktable beside it.

I swung the door shut behind me. "Spider, what's wrong?" I demanded.

He sank listlessly into his chair. "Oh... nothing..." He pasted on the painful-looking smile again. "It's been great to have the promotion; the extra money's really nice now that Linda and I are racking up bills for the wedding..."

"Bullshit." I pulled a chair over beside him and dropped into it, taking his hand to still the bony fingers that fidgeted with the armrest. His nails were bitten down to the quick.

"Talk to me, Spider," I coaxed. "What the hell's wrong?"

"Oh, Aydan..." His face crumpled. "Thank God you're back! You're the only person I can talk to-"

A knock on the door made him bolt upright and pull his hand from my grasp, his expression smoothing into composure that didn't quite hide the distress darkening his hazel eyes.

"Come in," he called.

The door swung ajar and Stemp's reptilian features appeared in the opening. "Kelly; Webb; good morning." His expressionless gaze fastened on me. "Kelly, I'd like a few moments of your time." He didn't add 'now', but he didn't need to.

I rose with a sigh. "Talk to you later, Spider."

He nodded unhappily, and I followed Stemp's sinuous stride down the hall.

In his office, Stemp closed the door and motioned me into the chair in front of his desk. I sat cautiously, my pulse ticking up a notch. Meetings with Stemp tended to end badly for me, but maybe today would be an exception.

"The cleanup crew is finished with the body," he said without preamble. "Drake Agnew Mallard, age twenty-four, a small-time thug with various convictions for assault, possession of weapons, uttering threats, breach of parole..." Stemp trailed off with a gesture that indicated 'et cetera'.

"The cash in his wallet was almost certainly a payment for the attack on you," he continued. The faintest hint of a frown creased his brow. "The usual deal is half up front and the other half on completion of the job, but five thousand dollars seems a paltry sum for a contract killing even for a bottom-feeder like Mallard. We did, however, find nylon zip ties and a strip of fabric that might have served as a gag in his car, so perhaps he was only intending to abduct you."

"Great." I held my voice completely flat to hide my surge of fear. "That might explain why he didn't have a shell chambered when he was waving that shotgun around. Was there any clue as to who might have hired him?"

"The analysts are forwarding a report to you containing the contacts and call data from Mallard's phone. Maybe you'll recognize something there. Forensic examination of the body and car yielded nothing, but there were fingerprints on the photo."

My pulse quickened. "Could you identify them? Or the handwriting?"

"There wasn't enough handwriting for a conclusive match, but we found four separate sets of fingerprints. Three of the four came up in the law enforcement database." Stemp's reptilian gaze raked over me as if to gauge my reaction. "One set belonged to Paul Hibbert."

I took a slow calming breath at the memory of Hibbert's bullet-riddled body bleeding all over my front porch last winter, and held my voice level. "Who did the other fingerprints belong to?"

"Drake Mallard. And Nicholas Parr."

"Oh, shit." The words squeezed out of my throat.

Please, not Fuzzy Bunny again. No matter whether they believed I was Aydan Kelly, the holder of classified network technology, or Arlene Widdenback, the porn-star fraud artist and arms dealer who had destroyed their organization, the end result would be a slow and agonizing death if they caught me.

"But Parr and all Fuzzy Bunny's guys are in jail, aren't they?" I silently cursed the pleading note in my voice.

"Yes, Nicholas Parr was convicted along with the members you identified in your sting four months ago," Stemp confirmed. "All the officers and directors of Fuzzy Bunny are currently imprisoned except Parr's wife, and charges are mounting against all of them except her as the investigation continues." He raised a restraining hand as I leaned forward to pounce on the clue. "The unidentified fingerprints are not Eleanor Parr's," he added, dashing my hopes. "Hers were collected during the investigation."

"So was she innocent?"

"Yes. She came from an old-money family with a long tradition of integrity and philanthropy, and no matter how deeply we dug we found no indication that she had any knowledge of her husband's criminal activities. It seems Parr married her for her connections, to lend legitimacy and credibility to his operation."

Recalling Eleanor Parr's blonde elegance and gracious kindness, I let out a breath. "Well, she seemed really nice when I met her. I can't imagine how she must have felt finding out her husband was a criminal mastermind."

"She refused to believe it," Stemp replied. "Even after he was arrested and convicted she stood by him. Right up until his death she was trying to launch an appeal."

"His *death*?" I gaped at Stemp. "He's dead? When? How?"

"He and his enforcer Kevin Barnett were killed in prison by their former underlings six weeks ago."

"Holy shit." I digested that for a moment, relief easing my shoulders. "Well, I guess that probably means Parr's not behind this. But poor Eleanor. What a shitty thing to have to deal with." I heaved a sigh and returned to the point. "Is there any chance of finding out who the fourth set of prints belongs to?"

Stemp's shoulders rose in a fractional shrug. "It likely wouldn't help. The unidentified prints were the oldest. All the others overlapped them."

"Shit. Whose were on top?"

"Mallard's. And Parr's overlapped Hibbert's."

I propped my chin in my hand. "So the photo went up the food chain before ending with Mallard. Our unidentified guy handled it first six months ago..."

Stemp's eyes narrowed. "What makes you say six months?"

I shrugged. "The picture shows me getting out of a red Subaru Legacy, and I only had that car for a couple of days before it got blown up at the end of October."

"Ah." Stemp nodded. "That was around the time Hibbert first contacted you. So perhaps the photo was given to him so he could identify you when he followed you to Las Vegas."

"Right, so his prints were next. Then the photo went from him to Parr, and then to Mallard..." I trailed off. "Could Parr have hired Mallard from jail before he died?"

"Unlikely. The analysts checked the prison records and Mallard wasn't there at the same time as Parr, nor did he visit."

I grimaced. "Yeah, and Parr wouldn't hire an idiot like Mallard anyway. If he was going to hire a contract killer, he'd get a professional."

And a professional undoubtedly would have succeeded. I hid a shiver.

"Probably true." Stemp frowned. "It's possible that someone in the lower echelons of the organization eluded us and acquired the photo, though if they did they were careful not to leave fingerprints. Perhaps they're seeking revenge. Or perhaps they're hoping to take over Fuzzy Bunny's previous arms deals and they simply want to eliminate the competition. It would be helpful if we could establish a motive."

"Yeah." I massaged the growing ache in my forehead. "My neighbour says there's been an SUV hanging around my place for the past few months. He didn't have a make or license number, but once I get Mallard's contact list I'll run a cross-reference in the database just in case one of his buddies drives a silver SUV." I swallowed the taut sensation in my throat. "At least we know whoever's after me doesn't have much of a budget if they're hiring guys like Mallard. If I don't come up with anything from Mallard's phone data I guess I'll just have to wait until his boss figures out Mallard didn't finish the job and sends somebody else."

Stemp eyed me with a trace of something that might have been concern. I looked again, but the flicker of expression was already gone.

"True," he agreed. "Meanwhile, I've passed the case details on to the RCMP and the Calgary city police. They'll carry on with the investigation, checking Mallard's known associates and so on."

He paused, measuring me with his gaze.

"Your mandatory post-mission psych evaluation is scheduled for Wednesday at ten hundred," he said. "I didn't expect you to be involved in anything of this magnitude so soon. I recommend you move to one of our safe houses until your evaluation is completed and Dr. Rawling approves you for active duty."

Shit, the psych evaluation. The only way I'd pass was if I lied my ass off. And even that might not work anymore. Despite my best efforts Dr. Rawling was getting to know me too well.

But, oh God, not a safe house. Imprisoned in a small space all day, every day. The blinds drawn, never going outside, no breath of wind or warmth of sunshine...

My heart accelerated to a rapid drumming. "Well, let's not rush into the safe house thing," I said evenly. "Any dumb shit who'd hire a guy like Mallard is bound to make mistakes. We should be able to figure out who's behind this pretty quickly."

"Perhaps." Stemp's gaze bored into my skull as if to examine my quivering brain. "Or perhaps they'll hire someone better and be successful next time."

"I'm taking precautions," I said hurriedly. "May I keep the night vision gear and the trank pistol I had in B.C.? I was going to turn them in today, but it would really help if I could keep them for a while."

"Give me one good reason why I shouldn't simply tranquilize you right now..."

A trank pistol appeared in his hand. Goddamn, the bastard was fast.

"...and ship you to a safe house to be restrained there until this is resolved," he finished.

"I'll give you two reasons," I said promptly. "Number one, I wouldn't cooperate at the safe house and you know what a pain in the ass I am when you're trying to restrain me." I gave him a narrow-eyed glare, and the corner of his mouth quirked. "And number two, if Mallard's employer sends another loser, it'll be easier to triangulate back to them," I finished.

That sounded weak even to my own ears. Stemp was right; they might send somebody more competent next time, and Stemp needed me alive.

"Oh, and number three," I added hurriedly. "Back in December you said you needed me to work on Tammy Mellor's project as soon as possible. It's probably even more urgent by now, and I wouldn't be able to work on it from a safe house."

"True," Stemp conceded. He gave me a long inspection over the sights of the trank pistol while I held my breath. "Tell me," he said in a conversational tone, "Are you making any progress in your claustrophobia therapy with Dr. Rawling?"

Bastard. No doubt he already knew the answer to that question.

I brazened it out as best I could. "I'm sorry, I don't see how that's relevant."

"It's relevant because if one of my valuable agents is suffering from a phobia that causes her to take unreasonable risks..." He paused and gave me a significant look over the pistol sights. "...then it's my responsibility to remove her from active duty until she can function effectively again. If you're avoiding the safe house simply because you fear captivity..."

Too right about that, but I couldn't let him see it. Lucky he believed I was a competent agent instead of a chickenshit bookkeeper.

I pulled myself upright in the chair and feigned indignation. "You seriously think I can't hold my own against some two-bit thug? I've faced far better men than him and come out on top. And whoever sent him after me has to be small-time, too, or they'd have hired somebody better. We can just let them make another move. If I've got the trank gun I can capture instead of kill, and we can question the next guy."

"Why did I know you'd say that?" Stemp asked, deadpan.

I held my expression as impassive as his. "Lucky guess."

"Indeed."

The trank gun disappeared as quickly as it had materialized and I drew a breath of relief.

He leaned back in his chair and regarded me over steepled fingers. "We'll revisit this issue after your evaluation on Wednesday. So. The situation with Tammy Mellor needs to be resolved as soon as possible. Have you come up with any ideas?"

CHAPTER 6

I tried to stifle my snotty rejoinder but it popped out anyway. "No, I was a little busy getting my ass shot up to save your parents."

"Yes." Stemp inclined his head graciously. "And I'm truly grateful. However, I'm under significant pressure to find a resolution to the problem Ms. Mellor poses."

He made a carefully controlled gesture that in any other man would have been arm-waving frustration. "Despite frequent reminders of the importance of confidentiality, Ms. Mellor's constant babble has proved uncontrollable. Dr. Rawling says that although she has normal intellect, she is functioning at the developmental level of the eight-year-old she was when she was taken from her family. She is fundamentally incapable of exercising the level of discretion required to protect our classified operations."

He pressed his fingers to the bridge of his nose as if to tamp down a headache and went on, "Agent Francis and her team are so worn down with the constant struggle to handle Ms. Mellor that Francis has requested a transfer. Twice. In the past two months. The only reason Ms. Mellor is not currently incarcerated to protect both herself and national security is because I promised you the chance to attempt to remove the classified information from Ms. Mellor's mind. I had originally intended to keep that proposal strictly between you and me, but since Ms. Mellor has proven so..."

He hesitated as if searching for the right word, still massaging the bridge of his nose. "...intractable..." he continued after a moment, "...it has become obvious that drastic action is required. The chain of command wanted to incarcerate Ms. Mellor immediately, but when I raised the possibility of simply editing her memories they reluctantly agreed to wait until you returned from B.C. to give you that chance."

I held my temper under careful control. I had already blasted him with my outrage over that idea. Blowing up again wouldn't solve anything.

"I already told you I wouldn't tamper with her memories without her knowledge and consent, even if I was certain I could do it without harming her," I said evenly.

"So you said," Stemp agreed. "But I have exhausted all other avenues so I am forced to give you an ultimatum. I leave it up to you to decide whether having Ms. Mellor incarcerated is less offensive to your sensibilities than subtly altering her memories. If you can propose an alternative solution I will be pleased to consider it, but if you haven't provided a solution by the end of next week, Ms. Mellor will be transferred to a secure facility where she will remain for the rest of her life."

'*Dickhead*' sprang to my lips but I managed to bite it back. I held my voice level. "I may need more time if I have to deal with assassins popping up all over the place."

Stemp allowed himself a tiny exhalation. "There will always be reasons to postpone this. The chain of command has made its decision. The deadline stands."

Profanity boiled at the back of my throat and I pressed my lips together to prevent it from erupting. We'd already had this conversation. I knew what a potential disaster Tammy Mellor's loose lips represented. And Stemp, for all his irritating qualities, had stood up to the chain of command to give Tammy a last chance for freedom.

A chance that depended solely on me.

God help poor Tammy.

My voice came out slightly seared by the heat of the words I was holding back. "I'll do my best."

Stemp gave me a tired smile. "I knew you would." His expressionless façade returned and he spoke with his usual clipped efficiency. "I have briefed Webb and Dr. Travers and assigned them to assist you in any way possible. No one else besides the chain of command is aware we're considering this action, though Kane will be briefed and will join your team when he returns from his leave on Monday. You, Webb, and Dr. Travers will observe Ms. Mellor's session this morning and as frequently as necessary thereafter to complete your research and recommendations."

His flat amber gaze pinned me with the weight of his authority. "You will not, under any circumstances, enter the network while Ms. Mellor is in it. We can't risk the data transfer if your minds accidentally collide in the network." He raised a hand to forestall my objection and went on, "I know Webb's solution worked the last time you tried it, but we have more at stake now. With only a week remaining until the deadline, it doesn't make sense to risk a potential security breach. If you choose to do so, you may attempt to edit Ms. Mellor's memories on the last day before she is transferred."

A few months ago I would have sourly observed that he was only making sure his own secrets were safely protected inside my brain. But I had a few potentially disastrous secrets of my own, and after what I'd learned about his parents only a few days ago, I was right on board with his paranoia.

Hell, why did people keep trusting me with their secrets?

Stemp was still talking. "...furthermore, you will not enter the virtual reality network at all for any reason until Dr. Rawling approves it, and even then not unless Kane is available to accompany you. You have been exposed to a far greater frequency of active missions than we consider optimal, and until Dr. Rawling is convinced of your psychological stability we won't risk the chance that you might accidentally harm yourself or others in virtual reality. You may access the network only via a desktop computer with a physical interface." His gaze bored into me. "Is that understood?"

I nodded dumbly. Not going to protest that. God, with the nightmares I'd had last night, I likely wouldn't even make it inside the virtual portal before my subconscious conjured up some fatal scenario.

Stemp returned my nod, his eyes narrowing suspiciously at my meek acquiescence. "Very well then." He glanced at his wristwatch. "The team will be assembling now, so you should begin as soon as possible. I have another item I wish to discuss with you, but it can wait until this afternoon. Dismissed."

I rose slowly, the weight of a woman's freedom bowing my shoulders, and trailed out of his office.

When I ducked into Spider's office a few minutes later, he looked up from the electronic gadget he was fiddling with, relief easing his face.

"Aydan..." he began.

The sound of approaching voices made him snap his mouth shut, wariness closing down his expression.

"Let's grab lunch later," he said.

"Okay..." I eyed him with concern, but he rose and headed for the door without saying another word.

I followed him into the hall in time to get caught in a wave of Tammy Mellor's prattle. Her round face was alight behind her dark glasses and one small plump hand deftly skimmed her white cane across the carpet while the other clutched the arm of Jill Francis, the hapless agent assigned as her handler.

"...but I just *love* strawberry jam, don't you, Jilly-bean?" Tammy babbled, barely pausing for breath before continuing, "My Terry *loved* strawberry jam, too, but you know it's *funny*, he just *hated* raspberry jam. Isn't that *funny*, Jilly-bean? When I was a little girl and I could still see, I knew they were both red berries but I can hardly even *remember* red now, but my *Terry* always used to tell me what colours things were even if I couldn't see them and I miss him so *much*, it was such a *tragedy* when he died-"

"Hey, Tammy," Jill interrupted in a voice so falsely animated I thought it might crack. "Spider's here and guess what? Aydan Kelly's with him! Hi, Spider; hi, Aydan!" She stepped forward to grip my hand in welcome. "It's great to see you," she added quietly. "We should go for drinks sometime soon."

Her voluptuous figure was tastefully accented with a fashionable sweater and scarf as usual and her makeup was as flattering and impeccably applied as always. But the vivacious sparkle I remembered from four months ago had vanished, and her usually warm smile looked strained.

I squeezed her hand. "It's great to see you, too. And drinks sound good. When do you want to-"

"How about tonight?"

I noted the desperate light in her eyes. "Sure," I agreed, and her shoulders sagged in relief.

"Aydan, how are you? I'm so glad you're back!" After an unprecedented ten-second silence, Tammy was back in full cry as she pressed forward, reaching toward me. I took her hand and submitted to her usual pat-down of my arms, face, and hair.

"Did you have a nice trip?" she bubbled. "Oh, I hope you *did*, and I *hope* we get to go into the network together today, I've been *so* looking forward to meeting your mind in the network. My Terry *promised* if I ever went into the network with another mage I'd get to see her memories, so I can hardly *wait* to see all your memories-"

Knowing it was futile to wait for a break in the deluge of words, I interrupted as gently as I could. "I'm sorry, Tammy, but Stemp said I'm not allowed to go into the network for at least a couple of weeks."

"Oh."

Disappointment clouded her features and my heart smote me. I could only imagine what it must be like to cling to the hope that she might someday see again, if only through another's eyes.

Her smile came back. "That's okay, I can wait. If *Charles* says that's the way it has to be, I'm *sure* he has a good reason. He's such a *nice* man and he's been so *wonderful* to me, I just can't tell you how *grateful* I am to him that he's given me such a nice *apartment* and such an interesting *job* and introduced me to a *wonderful* friend like my Jilly-bean!" She beamed in Jill's direction and Jill winced, her gaze sliding away down the hall.

"Oh, and here's Brock, too," Jill said without intonation.

I eyed the unprepossessing figure approaching us, wondering if Tyler Brock was any less annoying now than when I'd first met him four months ago. He didn't look any different. Still glittering with piercings in every square inch of his face; still shaggy-haired, patchy-bearded, and petulant-looking. I averted my gaze from the mustard-yellow jeans that hugged his skinny legs and concentrated instead on his Buddy-Holly-style glasses and the bulky toque and scarf that looked far too warm for the spring weather.

His ring-bedecked mouth twisted into a supercilious sneer as he joined us.

Nope. Still an irritating little shit. And he hadn't even opened his mouth yet.

"Yo," he said.

"Hi, Tyler!" Tammy turned a worshipful face toward him. "How's my *favourite* knight in shining armour today? Are you feeling *better*? I *hope* your headache went away, headaches are just *awful*, aren't they?"

Brock pushed past without responding, groping into his man-purse for a set of keys. When he unlocked his office door my jaw dropped. Black fabric shrouded the windows, reducing the morning sunshine to gloomy twilight. The walls were covered with music posters and a rack of stereo equipment dominated the back wall.

Extracting a small remote from his pocket, Brock pressed a button and black-light lamps illuminated on his desk while a cacophony of electric guitars shattered the air.

"*Jesus!*" I recoiled and clapped my hands over my ears, my hearing overloading into physical pain after the previous day's close-range gunshots. "Turn it down!" I shouted.

Everybody turned to stare at me and Brock's sneer widened. He pressed his remote again, raising the volume. His lips moved but his words were inaudible in the shitstorm of noise. Lipreading, I deciphered "My office, my music."

The frazzled threads of my composure snapped. In two long strides, I reached his stereo system and punched the power button with enough force to slam the unit back against the wall. In the sudden silence I crowded into his personal space, making the most of my three-inch height advantage.

"This time I turned it off with the button," I growled. "Next time I'll turn it off with a sledgehammer. Got it?"

The little snot paled and took a step back, but he wasn't smart enough to shut up. "Then I'll have you charged with vandalism," he snipped.

My fist shot out of its own accord to clench his funky scarf and haul his face within inches of mine. My words came out in a deadly hiss. "Yesterday I killed a man. The day before that I killed a man. Want to go three for three?"

"Aydan, no!" Spider clutched my sleeve, his voice shrill with alarm.

On my other side, Jill closed a firm hand on my shoulder. "Kelly, stand down!"

Brock's mouth opened and closed soundlessly and I unhanded him with a shove. "Lucky for you that you're not a man," I snarled. "You're not even worth my effort."

"Hello, everybody, sorry I'm late..." The melodious voice from the doorway trailed off uncertainly, and we all turned. Jack's flawless ivory forehead puckered slightly under her cloud of angel-blonde hair, her blue eyes widening. "Um, is... everything... okay?" she faltered.

CHAPTER 7

"Is that you, Dr. Travers?" Tammy spoke up eagerly. At Jack's cautious assent, Tammy gushed, "I *knew* it was you, you wear the most *beautiful* perfume and I know *you* must be *just* as beautiful as it is! And oooh, you just missed the most *exciting* thing, Aydan threatened to *kill* Tyler, it was just like an *audiobook*! But she was just *kidding*, weren't you, Aydan?"

Fortunately she didn't allow me a chance to reply.

"...Because nobody would *ever* want to hurt *Tyler*," she chattered on. "He's my knight in shining armour and I just love-love-*love* him to *death*! We have so much *fun* together, don't we, Tyler? I'm so *glad* I get to work with you every day, even if your music is kind of awful-"

"Will you shut up, you pathetic loser?" Brock flared, and Tammy's crushed look made my fist itch to crush him in turn. He drew a deep breath and adjusted his rumpled scarf and snotty expression before sidling past me. When he was safely at the door, he turned and looked down his pierced nose.

"I'm pressing charges, Kelly," he said. "You're going to jail. Bitch."

I felt my face twist with fury and he paled again and

scuttled away.

Jill planted herself in front of me before I could lunge after him. "Stop," she commanded. "Take a breath."

Jaw locked, I obeyed. One breath. Then another, hissing through my clenched teeth.

"Aydan?" Jack stepped forward to lay a gentle hand on my shoulder. "What happened?" she asked softly. "What did he do?"

I drew in a deep breath through my nose and let it out slowly through my mouth.

"I overreacted." My voice came out harsh despite my best efforts. "I overstressed my hearing yesterday. He cranked on the music and it hurt my ears and startled the hell out of me. Too much adrenaline. Then he acted like the little shit he is and I lost my temper."

"But you didn't hurt him, did you?" Jack directed a frown in the direction of the empty doorway. "He looked fine."

"He *is* fine." Spider's tone held more venom than I'd ever heard from my sweet-natured young friend. "He's just trying to stir up trouble the way he always does. He's a... a..." Spider flushed, blotches of red glowing on his cheeks. "An *asshole!*" he burst out, and blushed so hard the tips of his ears turned purple. He turned to take Tammy's hand. "You're not pathetic, or a loser. You're a really nice person and he's just a jerk. Don't let him make you feel bad."

A wobbly smile warmed Tammy's face and she threw her arms around him as high as she could reach, which was his skinny midsection. "Thanks, Spider. You're such a *sweetie*. But it's okay, I *know* Tyler didn't mean what he said. *Everybody* has a grumpy day sometimes."

"Try 'all the time'," Spider muttered.

"Well..." Jack looked from me to Spider to Jill. "What should we do? We can't go ahead without him."

I sank wearily into his chair and propped my feet on his desk, crossing my arms over my chest. "We wait. When he's done crying to Stemp, either he'll come back or Stemp will. Shouldn't take long..."

As the words left my mouth, Stemp appeared in the doorway, his expression impassive as always. "Kelly," he said emotionlessly. "In my office."

"It wasn't her fault!" Spider protested. "He provoked her and she didn't even hurt him even though he deserved it-"

Stemp silenced him with a quelling glance, and I dragged myself up to balance on suddenly-shaky legs. He wouldn't send me to jail, would he? Oh, God, and I'd thought the safe house was bad.

Stemp motioned me ahead of him and I tottered down the hall to his office in silence. I'd die in jail. Or kill myself. Or kill somebody else.

When I turned the corner into Stemp's office, the sight of Brock sent another sizzle of rage through my veins. Thankful Stemp was behind me, I gave Brock the full force of my glare before smoothing the expression from my face and pulling a chair up close beside his.

He gave me an uneasy glance and twitched his chair a little farther away.

I showed him my teeth. "Don't worry, Brock, I won't bite."

"No, you'll shoot me." He turned his self-righteous expression toward Stemp, who had just seated himself behind his desk. "I want to press charges! She threatened to shoot me! And she grabbed me and hurt me!"

I put every ounce of my self-control into an even tone. "Actually, I did neither."

"She's lying! I have witnesses..." Brock voice rose in a squeak of indignation.

"Brock." Stemp's dispassionate word silenced him effortlessly. "Where are you injured?"

"She grabbed me around the neck!" Brock shot me a look of hatred and clutched his scarf with a dramatic hand.

"Let me see." Stemp eyed him levelly across the desk.

Brock's air of victimhood faded as his normal personality reasserted itself. "You don't need to see." He sniffed. "I have three witnesses that will tell you she grabbed me by the throat."

"Except one of them is blind," I pointed out, holding onto my temper for all I was worth. "And the other two will confirm that I only grabbed your scarf."

Stemp rose and came around the desk. "Brock, take off your scarf and show me your neck."

"Well, you won't be able to see any marks by now," Brock huffed as he unwound the scarf.

Stemp studied his unmarred throat in silence before raising his reptilian gaze to transfix Brock like a rat before a cobra. The silence stretched.

Brock fidgeted with the scarf in his lap, his gaze darting away from Stemp's smooth deadly features. After several long moments he tossed his head. "Well, fine. She grabbed me by my scarf, not my neck. But she pushed me and I could have been badly hurt! And she threatened to kill me!"

"Kelly?" Stemp asked without removing his cold gaze from Brock.

I explained everything exactly as it had happened,

finishing with, "I overreacted, and I'm sorry."

Stemp eyed Brock expressionlessly. "If I interview the witnesses, will they confirm Kelly's story?" he asked.

"Probably," Brock said, a whine creeping into his petulance. "They're all buddy-buddy. They'd lie to protect her-"

"Enough." Stemp's voice didn't rise, but the word snapped out like a whip. "Webb is my most trusted analyst and he is scrupulously honest. Both Francis and Kelly have acted with integrity even under threat of death. You will not slander my staff. You will not press charges against Agent Kelly, and if you choose to do so despite my direct order, I will be pleased to inform the police of your lies to me."

He leaned closer to Brock. "You may recall that I have the power to make charges against my agents go away. I suggest you don't test that power. I further suggest that you make it a policy from now on not to deliberately provoke my agents. And..." His voice went ice-cold, making me shiver even though it wasn't directed my way. "...I *strongly* suggest that you never lie to me again."

Brock blinked and gulped. Then, unbelievably, he copped an attitude. "Fine." He rose and flung his scarf theatrically around his neck. "I should have known you'd turn this around on me. You'd do anything to cover up for your precious agents-"

"Kelly." Stemp's voice was so dangerous that my hand twitched toward my holster out of sheer reflex. "Wait outside."

I sprang up and scooted out the door, closing it behind me. A few paces away, I sagged against the wall, my heart thumping.

God, Brock had no sense of self-preservation

whatsoever. Even though I had hurled abuse at Stemp a few times myself, I had never insulted his integrity or objectivity. Brock's snide insinuation was a whole lot worse than calling Stemp a dickhead in the heat of anger.

Only a couple of minutes later Stemp's door opened and Brock tottered out looking as though he'd left behind several pints of blood and most of his entrails. White to the lips, he stared straight ahead while he felt his way along the corridor wall toward the men's room.

"Kelly." Stemp's emotionless voice made me twitch in spite of myself. "Please come in."

I re-entered his office cautiously, glancing around for evidence of the evisceration that had just occurred.

The office was pristine as always, and I eased into the chair Stemp indicated across the desk from him.

He studied me in silence. Only one of his hands was on the desk. I knew damn well he was holding that goddamn trank gun in the other.

Refusing to give in to the urge to talk just to fill the silence, I held his gaze as steadily as I could manage.

After several minutes, the corner of his mouth quirked up a fraction. "Very well," he said as though continuing an argument. "I've rescheduled your psych evaluation for this afternoon at fourteen-thirty. Can I trust you to control your violent impulses until then?"

Ignoring the burning in my cheeks, I nodded. "I'm sorry. I normally wouldn't have let him get to me. It was just the double whammy of a shot of adrenaline and pain. Fear and pain makes me instantly furious. I've been that way all my life."

"Yes." Stemp leaned back in his chair. "That was in your

psych report.   Dr. Rawling had some psychological explanation for it, but frankly..."

Was that a glint of humour in his eyes?

"...it seems reasonable enough to me," he finished.

The glint vanished without a trace, leaving behind nothing but cold steel.

"However," he said.   "Regardless of any personal empathy I may feel, your loss of control is unacceptable. It is never appropriate to threaten or physically engage anyone except as strictly required by the needs of a mission. Don't make the mistake of believing I'll make exceptions for you."

I held his gaze. "I wouldn't expect you to."

"Good."   He eyed me like a snake about to strike. "Ordinarily I would suspend you on the spot, but since Ms. Mellor would suffer the consequences of that, I'm going to offer you another chance..." He held up a hand to deflect the thanks already on my lips.   "...pending Dr. Rawling's evaluation," he went on. "If, in his opinion, you are capable of functioning as part of the team without further altercations, I'll allow you to continue. If he has any doubts about your ability to control yourself, I will confiscate your weapons and relocate you to a safe house for your own protection. Forcibly if necessary."

It was my turn to gulp, and I could feel the blood draining from my face. "Understood." My voice came out in a croak.

"Very well." He inspected me in silence again, and I held my spine straight with all the strength I could muster.

"Brock has gone home," he said at last. A rapier-thin smile flitted across his lips. "Something about a bad headache."

I would have smiled, too, if I hadn't been so busy

worrying about my own skin.

"...so you can begin brainstorming with Webb and Dr. Travers today," he went on. "And if Dr. Rawling approves, you can observe Ms. Mellor's session tomorrow. Furthermore..."

Oh, God, it was always the 'furthermore' that dealt the killing blow.

"I had planned to bring this up later," he continued. "...but since your observation of Ms. Mellor is effectively cancelled for today, I'll tell you now. The rest of the team is already aware that my position is up for review next Thursday. A representative from Human Resources will be contacting you for a peer review of my work sometime before then."

I hadn't thought it was possible for my stomach to sink any lower. "Oh, God," I blurted. "Please tell me they're not thinking of giving Dermott the director's position."

Impassive as always, Stemp replied, "Dermott would be the logical choice if my performance is found wanting."

"Oh, God, we're all going to die." I buried my head in my hands.

"Dermott is competent," Stemp said. "They wouldn't consider him for the position otherwise."

"Competent, maybe." I dragged my head up to face him. "But only *competent*. Not exceptional. You're a far better director than he could ever be." We stared at each other in silence, and I added, "I can't believe I just said that. But it's true."

One of Stemp's rare laughs escaped, softening his features and warming his eyes. "Thank you for the vote of confidence."

I filled the slightly awkward pause with the first question that came to mind. "Um... do you actually *want* to stay on as director?" The thought of his secret wife and daughter overseas niggled at me. "Or are you thinking of, um... retiring... soon?"

He sobered. "Retirement is my goal within the foreseeable future, but ideally not at this juncture." He gave me a significant look. "I want to be sure all loose ends are completely resolved before I leave this position."

Of course. Stemp the chessmaster. He'd be closing every loophole, making sure he and his family could live in safety even after he relinquished his access to classified intel.

"Well, you'll get a good review from me. For what it's worth." I gave him a tight smile and rose to head for the door. As I touched the door handle, he spoke again.

"Aydan."

Surprised by his use of my first name, I turned to face his penetrating gaze.

"Don't try to deceive Dr. Rawling in your evaluation this afternoon," he said softly. "If you go back to active duty when you're not ready, it could cost lives. Including your own."

I grimaced at the stab of guilt but refrained from any other comment.

CHAPTER 8

Like Brock, I wobbled away from Stemp's office to the washrooms. Surveying my bloodless face in the ladies' room mirror, I let out a sigh that came all the way from my toes and closed myself into a cubicle until I felt capable of facing Spider and Jack.

As soon as I thought I could fake composure convincingly, I plastered on a smile and strode back to Spider's office. When I tapped on the open door, Jack eyed me worriedly and Spider sprang to his feet.

"Come in," he said, and hurried over to close the door behind me. "What happened?" he whispered as I sank into one of his chairs. "Where's Brock?"

"Stemp sliced and diced us both." I let out a breath and slithered lower in the chair. "He did Brock first. I don't know what he said, but it only took a couple of minutes before Brock came out looking like a gutted fish and went straight home." I held up trembling fingertips a fraction of an inch apart and went on, "I came this close to getting suspended, and I might still end up that way if I can't convince Dr. Rawling I'm sane and stable this afternoon."

"But that's not fair!" Spider's eyes blazed above pinkening cheeks. "Brock deliberately provoked you! I'll go and talk to Stemp."

"No." I held up a calming hand. "Thanks, Spider, but don't. Stemp will let it go as long as Dr. Rawling okays me, so there's no point in rocking the boat. Let's just get to work on Tammy's project. I only observed her that one time four months ago, so what's new since then?"

"Well..." Spider began, but Jack interrupted him.

"Sorry, Spider; just before we get started..." She cast him an apologetic glance before continuing, "Aydan, Jill asked me to give you a message to meet her at seven o'clock at Blue Eddy's. If that doesn't work, give her a call on her cell but otherwise she'll see you there."

"Okay, that's fine. Thanks, Jack."

"And..." Jack hesitated before giving me a strained smile. "Are you free for lunch today?"

"Oh... uh... Spider and I are having lunch together..." I trailed off, fairly sure he wanted it to be a private conference.

"Would you like to join us, Jack?" he asked. If I hadn't known him so well, I might have missed the dismay he was hiding.

Jack's gaze darted between us. "Um... no... thanks. That's kind of you but, um... I'd better get some work done in my lab. Being on Tammy's project will cut into my regular research time." She gave me a beseeching look. "How about grabbing coffee after work? I have to pick up my children from their after-school care, but I promised to take them to the playground afterward. We could get some coffee and sit out and enjoy the nice weather while they play. That'll leave you lots of time to get to Blue Eddy's and meet Jill later."

"Okay..."

Concerned, I studied her more closely and noticed for the first time that her usually-flawless ivory complexion was marred by faint bluish circles under her eyes and tiny lines of strain bracketed her full lips.

My brain sprang into worry-mode while my mouth went on, "...that'll leave me just enough time to get to the lumberyard and buy my new doors before I meet Jill. Perfect."

God, was everybody hiding some stressful secret? And why were they all desperate to talk to me?

I sighed. "So, getting back to Tammy's project..."

By the time we finished our session at noon my tired brain was throbbing. I rose wearily and eyed Spider and Jack, seeing the same anxious frustration on their faces that I felt on my own.

I hissed out a breath between my teeth. "I hate to say it, but I don't see any way around this. It's either edit Tammy's memories or lock her up."

"No, there must be another way," Spider insisted. He raked his fingers through his hair, rumpling it into untidy peaks. "We've still got nearly a week. We'll think of something. And you always find a way to make things right." His trusting words made my guts clench.

I forced a smile. "Well, I'll do my best. Come on, let's get something to eat. Food always makes my brain work better."

"Are you sure you won't join us, Jack?" Spider inquired nobly, and managed not to look relieved when she shook her head.

When we left the building my feet turned automatically toward the Melted Spoon, but Spider touched my arm. "No, let's go to the Greenhorn instead," he said. "I'll drive."

"Okay." I fell into step beside him and we made the short walk to the Sirius parking lot in silence.

I slid into his lime-green Smart car and watched while he folded himself into the driver's side. When the doors were safely closed, he reached into his pocket, murmuring an apology when I had to plaster myself against the passenger door to avoid his elbow in the cramped space. He opened his hand to reveal a bug detector and let out a breath of relief at the indicator light's reassuring green glow.

"What's going on, Spider?" I demanded. "Why the cloak-and-dagger stuff?"

He sighed again and returned the bug detector to his pocket, necessitating another round of dodge-the-elbow. "Sorry," he said tiredly. "I just... I don't want Stemp to know I'm talking to you about this, and Brock... well, it's not that I don't trust him, exactly... but..."

"I wouldn't trust that little shit any farther than I could throw him," I said. "Hell, never mind that. I wouldn't trust him any farther than I could throw this whole damn car. With you and me in it."

"No... Well, I mean, yeah... but no; he's trustworthy. I mean, he's got top-level clearances and I know he'd never breach security," Spider mumbled. "I just meant... I mean, well... I don't trust him... um, personally."

I studied his unhappy profile as he ran his fingertip back and forth on the steering wheel.

"You mean he's the kind of guy who'd pry into your personal life to find out your deepest secrets just so he could use them to make you miserable," I said.

Spider gave me a single eloquent glance. "Yeah. Or make somebody you love miserable."

The embers of the morning's anger flared to life and my voice boiled out of my throat. "Spider, what is he doing to you? Or to Linda? Tell me."

His eyes widened. "Aydan, d-don't... I mean..." He gulped. "Um... could you please, um... don't take this wrong, but could you please stop looking like you're going to kill somebody? Promise you won't hurt him."

"No promises," I grated.

"Aydan, no! Please!" He clutched my hand, his fingers icy. "I don't want you to get in trouble. He's not worth it. Please promise me. If you don't promise, I can't tell you. And I really need to talk to you about this. Please?" The naked appeal in his eyes twisted my heart.

I swallowed the anger, smoothing my expression and steadying my voice. "Don't worry, Spider, I promise not to hurt him..." I mentally added, 'because I'll kill the little shit so fast he'll never even feel the pain', and finished aloud, "... and I'm sorry I scared you. Please tell me what's wrong."

His breath came out in a whoosh. "Oh, thank you, Aydan! I knew I could count on you!"

He backed out of the parking space and steered in the direction of the Greenhorn Café. We were barely under way when he burst out, "Oh, Aydan, everything's so messed up I don't even know where to start!"

"Start with Brock." My tone came out a little more dangerous than I'd intended, and Spider glanced worriedly in my direction before returning his gaze to the street.

"Okay," he said. "He's... well... I wouldn't say this to anybody but you, but... I mean, he's really smart and good at his job and everything-"

"Spit it out, Spider."

"He just... it's like he's always trying to show how he's better than me. He never says anything in our team meetings but as soon as we're in front of Stemp he picks my work apart. Any time Linda's around he makes fun of me and tries to make me look bad. I mean, I *know* I'm not cool, I never have been, and I *know* every guy in town has been chasing Linda ever since high school and she's 'way out of my league-"

"Stop right there!" I snapped.

He slammed on the brakes, staring wildly around us.

I chuckled despite my indignation. "No, I didn't mean 'stop the car', I meant 'stop that train of thought'."

"Oh." He resumed driving, a flush rising on his cheeks. "See, I'm such a doofus."

"You are not! You're the smartest, nicest guy I know." His blush deepened, and I went on, "Spider, Linda is *not* out of your league. She loves you and she's thrilled to be marrying you. Remember, she's the one who asked you out, not the other way around. And she's far too smart to fall for Brock's poison-tongue campaign. Stemp sees right through it, too, so don't worry. Don't let Brock spoil your happiness."

"Oh, no, I'd never doubt Linda!" Spider shot me a shocked glance. "No, I didn't mean that. I just meant... I don't know whether Brock just likes making me miserable or whether he's hoping to split us up so he can have a chance with Linda, but-"

My snort drowned out the end of his sentence. "Linda wouldn't give him the time of day. She'd kick his pathetic little ass so hard he'd end up with two new cheeks on the back of his head. And then you could call him a butthead in all honesty."

Spider grinned. "Thanks, I was pretty sure she would,

but it's nice to hear you say it." His smile disappeared as quickly as it had come. "But that's not really what's bothering me. I know Linda loves me and I love her more than anything in the world, but..." He pulled to a stop in the Greenhorn parking lot and turned a tormented face toward me. "This thing with Tammy... I can't do it, Aydan. I just can't! And it's going to spoil everything!"

"Spider..." I began.

"It was bad enough when it was just Brock controlling Tammy in the network without her knowing," he went on as if I hadn't spoken. "Even though you said she wouldn't mind and she'd be happy to do it, still... it bothered the heck out me. But now..."

He faced me, squaring his shoulders even though his lips quivered. "I won't tamper with her memories. I *won't*. I'll quit first. And if they go ahead anyway I'll tell her about it, even if Stemp sends me to jail for breaching security."

He gulped and went on, his voice trembling. "If I'm in jail I can't expect Linda to wait for me, and even if I don't end up in jail, I'll never be able to work in any high-security position ever again. Flipping burgers is the only job I could get here in Silverside, and if I wanted a regular tech job I'd have to move to Calgary."

Emotion drove his voice higher and his words tumbled out. "Linda didn't sign up to marry a burger jockey, and she doesn't want to live in Calgary. I know she'd move to be with me anyway, but I don't want her to sacrifice her whole life. She loves her job at the hospital and her whole family is here and she has the store, too; she can't leave Lola to run Up & Coming all by herself..."

"Whoa, slow down." I held up a hand to stem the torrent

of anguish, but the dam had burst.

"...and if Brock finds out about any of this, this... crap... with Tammy he'll blab it to Linda and she'll be so hurt because I didn't tell her, and she'll be worried, too, and she's so happy right now planning the wedding and it'll spoil everything..."

"Spider, stop!" I gripped his shoulder and gave him a little shake. "Take a breath."

He obeyed, blotches of colour burning in his cheeks while he blinked back tears.

"It's going to be okay." I rubbed a soothing circle on his shoulder in lieu of trying to hug him in the cramped space. "I promise we won't even consider altering Tammy's memories. I've already told Stemp I won't do it. It's just not an option, so don't worry about it anymore. You and Jack are two of the smartest people I know, and we've got nearly a whole week. We'll figure out something. And Stemp knows Brock is a backstabbing little rat so you don't need to worry about that either. In fact, Stemp said this morning that you're his most trusted analyst."

"I won't be if I spill the beans to Tammy," he mumbled.

"We'll make sure you don't have to," I said firmly despite the sinking sensation in my stomach. "And we'll figure out a way to get Brock off your back, too. Trust me, we'll fix this and you can go back to loving your job and planning your wedding without a care in the world."

He swallowed hard and brushed the moisture from his eyes. "Thanks, Aydan." Somehow he managed to get his arms around me despite the lack of space and nearly hugged the life out of me. "I knew you'd make everything better," he said earnestly. "Thank you." He let out a long breath. "Let's go get some lunch."

"Sure," I agreed, and levered myself out of the tiny vehicle to plod into the restaurant, my stomach churning at the magnitude of the lies I'd just told.

I didn't have a clue how to resolve the problem with Tammy. And short of killing Brock outright I didn't have a clue how to make him stop tormenting Spider, either.

CHAPTER 9

His optimism miraculously revived, Spider chattered cheerfully while I forced a sandwich down my dry throat. When we returned to work after lunch, I was so abstracted that I accomplished nothing besides increasing the intensity of my headache. Judging by the way Jack was massaging her temples, I wasn't the only one suffering.

But I was the only one who had to face Dr. Rawling's scrutiny.

Promptly at two-thirty I drew a deep breath, summoned my best acting skills, and tapped on his office door.

At the sound of his 'Come in', I swung the door open and entered with a brisk stride. Repressing the impulse to slink into the chair that offered a coffee table as a barricade between us, I sat undefended directly across from him, arranging my posture into calm confidence. Letting my arms rest easily on the armrests, I kept my hands loose, feet comfortably apart, knees relaxed. I offered him a disarming smile.

He returned a kind smile of his own, but I wasn't fooled. Already his keen eyes were trying to dissect me.

"It's nice to see you again, Aydan," he said. "How have you been?"

Standard opening line. Easy.

I went for wry humour. "Pretty much the same as when I talked to you on the phone two weeks ago, except now I've got a couple more notches on my gun."

Shit, that had come out too flippant.

"And how do you feel about that?" he inquired gently.

Go for some fake honesty. "Terrible, to tell you the truth," I said.

Damn. Shouldn't have said 'to tell you the truth'. All liars say that.

I let out a breath and coaxed my shoulders back into their relaxed posture. "I'm getting through it," I added. "Sorry about the black humour; it's just whistling in the dark. But I'll be okay. You know I've been through the process a few times, so I know how to deal with it."

"Yes, you've been 'through the process', as you put it, far more frequently than we'd like." Dr. Rawling adjusted his wire-rimmed glasses and offered me one of his trademark sympathetic smiles. "Of course, we'd like it better if you never had to kill, but..." He trailed off with a rueful twist of his lips before asking, "How have you been sleeping?"

I almost blurted, 'In my garage', but that didn't seem wise. I tilted my hand in a 'so-so' gesture that was a lie, and said, "The usual", which was the truth.

Fortunately only Kane and Hellhound knew that my 'usual' was more-or-less-constant screaming nightmares.

"So a few nightmares, then?" Dr. Rawling asked.

"Yeah."

Anything more than three was 'a few', right?

The monosyllabic answer didn't sound cooperative enough, though. Better say something else that sounded sincere.

I added, "It was pretty upsetting to have that guy blow a hole in my front door. I hate it when bad stuff happens in my house; it always shakes me up."

"Yes, that must have been very upsetting." He studied me, a deceptively mild little man poised to swoop in for the kill. "Do you think that might have contributed to the way you reacted to Tyler Brock this morning?"

Yep, there was the first attack.

I parried. "Indirectly, yes. Have you ever had a firearm discharged next to your head in an enclosed space?"

Any other man might have sounded defensive, but Dr. Rawling's response was as tranquil and accepting as ever. "No, I haven't. It must be quite distressing."

I blinked. "Um, no... not really *distressing*. Not if you're used to guns. It's just that it's really fu-" I bit off the f-bomb and substituted, "Really loud. Deafening; literally. And I don't know how it affects other people, but it makes my ears supersensitive for a while afterward. So when Brock cranked on his music, it physically hurt me. And it startled the hell out of me, too, so I had too much adrenaline in my system. That's why I overreacted."

The doctor settled more comfortably in his chair, as though we were having a cozy little chinwag with no consequences. "Would you like to talk about that?"

Yeah, sure. And I'd like to hopscotch through a minefield, too.

But if I volunteered the information I'd look all nice and sane. I suppressed a telltale sigh and reminded myself to keep my posture relaxed and open.

"It was just one of those stupid things you say in the heat of the moment," I began. "And I was exaggerating anyway.

I've only killed two guys this week, not one a day like I told him."

Shit, that was probably the wrong tack.

"I mean, *you* probably don't say stuff like that, being a psychologist and all," I amended. "But what I meant is that it was just an empty threat. Honestly, the thought of really killing Brock... like I killed those other guys..." Despite my best efforts, my arms abandoned their fake relaxation to hug the queasiness in my midsection. I swallowed nausea. "It just about makes me sick. He's an annoying little shit, but-"

Suddenly remembering where I was and why, I straightened and replaced my arms in their easy posture. "Sorry, that wasn't very constructive," I backtracked. "What I meant was, um, he and I don't really see eye to eye. But no matter how much he might annoy me, I wouldn't actually kill him."

Dr. Rawling nodded and smiled his innocuous little smile. "What do you think might have happened if your co-workers hadn't intervened this morning?"

I stared at him, confused. "They didn't."

He made no response, just watched me with those dangerously kind eyes.

Apparently that was the wrong answer. Frowning, I thought back.

"Well, okay," I conceded. "I guess Spider and Jill said something, but it wasn't like they were physically holding me back. If I'd really wanted to hurt Brock, they wouldn't have been able to stop me."

Should I have said that? But since he believed I was an agent he'd expect that to be true.

"But they did intervene, nonetheless," the doctor

reiterated gently. "What do you think might have happened if they hadn't been there?"

I shrugged. "Nothing. Or, well, I guess exactly what happened. I'd have threatened him and then backed off."

"Even if he had escalated the confrontation? What if he had fought back? Struck you?"

I pressed my lips together to smother the words 'I'd have flattened the little fuck', and stared at Dr. Rawling in silence.

"After all, he had legitimate reason to fear for his life," he persisted. "You threatened to kill him and you physically accosted him. What would you have done if you were in his shoes?"

Probably a bad idea to answer that question.

"I wouldn't have hurt him," I said instead. "If he had fought back I wouldn't have just stood there and let him beat me up, but I wouldn't have beaten him to a pulp, either. I can tell the difference between a legitimate threat and an annoyance even if I've been taken by surprise. It's no different than the shooting simulation exercises. If a target pops up and startles me I aim at it, but I don't fire unless it's a valid target. Metaphorically speaking, I took aim at Brock this morning but I didn't fire. And I wouldn't have unless he was actually a threat."

The doctor gave me one of his treacherously mild smiles. "That's an excellent example, though it's important to note that in the shooting simulation you know it's a simulation. You *know* none of the targets are capable of hurting or killing you so there's a reduced perception of threat."

"True," I admitted. "But have you ever done one of those simulations? There's a hell of a lot of adrenaline pumping through you."

"No, I haven't." He gave me another gentle smile. "I

have never fired a gun so I would undoubtedly not do well in the simulation. But getting back to you: Do you think it's possible that you might have a heightened perception of threat at the moment?"

I clamped my teeth on my tongue to prevent myself from snapping 'Ya *think*, Sherlock?'

I held my voice calm and level. "Heightened, yes, but I wouldn't say it's disproportionate to the threat, considering that somebody is actively trying to kill me."

He nodded as though we were in complete agreement and asked, "Do you think perhaps your heightened threat perception might cause you to overreact in non-lethal situations?"

Bastard. He'd cornered me.

My heart lurched into my throat and lodged there in an unwieldy lump. I had already admitted I'd overreacted. How the hell could I answer his question without buying myself a ticket to safe-house prison?

With a gargantuan effort I kept my hands from clenching into fists and kept my voice even. "I think we've already agreed that this morning was an overreaction in the larger sense. But as you know, that's a normal reaction for me. Ever since I was a kid I've always gotten angry when I'm hurt and scared. So no; I wouldn't say my reactions in non-lethal situations have really changed."

He nodded, his little half-smile as unreadable as ever. "Aydan," he said in his pleasant non-confrontational tone. "I feel as though you're trying to avoid going to the safe house."

No shit. And never mind how he *felt*; Stemp had probably told him exactly that. No point in denying it.

"Yes, that's true," I said, trying not to sound grudging.

"Why is that, Aydan?"

Go for just the right mix of honesty...

I leaned back in my chair, holding onto my relaxed posture for dear life. "Well, as you know I'm not fond of being..." I almost said 'trapped', but substituted a more moderate phrase at the last instant. "...closed in." I couldn't quite prevent the convulsive swallow that accompanied the thought, dammit.

"...but it's not just that," I went on determinedly. "You're aware of the situation with Tammy, of course..."

Dr. Rawling nodded and I went on, mindful that he wasn't privy to classified information. "Stemp believes I can help with that, but I only have a week before the deadline. I can't tell you the details but it's something only I can do, and if I fail there will be life-changing consequences for Tammy. And Stemp and I both believe that this situation with the assassins can be resolved more quickly if I stay in their sights."

"And do you think the consequences to Tammy would be so severe that it's worth risking your life to prevent them?"

"Hell, yes!" The words popped out before I had a chance to think them through, but even in retrospect it was the truth. The thought of sweet child-like Tammy spending the rest of her life imprisoned made my spine stiffen with determination. I wouldn't let them do that to her, dammit.

He nodded his usual accepting little nod, and our interview continued with some general discussion of Brock and the team before seguing into the standard post-mission psych evaluation. I fielded the questions as best I could, nudging the truth into more attractive shapes whenever possible.

Finally Dr. Rawling studied me in silence and I held my

breath. I was pretty sure I had gamed the post-mission questions well enough. And after counselling Tammy for the past several months, he must feel some empathy and concern for her. If I had made the consequences to her sound dire enough...

"All right, Aydan," Dr. Rawling said at last. "I'll clear you for modified duty only. No new missions, but I'll give you a chance to deal with the current situation. If anything changes we'll discuss this again, and certainly if you have any concerns or if you'd just like to talk..."

He trailed off as if realizing the unlikeliness of that. "I want to see you again first thing next week," he added. "Will Monday at two-thirty work?"

I agreed and vacated his office as rapidly as it was possible to do without actually breaking into a run.

CHAPTER 10

Another fruitless hour of brainstorming with Spider and Jack accomplished nothing except to wind the tension in my neck and shoulders even tighter. Jack looked at her wristwatch so often that her anxiety transferred itself to me, and when four-thirty finally arrived she sprang to her feet as though she had been jabbed by something in her chair.

"Well, we'd better get going," she said in an unconvincing imitation of nonchalance. "The day-home operator gets antsy if I don't pick up the children by a quarter to five."

My heart thumped a little faster and I rose, too. "Okay, I'll swing by the Melted Spoon and pick up our drinks, and I'll meet you at the park. What can I get you?"

"Oh..." She blinked as though a beverage was the last thing on her mind. "Um... a skim-milk vanilla latte with no sugar. Thanks, Aydan." She gave me a faux-cheery smile. "See you in a little while."

"See you," I replied, but she had already hurried out.

Spider turned a worried face toward me. "Something's wrong, I'm sure of it. Jack hasn't been herself for the past month. I've asked her about it but she always says everything's fine."

I hissed air out between my teeth. "It doesn't look good, does it? I hope it's nothing serious."

"I hope not, too." He knotted his fingers together anxiously. "Let me know if there's anything I can do to help."

"I will, Spider. Thanks. I better get going." I gave him a grimace that was supposed to be a smile and hurried out.

When I arrived at the small park, Jack was already seated on a bench while her son and daughter, easily identifiable by their bright blonde hair, scampered on the playground.

Pulling my truck to a stop in the parking lot, I cast a nervous glance at the trees that surrounded the park. Twice before, clandestine activities in those trees had nearly cost my life. If a gunman was hidden in the woods today, my third time might prove unlucky.

My pulse sped up while I calculated angles and sight lines and escape routes. If somebody started shooting at me, Jack and her kids would be caught in the crossfire.

Childish squeals of delight floated to my ears through my open window. Brendan swarmed up the climbing frame like a towheaded chimpanzee while little Ivy twisted up the chains of her swing until her feet left the ground. The unwinding chains spun her around and around, her mouth open in peals of silvery laughter, flaxen ringlets flying.

God, if anything happened to them...

The thought of small bodies motionless in pools of blood made my stomach lurch into my throat. I gulped down the bile and scrubbed both hands violently over my face.

Don't think about it.

Don't let it happen.

Jack spotted the truck and waved, and with a curse I bent to transfer my Glock from my ankle holster to the waistband of my jeans for quicker access. The trank pistol went in beside it, turning the jeans into an uncomfortable tourniquet. I pulled my sweatshirt down over them, still muttering profanities. Should've worn my waist holster today, dammit. And brought my shoulder rig.

But I needed both weapons within easy reach. I'd prefer to leave any attacker tranquilized and alive for questioning, but if the children were endangered, I'd need the greater range and accuracy of the Glock.

Gripping the cardboard takeout tray and my courage with equal firmness, I deserted the safety of the truck and headed for the bench. At least if he was aiming at me from the trees beside the lot, his shooting line wouldn't cross the playground.

I shook off the thought.

Get real. There wasn't a shooter in the trees. Nobody could have known I'd go to the park after work today. I hadn't even known myself.

But if somebody had followed me...

Just settle down. In a town the size of Silverside I would have noticed a tail. God knew I'd been paranoid enough about watching for one.

"Hi again," Jack said as I approached, and I returned the greeting and handed her the latte before perching on the bench beside her with one more uneasy survey of the trees.

Jack turned a worried face toward me. "Aydan, I'm sorry to bother you the first day you're back to work, but there's something I need to tell you."

I took a gulp of my chamomile tea in an attempt to swallow the spiky ball of tension in my throat. "Okay, what is it?"

She glanced around and leaned toward me as if afraid to be overheard. "Did you know Charles is up for review this coming Thursday?"

"Ch...?" I bit off my incredulous question. So it was 'Charles' now instead of 'Stemp'. That didn't bode well.

"Um, yeah, he told me," I replied.

"This is bad, Aydan."

"Yeah, I know..."

I trailed off, wondering why she looked so upset. Losing Stemp would be a disaster to clandestine operations, but it likely wouldn't affect the research department. I gulped. Oh sweet Lord, please tell me she's not secretly in love with Stemp.

She leaned nearer. "Dermott would be his replacement." Dermott's name came out in a hiss, and I suddenly recalled how much Jack disliked him. And vice versa.

"Oh." I eyed her with concern. "Yeah. That would be bad, wouldn't it?"

"You don't know the half of it." She glanced around again. "Are you involved with the Spring Thing?"

"Uh... what?" I frowned, struggling to catch up with the sudden change of topic.

"The Spring Thing. You do know what the Spring Thing is?"

I held up a hand to forestall an explanation. "Yeah, I know. I was going to see if I could ride on the Sirius Dynamics float."

"Don't," she said darkly. "Take my advice: Stay far, far away."

"Um... okay... but..." I did another nervous inventory of

the surrounding trees, wishing she'd get on with it. "I don't know what that has to do with Stemp," I said, trying not to sound impatient.

"Every year the social committee decides on a theme for the float," she explained. "Spider and I usually serve on the social committee along with a few other researchers. We form the core group from year to year, and often agents who are on administrative leave will join just for a break from the monotony. This year Jill has joined us, along with another agent, Greg Holt. Do you know him?"

I nodded and she went on, "And..." Her nose wrinkled fastidiously. "Tyler Brock."

"Ew. You have my sympathy."

"Yes, well, he's certainly been an annoyance, but that's not the problem." Jack frowned. "Greg Holt has been... um... offering me a great deal of attention..."

I read between the lines. Jack's radiant blonde beauty and jaw-dropping figure would bring any red-blooded man to his knees. Holt was clearly no exception.

"...which is really quite... unfortunate," Jack went on. "He's not particularly... er... well, you know I don't date agents. And in any case he's really not my type."

Recalling Holt's craggy features, lantern jaw, and volatile temper, I nodded again and sipped my tea.

"But..." Jack blushed. "I'm rather ashamed to say I've been pumping him nevertheless."

Tea shot out my nose. Groping frantically for a napkin, I choked, "I beg your pardon?"

"Pumping him for information," Jack qualified with icy primness, but mischief sparkled in her eyes.

"That wasn't nice," I admonished, blotting the wet spots on my sweatshirt.

"No, but it was fun." She grinned, but sobered immediately. "But what I've discovered isn't funny at all. Holt hates Charles. Apparently there was friction between them when Charles put him on administrative leave originally. Then Dermott reinstated Holt briefly, but as soon as Charles returned he pulled Holt from active duty again."

"Yeah, I knew about that. I was glad he did. Holt's a good agent but he had major anger issues after a mission went bad on him. He wasn't ready for active duty, but he and Dermott are buddies."

"Oh. Good, so you understand the dynamic." Jack nodded, frowning. "So here's where it gets bad. Remember when Dermott fired Spider for refusing to control Tammy in the network? And then he had to eat crow and re-hire Spider? And then Charles promoted Spider and complimented him for his good work?"

I nodded along with her points, knowing she wouldn't be hurried through her step-by-step analysis. Usually I admired her scientific mind, but today I could barely throttle a scream of impatience.

"So..." Jack eyed me worriedly. "According to Holt, if Dermott takes over the director's position there are going to be, as he puts it, 'shakeups'. Aydan, Dermott will reinstate Holt despite Dr. Rawling's recommendations. But that's not the worst of it. He'll fire Spider and promote Brock to team lead."

"Oh, *shit!*"

"Exactly." Jack rubbed her temples as if fighting off a headache. "So you see why I couldn't say anything in front of Spider, but this has been driving me to distraction ever since I found out about it a month ago. I've been trying to drum up support for Charles wherever I can, but..." Her shoulders rose and fell in a despairing shrug. "He doesn't make himself popular. He just does the best job he can and lets the chips fall where they may."

She turned an imploring face toward me. "Aydan, I know you don't like Charles, but will you support him?"

"Of course. I told him I would as soon as he mentioned the peer review. Dermott would be a bloody disaster."

"Oh thank heaven!" Jack fell back against the bench. "I was so afraid... as one of the top agents your recommendation carries a lot of weight. I was..." She drew a breath. "Do you think John Kane will support him, too?"

I choked down my dismay at the thought of being considered a top agent and assured her, "I'm pretty sure he will. He doesn't like Stemp much either, but he wouldn't let his personal feelings take precedence over the good of the Department."

"Oh, thank goodness." She took a sip of her latte as if seeking strength, her hand trembling slightly. "I spoke with Carl Germain before he shipped out to his current mission and he supports Charles. Jill does, too." She let out a breath. "Most of the top agents do. Thank goodness you're all so dedicated to results that you can put aside personal differences."

"Uh... yeah..." I eyed her. "Look, Jack, I know you don't like Dermott, and this thing about Spider is really bad, but I'm getting the feeling it's a little more than that."

She flushed. "Well, yes. It is a little more than that. I admire Charles a great deal. More to the point, I admire the way he approves my research budget so promptly every year. If Dermott takes over, I really don't believe he has enough strength of character to put aside our personal differences.

There's a very good chance that I'd be demoted or fired, too."

I stared down a long bleak future of Brock's petulance, Holt's unpredictable rages, and Dermott's bluster, all without the expertise and camaraderie of the two best friends I had at Sirius Dynamics. I swallowed hard.

After a short silence I offered, "I could shoot Dermott."

Jack's horrified expression completely destroyed my attempt at remaining deadpan and I laughed aloud.

"That wasn't nice," she snapped.

"No, but it was fun." My amusement ebbed rapidly and I sighed and slouched back in the bench. "Well, if all the top agents are rooting for Stemp, there's probably nothing to worry about. His track record is excellent. As long as he hasn't antagonized anybody up the chain of command..." I trailed off at the sight of her expression. "Oh, shit, has he?"

Jack hunched her shoulders miserably. "Potentially. There were some very ruffled feathers when he left the country with that top-secret weapon back at Christmas without informing any of his superiors. They settled down when he broke that giant case with Interpol as a result, but... some of those army types take a very hard-line stance."

I shuddered in agreement, remembering a certain hearing with Kane's military chain of command. "So... what can we do, besides worry about it?"

Jack sighed. "Nothing I know of. But I'm worrying as hard as I can. I was hoping you'd be able to think of something."

I suppressed a groan. "I don't know what I can do, but I'll try."

CHAPTER 11

With my new doors safely stowed in the back of my truck, I pulled into the parking lot at Blue Eddy's Saloon at a quarter to seven and turned off the ignition with a sigh.

I had already driven by once to scope out the nearby roofs and alleys for potential access points for an assassin. I hadn't seen anything threatening, but what did I know? I needed Kane's ability to effortlessly assess every detail of a site in a single glance.

Hell, who was I kidding? I needed Kane himself, and Hellhound, too, to watch my back.

And warm my bed, though I had no idea which of them I'd choose if they were both here.

But with my shitty luck they were probably male-bonding during their motorcycle trip and making a pact to dump me. After all, their brotherhood went back decades. I was only a blip on their timeline.

I pushed that dismal thought aside and climbed wearily out of the truck. Bracing myself for another litany of woe, I trudged toward the back door. Even if I wasn't really in the mood to listen, I couldn't blame Jill for wanting to vent. If I were her, I'd be ready to jam sharpened sticks in my ears just to escape Tammy's constant babble.

When I walked in Jill was nowhere to be seen, but Eddy's face split in a grin as he hurried out from behind the bar.

"Aydan!" He enveloped me in a bear hug and I silently thanked my lucky stars I'd transferred my weapons out of my waistband before I left the truck. "It's great to see you!" he exclaimed.

Finally, one of my friends looked happy. Thank God.

"It's great to see you, too, Eddy," I said with feeling. "How have you been? I've missed you!"

"I missed you, too," he replied. "The bookkeeper who was filling in for you did a good job, but she was a little, um... well, I'm really glad you're back, is all. Would you like a beer?"

"Eddy, after the day I've had, I'd like a keg. But I can't. I'm driving."

He nodded understanding and turned back to the bar.

Some small childish part of me rebelled.

Dammit, I'd been stuck on an alcohol-free commune for the past four months. After enduring Dump-On-Aydan Day I had a headache the size of Alberta, and I might not even be alive by tomorrow if my unknown enemy had hired a more competent assassin. And if I was going to present any kind of sympathetic ear for Jill tonight, I was damn well going to need a beer.

No; several beers.

"You know what, Eddy? Forget it. Bring me a pint of draft."

He turned, frowning. "That's not like you."

I sighed. "I'm not feeling much like me today, but don't worry. I won't drink and drive. I'm not going to stay late, so I'll call Spider when I'm ready to go. He can drive me home in my truck and Linda can follow in her car and bring him back."

Eddy nodded, his smile returning, and I headed for my favourite table in the corner. Sliding into the chair with my back to the wall as usual I eased out a sigh, relaxing into the welcoming arms of the blues music.

Eddy arrived with my beer a few moments later. Sucking in a mouthful of suds, I closed my eyes in gratitude as the nectar of the gods slid down my throat. I groaned and opened my eyes. "Thanks, Eddy, I might just live now."

"Sounds like a tough day," he replied, the usual twinkle in his eye fading to seriousness. "Do you want to talk about it?"

I gave him what felt like my first real smile of the day. "Thanks, but I'm okay. This is exactly what I needed." I took another drink and added, "Well, this and one of your fabulous burgers. I'm starving."

"Coming right up!"

Eddy hurried away and I settled back in the chair and applied myself to his excellent draft.

A few minutes later Jill appeared in the doorway, her gaze flicking over the room in an agent's seemingly-casual assessment before she strode over to join me.

Eddy returned from the kitchen, and I beckoned to him. "Eddy, have you met Jill Francis? We work together at Sirius Dynamics."

"No, I haven't. Nice to meet you, Jill." Eddy offered his hand and Jill shook it with a smile. "What can I bring you?" Eddy added.

"Do you have a house red?"

Eddy nodded. "Cabernet Sauvignon or Shiraz?"

"Cabernet." The word issued from Jill's lips in a tone

that might have been used to say 'Heaven'. "Please," she added. "And thank you."

"Would you like to see a food menu, too?" Eddy inquired, and Jill shot a glance at me.

"Aydan, what do you like here?"

"Everything," I said promptly. "But my favourites are the burgers, hot wings, and Caesar salad."

"Burger, please," she murmured. "With Caesar salad."

Eddy returned in moments with a glass of red wine, and Jill's first sip went down with a moan of satisfaction that echoed mine earlier.

Eddy smiled and withdrew, and Jill took another appreciative mouthful, her eyelids drifting half-closed and her shoulders relaxing.

"Oh, thank God," she breathed, and leaned back in her chair.

I grinned and raised my pint. "Here's to alcohol and whoever invented it."

"You can say that again. Cheers."

After we drank, I said, "You must really need that. I don't know how you're still sane and sober. Tammy is sweet, but, yikes."

Jill gave me a twisted smile. "My sanity is questionable, and I'm planning to ditch the sobriety as soon as possible."

"Good strategy." I twisted my pint back and forth on the coaster, waiting for the outpouring of angst.

None came. Instead, Jill sipped more wine, relaxing in her chair and tapping her fingertips to the beat of the music.

I braced myself and broached the subject. "I got the feeling there was something you wanted to talk about."

"Huh? Oh. No, nothing in particular. I liked you when

we met at Christmas and I thought it'd be fun to get to know you." A faint flush rose on her cheeks. "And, sorry, don't take this the wrong way, but I really need to get hammered. I don't drink alone and I never get drunk with anybody who doesn't have a higher security clearance than me. That way if I accidentally let something slip it doesn't matter. But it really limits my drinking buddies."

I sat back in my chair, my surprise fading into a relieved grin. "So, no agenda, just a chance to relax and blow off some steam."

"Yep." She raised her glass, then paused. "Unless there's something you want to vent about. Go ahead, I'm a good listener."

I laughed. "With Tammy, do you have a choice? But, no. I just had my post-mission psych evaluation. I may never talk again."

"Good Lord." She nodded toward my beer mug. "I'll buy your next one. You need it."

"You have no idea." I took another drink, stalling while I searched for a topic of conversation. God, when was the last time I'd gone out for a drink with a new potential friend? Granted, I wasn't much of a social butterfly by nature, but it was pretty sad that I had to count back years.

"*Yes!*" Jill's shout made me jerk violently in my chair. "Sorry," she added as I took a shaky swig of beer. "We just scored." She nodded toward the TV screen.

"Oh." I squinted at the on-screen display. "So you're a Calgary Flames fan."

"Oh, hell, yes!" She grinned, then glanced at the screen again. "Way to go, boys!"

I dredged up my rudimentary knowledge of hockey, and we settled down to a pleasant evening of cheering for the team, interspersed with lively conversation and frequent drinks. Even the sight of Tyler Brock arriving in a group of skinny young men adorned with piercings and sneers wasn't enough to spoil my evening. I ignored him thoroughly, and he returned the favour.

Quite a while after the final buzzer had sealed the Flames' victory, Jill leaned forward, her eyelids drooping and her expression serious.

"Y'know, Aydan, sometimes I really hate my job."

"I hear you," I mumbled with a tongue that felt too big for my mouth.

"I mean..." She stared down into her wineglass before taking a gulp and continuing, "Tammy's sh... sweet, but she'sh sho..." She blinked and tried again, "...she's... so..."

She couldn't seem to think of the word. She made an eloquent gesture with both hands instead, barely keeping the wine inside her glass.

Apparently the word she had in mind was about the size of a breadbox. I nodded in perfect understanding through my warm and fuzzy alcoholic haze.

"She thinks we're friends," Jill went on. "All of us. Me, the an'lysts that cover for me..." She swallowed more wine. "An'... an' then sooner 'r later, POOF!"

I recoiled at the sudden loud word, which turned out to be fortunate since it was accompanied by a dramatic gesture and a small splatter of red wine.

"*Poof*," Jill repeated with slightly less emphasis. "Our mission's over an' we're reassigned an' all the friends she thought she had 'r gone. Gone like the wind," she repeated sadly. "Gone like... like... Carl."

A small arrow of concern jabbed through my comfy

blanket of inebriation and I sat up. "Carl's gone? You mean, like, *gone*-gone?"

"Oh. No. Not *gone*-gone. Jus' gone. Mission." One of Jill's eyelids lowered in a wink and forgot to reopen. "Wouldn't let a hot piece of man like that get away. Oh, *Lordy*, Aydan, what a body! And what that man can do in bed!"

"Uh..." I began, but she was already elaborating.

Elaborately.

I blinked in silent awe, too drunk to exercise the level of good taste required to make her stop, but with a growing certainty that I was going to have a hell of a time looking Germain in the eye the next time I saw him.

Just as Jill finished describing activities involving a certain household appliance that I'd never look at again without having a hot flash, a tall angular woman appeared beside our table.

I twitched. I'd been so engrossed in Jill's narrative I'd almost forgotten we were in a public place.

Jill stopped speaking, and I felt a small pang of regret that now I'd likely never find out what had happened with the western saddle and cherry Jello.

"Oh, hi, Mary," Jill said, unsurprised. Then again, she was several glasses of wine past the ability to be surprised. She waved an inaccurate hand in the woman's direction. "Aydan, this's Mary. She's anana... anan... uh..." she trailed off, frowning, then shrugged and swallowed the last of her wine.

"Hi, Aydan," Mary said. "I've heard a lot about you so it's nice to finally meet you. What Jill's trying to say is that I'm an analyst. I and another woman spell off staying with Tammy in the evenings to give Jill a break from her handler's duties."

"Nice t'meetcha," I slurred.   Somehow it seemed as though I should say something else, but I didn't know if the proper words were bigger or smaller than a breadbox so I offered a bleary smile instead.

"How smart'm I?" Jill mumbled. "Asked Mary to come'n get me when her shift's over."

"Fuck'n smart," I agreed.

"Well, back to the grind," Jill said, and lurched to her feet only to stagger sideways. "Oops. Gimme a hand, Mary?"

Mary looked slightly less than enthusiastic, but she allowed Jill to drape an arm over her shoulders and they made erratic progress to the bar. Jill handed a wad of cash to Eddy and offered me a cheery if uncoordinated wave before she and Mary navigated to the door and disappeared.

I stared down into the dregs of my latest pint. I'd lost count a while ago. That probably wasn't good.

Without Jill's convivial company I suddenly realized my mouth felt like I'd been drinking glue, and a one-eyed squint at my wristwatch made me groan. After midnight. I couldn't call Spider now.

And I'd be stupid to go home drunk anyway. If I got attacked, I'd be a sitting duck. Never mind aiming my pistol; I was having enough trouble finding my mouth with the beer mug.

Speaking of which...

I gulped the last of the beer and stared morosely down at the foam streaking the inside of the mug.

I was so totally fucked.

Lucky I was too snockered to care.

I was considering laying my aching head down on the

table when two Eddys appeared beside me.

"How are you doing, Aydan?" they inquired in stereo, and I frowned and blinked until they reluctantly merged into a single Eddy, regarding me with a mixture of concern and amusement.

I sighed. "Shit-faced."

He chuckled. "That was my professional opinion, but I didn't like to say so. If I didn't know you so well I'd have cut you off two beers ago."

A groan escaped me. "You prob'ly should've, but thanks."

"Do you want me to call Spider for you?"

"No." A beery urge to burst into tears seized me and I let my head fall forward to thump gently against the table, but my depth perception was off.

"Ow." I rubbed the painful knot rising on my forehead. "'S too late, Eddy." I sniffled, feeling colossally sorry for myself. By morning I'd be dead, shot by some two-bit assassin. "'S too late," I repeated in lugubrious tones. "'S'all over for me."

Eddy patted me on the back and gently prised the empty beer mug from my grasp. "Yep, that's all for you tonight. Give me Spider's number and I'll call him for you."

"Can't." Realizing how pathetic I sounded, I sat up straighter and marshalled my tongue as best I could. "'S too late t'call him now. That'd be rude."

"Well, you can't drive home," Eddy said firmly.

"God, no!" I stared at him in horror. "I'd never... People die! Or survive; that's worse." I shuddered, my stomach doing a slow roll at the memory of raw-throated screams and supplicating hands clawed in agony.

"Okay, Aydan," Eddy said with the kindly patience only

possessed by career bartenders and trusted friends. "Who can I call for you?"

"Nobody." The sniffles were back. I straightened my spine and muttered, "Get it together."

"I'm sorry, what was that?"

I forced my clumsy tongue into a semblance of cooperation. "Would it be 'kay if I jus' slep' in your office t'night, Eddy? I could jus' curl up..." I smothered a hiccup. "...onna floor. I'd be no trouble, promise."

He studied me for a moment. "You really did have a bad day, didn't you?" he said softly. "And you don't want to go home, is that it?"

His sympathy brought tears to my eyes and I blinked them back, focusing on the coaster I was turning over and over between my fingers.

"It'll be okay, Aydan," he comforted. "I can just run you over to the hotel..." I was already shaking my head, and he hesitated before brightening to say, "Or, tell you what, if you want to stick around until closing you can stay at my place tonight."

"No."

The bluntness of my refusal made him blink, surprise flickering across his face before dismay replaced it. "I'm sorry!" he exclaimed. "I'm not propositioning you, I swear I wasn't thinking that!"

"No! Oh, God, no, Eddy, sorry, I didn' mean that." I clutched his hand. "I didn' think you were; I jus' have loud nightmares 'n' didn' wanna keep you awake. An' you're such a nice guy, I'd sleep with you inna heartbeat... Oh, Jeezis." I knotted my fists in my hair. "I didn' mean that, either, I jus' meant if I *wanted* t' sleep with somebody right now, you'd be... oh shit, I'm jus' gonna shut up now." I gave him an imploring look. "Are we still friends?"

He laughed. "Of course. And I can do better than my office floor. The original owner used to live above the bar and there's still an old couch up there. It's not the Ritz, but..."

"Eddy, you're a prince!" I managed not to burst into tears or kiss him.

"Come on," he said, and held out his hand. "I'll help you up the stairs."

"'S'all right," I mumbled. "Corndation... Oops, cro... I mean cord... fuck it, *balance*... 's the las' thing t'go..." I stood and managed a straight line over to the bar, where I proffered my credit card despite Eddy's objections. The stairs were an exercise in concentration but I made it to the top without incident.

Eddy bustled around closing blinds and fussing because there were no blankets or pillows, but I made grateful noises until he wished me a good night and closed the door behind him.

I guzzled the mug of water he'd left me and fell onto a dilapidated sofa that smelled of stale beer and wet dog. It looped once; twice; dizzying spins that made me utter a feeble "Whee!"

Then I knew no more.

CHAPTER 12

My stomach was vibrating.

I groaned and clamped my hand over it, but the vibration transmitted itself to my palm.

I pried an eye open and fumbled my phone out of my waist pouch as it vibrated a third time. Squinting one-eyed, I identified the answer button and pressed it before squeezing my eye shut again and holding the phone to my ear.

"'Lo?" My croak elicited a moment of silence on the other end of the line.

"Is Aydan there?" a familiar gravelly voice inquired.

"Arnie!" My cry of delight subjected my nasal passages to my own foul breath and I dragged myself upright, gulping distastefully. "God. Gross. Hang on..." I swallowed a couple more times. "Jeez. Fall asleep for a few minutes and somebody goes and eats shit with my mouth."

Hellhound's voice took on a worried note. "What's wrong, darlin'? Are ya sick?"

"No." I ran a fuzzy tongue over my dry lips and sucked at my cheeks in an attempt to generate some spit. "Drank too much last night."

A raspy chuckle tickled my eardrum. "Ya celebratin' somethin'?"

"No, drowning my sorrows." Giving up verticality as a bad job, I fell back on the couch. "It's good to hear your voice. Um... it's not Sunday is it?"

"Nah. Only Saturday. Ya sure you're okay? How long've ya been passed out?"

I laughed. "I drank more than I intended to, but I didn't pass out. I just thought you weren't coming home until tomorrow. Are you calling from California?"

"Nah, I'm home. Been off work for too long an' needed to get caught up on a coupla my cases."

Guilt nudged me. He was behind in his P.I. business because he'd dropped everything to rescue me last week.

I pushed away the thought. That wasn't the whole reason. Nobody had twisted his arm to join Kane on that motorcycle trip afterward. I suppressed a sigh. But he had known Kane needed his companionship. He always put himself last.

"Well, welcome home," I said. "Did you have a good trip?"

"Hell, yeah." I could hear the grin in his voice. "Woulda been better if I had my own bike, but that new hog I rented was pretty sweet. How 'bout you? When did ya get home from the commune?"

"Wednesday afternoon. I had to stay there a few days after you guys left just to tie up the last of the loose ends." I hesitated. "How did it go, uh..." I wasn't quite sure how to phrase the question. "How's John?"

"Okay, I guess..." Hellhound sounded uncertain. "Actually, darlin', that's kinda why I'm callin'."

"Shit." I sat up, anxiety displacing my lassitude. "What's wrong?"

"I dunno if there's anythin' really wrong." I imagined his

battle-scarred face creased with the concern I could hear in his voice. "But his last mission was a helluva bitch. Did he talk to ya about it?"

"Some. He said there was a little boy involved, and I could tell it really hit him hard."

"Yeah." Arnie's voice was grim. "He's gonna need some help with this one. I wanted to give ya the heads-up in case ya didn't know." He hesitated. "An', uh... I got the feelin' he was kinda freaked out about our little threesome."

"It wasn't a threesome!" I protested. "Jeez, we just slept in the same tent. Not even really in the same bed."

"Well, yeah, but... when I brought it up he said he didn't wanna talk about it. We had a good trip otherwise an' shot the shit just like old times, but... I dunno. I'm pretty sure it's buggin' him."

"Well, he's dealing with a lot right now." I sighed. "Maybe that's all it is."

"Maybe. Or maybe he'll talk to ya about it."

"Mm," I agreed. The thought of having that conversation with Kane made my already-complaining stomach tie itself in knots.

"So what sorrows were ya drownin'?" Hellhound asked.

"Um..."

Shit, if I said somebody was trying to kill me he'd drop everything to run to my rescue again, and that would put him in the line of fire.

But having somebody I trusted to watch my back would be heaven.

"Just some back-to-work bullshit," I semi-lied, trying to ignore my guilty conscience.

It wasn't a complete lie. Assassins were part of my

working life now.

"Anythin' I can do?"

"Not just now, but thanks for asking." I hesitated, the words 'When will I see you again?' hovering on the tip of my tongue. How could I ask without making it sound like I was pressuring him?

"Are ya gonna be around at the end a' the week?" Hellhound asked. "I gotta be up there Thursday mornin' for the parade, an' then I'll stick around an' jam at Eddy's Thursday night."

"You're in the Spring Thing parade?"

"Yeah. Eddy sets up a sound system on a flat-deck an' everybody rides it an' jams. This's the first time I've been able to make it, but the other guys say it's a blast."

"Oh... that sounds great..."

I swallowed my dismay. So much for riding on Eddy's float. There was no place in that talented group for a woman whose musical ability consisted of drumming on tabletops and singing off-key.

But oh, please, don't let me get stuck with the screaming kids...

"Give me a call when you know for sure when you're coming," I said. "It'll be good to see you. Oh, and by the way, I changed the combination on the gate lock." I recited the new combination, knowing it would be instantly stored in his phenomenal memory banks.

"Thanks, darlin'. Take care, an' I'll see ya later. An', uh... if ya talk to Kane, gimme a call an' lemme know how he's doin', okay?"

"I will. You take care, too. 'Bye."

I disconnected and flopped back on the couch to stare at the ceiling. More to worry about. Great.

"Should've stayed at the damn commune," I mumbled, and hauled myself to my feet.

When I descended the stairs cautiously so as not to jar my headache too much, Eddy looked up from behind the bar.

"Good morning," he said quietly. "How are you feeling?"

"Fine, other than a nasty dry mouth and a bit of a headache. Thanks for letting me stay." I glanced at my watch. "Hey, it's nearly eleven. Why aren't you playing the piano?"

He gave me an incredulous grin and spoke at his normal volume. "Are you kidding? I thought you'd have the granddaddy of all hangovers this morning. I was trying to be quiet."

My heart swelled at his thoughtfulness. "Aw, thanks, Eddy, you're the best! I don't really get hangovers, though. It's this fast metabolism of mine. I feel like absolute crap about two hours after I go to bed, but I'm usually okay in the morning as long as I drink lots of water the night before."

"I guess you won't need my patented hangover cure, then," he teased, and removed a glass filled with red fluid from the bar fridge.

"If it's got tomato juice in it, I'll take it," I assured him. "And then I'm going to go hunt down the greasiest breakfast I can find. Fried eggs and sausages and hash browns and buttered toast and bitter black coffee. It's funny, the only time I ever want a greasy breakfast with coffee is after a night of drinking." I took a swig from the glass he handed me and sighed. "Ah. Thanks, this tastes so good!"

"You don't have to go hunting for breakfast," he protested. "Remember, we do breakfast from eleven 'til one on weekends. The kitchen will be open in about ten minutes, and yours can be the first grease off the grill."

"Fabulous! I like it here. I think I'll just move in upstairs," I joked as I slid onto a bar stool and sucked back some more ice-cold tomato juice.

Eddy smiled, but his keen gaze appraised me. "Did you get through the night without too many bad dreams?"

I shrugged, embarrassed that I'd revealed my weakness to him. "If I had any, I don't remember."

"If you want to talk, remember I'm a bartender," he quipped. "Cheaper than a shrink and tight-lipped as a priest." He sobered. "Seriously, though, is something bothering you? If you're having nightmares that often..."

"Um, no, not really..." I mumbled, cursing myself for blabbing the truth. "I was just afraid that if I was drunk I might... um... not sleep as well as usual."

"Drinking brings on the nightmares?" He eyed me shrewdly. "Last night when I told you not to drive... The way you reacted... did that have something to do with it?"

I drew a breath of relief at the realization that I could tell him a truth without revealing anything about my current nightmare-inducing life.

"Um... yeah." I studied my glass, not really wanting to tell him. But it gave me a plausible excuse for the nightmares, and it didn't include secret government agencies and assassins.

I sighed. "About ten years ago a drunk driver ran a biker off the road right in front of me." I took a gulp of tomato juice as my throat closed at the memory. "It was... really bad." My voice came out in a whisper. "The biker was thrown. Landed on a fence post. Impaled."

Eddy went still. "Oh, God, Aydan, I'm sorry."

"But he didn't die." The thin distant voice trickled from

my lips even though I tried to stop it with all my might. "He was conscious the whole time. Screaming. Horrible screams. Begging to die..."

My hand curled unconsciously into a bloodless claw, making me shudder at the memory of the biker's reaching hands, so taut with agony the bones and tendons nearly split the skin.

"I was pinned. In front of him. Couldn't help him. Couldn't even look away..." My voice mercifully choked off.

I clutched the glass in icy fingers. When I raised it shakily to my lips it clattered so violently against my teeth that Eddy reached out to steady my hand.

"So that's why I never drink and drive," I finished, the words falling like hollow pebbles into the well of silence between us. "Because if I had even one drink and something like that happened, I'd always wonder if I could have prevented it if I'd been stone-cold sober."

Eddy stood immobile for a moment. Then a shudder shook him and he relinquished my hand to pour himself a shot of whiskey, which he downed in a single gulp.

He tilted the bottle wordlessly in my direction and I shook my head. "No. I have to drive."

He shuddered again and rounded the bar to fold his arms around me. I leaned into him for a moment, taking comfort.

"I'll go and find you some breakfast," he said.

Shortly before noon I dragged my grease-distended belly out of Eddy's. Emerging from the windowless back door with my customary paranoid sidestep, I kept my back to the wall and snapped a glance around the parking lot and rooftops.

A couple of incoming patrons gave me quizzical glances, but I returned a bland smile and headed for the truck. Climbing into it, I settled in the seat and rechecked my phone for text messages just in case.

No 'call home' or 'I've been thinking of you'. So everything must be quiet around my house and the analysts had no further information about the identity of my enemy. I let out a breath and put the key in the ignition.

A sudden thought froze me in place.

I had left my truck unguarded for hours. Between closing time last night and Eddy's arrival to open the bar this morning, there wouldn't have been any passersby to witness anybody tampering with it. Any assassin with even a speck of competence could have wired a bomb to my ignition.

A too-vivid memory of my red Legacy engulfed in a fireball made me leap out of the truck. Crouched on the pavement beside it, I studied the mud-caked undercarriage and wheel wells.

Thank God I lived on a gravel road. I'd be able to spot any areas where the dirt had been disturbed.

There weren't any.

Drawing a slow breath, I reached into the cab to disengage the hood latch. When I went around to gingerly open the hood, the familiar twang-clunk of the ancient springs made me flinch in spite of myself.

The old engine looked the same as always. Maybe a bit more oil caked around the valve covers. Should clean that up and replace the gaskets one of these days.

I hunkered down to look under the front bumper, then stood again to give the engine a final inspection. No packages that looked like grey modelling clay. No clean new wires anywhere.

"Need help?"

"*Agh!*" I spun to face the source of the voice, my hand diving toward my holster.

At the sight of an alarmed-looking man taking a rapid step backward, I converted my grab into an odd scooping motion ending in a convulsive clutch at my chest.

"Jeez! Sorry, you scared me." I sucked in a breath and patted my heart back to where it belonged.

"Sorry." He eyed me warily and nodded toward the open hood. "Engine trouble?"

"Oh. No. It's fine." I drew another breath and managed to bring my voice back down to a normal tone. "It's just got a sticky choke plate, so when I'm starting it cold I sometimes have to manually reset it." I tried a chuckle. "I call it my anti-theft system."

"Oh. Ha-ha. Good one." His laughter didn't sound any more convincing than mine. "Well, I'm glad everything's okay." He backed away.

"Yeah, thanks for asking." I pasted on a smile and turned away from the awkward encounter, then snapped a glance over my shoulder to make sure he wasn't sneaking up on me.

He wasn't. He was hurrying away, undoubtedly resolving never to play Good Samaritan again. Poor bastard.

I stifled a groan and slammed the hood with a little more force than necessary.

A couple of hours at Sirius Dynamics running Drake Mallard's contacts through the law-enforcement database gleaned nothing but a list of petty criminals I didn't recognize and a resurgence of my headache. At last I gave up, checked the truck over one more time, and headed home.

CHAPTER 13

I cruised slowly past the woods and creek that separated Tom's farm from mine, straining my eyes. The still-leafless branches formed a complex network of browns and greys, but I didn't spot anything that looked like a camo-clad gunman. Still, when I got out to unlock my gate, it took all my willpower not to cringe and scuttle back to the truck.

Hissing out a breath between my teeth, I deliberately slowed my stride when I got out again to close the gate behind me. Dammit, I wouldn't give in to fear.

A dull report from the direction of the creek made me yelp and dive behind the truck, my body already in motion by the time my brain identified the familiar sound of Tom splitting wood.

As the regular thumps continued I crept back to the driver's seat, trying not to hyperventilate.

Cursing quietly, I drove to the house and backed the truck up to the front porch. The plywood barricade behind the screen door looked exactly as I'd left it. A tense scrutiny of the surrounding hills and fields assured me that I was as safe as I was likely to get, and I abandoned the shelter of the truck to scoot around to the back door.

Inside, I resisted the urge to clear the house. The

analysts would have notified me if anybody had been caught on camera. Nobody could possibly be hiding inside.

Don't give in to fear.

My resolve lasted precisely fifteen seconds. Then I drew my Glock.

Okay, so maybe I'd give in to fear a little bit.

But only a little. With an effort of will I re-holstered the Glock and drew the trank pistol instead.

I cleared the house, cursing my own weakness but unable to stop myself.

Several long minutes later I finished in the last corner of the basement and drew a deep breath as I climbed the stairs again.

Okay. Now I was okay.

Reaching for the blinds, I stopped myself before I could lower them.

"Cut it out," I snapped. "If you want to hide behind closed blinds, call Stemp and go to the damn safe house. Otherwise get it together, chickenshit."

I squared my shoulders. I'd take reasonable precautions. Nothing more.

My answering machine's light was blinking, and I skirted the bright flood of sunlight from the window to head for it. As long as I stayed in the shadows, nobody could get a scope on me.

When I pressed the button, Tom's voice issued from the speaker. "Hi, Aydan, it's Tom. I just wanted to let you know that guy in the silver SUV was hanging around again. I told him to take a hike and he won't be back, so don't worry about it. Talk to you later. 'Bye."

Heart pounding, I stood staring into space while my mind rocketed from dismay to irritation to fear.

Shit, that silver SUV was the only clue I'd had. And if Tom had intervened, did that mean he was in danger now, too? Dammit, I should have known better than to go over there for dinner. I should've just dropped off a cheque with a polite but distant thank-you.

But, hell, I hadn't had much choice.

Growling, I picked up the handset and punched in his number.

The phone rang several times and I was mentally composing my message for his answering machine when he picked up with a breathless, "Hello?"

"Hi, it's Aydan. Sorry, I must have gotten you from a long way away."

"I was just finishing up splitting some wood." I could hear the smile in his voice. "You know the old joke. It warms me up twice: once when I chop it and once when I burn it."

"Right." I managed a chuckle. "So I got your message. What was that all about?"

"Oh, yeah. I saw that silver SUV cruising by again yesterday. I was eating lunch and just happened to glance out the window as it went by. I thought about chasing after it but I figured by the time I got out the door and into my truck it'd be gone again."

"But you said you talked to him."

"I did. A few minutes later he drove onto my yard."

I swallowed, my grip turning sweaty on the handset. "So what happened?"

"Well, it was like this," he began in his laid-back manner, and I stifled my impatience with an effort. "He drove onto the yard," Tom went on. "Knocked on my door and asked if I knew whether Arlene Widdenback had been home lately. So I knew right away he must have read that newspaper article that got you mixed up with that porn star back in October. I told him you were Aydan Kelly, not Arlene Widdenback or Arlene Cherry, and I said you were at work and by the time you got home he'd better be gone. He tried to argue, but I told him the newspaper had gotten it wrong and you weren't Arlene Widdenback, and if I saw him hanging around your place again I'd get out my shotgun."

I thumped my forehead with a fist, clamping my teeth on my tongue so I wouldn't say something I'd regret. When I spoke my voice came out surprisingly calm. "Thanks, Tom, but I don't think you should have threatened him."

"Huh." The single syllable came out laden with disdain. "I know his type. If you don't face them down they never go away. This isn't the city, Aydan, and the police aren't right next door. The best restraining order out here is the business end of a shotgun."

I eased my tension out in a sigh. No sense in arguing. "You're probably right," I agreed. "Did you get a license number just in case?"

"Uh... no." Tom sounded slightly less sure of himself. "He drove in and backed out so I couldn't see his plate." His voice firmed. "But I got the make of the SUV. It was a Hyundai Sport."

"Oh... Good... Thanks."

No, *not* good. Totally bloody useless.

I kept my voice calm through sheer force of will. "What did he look like?"

"Uh... I don't know, just average, I guess."

I tried again, holding onto my patience with all my might. "How tall do you think he was? What kind of build?

What colour eyes and hair?"

"Well... he was a few inches shorter than me, so I'd say a little less than six feet. Not fat but not skinny, either. He was wearing a ball cap and sunglasses, so I didn't see his hair or eyes, but he had a brown beard."

Patience. Do not bite the phone in half from sheer frustration.

"What kind of beard? What about the shape of his face? Skin colour? Any scars or tattoos? Unusual clothes?"

"Uh..." Tom sounded crestfallen. "I'm sorry, Aydan, I don't really know. He was just kind of... ordinary. He was white, I'm pretty sure. His beard was just ordinary, too, not really short or long, just in between. I don't really notice clothes, but I think he was wearing jeans and kind of a grey jacket."

"What kind of jacket? You mean like a sports jacket?"

"No, just a regular jacket. With a zipper," he added as though that helped. "But it might have been beige or light blue. I'm a bit colour-blind."

Oh, for chrissake.

My voice came out slightly strangled. "Okay, well, thanks for dealing with it, Tom. If it happens again, maybe you could try to get a description. If he turns out to be a stalker and I have to make a police report I'll need as much information as I can get."

"Okay, I will, Aydan. I'm sorry I didn't pay more attention."

"It's all right." I stifled a sigh. "Well, I guess I better get back to work here. I'm putting in my new doors today."

"Do you need a hand? Those steel doors are pretty heavy."

I hesitated. The two pre-hung door-and-frame units were damn heavy, but I didn't want Tom in the line of fire if another assassin showed up.

But shit, if he'd already antagonized my enemy, he might be safer here where I could protect him.

"Um... I could use a hand unloading them in about half an hour," I agreed.

"Okay, I'll head over around a quarter after one, then. See you later."

"Okay, thanks. See you." I hung up the phone, wondering if I'd just signed his death warrant.

I hissed out a breath between my teeth. Too late to second-guess myself.

And I only had half an hour to take down my barricade of plywood and tear out the wood casing with its incriminating sprinkling of buckshot holes.

I pulled out my crowbar and got to work.

Promptly at one-fifteen my phone rang, making me jump. I dropped my crowbar and snatched the handset up from the porch beside me.

The analyst's tense voice slammed my heart rate into overdrive. "Incoming with shotgun from south, fifteen yards from back door and closing."

My Glock was already in my hand. As an afterthought, I jammed the phone receiver between my ear and shoulder and bent awkwardly to draw the trank gun left-handed from the holster I'd secured on my other ankle.

"Six-two, one-seventy, short brown hair. Walking, looks casual." The analyst went on reeling off data. "Veering east now, heading around the house to the front. Cowboy hat-"

"Shit!" I ducked through the gaping door opening to flatten my back against the wall beside it. "Is it my neighbour? Tom Rossburn?"

"Facial analysis still working. He's rounding the front of the house now."

I raced for the basement, praying the facial analysis would return an answer before I either jumped out at Tom with my gun levelled or stepped out in front of an assassin unarmed.

"Identity confirmed. Tom Rossburn," the analyst said at the same time Tom's voice called a cheery hello from upstairs.

"Thanks," I whispered into the phone, and stuffed my weapons back into their holsters.

"Aydan! Hello! Anybody home?" Tom called. His footsteps paused in the entry above.

"Hi, Tom, I'm in the basement! Be right up!"

I took a slow deep breath, wiping my clammy palms on my jeans. My knees trembled so violently I wasn't sure if I could make it up the stairs.

After a few more moments I made the attempt. When I emerged on the main floor with my smile clamped firmly in place Tom eyed me quizzically, taking in my sweaty dishevelment.

"You look like you've been hard at it already," he said. "I could have come earlier."

"Oh, no, that's okay. I was just prepping the opening." I indicated the hole. "The old door was so cheap and light I could carry it to the shed myself, and I just finished taking the old frame and casing there, too. I wanted to be ready to put the new unit in place when you got here." I nodded toward the back door. "But if you're feeling left out, there's still the back door to do."

"Sounds good."   He glanced around the kitchen. "Where's a good place to leave my shotgun?" He gave me his crooked grin. "After I promised to show it to your visitor, I figured I'd better have it with me. And it was such a nice day I decided to take a page out of your book and walk over."

"Over there in the corner's fine. And thanks, I appreciate you coming over."

"Happy to help." He placed the shotgun carefully beside the kitchen table and straightened with a smile. "I'm all yours. Let's get started."

I nodded toward the tailgate of the truck.   "Okay, cowboy, time to flex your muscles."

Shit, that had come out more flirtatious than I'd intended.

Tom's grin widened and a glint appeared in his eyes, but he turned toward the truck without comment. I drew a breath of relief that morphed into lustful appreciation of his receding rear view.

Damn, nothing like a man in cowboy boots and well-fitting jeans.

Only a few minutes later we had extracted one of the door units from the truck and stripped off its packing to stand it next to the opening in the wall. I had managed not to embarrass myself with any double entendres or conspicuous drooling, and I was beginning to relax when the phone rang again.

Pouncing on it, I snapped, "Hello!"

"Hi, Aydan. Did I catch you at a bad time?" Kane's warm baritone somehow managed to both relax me and wind me up tighter.

"Uh, no, that's okay. I was just, um... working on my front door," I stammered.

"Oh, good. I'm on my way home from Calgary. I'm just coming up to your turnoff and thought I'd drop by if you're not too busy."

"Oh. Um..." I swallowed. "Okay..." I hesitated, wondering if I should mention Tom's presence, but it was already too late.

"See you soon, then," Kane said, and hung up.

I stood there holding the phone to my ear, my mind whirling. This wasn't going to end well, I just knew it.

"Is everything okay?" Tom asked.

"Um... yeah. That was John. He's on his way over. Should be here in a few minutes."

"John Kane?" Tom's eyes narrowed.

Oh hell, here we go...

"Is that who you meant when you said you were seeing someone?" Tom asked.

"Um, yeah." It seemed like the simplest answer.

"Oh." His suddenly stiff shoulders radiated waves of disapproval. "You don't seem very happy that he's coming."

"Of course I'm happy; I just know you don't like him so I'm feeling uncomfortable," I half-lied.

"It doesn't matter whether I like him or not." The corded muscle in his forearms rippled as his hands closed into fists, then released. "I just want to be sure you're safe. And happy."

"Thanks, Tom, I appreciate that..."

The sound of approaching tires on gravel made me trail off, and we stood in silence while Kane's shiny black Expedition turned into the drive and stopped at the gate. I waved as he got out to swing the gate open, but he didn't return the salutation. My hand drifted down again as he got back in the SUV and drove it through the gate, then returned to close it behind him.

I mumbled, "Shit, I must have forgotten to lock the gate."

Of course I'd forgotten. I had freaked out at the sound of Tom chopping wood and jumped back in my truck without closing the padlock. Dammit, I couldn't afford that kind of carelessness.

"Do you want me to tell him to leave?" Tom asked.

I blinked, realizing he had ducked back into the house to retrieve his shotgun, which was now cradled comfortably in the crook of his elbow.

"No! No, of course not," I said as the Expedition pulled to a halt in front of us. "I didn't mean I was trying to keep him out, I was just annoyed with myself because I forgot to lock the gate."

Kane swung out of the driver's seat, sparing a single glance at Tom before focusing a gaze like grey lasers on me. He strode up the walk and took the stairs in an easy bound.

"Aydan," he said in a tone of deep satisfaction.

Before I could respond, he swept me into his arms and kissed me.

CHAPTER 14

It was not a quick platonic peck. Kane's fingers wound into the hair at my nape, positioning my mouth where he wanted it while he devoured my lips like a starving man. Despite the discomfort of Tom's presence, warm tendrils coiled into my belly and weakened my knees.

Kane pulled away at last and smiled down at me, ignoring Tom entirely.

"Uh... hi," I stammered. "Welcome home."

I shot an anxious glance at Tom's rigid posture. His lean powerful six-foot-two seemed much smaller beside Kane's massive musculature and two-inch height advantage, but I sensed his readiness to fight nevertheless. Testosterone smoked in the air.

Then Tom gave me a stiff nod. "Well, I guess I'll be going. Give me a call if you need anything, Aydan."

"Thanks for your help," I said faintly, but he was already striding away.

When he disappeared around the corner of the house I turned to face the small smile tugging at Kane's lips.

"What the hell was that?" I demanded.

His smile widened. "I was glad to see you." The smile grew predatory. "And I wasn't in the mood for a pissing match."

"So you just whipped out your big honkin' fire hose and sprayed down the whole place," I snapped, caught between irritation and amusement.

Kane grinned. "I'm going to take that as a compliment," he said complacently. "Thank you."

Amusement won. I laughed. "Think rather highly of yourself, don't you?"

A wicked spark kindled in his eyes. "You're the one who called it a fire hose. And you should know."

"Uh... yeah..." I licked suddenly-dry lips.

The spark in his eyes flared hotter as his gaze locked onto my mouth. "Ahhh." His rumble of satisfaction vibrated all the way from my ears to my toes, stimulating some very interesting places in between.

"I missed you," he said, and reached for me.

Expecting one of his incendiary kisses, I was surprised by the gentleness of his touch. Holding me close and smiling down at me, he stroked back the wisps of hair that had escaped my ponytail.

He smiled. "Finally." The word came out on a breath. "A chance to be alone with you when we have time and safety."

His lips were descending toward mine when I came to my senses.

"Shit!" I jerked back. "It's not safe!"

I tried to pull him through the door opening, but he was already lunging toward me. He slammed into me as I stepped back and my foot caught the edge of the doorway. We crashed to the floor and I lost track of which way was up as he rolled us around the corner, fetching up against the wall with a thump. Pinned by the weight of his protective body, I blinked up at his taut features as he snapped a look around us, his pistol at the ready.

"Uh... I mean... we're not in immediate danger," I amended weakly. "I just meant, um..." My voice died in my throat at the intensity of his gaze.

"What is it, Aydan? Tell me!" He hadn't holstered his Sig, and steel-cable tension thrummed through the length of his body.

I eased out a breath. Speaking of overreacting in non-lethal situations...

"John," I said gently. "We're not under attack." Honesty compelled me to add, "At least not at the moment." I smoothed my palm over his cheek. "Put your gun away and let me up, and we can talk about it, okay?"

He stared down at me for a long moment. Then he relaxed and let out a long breath, easing down to rest his forehead against mine.

"Sorry," he said.

I hugged him before letting go to give him a gentle push. "It's okay. Now could you please take your knee out of my crotch? There are some sensitive bits down there that I'd really prefer un-smushed."

He rolled to his feet and extended a hand to help me up, the wicked humour rising in his eyes again. "I could kiss the sensitive bits all better."

I gulped, suddenly breathless.

He sobered and holstered his Sig. "But not until you tell me what's wrong. What exactly did you mean by 'we're not under attack at the moment'? And if we're not in immediate danger, why did you duck and cover?"

"Sorry." I rubbed my elbow where a bruise was

beginning to form. "I've got a bit of a situation going on here, but that wasn't what I was thinking of on the porch. I was worried about the analysts watching our every move from the surveillance cameras. We could pass off that first kiss as a tactic to get rid of Tom, but anything more than that would be really hard to explain."

Kane shook his head, relaxing into a smile. "We don't have to explain anything. When I requested my transfer off your project in December, I told Stemp why. He knows I have feelings for you. That would be a problem if we were working together, but we aren't."

"Uh, don't be too sure about that," I said. "Stemp's planning to assign you to my project again on Monday."

"Oh." Kane looked momentarily nonplussed before his smile came back, edged with mischief. "Fortunately, I don't officially know about that." The smile dissolved. "Now, tell me about this 'situation'."

"Oh. Um..." There didn't seem to be much point in beating around the bush. "Somebody's trying to kill me. Or maybe abduct me. We don't know who or why yet, but some guy came through my front door with a shotgun the day before yesterday. That's why I'm replacing the door."

Kane's face hardened. "'Came through the door', meaning..."

"Shot off the lock and kicked the door in," I confirmed. "It was just his bad luck I was sitting here at the kitchen table reloading my Glock."

"Didn't the analysts warn you?" he demanded.

"They tried, but he was too fast. He had the combination to my gate lock so he let himself in without anybody knowing. Then he jumped out of his car, pumped a load of buckshot into the lock, kicked the door in..." I shrugged.

"...and died pissing and bleeding all over my floor, the asshole. Fortunately Stemp let me have a cleanup crew this time."

"Any demands? Any other suspicious activity?" Kane was in full cop-mode, his expression shuttered.

"Nothing yet. This guy was strictly small-time, so we figure it'll take a few days for whoever hired him to figure out that he didn't do the job and hire the next loser."

"Why aren't you in a safe house?" Kane demanded. "You're fresh off your last mission and you shouldn't be dealing with anything of this magnitude until you're cleared for active duty again."

I shuffled my feet. "Dr. Rawling kind of cleared me."

"Kind of?" Kane's eyes narrowed. "You lied in your psych evaluation, didn't you?"

"Um... not really..."

"Dammit, Aydan!" he barked. "Those evaluations are for your own protection and everybody else's, too! It's your duty to be honest-"

Defensive anger made my voice louder than I'd intended. "There's more to it, all right? Just back off!"

We glared at each other in silence for a moment.

"Can you tell me about it?" he asked, his voice controlled.

I hesitated. If he got up on his high horse about 'duty' he might rat me out to Stemp thinking it was for my own good.

I matched his even tone. "There's a lot of stuff going on, and I can't give you the whole story right now. Sorry. You'll just have to trust me." The last sentence came out a little more challenging than I'd intended, and his shoulders stiffened.

"Of course I trust you," he said curtly.

"Good!" Oops, that had come out pretty challenging, too.

"Fine!" he snapped.

We eyed each other across a few feet of floor that felt like the Grand Canyon.

Kane let out a breath. "Look, Aydan, I don't want to fight. I really do trust you. If you say that's the way it has to be, I believe you." He spread his hands, palms up. "Can we please not fight?"

Guilt twisted my guts. "I'm sorry, too. I flew off the handle. I'm..." I made a helpless gesture toward the gaping hole in my wall. "...a little stressed. I don't want to fight, either."

He stepped forward to take my hands, a teasing smile curving his lips. "Somebody's trying to kill you and you're a little stressed? I know you don't express your emotions easily, Aydan, but I think that might be a bit of an understatement even for you."

I sighed and stepped against him to tuck my head under his chin. His arms closed around me, and I pressed my face into his chest.

"I'm..." I started to say 'totally freaking out', but I couldn't quite trust him enough. "...really glad you're back," I finished. "I was worried about you." I pulled back to look up into his face. "How are you doing?"

"I'm messed up," he said flatly. "I've already told Stemp I'm not fit for active duty now or for the foreseeable future. Maybe never again. I've talked to Dr. Rawling a couple of times on the phone and I'll be seeing him regularly now that I'm back."

"Oh, John." I held him close. "I'm sorry."

His shoulders rose and fell in a shrug. "It is what it is.

Maybe it's fate's way of telling me it's time to pack it in. I'm getting too old for this game." The defeat in his voice twisted my heart.

"But you're not even fifty yet," I protested.

"Most agents retire to a desk job in their forties. Stemp did it in his late thirties." Kane's lips twisted. "He's smarter than I am. Quit while you're on top instead of when you find out you can't cut it anymore, at the cost of an innocent life."

My heart sank. "But... you said you got that little boy out. You said he'd live."

"Barely." Kane stared down at me, his eyes haunted. "I barely got him out. I had to carry him all the way. It should have been easier. I wasn't in top shape, and I should have been. If I'd had to stop and rest, we'd both be dead, and I... it took everything I had." He scrubbed his hands over his face and turned away. "Everything I had," he repeated quietly. "I barely made it."

I ran my hand over the muscled contours of his shoulders, hardly believing that such strength could fail. "But you did make it, John," I said softly. "How old was the boy? And how far did you carry him?"

He didn't turn to face me. "I don't know how old. Maybe six or seven. And it was about sixteen miles."

"Sixteen..." I gaped at his back for a moment. "What kind of terrain? And what else were you carrying?"

His shoulders twitched in an irritable shrug. "Rough terrain. The usual gear. But it doesn't matter, Aydan. Ten years ago I could have-"

"No!" I strode around in front of him to seize his shoulders. "No, that's bullshit! I don't care what you could have done ten years ago. You did it *now*. And today, the way you are right this minute, there's still nobody else in the Department who could have done what you did..."

He began to speak, but I kept talking. "...and I know for a fact that you're not telling the whole story. You were recovering from getting shot, you hadn't slept for days, you probably hadn't eaten, it was probably dark and raining..." He didn't deny it, and I challenged, "Name me one other agent who could have done that!"

"Germain," he said immediately.

I hissed frustration through my teeth. "Okay, fine. Name me another one."

"Hellhound could do it."

"He probably could. But he's not an agent so he'd never be in that situation."

Kane hesitated. "Probably Wheeler..." he began.

"Bullshit! Don't give me 'probably'! You're still the best of the best, and you damn well know it!"

We locked eyes, and he dropped his gaze first.

"John." I stroked down his arms to take his hands. "If you were talking to a young agent who'd just been through the same experience, what would you tell him?"

"That's not the point, Aydan-"

"Yes, it is the point! Tell me. Tell me what you'd say."

His shoulders sagged and he spoke to the floor. "I'd tell him everybody has a physical limit. You can push the limit with adrenaline and guts and willpower, but there's a point where you just... can't..." He trailed off.

I softened my tone. "And if that young agent wasn't as physically fit and strong as you, would you tell him to quit the Department because he might not be able to do what you just did?"

"No, of course not," Kane mumbled.

"So, John..." I let go of his hands to cup his face and make him look at me. "If you need to quit the Department because you've had enough, or if you want to quit because you've given your entire life to it and it's time to do something for yourself for a change, that's fine. Quit and don't look back. But if you still want to be an agent, don't ever believe you're a liability just because you've got a big birthday coming up next year."

He started to shake his head, but I went on, "That little boy is alive today because of you. If any other agent had been in your place, he wouldn't be." I held up a hand to forestall his objection. "Okay, except Germain, but the point is that even if you or any other agent had tried and failed, at least that little boy would have died knowing somebody cared enough to give their life for him."

I linked my arms around his hips and smiled up at him. "And anyway, a very wise man once told me 'What *almost* happened doesn't matter'."

Kane's face softened. "Do I know this wise man?"

"Yep. He's your dad."

The tension eased from his shoulders. "He is a very wise man, isn't he?"

"Uh-huh." I stepped away to plant my hands on my hips in mock indignation. "So, you sonofa-wise-man, you chased away my help. You'd better be ready to work now."

Kane laughed. "I'm no carpenter, but I can hold the dumb end of a measuring tape and I follow orders well."

"Good." I grinned up at him. "Then hand me that level and get ready to flex those muscles."

CHAPTER 15

I was acutely aware of Kane's flexing muscles. Thigh muscles, to be exact. Inches from my nose while I knelt in the doorway trying to concentrate on the bubble in my torpedo level instead of the heat rolling off that luscious...

"How's that?" he asked.

"Stupendous," I breathed before blinking my attention back to the job at hand. "And the door frame's pretty good, too," I added. "Just push it toward me a bit."

His thigh flexed again and I exerted all my willpower to keep from sinking my teeth into that heavy ridge of muscle and nibbling all the way up to...

"There," I said faintly, and secured a shim in the gap.

Then I pushed in another shim, trying to ignore the sexual connotation of rigid wood driving into the waiting, wanting aperture...

"Jesus," I muttered, and stood.

"Sorry, what was that?" Kane asked.

"I said 'just'... um... just hold it there for a second while I grab a couple more shims."

"They're here by my foot." His arms still braced in the doorway, Kane nodded toward the floor.

Caught by the sight of his biceps swelling and curving

into the mountains of his shoulders, I was a little slow to follow the direction of his gaze. When I didn't respond immediately he glanced up and caught me ogling him.

A slow smile started at the corner of his mouth. Holding me with a smouldering gaze, he shifted his hips ever so slightly. My mouth went dry at the memory of those hips circling in a sensuous dance.

"Ms. Kelly," he rumbled, his baritone stroking me like hot hands. "The help wants to know..." He shifted again, invitation sizzling in every line of his body. "...what you want to do next."

A dizzying rush of arousal stole my breath for a moment. Then I gave him a slow smile of my own and prowled toward him. "Are you saying I'm the boss?" I inquired silkily.

Kane glanced down at himself, spread-eagled in the doorway. "It certainly looks that way."

"Well..." I leaned closer, inches away from his lips. "The boss says..." I traced the square line of his jaw with my lips, shivering at the fine sandpaper of his five-o'clock shadow. "...don't move," I whispered.

God, that brain-melting gun-oil-and-leather scent. Heat rolled through my body, half-closing my eyes. Without my permission, my tongue tipped out to flick into the hollow behind his jaw. Ohmigod, that salty, musky flavour that was one hundred percent pure Kane...

He shifted again, leaving only an inch of supercharged air crackling between us.

I went up on tiptoes to nip his earlobe. "I said, don't move."

A growl rumbled up from his chest, melting what was left of my brain into a puddle of lust.

I stepped away before my knees could melt along with it, letting my hand coast down his arm. Over the hot muscles of his chest to bump over the washboard of his abs. Then down...

The growl rumbled louder when I teasingly bypassed the bulge in his jeans to fondle that toothsome thigh.

"Don't move," I reminded him, and bent to retrieve my shims.

Securing the door in the opening was sweet torture. Brushing against Kane's hard body as I moved back and forth, I felt each contact like an electrical charge.

Once again I cursed Drake Mallard. If not for him I'd be getting happily laid instead of interspersing my enjoyment of Kane's considerable attributes with uneasy glances toward my yard.

At last I drove in the final screw and rose. "Okay, you can move now."

An instant later I was wrapped in Kane's arms, his mouth savaging mine while I ground against his breathtaking erection. Just as I was considering throwing caution to the wind and dragging him to the bedroom regardless of the danger, he broke the kiss.

"We'd better finish," he said against my lips.

"I'm halfway there already," I assured him.

He chuckled. "Good to know, but I meant the door."

I sighed and extracted myself from his embrace. "Yeah. And I still want to get the back door done today, too." I aimed a half-hearted kick at the door jamb. "This sucks." I sighed again and picked up my crowbar. "Can you do the expanding foam while I start pulling out the back door?"

Kane grinned and gave me a superheated look. "You're the boss."

I shivered with sheer desire and determinedly plodded off to the back door.

Some time later, my stomach let out a ravenous growl as I was kneeling to secure the last of the shims.

"'Scuse the comments from the peanuts section." I massaged the complaining region before returning to my shims.

"You must be starving." Kane looked down at me with concern from his Atlas-like pose inside the door frame. "It's nearly six and you didn't even stop for a snack."

"Yeah." I held out my hand to gauge its tremor before flashing him a rueful smile and returning to my work. "But I really wanted this done. There. You can let it go now."

He stepped out of the doorway and reached down to help me up. I rose slowly, grimacing at the crackling under my kneecaps.

"God." I hobbled a few steps before my knees deigned to cooperate again. "Speaking of getting too old for this shit..."

"Come and sit down," Kane urged, shepherding me toward the kitchen table. "Relax while I cook supper. Let me get you a drink."

Dazzled by the glorious thought of a rest, a drink, and one of Kane's gourmet meals, I sank into a kitchen chair. A moment later I came back to reality. "I don't have much to cook with. I was so eager to be home I only bought milk and eggs. I've still got carrots and onions and garlic and potatoes from last summer's garden and there's stuff in the freezer, but..."

Kane was already inspecting the contents of my fridge

and freezer. He extracted two beers and popped their caps before handing me one. Taking an appreciative swallow of his own, he held up one of the bags from the freezer. "Peppers?" he asked.

"Yeah, I cut them up and freeze them so I always have some on hand. Those are the bell peppers and there should be some jalapenos in there somewhere, too."

"Ah." He nodded, looking pleased while he continued to excavate the freezer. "Chicken breast. That'll do... oh good; prawns, too." He turned, packages in hand, and smiled. "And I'd be willing to bet a month's salary that you've got peanut butter."

I took a satisfying swallow of beer and leaned back in the chair, returning his smile. "Always a safe bet. I have panic attacks if my peanut butter jar is more than half empty."

"Noodles?"

I nodded. "Rice vermicelli or egg noodles, whichever you want. In the cupboard to your left."

"Excellent. I can do an Asian noodle bowl."

I sighed in pure bliss and slouched lower in the chair to stretch out my legs. Sipping my beer and occasionally directing Kane to utensils and ingredients, I watched him prowl around my kitchen with his distinctively powerful fluid movements.

Soon delicious smells began to emanate from the region of the stove. I raised the beer bottle again, but desisted when I realized the first few swallows had already hit my calorie-deprived system hard. I sighed and pushed the bottle away. This cozy safety was only an illusion. Stay alert.

As if reading my mind, Kane reached for the window blind. "Do you mind if I close this?" he asked. "I feel too exposed with my back to a window."

Relieved that I didn't have to second-guess my own paranoia, I nodded. He lowered the blind before resuming his work at the cutting board, conversing easily while his hands deftly sliced and chopped as though of their own accord.

The promise of the enticing aromas was fulfilled a short time later, and I let out a small moan as I gobbled succulent chicken and prawns in spicy peanut sauce.

"Thank you," I mumbled around a mouthful of noodles. "This is amazing. *You're* amazing."

He smiled. "Thanks, I'm glad you're enjoying it."

"Mmhmm!" I confirmed, and wasted no more breath on conversation while I devoured the delicious meal.

At last I leaned back and eased out a long breath. "Ohmigod. That was so good. Thank you again."

"You're welcome." Kane laid aside the chopsticks he'd been wielding with casual expertise and leaned back in his chair, too. "It was nice to cook for a change instead of eating restaurant meals."

"Right, I suppose that part of the trip wasn't really a treat for you," I agreed. "But did you enjoy it otherwise?"

"Yes. Hellhound and I had often talked about making that trip, so it was good to finally do it. And it was good to have his company. I needed it." Kane drained his beer bottle and set it down on the table in a way that looked like a decision. He gave me a level look. "Hellhound brought up the night we spent together in your tent. I told him I didn't want to talk about it."

My post-dinner contentment drained away into an anxious void. "Oh. Okay..."

"I didn't want to talk to him about it because it's not

about him and me." Kane gave me an intense look. "It's about you and me."

My stomach contracted into a queasy ball. "Okay..." I tried to keep my face under control but I knew I hadn't managed to hide my dread.

Kane eyed my expression and sighed. "Aydan, I know how uncomfortable you are with conversations like this, so I'm going to make you a promise. This will be the second-last time I'll ever bring up the subject of you and me. And you don't even need to talk this time. Just listen."

"The *second*-last...?" I realized I had unconsciously pushed my chair back a few inches, and I drew a deep breath and relaxed my rigid leg muscles.

"Yes," Kane said firmly.

I sprang up. "Do you want another beer? I could sure use another beer-"

"No."

The word landed between us like a rock and I hesitated, trying to decide whether to grab another beer or just take a page out of Eddy's book and go for a shot of straight whiskey.

"And, frankly, I'd prefer it if you didn't, either," Kane added. "I don't want any misunderstandings between us and alcohol won't help that."

"Oh..." My voice crept reluctantly from my throat.

My feet tried to flee for the door but I overpowered them and forced them into an ungraceful shuffle back to my chair. My knees didn't want to bend, but I subdued them, too. Perched on the edge of the chair, I gulped at the constriction that felt like a noose around my throat and braced myself.

CHAPTER 16

"Okay," I whispered through dry lips. "Shoot."

Kane hesitated. Then he scrubbed his knuckles through his hair and muttered, "Why am I even doing this?"

"If you'd rather do it another time..." I began hopefully.

"No." He squared his shoulders. "This is important, and it's long overdue." He drew a deep breath. "Aydan, I haven't been completely honest with you. Or with myself, for that matter."

"It's okay," I said hurriedly. "I know you can't always be as honest as you might like. It's just part of the job-"

"No!" His fists clenched, then released. "Aydan, I need to say this and it will help if you can just let me say it-"

"Without interrupting, okay," I interrupted, then realized what I'd done. "Shit. Sorry." I knotted icy fingers together in my lap. "I'm shutting up now. Please go ahead."

Kane drew another breath and let it out halfway in the same ritual I used to calm my pulse while sighting a gun. "I told you I love you," he said abruptly. "That was... is... the truth."

I almost spoke aloud the 'but' that was hanging in the air, but I managed to hold back.

"...but I lied when I said it didn't bother me that you

didn't... don't... want an exclusive relationship with me," Kane went on. "It does bother me. It bothers the hell out of me." His fists clenched. "I told myself a casual relationship was what I needed right now. That the job makes it impossible to have any other kind. I told myself that everything was perfect the way it was." His lips twisted. "More lies."

I gripped the seat of the chair to prevent myself from jumping up and running away.

Kane eyed my glowing white knuckles and passed a hand over his face. "This last mission..." He trailed off, staring into the past for a moment before he gave his head a slight shake. "This last mission was a gut-punch. That abused child... that would upset anybody. But it was more than that for me."

His gaze bored into me and I suppressed a shudder at the bleak iron-grey of his eyes. "Aydan, this mission woke me up. Made me think about my priorities. And I want more than just a... a..." The muscles in his jaw rippled. "A fuck-buddy," he said tightly, the uncharacteristic word sounding impossibly vulgar coming from his lips. "I want a committed relationship." His jaw muscles rippled again. "No," he ground out. "No, dammit, I'm going to be completely honest with you. I want a wife. A family. And I'm running out of time."

I began to speak but he silenced me with a raised hand. "Please. I'm not finished yet."

I bit my lip and nodded, my pulse pounding in my temples.

"I know you don't want that," he went on. "Not now, maybe not ever. Or maybe just not with me." The pain in his words stabbed my heart, but he went on without a change of expression, his cop face impassive. "I know better than to make any major decisions until I've got my head on straight. I don't know how long it will take, but I seriously doubt it'll be soon."

Kane faced me squarely. "But when I'm ready, I'll bring up our final relationship conversation. I'll ask you to consider making a commitment to me. If you say no, I'll move on."

My fingers were numb, small tingles of protest zipping up into my wrists. I tried to loosen my grip on the chair but failed. Frozen, I heard his words as if from a great distance.

"I love you, Aydan." The clear grey of his eyes held me helplessly immobilized. "If you're not ready when I ask but you're willing to consider it down the road, I'll wait for you." He leaned forward and gently pried my hand loose from the chair, stroking my whitened fingers. "But I'm sorry, Aydan, I won't wait forever."

"I..." The word was a dry croak, and I cleared my throat and tried again. "I don't expect you to." Blinking furiously at the burning behind my eyes, I pulled my hand from his grasp and stood so I could turn away. "And I think it would be best for you to start looking for another relationship now." My voice came out dead level. "I can't be the wife you want, and I can't have children. Don't waste any more time here."

"Aydan, dammit, I didn't say my time with you was wasted!" His voice was raw behind me. "And I don't even know what I want or when I'll want it, so you can't possibly know it won't work. I know you're not ready to think about this decision now. Neither am I. I just wanted to be up front about how I'm feeling so you aren't blindsided when the time comes."

"Okay. Thanks." I squashed the tears down into the small cold place that had never healed in my heart and turned back to him, holding my face in the bland expression that had served me well during my first miserable marriage. "I'm going to have that beer now," I said lightly. "Do you want another?"

"No!" He sprang up and seized my shoulders. "Dammit, Aydan, don't shut me out!"

I couldn't help flinching just a little. He let go as though my skin had burned him and clenched his fists by his sides.

"God *damn* it!" He sank back into his chair, elbows on knees, and scrubbed both hands over the back of his hanging head. "I'm sorry," he said quietly to the floor.

My heart contracted sharply. After all the suffering he'd been through, I was kicking him while he was down. The ugly voice from my past replayed in my mind.

Cold heartless bitch.

I dropped to my knees beside his chair and slid my arms around him. "I'm the one that should be apologizing. I'm sorry. I know you were just trying to be honest, and I appreciate you giving me the advance notice." I couldn't bear to hurt him again, so I went for a vague platitude. "Like you say, neither of us is in any shape to make life-altering decisions right now. Let's just take it as it comes, okay?"

Kane met my eyes with a bleak gaze. "For now, yes. But when the time comes, don't be kind to me, Aydan. I need the truth."

No matter what I said, it would hurt him. I did the only thing I could think of.

Cupping his face in my hands, I leaned in. "This..." I kissed him softly, taking my time. "This is the truth," I whispered against his lips.

His arms closed around me and I teased his lips with the tip of my tongue. As I pressed closer, he broke the kiss and distanced me with gentle hands on my shoulders.

"No," he said quietly. "It's not the truth. It's just an illusion of happiness. I can't do this anymore, Aydan. Until or unless you commit to me, the physical part of our relationship is over."

"It's..." I gaped at him. "Wha...?"

I sputtered uselessly for a moment until my brain connected to my mouth again. "*Seriously?* You're hitting me with a 'no-sex-before-marriage' speech?"

Hurt and surprise morphed into anger and my voice rose as I jerked out of his grip and leaped to my feet. "After I told you up front that I'd never want commitment and you talked me into your bed anyway? When you fuck every goddamn female spy you've ever met and call it 'duty'?"

Pure red rage exploded into my veins. "YOU FUCKING BASTARD!" The yell tore my throat, but I barely felt the pain. "I can't *believe* you'd try to manipulate me like this! Get out! Get the hell out of my house, get the hell out of my life, and take your fucking sanctimonious bullshit with you!"

It was his turn to gape, shock written all over his face. "I didn't mean it as a manipulation..." he began, but I had only paused long enough to suck in a breath that burned like fire.

"*Out!* Goddamn you, *get out!*" I grabbed his arm and yanked, nearly pulling him off the chair. "OUT!"

He lurched to his feet, hands outstretched. "Aydan, wait, let's talk-"

"*OUT, OUT, OUT!*" I emphasized each shout with berserk two-handed shoves against his chest, driving him toward the door.

"Aydan, stop!" He grabbed my wrists and held them in an iron grip. "Calm down-"

"*Calm?* You want fucking *calm?*" I drew a breath that hissed between my clenched teeth. "I'll give you calm," I ground out in the lowest, deadliest voice I could manage. "You come in here trying to emotionally manipulate me and when that doesn't work you physically overpower me. Fine, Mr. Big-Man-With-A-Black-Belt-In-Everything. Go ahead. I can't stop you. But sooner or later you're going to have to let go of me. And when you do, you'd better run and keep on running because I will fucking destroy you. Got it?"

His face turned to icy stone and he dropped my wrists. "Got it." He turned on his heel and strode out, slamming my new steel door behind him.

"*ASSHOLE!*" I bellowed, and kicked the nearest kitchen chair with all my strength. It slammed against the table, rebounding violently and smacking into my shin as Kane's empty plate jolted over the edge of the table to shatter on the floor.

Shrieking inarticulate cries of rage and pain, I swooped down to seize the fallen chair with every intention of beating it to splinters against the floor.

The phone rang.

I froze, the chair poised over my head, my breath jerking in and out in a choppy rhythm above the thunder of my heart.

Ohmigod.

I was going to be attacked and I'd just banished the one man who could save me.

I dropped the chair and fled for the phone, snatching it up to gasp a frantic 'hello'.

Still panting uncontrollably, I could barely hear Tom's

urgent voice. "Aydan, what's wrong? Are you all right?"

Shit! Check the goddamn call display next time, idiot!

"Fine." I gulped a few more harsh breaths, knee-trembling relief mingling with fury. "I'm fine."

"I don't think you are. I'll be right there-"

"*No!*" My panting was edged with whimpers of sheer frustration.

"Aydan," Tom said firmly. "Tell me what's happening or I'm going to hang up and call the police and then I'm coming over there with my shotgun."

"For chrissake... don't do that!" I fought for control, my words coming out between gasping breaths. "I'm just... upset. I just had... a huge fight... with John and... kicked him out."

I was pretty sure Tom was trying to suppress the note of triumph in his voice, but he didn't quite succeed. "So he's gone for good?"

"Yes. The prick." The words gave me no satisfaction. An ache squeezed my chest, my breath slowing as my heart plummeted. I swallowed hard and held my voice level. "Sorry, I didn't mean to dump on you. Did you want something?"

"I was just calling to see how the door installation went and whether you still needed a hand. Are you all right? Do you want some company?"

"Thanks, Tom, but no." The ache was tightening my throat now, threatening to choke me. "I just want to be alone." The last word came out in a thin quaver, and I summoned every shred of self-control I had left to stabilize my voice. "I'll talk to you later, okay? 'Bye."

I barely heard his 'goodbye' as I clicked off the handset

and stood rigidly with it clenched in my hand.

Dammit, I was not going to cry over this.

I was *not*.

I slapped the handset back on the base unit and got to work on the wreckage.

The kitchen cleanup did nothing to soothe me. Vacillating between shame over my meltdown, residual fury at Kane, and misery over the destruction of our friendship, I scrubbed the kitchen within an inch of its life, then sanded and painted my drywall patches. I had just finished cleaning the paint tray when my phone rang again.

CHAPTER 17

Heart pounding, Glock in hand, I sprang over to the phone and checked the call display.

Shit. Hellhound.

Really didn't want to talk to him just now.

My hand hovered above the handset. If I didn't pick up, he'd call my cell. If I didn't answer either of my phones he'd worry, and when I did finally talk to him I'd have to come up with an excuse.

I growled and pressed the Talk button.

"Hey, darlin'." Hellhound's cheerful rasp made me feel a little better. "How ya doin'?"

"Okay," I equivocated. "How about you? What's up?"

"I'm good. Just tryin' to track Kane down. He ain't answerin' his home or cell. When he left this mornin' he said he was gonna drop in an' see ya, so..." I could hear the suggestive grin in his voice. "I figured he might still be there."

My spirits nose-dived all over again. "No. He left."

"Oh." Hellhound hesitated. "Did ya talk to him about, uh... How was he?"

I briefly considered avoiding the question, but what the hell, he'd find out soon enough anyway.

I held my voice level. "He was a fucking dickhead and I threw him out."

"Wha... Aw, shit. What happened?"

"I don't want to talk about it."

"Come on, darlin', give." His voice took on a teasing note. "Ya might as well tell me now so I know whether to kick his ass or yours. Or both."

Sudden tears throttled me and my voice came out small and tremulous. "Please don't kick my ass." I gulped hard and forced a bantering tone. "Ass-kicking hours are over for today, but if you want to get in line for tomorrow I can probably squeeze you in near the end of the day."

"Aw, darlin'." His soft rasp made my tears threaten all over again. "Sounds like ya need a beer an' a hug. D'ya want me to come up?"

I stiffened my spine and held onto control. "Thanks, Arnie, but you just got home. I'm okay; it's just been a tough day. Tough couple of days."

"Talk to me, darlin'. Tell me all about it," he encouraged, his warm concern crumbling my defenses. "Was he upset about our threesome?"

"Stop calling it that!"

"So I'm gonna take that as a 'yes'?"

I sighed and gave in. "Yes and no. It was his mission that upset him more than anything. He said it made him rethink his priorities. And he said he wanted a commitment from me."

"Aw, shit." I could practically hear Hellhound's wince at the other end of the line. "So ya freaked out," he deduced.

"Yeah. Well... no. Not right then..." I trailed off, the anger rising all over again. I tried to hold it back, but it burst out in spite of me. "The bastard gave me a big sob story about how he needs commitment; how he loves me and he'll wait for me and all that bullshit, and then he tried to coerce me by withholding affection! And he twisted it around so *I* apologized to *him*, when I've told him right from the start that I didn't want commitment-"

I bit off the furious torrent of words and took a breath, fighting my voice back under control. "Anyway, it doesn't matter. It's done."

Hellhound's rasp hardened to a steely edge. "What d'ya mean he tried to coerce ya? 'Cause I don't care if we been brothers for forty-some years, I'll kick his fuckin' ass if he tried to strong-arm ya."

"He didn't. And it doesn't matter, Arnie. Let it go."

"I'll let it go soon's ya tell me what ya meant."

He wasn't going to let up. Damn.

I drew in a long breath. "He said the physical part of our relationship was over unless I committed to him. And I..." I gulped down the lump that was forming in my throat. "I went totally nuts on him and threw him out."

"Hang on..." Hellhound sounded bemused. "So ya didn't freak out when he was talkin' about commitment, but when he said 'no nookie' ya lost it?"

"Do you know what it's like to be trapped in a relationship with no physical affection?" I demanded. "Day after month after year until you're so desperate you beg for even the tiniest contact? To look forward to sex because it's the only time he touches you, even though he just fucks you like a whore and walks away? I've got no use for a man who uses love as a weapon."

"But, darlin', sex ain't love," Hellhound pointed out gently. "He prob'ly didn't mean-"

"Oh, sure, so I'm being unreasonable!" Suddenly I was shouting. "And pretty soon everything I want or feel or say is unreasonable and I'll keep feeling guiltier and apologizing more until finally I won't even speak up when I'm about to be killed in a car crash because if I even mention a car's coming at us he'll punish me for days for criticizing his driving, and even then I'll stay because I took a marriage vow and that tiny shred of self-respect is all I have left..."

My voice broke, mercifully ending the humiliating outburst. "I have to go," I croaked. "'Bye."

"Wait!"

His shout stopped me as I was lowering the phone. I hesitated.

"Aydan, are ya there? Aydan!" His voice crackled faintly from the speaker. "Come on, darlin', talk to me. If ya hang up I'll just keep callin' ya back."

And he would, too. God *damn* it.

Overcome by fatigue, I dropped into a kitchen chair and laid my head on the table, propping the handset against my ear. "I'm still here, but I'm done talking about this."

"Thanks, darlin'." His words came out on a breath and I imagined him sinking back in his favourite chair. He'd be reaching over to touch his beloved guitar for reassurance, and Hooker the cat had probably already settled in his lap. The cozy picture made me feel even worse.

"So I couldn't quite figure out what ya were talkin' about a few minutes ago," Hellhound began cautiously. "What was that about Kane gettin' in a car accident?"

"Forget I said all that crap." My voice was as flat as the tabletop pressed against my cheek. "How are your cases going?"

"Fine, darlin'. Ya were talkin' about your ex, weren't ya?

How he mind-fucked ya 'til ya didn't know which way was up anymore."

"Let it go, Arnie. How's Hooker? Did he give you a big welcome when you got home?"

"Yeah. So Kane triggered some bad shit an' ya flashed back an' reacted like he was your ex, is that it? It ain't the end a' the world, darlin', just explain it to him an' everythin'll be okay."

I thudded my head against the table. "That's not the problem!" I sucked in a tremulous breath. "Look, Arnie, I'm permanently fucked up. Programmed to do whatever he wants. And I can't go through that again." My voice choked to a broken whisper. "I can't, Arnie. I'd rather die."

Alarm flared into his tone. "Hang on, darlin', nobody's gotta do any dyin'. Ya don't hafta do anythin' ya don't wanna do. Kane ain't gonna force ya."

"No, he won't." Bitterness burned my throat. "But he'll point out that I'm overreacting because I was in a bad marriage before. Hell, that's what you said, too. And I know you're both right, so it's only reasonable to do what you want. And as soon as I give up what I truly want because somebody else tells me it's unreasonable, the whole ugly circle starts again."

"But, Aydan, ya know it doesn't hafta be that way. Ya got outta that shitty marriage an' ya remarried an' got it right the second time-"

"Because Robert kept pushing until I gave in," I interrupted. "Because I never had an opinion and always went along with whatever he wanted. It was only sheer dumb luck that he was a nice guy and not a sociopath like Steven."

"But ya know better than that now..." Hellhound began.

Sudden anger propelled me up from my slumped position. "Why are you trying to push me back into the cage?" I blazed. "Is this some man thing? A woman gets uppity and thinks she can live alone so you have to cut her down to size, remind her she's nothing more than a piece of dirt on the bottom of your shoe and a wet hole to fuck?"

"Whoa, hang on, Aydan!" The shock and hurt in his voice made my heart twist with guilt.

Way to go, stupid. I'd already driven Kane away. Nothing like going two for two.

"I'm sorry," I muttered miserably.

"Aw, darlin', it's okay." His soft rasp brought tears to my eyes. "I thought I could help, but I ain't a shrink. I'm just a dumbfuck, an' I don't blame ya for getting mad."

"You're not a dumbfuck, and I'm not mad at you, Arnie. I'm just... really messed up right now. I shouldn't have said that stuff. I know you were only trying to help."

"Overcompensatin' a bit, actually," he said wryly. "Truth is I really want what's best for ya, but I'm kinda hopin' ya don't end up married. I don't wanna go lookin' for anybody else to warm my bed."

Relief turned my spine to jelly and I fell back in my chair with a tremulous laugh. "I don't know what you're worried about. You've never had any shortage of bed partners."

He laughed, too. "Yeah, but ya spoiled me. I'm gettin' lazy about findin' new ones an' havin' to go through the whole 'no commitment' speech every time."

"Aw, gee, it sucks to be you," I teased.

I sobered, hesitating. Should I ask? Or would I just open another can of worms?

What the hell. I really wanted to know.

"Arnie... can I ask you something personal?"

"Well, hell, darlin', I just finished pryin' into your personal shit. I'd say it's your turn."

"It seems like you're always trying to encourage me to have a so-called normal relationship. Is it because that's what you want? Have you ever felt like it might be nice to come home to somebody?"

"Maybe once or twice." Hellhound chuckled. "But if that happens I just take a coupla blondes an' lie down 'til I feel better."

I laughed in spite of myself. "Smartass."

"Seriously, though?" His tone turned introspective. "Nah. Even if I wasn't so fucked up, even if I didn't think I'd turn into my fuckin' ol' man if I ever had a fam'ly... It's nice comin' home to somebody for a day or two, but then I get the cold sweats an' I gotta hit the highway. Even when you're stayin' at my place or I'm stayin' at yours, I like it for a coupla nights an' then I want out."

"And... how do you deal with it? When people tell you that you're wrong and sick to live that way and you should settle down with somebody?"

He barked out a laugh. "Hell, darlin', I don't give a shit what anybody says. Fuck 'em all. An' if they're good, fuck 'em twice."

I laughed and rephrased. "Okay, I guess I didn't ask that question right. I don't care what anybody says, either, until they get... important to me. That's when the programming kicks in. So what if somebody you cared about said it? What if... don't get me wrong, it's the farthest thing from my mind, but what if I asked you to move in with me?"

"I'd run like hell." His answer was swift and firm.

"That's it? No second-guessing, no guilt?"

"Guilt?" He hesitated. "I dunno. I'd hate to hurt ya, but I wouldn't feel guilty about runnin'. We were clear up front about what we wanted. It ain't my fault if ya change your mind."

I sighed. "In my next life, I want to be a man."

Hellhound laughed. "Don't be in a hurry for that. Guys don't do it for me."

"Oh, sure, always looking out for yourself," I faux-griped.

"Hell, yeah, darlin'. Gotta take care a' Number One. When life gets tough, a man's best friend is his own right hand."

"Uh-huh." Comforted by our repartee, I relaxed into the chair and tucked the phone closer to my ear, smiling. "Tell me more about your best friend. What are you doing with it right now?"

"Well, darlin'..." Hellhound's voice dropped to a sexy growl. "What d'ya want me to do with it?"

Some time later, Hellhound let out a breath that was half-groan, half-purr. "Damn, darlin', I shoulda come up there after all."

I grinned and stretched languorously as I emerged from the closet where I'd hidden just in case an assassin showed up while I was otherwise occupied. "You came down there. I came up here. It's all good."

He chuckled. "Phone sex's fine, but there ain't nothin' like the real deal. Maybe I could take a bit a' time off tomorrow, get out the Harley an' ride up your way..."

Tension re-knotted my muscles. "Uh... Actually, Arnie, I've got a bit of a situation here so I'd rather you stayed away for a few more days."

His tone lost its lazy satisfaction. "What kinda situation? Is this the 'back-to-work bullshit' ya were talkin' about?"

"Yeah. I'm not quite sure how it's going to shake out, but..."

I hesitated, wanting him with me almost as much as I wanted to protect him. I squared my shoulders and kept my voice calm and confident.

"...if anybody's hanging around me it might mess things up," I finished. "I hope I'll be ready for company by Thursday, though."

"Okay..." He sounded suspicious. "How dangerous is this 'situation', Aydan?"

"Um..."

I hesitated too long.

"Fuck," he said. "Ya sure ya got it under control? Ya got any backup?"

I sighed. "No; and no. But I don't have any choice."

"Fuck," Hellhound repeated. "Lemme come up an' watch your back. I'll stay away from ya if that's what ya need, but I could-"

"No, Arnie. Thanks, but that won't work."

He sighed. "Shit. I figured there hadta be some bad shit happenin' to make ya melt down like ya did earlier." He hesitated. "I know ya can't use any help with your mission right now, Aydan, but how about gettin' some help with your personal stuff? Doc Rawling-"

"It's none of his business," I interrupted.

"Darlin', he's a shrink," Hellhound said gently. "It's his business."

"No. I'm not going to give him any ammunition."

In the lengthy silence that swamped the line, I imagined Hellhound considering and discarding responses. "Listen, Aydan," he said at last. "I know ya got good reasons not to trust people, but..." He trailed off.

"I know I'm a paranoid freak, but I'm not quite as nuts as that sounded," I explained. "It's just that I'm kind of on probation at the moment."

"Why?"

"Long story, but the short version is I lost my temper at work and if I can't convince Dr. Rawling I'm stable they might lock me up in a safe house." I did my best, but the last part of the sentence still came out sounding squeaky.

"Shit, Aydan, what the hell?" He blew out a breath. "It's okay, I know ya can't tell me. Just promise me this. If there's anythin' I can do to help, call me any time a' the day or night."

The tension eased from my shoulders. "Thanks, Arnie."

"You're welcome, but I didn't hear ya promise."

"I promise."

"Thanks, darlin'. Be safe. Love ya."

"I love you, too." I disconnected and cuddled the handset close for a moment.

"Don't be so fucking pathetic," I said aloud, and dropped the handset back on its base.

CHAPTER 18

After a slightly more restful sleep in the garage, I rose in the morning with new determination. The previous evening's sexy sojourn in the closet had done more than relax me; it had given me an idea.

A few minutes in the basement with a measuring tape confirmed that I'd be able to build a small hidden room concealed by my furnace and water heater on one side and the storage room on the other. The intricacies of its planning calmed me enough that I braved the bathroom for the world's most awkward shower, soaping and shampooing left-handed while holding my trank pistol outside the shower curtain with my right.

After a quick breakfast I carried in the leftover studs from the garage addition and began framing, my pistols strapped to my hips like an old-west gunslinger and the telephone handset within easy reach.

I had relaxed into the comforting rhythm of construction and was securing the last piece of drywall when the ring of the phone jolted me back to unpleasant reality.

I snatched my Glock out of its holster, then cursed. Capture, don't kill, idiot. I swapped it for the trank pistol and grabbed the phone left-handed to snap, "Hello?"

"Hi, Aydan, it's Lola. Did I catch you at a bad time?"

"Oh. No." I let out the breath I'd been holding and holstered my gun. "It's great to hear from you! How are you? And you're not interrupting anything, I'm just working on some renovations."

"Honey, you never stop, do you? You work too hard." Her motherly voice warmed me like a hug. "Did you have a nice vacation out on the coast?"

"Yeah, I did." Wistfulness overwhelmed me at the thought of peaceful commune life guided only by the natural rhythms of sunrise and sunset, rain and fair weather. I had felt safe out there.

Vegetarian food wasn't so bad.

But no personal vehicles allowed.

And no beer.

And then there were the spies and terrorists...

"...but I'm glad to be back," I added. "I missed you. What are you up to these days?"

"Actually, that's what I'm calling about. The Chamber had a meeting last week and I volunteered to call you. The Spring Thing Committee wants to know if you'll drive your fancy car in the parade on Thursday."

"I'd love to, Lola, but the cam's so radical and the timing's so advanced it won't idle low enough."

"Car stuff. I don't have a clue what you just said."

I grinned. "Sorry. Translation: I'd like to, but I can't."

"Well, you'll have to contribute somehow. It's a membership requirement." She paused reflectively. "They're always looking for help with the kids-"

I interrupted as politely as I could. "No kids. What else can I do?"

"Well, honey, I thought you'd never ask. I have a great

idea!"

My brain served up a vivid montage of Lola's previous great ideas, and I shivered. "Stop it, you're scaring me."

"No, this will be fun! This is the first year we're entering a float in the parade to advertise Up & Coming, and you'd be perfect to ride on it."

"Ride on it and do what, exactly?" I demanded with justifiable suspicion.

"Just ride on it and wave to the crowd. That's all. Oh, and throw candy. I was going to do it myself, but you'd be perfect!"

"I know you better than that. There's an 'and' or a 'but' in there somewhere. Knowing you, probably a butt. My butt." My suspicion flared into certainty. "You want me to dress up in some leather contraption, don't you? Or those damn thigh-high boots?"

"No, no, of course not," she soothed. "This has to be tasteful and G-rated for the kids."

"Lola. You own a sex shop and you have a truly twisted sense of humour. You have no concept of 'tasteful' or 'G-rated'."

"Oh ye of little faith," she said with completely implausible injured innocence. "You're as bad as the Spring Thing Committee. They made me submit a sketch before they'd approve my float." I imagined her drawing herself up to her full four-foot-ten-and-a-half-inch height. "And I'll have you know that my design passed with flying colours."

"Really?"

"Really. I'm going to borrow a little pickup truck from one of Spider's friends and wrap it completely in brown paper. Plain brown wrapper, get it?"

"Got it. And...?"

"Oh, just some balloons for decoration," she said in an airy tone that red-lined my bullshit meter. "And I'll ride in back and throw candy."

"What *didn't* you tell them?" I asked cynically.

"What makes you think I-"

"Lola. I know you."

Her giggle made every hair stand up on the back of my neck. "They're going to have an absolute cow," she said with evil satisfaction. "The balloons will be inflated condoms. We've got all colours so it'll be really bright. The little kids won't get the joke but every single adult will, and none of them will be able to say anything because if they do they'll have to explain it to the kids. And I'll be wearing a short trench coat with high heels and a push-up bra."

My mind's eye outdid itself with a detailed mental image of Lola's still-shapely legs protruding from an inadequate coat, surmounted by bountiful but wrinkled cleavage. Imaginary-Lola gave her characteristic wicked grin and gripped the lapels of the trench coat, clearly ready to expose more than I even wanted to imagine.

I grimaced, willing the vision away. "Lola, you can't flash the entire town of Silverside! Not even you could pretend that's G-rated!"

"No, of course not, honey. I won't flash anybody, I'll just do sexy poses, you know, like the old-time burlesque dancers. And I was planning to wear a bathing suit under the coat. Some of those little kids are pretty low to the ground and if I'm standing in the back of the truck, the angle might be bad. I don't think they need to see this old lady's kitty-cat." I was shaking my head in resignation when she continued, "That's why I need you to ride instead of me."

"What?" The word came out in a yelp, and I hurriedly added, "Wrong! Wrong-wrong-wrong! My kitty-cat only comes out to play in private."

"Aydan, what kind of sicko do you think I am?" I knew she was trying for indignation, but the effect was spoiled by her snicker a moment later. "You're so much fun to tease, honey. No, I don't want you to expose yourself. But with your long legs you'd look great in a short trench and high heels. And you're 'way younger and prettier than me. We're already going to be throwing candy to the kids; we should give the big boys some eye-candy, too."

"No," I said with as much dignity as I could muster. "There is no way in hell I'm going to ride the parade in a pickup truck decorated with condoms while the wind whistles up the crack of my ass. Trust me on this, Lola, goosebumps are not sexy."

"Hmm. That's right, I forgot it could be nippy out."

I imagined her frown of concentration and crossed my fingers.

My unspoken wish was not to be.

Her voice rose in triumph. "Ha! I have the perfect solution!"

"Dare I ask?" I inquired cautiously.

"No goosebumps required. I'll dress a blow-up doll in the trench coat; she won't mind a bit. And we can make up a little bed for you in the back, you know, with a fancy satin coverlet and pillows all over the place, very sexy. You can be cuddled up all nice and warm, and you can tuck the bucket of candy between your knees under the covers so it'll look as though you're pulling it out of your-"

"NO!"

Her bigger-than-life laughter filled my ear. "Okay, I was only kidding about that part. You're just so much fun to tease. Come on, Aydan, it'll be fun! Will you do it?"

I seized the only lifeline I'd spotted. "I don't think you need me," I demurred. "Your blow-up doll will have the long legs and high heels, and you can throw the candy."

"But you'd be so much better as the candy-thrower. And you have to be involved in the Spring Thing somehow."

"I'll think about it and get back to you," I lied. "Well, gee, look at the time! I've got to get back to work here before, um... before my drywall mud dries up. Talk to you later."

"Chicken." Her laughter filled the phone before she hung up.

Shaking my head, I exchanged the phone for my cordless drill and drove in the last few drywall screws.

By the time I finished, I was slightly unnerved to realize I was actually considering Lola's offer despite my misgivings. Riding in the back of a pickup truck and throwing candy didn't sound so bad. And it would be fun to watch the adults' expressions when they identified the true nature of Lola's balloons.

But Lola's schemes had a way of backfiring in truly mortifying ways. And while most of my bookkeeping clients were as easy-going as Blue Eddy, I wasn't sure all of them would see the humour in their bookkeeper promoting the sex shop that had polarized the tiny town into heated debates over morality.

My stomach growled, cutting short my deliberations. I collected the phone and headed upstairs to the fridge, but the sight of Kane's lovingly-prepared leftovers made my appetite shrivel and die.

"Don't be stupid," I said aloud, and served up a generous helping.

The scent of garlic and ginger wafting from the microwave oven should have made my mouth water, but it made my eyes water instead.

"For shit's sake, cut it out!" I scrubbed the moisture away and carried the warm plate to the table, where I determinedly shoved noodles past the lump in my throat.

By occupying my mind with the construction of my secret room I managed to finish the whole meal. As soon as the plate was empty I rose and dropped it into the dishwasher, concentrating on the design of the hinged panels that would provide access to my hidey-hole while looking like solid walls. Surely the internet would yield some kind of specialty hinge I could use.

When I plopped down in front of my computer, I reflexively checked my email. My heart clenched into a small hard ball before clattering to the pit of my stomach.

A message from Kane.

Trying to ignore it, I dealt with the rest of my email, but its subject line nagged at me.

"Important: Please read."

No.

No, dammit, this had to end, and the sooner the better.

I clicked on the message, trying not to look while my cursor tracked to the Delete button.

The preview screen sprang up. "Dear Aydan, I realize it's over between us and I want to apologize."

"Fuck," I said, and gave in.

"I'm sorry," the message went on. "I never wanted to hurt you, and I hope you can forgive me enough to remain cordial. If you can't, please reply to this email with the word 'no', and I'll contact Stemp and apply for an immediate transfer. Please believe that I never intended to manipulate you and I am truly and deeply sorry for causing you pain. Sincerely, John."

"Oh, Jesus," I choked through a tear-clogged throat and lurched up from my chair to pace.

He knew exactly how to push my buttons.

Oh, God. What had Hellhound told him?

I snatched up the phone, my shaking fingers getting Hellhound's number wrong twice before the call finally went through.

"Hey, darlin'," he greeted me. "How ya doin'?"

"Fine." I forced the word out through a throat that felt too small for the words. "How about you?"

His tone sharpened with concern. "Ya don't sound fine. What's wrong, Aydan?"

"Nothing," I said faintly. "Have you, um... did you talk to John?"

"Nah, he never called me back last night. I figure he's prob'ly still pissed over your fight so I'll try him later. Why, what's wrong?"

"Oh, good." The constriction in my throat loosened. "Arnie, can I ask you a favour?"

"Sure, darlin'."

"Would you, um... Would you please not mention to John what we talked about last night?"

"What d'ya mean?" Hellhound asked cautiously. "Ya mean when we talked about your ex?" His tone turned teasing. "Or ya mean the part about my right hand?"

My laugh was a poor counterfeit of the real thing. "You can tell him whatever you want about your right hand and what you did with it last night. I'm sure he'll be riveted. Not."

"Why, darlin'?" Arnie's gentle rasp threatened to shatter my veneer of composure, and I forced another laugh.

"Probably because he doesn't swing that way, but I'm only guessing. Who knows, maybe he's dying to hear about your big date with Rosy Palm and her five daughters."

He chuckled. "Funny. But that ain't what I meant, an' ya know it."

"I know. I just..." I drew a steadying breath. "Please... I don't want him to know."

"Darlin', he already knows ya went through hell with your ex. Ya told him yourself."

"But he doesn't know..." I had to stop and swallow. "...any specifics. And I'd like to keep it that way."

"But, Aydan..." Hellhound hesitated. "Look, darlin', I know you're just tryin' to protect yourself, but I've known Kane since we were kids. He ain't gonna do that stuff to ya."

I blew out a breath and reined in my emotions. "I can't let him have any more weapons to use against me."

"But he ain't-"

I kept talking over his protest. "Don't you see? As an agent he's trained to manipulate people. When he was my handler, he had full access to all my psych evaluations. If he decides to use that knowledge and those skills on me, I won't have a chance." I yanked shaking fingers through my hair. "Hell, he's already doing it. I *don't* have a chance. And if... when... he wins... I just..."

My voice choked off and the silence on the line expanded. Finally I drew a trembling breath. "As long as I think he doesn't know exactly how to hurt me, I can keep believing he's not doing it on purpose. It's... It's the only way I can get through it."

The silence on the line felt too fragile.

I had revealed too much. Trying to protect myself from Kane, I had left myself completely vulnerable to a man who was, first and always, his best friend. Dark sickness consumed me.

"Aw, darlin'," Arnie said at last, the tenderness in his voice making tears burn my eyes. "I wish ya could see how wrong ya are, but don't worry. I ain't gonna say anythin'."

I swallowed hard, afraid to reach for the small gleam of hope. "P-promise?"

"Promise. I ain't a shrink an' I sure as hell ain't gonna play Cupid." His serious tone dissolved into playfulness. "'Cause I'm thinkin' a diaper an' a little bitty bow an' arrow ain't really a good look for me."

I squeezed my eyes shut so tightly I saw stars. "Thank you so much..." I quavered before clamping down on composure to add, "...for a mental image no amount of brain bleach will ever erase."

Hellhound laughed. "No problem, darlin'. What're friends for?"

"You always hurt the one you love," I quipped, suddenly feeling a hundred pounds lighter.

"Yeah." The humour was gone from his voice. "An' I wanna go lay a world a' hurt on your fuckin' asshole ex."

"Don't hurt him," I said hurriedly.

A moment of silence quivered on the line. "Fuck, darlin', that is some serious programmin'," Hellhound rasped. "That was a total knee-jerk, wasn't it?"

"Not really," I semi-lied. "It's just that I haven't seen him for years, and I don't ever want to again. And I especially don't want to see him in a courtroom where you're on trial for assaulting him."

"I could just kill him," Hellhound offered helpfully. "Or call up Weasel an' get one of his slimeball buddies to arrange a little accident."

I was pretty sure he was joking. But not positive.

"No, that's..." I began.

Inspiration struck like a lightning bolt and I sprang up from my chair, excitement sizzling in my veins.

"...brilliant!" I finished, grinning. "Arnie, you're a genius!"

CHAPTER 19

"Good. Gimme his full name an' birth date," Hellhound said with chilling efficiency. "Identifyin' scars an' marks, his parents' names, any brothers an' sisters, friends' names, an' the place he was workin' when ya saw him last."

Gulp.

He hadn't been joking.

"Uh, no, Arnie, I didn't mean I wanted you to kill my ex," I backpedalled rapidly. "I just meant you'd given me an idea for this case I'm working on."

"Oh." He sounded slightly disappointed, and I made a mental note never to wish anybody harm in his earshot unless I was serious about it. "Well, that's good, I guess," he added. "But why does that give ya an idea? D'ya think your ex's behind this case you're workin' on?"

"No, I'm sure he's not. I had just forgotten about Weasel and his contacts in the underbelly of society. Could you do me a favour? Could you please ask him if anybody's been sniffing around looking for a cheap assassin lately? Or a kidnapper," I added after a moment's thought. "I'm not really sure which."

"Sure, darlin'. Who's the mark?"

"Oh..."

Shit. Me and my big mouth.

"Uh... me." Tense silence vibrated on the line and I squeezed my eyes shut, waiting for his explosion. "Actually Arlene Widdenback," I added nervously into the void.

After another moment of silence, Hellhound spoke, his voice tightly controlled. "Okay. What d'ya want me to do if I find out somebody's gunnin' for ya?"

I dropped back into my chair, trembling with relief. "Have I told you lately how much I love you?"

A little humour seeped back into his tone. "Just last night, so don't do it again for a while or you'll freak me the hell out." The killing-machine voice returned. "So what d'ya want me to do?"

"Nothing, just let me know anything you find out. A name would be ideal, but times, dates, descriptions of the people involved, places; anything at all would help. And remember, Weasel thinks my name is Jane."

"Yeah, I remember. Ya wanna tell me the whole story now? Is this the 'back-to-work bullshit' ya were talkin' about?"

I sighed and capitulated. "Yeah. Some idiot blasted his way through my front door with a shotgun Thursday morning. He didn't survive the experience so I couldn't question him, but he had my picture and stats, and some nylon zip-ties in his car. He was strictly small-time, so we're waiting for the next one to show up so I can trank him and interrogate him."

"Waitin' for the next one..." Hellhound trailed off incredulously. "Shit, Aydan, no wonder you're so fucked up right now." I took no offense as he went on, "Ya shouldn't be dealin' with this shit straight off your last mission. Why doesn't Stemp put ya... in..." His words slowed to a halt.

"A safe house," I finished wryly. "So you see my problem."

"Shit. Yeah. Okay, darlin', I'll talk to Weasel an' see what the word is on the street. Tell me about your shooter."

I gave him all the details, confident that his infallible memory would store it and relay it with perfect accuracy to Weasel.

"...and that's all I know so far," I finished.

"Awright. Soon's I hear anythin' I'll let ya know. But lemme come up there an'-"

"No, Arnie. Thanks, but no."

He blew out a breath. "Okay. Same thing goes, if ya need anythin', call me right away." He hesitated. "Don't take this wrong, but... I love ya. 'Bye."

"Thanks," I said, but he had already hung up.

Smiling, I turned back to my computer only to be confronted by Kane's email again.

"...*reply to this email with the word 'no'*..." The words stood out in the message as if rendered in blood.

I seized the sand-filled rubber stress ball that sat beside my keyboard and mangled it left-handed while I browsed for specialty hinges, ignoring the email as hard as I could.

My search was half-hearted while my mind circled, darting fearfully toward a decision only to break off at the last instant and shudder away.

The kindest thing for everybody would be to simply reply 'no'. It would be a clean break for Kane, and he could go on to find the relationship he deserved.

I tortured the stress ball a little more.

But if I believed Kane deserved a good relationship, didn't that mean I thought he was a good person? And if he was a good person, why should I avoid being with him? My fear was far out of proportion; I knew that. I should just be reasonable. Give him what he wanted...

A tiny terrified voice yammered, "*No-no-no-no!*" in the back of my brain, and I tried to shush it long enough to finish my train of thought.

Kane had made it clear that he was giving me space. Didn't that prove I was safe with him?

My knuckles began to ache and I switched the ball over to my right hand. A sudden thought drove my fingertips deep into its rubber in a deathgrip that jabbed a spear of hot pain through my arthritic thumb.

No. It only proved he knew how to manipulate me effectively. It was the only message that could have made me second-guess myself. Threatening, cajoling, demanding; none of those would have worked. But this...

I stared blindly at the computer screen.

He wouldn't manipulate me like that.

Would he?

No. I knew he wouldn't. I was almost certain.

Well, mostly certain...

I hissed out a breath and rotated my head in a futile attempt to ease my knotted neck muscles.

But suppose he wasn't trying to manipulate me. Suppose he truly wanted a loving, healthy relationship. It would be unspeakably cruel to keep him hanging on and hoping for something I couldn't give. To let my aloofness slowly corrode his heart and soul until he was just as damaged as I was. The thought made me sick.

Don't be a cold selfish bitch. Set him free.

I switched back to the email and hit Reply. Stress ball

locked in a frozen grip, I watched my trembling left forefinger press the 'N'.

Then the 'O'.

Hovering over the Send button, my hand began to shake so violently that I snatched it away from the mouse before it could do anything irrevocable.

The 'no' glared accusingly from the screen.

How could I shut him out now, while he was still reeling in the aftermath of his hellish mission? A transfer would force him to abandon his cozy house here in Silverside; force him to leave behind any familiar contacts and routines that might give him comfort. And it was easy for me to say he could find another relationship, but there would be lonely days and nights until then. And even when he did find someone, she couldn't possibly understand what he was going through because he couldn't reveal his identity as an agent. He would be utterly alone in his torment.

Because I was a cold selfish bitch.

"Shut up!" I shouted at the ceiling only to wince a moment later, glad there was nobody around to witness that little lapse into crazy.

Shit, I was definitely losing it.

Relinquishing my grip on the stress ball, I laid it beside the keyboard again and carefully backspaced away the 'no'.

"Goddamn you," I mumbled. Sudden anger took me by surprise and I sprang to my feet. "Goddamn you!" I yelled at the screen. "You said you wouldn't make me choose right away and now you're forcing me to choose! *You asshole!*"

Snatching up the stress ball, I hurled it at the wall with all my strength. My aim was off and it struck the corner of my filing cabinet, exploding into a sandstorm of fine grit.

"FINE! FUCK YOU, TOO!"

I stormed out of the office before I could destroy anything else and made a beeline for the front door, where I laced on my running shoes.

Pounding down the gravel road at a too-fast run a few minutes later, I savagely wished the best of luck to any assassins who might be lurking around my farm.

Go ahead, assholes. Shoot me. Put me out of my goddamn misery.

They didn't, of course.

Limping back to the house nearly an hour later nursing the half-healed ankle I'd twisted a week ago, I muttered imprecations with what little breath I had left. Slamming my new steel door behind me, I kicked off my shoes and stomped directly to my office, where I brought up my email program.

I deleted Kane's email without a second glance.

Then I grabbed the phone.

CHAPTER 20

Kane answered on the third ring. His 'hello' was reserved, and my bravado nearly deserted me.

But not quite.

"It's Aydan," I said. "I just deleted your email."

"Oh."

He sounded completely emotionless. His stony cop-face hovered in my mind's eye.

"If you were trying to manipulate me, congratulations," I went on. "It worked."

"Aydan, I swear to you I wasn't-"

"It doesn't matter." I swallowed hard and forced the words out. "No matter what you say or how many times you deny it to me, the truth is that you're a spy. I'll never be able to trust anything you say without wondering whether you're sincere or just playing me. Your entire career is built on lies and manipulation."

Silence stretched between us, impossibly brittle.

"But you're also a friend." My voice trembled, and I fought back the fear. "Or at least I choose to believe you are. Maybe I'm wrong, but I have no way of knowing. You said I didn't have to make a decision right now, so I'm not. If you still want to have anything to do with me after the things I said, I..."

The words didn't want to come.

The small terrified voice inside my head shrieked, "Danger! Abort! Abort!"

I squashed it.

Locked my trembling fingers around the phone and squeezed my eyes shut.

"I'd still like to be friends." The phrase fell from my lips in a voice that didn't belong to me.

My heart flung itself against my ribcage over and over, desperately trying to escape.

The hiss of exhaled breath on the other end of the line did nothing to reassure me.

Silence expanded to smother everything. The ticking of the wall clock faded into oblivion.

"I'd like that," Kane said hoarsely.

My tension burst like a helium balloon, driving my voice up to cartoon-character pitch. "You would?" I cleared my throat and tried for a more normal tone. "Oh, well, that's good, then."

"Yes." Apparently Kane was having trouble with his voice, too. "That's good."

Another silence descended.

"So..." I drew my first deep breath in about a century. "I'm going to go and hide in the closet and have a panic attack, and then I'm going to Fiorenza's for pizza. Do you want to come?"

A chuckle rewarded me. "For the pizza or the panic attack?"

"Pizza. Or both, if you want. It's a big closet."

He laughed, strong and deep. "I'll meet you at

Fiorenza's. In about half an hour?"

"See you there," I agreed, and hung up before I could say anything stupid to spoil it.

Then I realized it was only four o'clock and I'd just eaten a couple of hours ago.

"Well, aren't you the smooth one?" I said to thin air, and headed for the bedroom to change my clothes.

I managed to resist the temptation to hide in my closet, but eyeing my nervous-looking reflection while I brushed my hair, I began to second-guess my decision.

What was Kane feeling right now? Relief? Triumph? Evil satisfaction? Hope? Fear? Or was he wishing I'd said no so he could leave behind my particular brand of fucked-up-ness and find a normal woman?

"And why am I worrying about how he feels?" I demanded of my reflection. "I don't even know how the hell *I* feel."

That was a bald-faced lie. Terror still fluttered dark wings inside my chest, but my reflection tactfully refrained from pointing that out.

I sighed and made for the door.

Bolstering myself with lavish mental praise for not driving as fast as possible in the opposite direction, I pulled into Fiorenza's parking lot right on time. Kane's black Expedition was already there, and as I parked he swung out of the driver's seat and strode over.

Too late to run.

I squared my shoulders and got out of the car.

"Aydan." His grey gaze searched my face. "I... It's good to see you." He reached as if to take my hand at the same time as I opened my arms to hug him, and we succeeded in rapping each other's knuckles smartly.

"Oops."

"Sorry."

Our words came out simultaneously as Kane switched and went for the hug while I tried for his hand, stymying each other again in a display of awkwardness that could only be rivalled by a pair of drunken dancing bears.

A smile crinkled the corners of Kane's eyes and he held his arms out from his sides and stood still. "I'm just going to stand here while you do whatever you want," he said.

Nerves pushed a smartass rejoinder out my mouth before I could stop it. "Really? Anything?"

His smile hooked into a wicked grin as my face went fiery.

"Well, I don't promise to stand completely still," he rumbled. "Depending on what you do."

"Sorry," I muttered, and gave him a quick hug before pulling away.

"Don't apologize." His arms captured me and held me close. "I'm sorry you felt manipulated," he murmured into my hair. "I didn't realize the physical part of our relationship meant anything to you. You always say 'it's only sex', so I was trying to keep it from complicating the way I feel-"

"It's okay," I interrupted. "I was a little too stressed. It wasn't that big a deal, and I'm sorry I overreacted."

"Shh." His arms tightened before releasing me to look down into my eyes. "No more apologies. Let's start with a clean slate. Just friends going out for pizza; no baggage, no agenda." He held out his hand. "Shall we?"

I took it, easing out a breath. "Okay."

Hand in hand, we headed for the entrance. Just as we reached it, Eddy emerged.

"Hi, Eddy," I greeted him. "It seems so weird to see you outside the bar. I keep forgetting you actually have a life."

He laughed. "Hi, Aydan; hi, John. Yes, I like to get an early supper so I can let my serving staff go home. It's so dead on Sunday nights, I can handle all the serving and bartending myself."

"Okay, well, have a good night," I said, feeling vaguely guilty for eating at Fiorenza's instead of Eddy's.

"You, too... oh, wait," he added as we moved toward the door. "Your nephew was looking for you Saturday afternoon. Did he find you?"

My heart lurched into my throat. "My nephew?"

"Yes. Tom Rossburn mentioned your nephew was in town...?" Eddy surveyed me with a slight frown as though wondering if I'd drowned a few too many brain cells Friday night. "You must have crossed paths on your way home without realizing it, because he just missed you at the bar."

I suppressed a shiver.

"Are you sure it was my nephew?" I asked. "Because he dropped by my place Thursday morning but I haven't heard from him since. Did he say he'd tried to call me?"

"No, I was busy with the brunch crowd so we didn't really talk. He only asked if you'd been in recently, and I said you'd just left. He looked about the right age, so I assumed he was your nephew."

"Did you ask him if he was?"

Eddy was beginning to look worried. "No. Why, is something wrong? You're not in danger, are you?"

Shit. After witnessing my abduction and being given the subsequent cover story over a year ago, Eddy took his duty as my unofficial guardian angel seriously. Seriously enough to put him at risk if he challenged the wrong person.

I put as much reassurance into my tone as I could muster. "No, don't worry, Eddy, nothing's wrong. But I doubt if he was my nephew. He might have just been a new client looking for bookkeeping services."

Eddy made a dubious face. "Didn't really seem the type. He looked like one of those artsy-rebel-alternative-music types that plays in a band where they abuse their guitars and scream like tortured ferrets. You know, with the beard and funky clothes and piercings everywhere."

I couldn't hold back my grin of relief. "That sounds like Tyler Brock. I work with him at Sirius Dynamics."

Eddy's eyebrows climbed his forehead. "He actually has a day job?"

"Yeah. He's a computer geek," I oversimplified cheerfully. "Thanks for letting me know, Eddy. I'll talk to him at work tomorrow."

"Okay, good," he replied. "I'm glad it's nothing to worry about. See you Tuesday, then."

"If not before," I agreed, and we parted with a smile and a wave.

Once we were seated at our usual table with our backs to the wall, Kane leaned closer, holding the menu in front of him as though discussing its offerings. "So your nephew is in town. Which nephew is this, and why does Rossburn know about him?"

His quiet tone masked any emotion, but I thought I detected a jealous edge.

I raised my own menu to point at a selection. "You know I don't have any nephews. Tom showed up at my place right after I shot Drake Mallard, and I had to explain his car in my driveway somehow. I would've made up a better story about a bookkeeping client, but Mallard's car was such a piece of shit Tom wouldn't have believed it."

"So you've been seeing a lot of him."

I deliberately misunderstood. "I'd never seen him before in my life until he turned up with that shotgun. But I asked Arnie to check with his contacts and see if anybody's been trying to hire any cheap goons lately."

To my relief, Kane accepted the diversion. "Good thinking," he said, and laid down the menu. "I'm going to go for the all-meat pizza with extra cheese. What about you?"

Later, we leaned against my car in the long rays of the late-afternoon sun, chatting companionably about nothing in particular. I had gradually relaxed during the meal, and by the end of it we had nearly regained our usual camaraderie.

At last, Kane straightened with a smile. "Well, thanks, Aydan. This was..." He let out a breath. "...good. Someday I'd like to have a meal with you where I don't have to do a visual check for concealed weapons every time a new customer walks in, but at least there was no bloodshed this time."

"Physical or emotional," I agreed. "That was really nice."

He winced, and I gave myself a mental slap to the head. "I'm sorry," I said hurriedly. "I didn't mean that as a dig, I just meant I liked being with you... as a friend. With no baggage or agenda."

His shoulders relaxed. "Thank you, that's nice to hear. Well... good night."

This time I let him take the initiative. He gathered me into his arms and lowered his lips to mine in a brief soft kiss that somehow managed to be both unsatisfying and hot as hell.

Then he stepped back.

"See you tomorrow," he said, and strode away.

"Yeah..." I said to nobody in particular, and slid into my car, frowning.

Driving home, I pondered why Brock would be looking for me. Other than our clash on Friday, I'd never really interacted with him before. If he needed something business-related, the Sirius Dynamics phone list was available to all internal personnel. Phoning me would make far more sense than wandering aimlessly around looking for me.

But if Eddy's visitor hadn't been Brock, then who was it and why was he looking for me? Could he have been Assassin Number Two?

At home, I spent an uneasy evening startling at every noise. When I finally retreated to my mattress in the garage, dark figures stalked my dreams and woke me screaming again and again.

CHAPTER 21

Morning came both too soon and not soon enough. Aching and exhausted, I dragged myself out of bed wishing for more sleep but thankful for an end to the nightmares. I couldn't bring myself to brave the shower, so I gathered my workout clothes and hauled my tired ass to the gym.

Even there, showering after my workout was an exercise in paranoia. I tensed at the slightest sound from the locker room, and when someone slammed a locker door the metallic clang nearly sent me through the shower ceiling.

"Get it together," I growled softly, patting my racing heart with a shampoo-lathered hand. "There'd be a hell of an outcry if some guy charged into the women's changing room with a gun."

I pushed my head back under the shower, but a sudden thought made me freeze, my pulse pounding.

Gender bias. Shit, I hadn't thought this through. I had been expecting a man, but if they sent a female assassin I was toast. I'd left both my guns in my locker.

I skipped the hair conditioner and stumbled out of the shower to make a dripping beeline for the lockers. My shaking hands muffed the padlock's combination twice before getting it right while I shivered with cold and nerves.

When the door finally opened I felt slightly better, but if I needed my guns in a hurry I'd still waste precious seconds unearthing them from the bottom of my duffel bag where they were hidden.

I didn't draw a full breath until I was back in my car, hair still in wet snarls that soaked my sweatshirt while I transferred the pistols back onto my body. Foregoing pride, I drove directly to Sirius Dynamics where I signed in under Leo's quizzical scrutiny.

"Running late," I muttered, and scurried upstairs to the safety of the ladies' room.

Inside I dropped my duffel bag and leaned both hands on the counter, letting my head hang while I waited for my heart rate to return to the vicinity of normal. At last I let out a long breath and straightened to survey my haggard face and wild hair in the mirror. Suppressing a groan, I rummaged in my duffel bag for my hairbrush and blowdryer and did the best I could.

By the time I emerged I had exchanged 'soggy and shivering' for 'frizzy-haired and cranky', but all in all it seemed like a good trade. I stopped in at the lunchroom to brew a cup of green tea and grab a cereal bar before heading for my office.

Gratefully inhaling the aromatic steam from my mug, I rounded the corner of my desk and sank into my chair.

A thunderclap of close-range guitars galvanized every nerve in my body and I launched to my feet with a yell, arms flailing, tea splattering everywhere.

The noise cut off abruptly, leaving me gasping with shock and adrenaline, my chest vibrating under the pummelling of my heart.

Spider dashed in wide-eyed. "Aydan, what was that?"

"I'll..." I had to stop and pant a few breaths. "I'll kill him... I'll kill the little fuck..." I braced my violently shaking hands against my desk. "...as soon as I can walk again..."

At Spider's look of confusion, I jerked my chin savagely toward the footwell of my desk. "Brock," I snarled.

Spider came around beside me and knelt to retrieve a small black box with a speaker from beneath the desk. Scowling, he peered at my chair before removing a second small device from the underside of the seat.

"Pressure switch," he said in the closest thing to a growl I'd ever heard him utter. "It closed the circuit when you sat down."

"I... will... fucking... *kill* him!" I ground out.

Spider rose, his frown dissolving into worry. "You can't, Aydan, you know you can't. And I don't want you to get in trouble. We'll report this to Stemp..."

"No, we won't," I growled. "Brock will just deny it, and I'll look like a fucking idiot." I drew myself upright, scowling at the puddles of tea on my desk. "Scratch that; like *more* of a fucking idiot."

"I bet we can prove it was him," Spider argued. "He probably left fingerprints on this, and I'm pretty sure I recognized the music. It's the same song he hurt you with on Friday morning, one of the ones his band does."

"He has a band?"

Spider made a face. "Yes. The Ballistic Rutabagas. Every now and then they get a gig at one of the alternative clubs in Calgary, and Brock thinks he's cool because he's the lead singer."

Well, shit. Chalk one up for Blue Eddy's snap character assessment. Maybe Sirius should hire him as a secret agent instead of me.

Spider was still talking. "He doesn't even play an instrument; he just screams at the microphone. Hellhound has more talent in... in his *beard* than Brock has in his whole body. Come on, Aydan, let's go talk to Stemp."

"No." I peeled off my tea-blotched sweatshirt and used it to sop up the remaining tea on my desk before hesitating. Damn, I couldn't walk out into the corridor with my guns in plain view. If one of the civilian researchers came along...

I swore and pulled the damp garment over my head again before marching for the door. "Time to end this."

"Aydan, no!" Spider squeezed out the door at the same time to scamper beside me down the hallway, clutching my wrist. "You can't, Aydan, you'll go to jail, please don't do it, *please...*"

Kane emerged from the doors at the end of the hall and strode toward us.

Spider cried, "Kane, help! Don't let her kill him!"

Kane's eyebrows snapped together and he quickened his pace. "What's happening?" he demanded as he closed the distance between us in a few long strides. "Aydan? What's going on?"

My lips stretched in a wolfish grin at the sight of Brock's pinched face poking out of his doorway like a rat from its hole. "I'm just going to talk to Brock."

Brock paled, but drew himself up with a small vicious smile. "Kane," he said. "I'm glad you're here. Kelly attacked me on Friday, and now she's coming back for another try. She's obviously unbalanced."

Kane surveyed him, his eyes like grey glaciers. "Is that so?" He took a couple of leisurely strides toward Brock to lean one massive shoulder against the wall beside Brock's door. Looming over Brock's expression of growing uncertainty, Kane smiled down at him. "Well, let's just see what happens. Innocent until proven guilty, you know."

"No, you have to protect me! It's your duty!" Brock's tone developed a whine as I paced slowly toward him. "You have to! If you don't, I'll report you to Stemp and you can go to jail right along with this bitch!"

Kane straightened, eyeing Brock as though he'd discovered something slimy and malodorous on the bottom of his shoe. "Oops," he said in a voice as hard and cold as his eyes. "I just remembered I left my SUV running."

He turned on his heel and strode down the hall. The click-clang of the security door closing behind him sounded abnormally loud.

Brock backed away from my pointy-toothed grin. Spider was still clinging to my wrist and making frantic noises, but I ignored him.

"Well, Brock," I said pleasantly. "I enjoyed your little practical joke this morning. I didn't realize you were such a funny guy."

"It wasn't me! I didn't do anything! I don't know how that speaker got there, it must have been the cleaning staff..." He trailed off as if suddenly realizing he'd admitted his guilt.

"Oh, that's okay, don't worry. I'm not mad." I bared my teeth at him and he twitched. "In fact, I'm really looking forward to working with such a joker," I went on in my fake-pleasant voice. "I love exchanging practical jokes. Now it's my turn. I won't do anything right away 'cause the surprise is part of the fun. But once I get going, you're going to absolutely *die* laughing."

He went even paler, but his lips curled with venom.

"Watch it, Kelly. You don't want to push me. If what I know about you gets out..."

A burst of icy fear cooled the heat of my anger, and I lowered my voice to a deadly hiss. "Gee, Brock, you're not saying you'll leak classified information, are you? 'Cause I hear the higher-ups get a little tight-assed about stuff like treason."

His sneer turned into a shocked gape. "No, of course not! I'd never breach security!" He looked so sincerely horrified at the thought that I actually believed him.

But a moment later his sneer came back. "I don't need to leak anything classified. All I have to do is say the right things to the right people and your dirty little secrets will be all over town. And Stemp will discharge you so fast it'll make your head spin."

"And which dirty little secrets would those be?" I inquired, racking my brain for anything shameful I'd done lately and coming up empty. Hell, I'd only been home for a few days. I hadn't had time to do anything shameful yet.

Brock shot a triumphant glance at Spider's worried face before turning his gloating grin on me. "Your drinking problem and your affair with Blue Eddy."

A bark of laughter escaped before I could stop it. "*What?*"

"Drinking problem. I saw you at Blue Eddy's Friday night, totally blotto and then propositioning Eddy right before he helped you up the stairs to his *private* apartment where you stayed the night. And you haven't slept at home since. The analysts' surveillance footage proves it."

Shit, I should have known his apparent disinterest on Friday night was too good to be true. And that must have been him sniffing around Eddy's bar Saturday morning, too, checking to see if I was still there. And the little slimeball had been snooping in my home surveillance footage. The garage was outside its range so it would look as though I hadn't been sleeping at home. Damn his low morals and high security clearance.

"Where I sleep is nobody's business but my own," I snapped. "And I'm not sleeping with Eddy but even if I was, I wouldn't be ashamed of it and nobody in town would care. And I didn't need help up the stairs."

"Oh, I don't know about that," Brock said snidely. "Eddy's *girlfriend* might care. And I notice you didn't deny your drinking problem. Stemp will confiscate your weapon and dishonourably discharge you if he finds out about that, and then we'll just see how tough you are without your gun. So you'd better be nice to me."

"Listen, you pathetic little louse," I began just as Stemp came through the security doors. I briefly considered trying to backtrack, but it was far too late. He had obviously heard.

Fine. This could work.

"Don't you dare spread lies about me or my friends," I snarled at Brock as Stemp approached. "And don't booby-trap my office again, either."

"What is this about?" Stemp demanded.

Spider's eyes lit with the unholy glee of a pacifist pushed too far. "Brock tried to goad Aydan into attacking him," he said. "And now he's threatening to spread lies about her." Even then he was too nice to turn a triumphant look on Brock, but Brock's cheeks turned crimson nevertheless.

Stemp's expressionless façade never altered, but I got the distinct impression of strained patience. "In my office, all of you," he said.

We trailed behind him like guilty children summoned to the principal's office, a similarity that was heightened when Brock stuck his tongue out at me. The childishness of the gesture was negated by the way he wiggled the tip obscenely, a silver dumbbell twinkling in the pale revolting flesh.

I held my face completely devoid of expression, fighting the urge to yank out the piercing and listen to him scream. Spider shot me a wide-eyed sidelong glance, but I didn't acknowledge him, either.

Inside Stemp's office, we weren't invited to sit. Stemp eyed us in silence across his desk.

Of course. He'd do the silent treatment until somebody blurted out something incriminating. Amusement bubbled up, but I stifled it and kept my face expressionless.

Spider was the first to crack.

"This isn't working," he said. His uncharacteristically grave and decisive tone surprised me. My endearing man-puppy was gone, replaced by a competent professional. He turned to Brock. "I've been putting up with your attitude because you're an excellent analyst. You do good work, but this kind of toxic stuff can't go on." Spider's cheeks were flushed and his fingers trembled where they knotted together behind his back, but his voice was steady. "You've been disrespectful to me, you've been abusive to Tammy, and your attacks on Aydan are not only childish, they're malicious and dangerous. That stops now. Or you'll be replaced."

I stared at Spider, holding my mouth closed while pride swelled inside me. That's my boy. I knew he had it in him.

Brock tossed his head. "Too bad there's nobody else with a high enough security clearance for this project. And when things start changing around here, you're going to wish you'd treated me with a little more respect."

I could see Spider didn't have a rejoinder for that, but Stemp's voice cut across the silence with the cool precision of a razor blade. "You have been treated respectfully, and you have not returned the courtesy. Though it's true we currently don't have any other analysts with sufficient clearances, that can and will change if necessary."

Brock turned his sneer toward Stemp. "If you're still director by next week."

Stemp's stony façade remained impregnable. "Indeed. Meanwhile, if there are any other incidents, you will be suspended without pay."

"You can't do that!" Blotches of colour flared into Brock's pasty cheeks.

"On the contrary, I can." Stemp levelled a deadly gaze at him. "And I won't hesitate to do so. You and Webb are dismissed. Kelly, stay."

Brock opened his mouth as if to protest more, but a fractional lift of Stemp's eyebrow made him press his mouth shut and flounce out. After an anxious glance at me, Spider followed.

Stemp and I eyed each other in silence for a moment. Then he inquired, "What was the booby-trap? And what lies is he spreading?"

I sighed and massaged my temples. God, I had a crashing headache and it wasn't even nine AM yet. That had to be some kind of record.

"I'm sorry," I said. "I wasn't going to bother you with it. It was just a high-tech version of a whoopee cushion; a pressure sensor under my chair that set off a blast of noise."

"And the lies?"

"He wants you to think I have a drinking problem so

you'll fire me. And he threatened to tell Blue Eddy's girlfriend that I was sleeping with him."

Stemp pressed his fingertips to the bridge of his nose. "And do you have a drinking problem?"

I couldn't help it. It was such a classic straight line that the punchline just popped out.

"Hell, no. I drink, I get drunk, I fall down. No problem." Horrified, I clapped my hand over my mouth too late.

A spark flared in Stemp's eyes, but I wasn't sure if it was amusement or irritation.

I unmuzzled myself slowly to make sure no more asinine comments were going to fall out of my mouth and added, "I'm joking. No, I don't have a drinking problem. I went out with Jill Francis on Friday night and had a little too much, but other than that I've only had two drinks in the past four months."

"Very well." The corner of his mouth quirked. "I got the joke. However, I suggest you choose your audience carefully for that sort of humour." He sank into his chair, looking uncharacteristically tired. "I won't dignify the other allegation with questions, since it's irrelevant to your job and therefore none of my business. Dismissed."

As I turned to go, he added, "Be prepared for another incident. I seriously doubt Brock will let this go."

I sighed. "Yeah. That's what I figured, too."

CHAPTER 22

When I returned to my office, Kane, Spider, and Jack were assembled inside. As I stepped through the door their accusing expressions made me trail to a halt.

"What?" I asked wearily. "What have I done now?"

"You didn't mention somebody tried to kill you last week." Two variations on that theme from Jack and Spider.

"You didn't mention you'd had an altercation with Brock last week." That was from Kane.

"Sorry..." I began, unsure which to address first. Deciding the answer was actually the same for both, I added, "It wasn't really relevant to what we were discussing at the time." I trudged over to drop onto my sofa. "In fact, it's still not. What's the plan for today? John, have you been briefed?"

"Yes," he said slowly, as if unwilling to let the subject drop. "But I'm not sure what use I'll be unless you need my protection in the network. I don't have enough scientific background to contribute anything else." He hesitated. "And I'm not really sure what you're researching anyway. As far as I understand it, you're basically just deciding if you're going to edit Tammy's memories or not."

"Not," Spider and I said simultaneously.

Kane turned a puzzled face toward us. "So what are we doing here? If you don't edit her memories, she'll have to be placed in a secured facility."

"Jail," I said bitterly.

"No..." Kane frowned. "She would be allowed to leave under escort-"

"Under guard," I interpreted unhelpfully. "For a few hours at a time, maybe, and then she'd be locked up again."

"Well... yes." Kane's frown deepened. "But she wouldn't be a prisoner. Her preferences would be accommodated whenever possible-"

"At someone else's convenience," I interrupted again. "It's a jail. A nice friendly jail, but a jail nonetheless."

"I think you're letting your own biases colour your perception..." he began, but apparently my expression convinced him that was a battle not worth joining. "...but it doesn't really matter at this point," he finished smoothly. "So I'm back to my original question. How can I help?"

"You can help us brainstorm," Spider said. "A fresh look from a non-scientific perspective might be just what we need."

"All right." Kane leaned back in his chair and stretched out his legs. "So help me understand this. Aydan, if you don't want to edit Tammy's memories, why don't you just... change her mind? Put in a subliminal command to not talk about anything that's classified?"

I sighed. "I'd love to, but I can't alter how her brain works. A memory is like a simple text document. Putting in a subliminal suggestion would be like rewriting a computer's operating system."

"Couldn't you just add a lot of memories of people telling

her not to talk about certain things?"

"I might be able to..." I tugged on a lock of hair. "But I don't think it would help. She's already been told dozens of times, but according to Dr. Rawling she doesn't have the ability to act on the memories appropriately."

"Well..." Kane frowned. "Let me play devil's advocate for a minute, then. You're fairly sure you can edit her memories if you need to, is that correct?"

I fought down the reflexive urge to deny the possibility. "I'm fairly sure I can remove memories, but that's not the same. When I did it before, I was just taking out the memories that were mine to start with, so it was easy..." I trailed off at the chorus of disbelieving noises that greeted my statement.

"You forget; we were all there," Kane said. "It nearly killed you."

I grimaced. "Okay, easy was the wrong word, but I could do it. But with Tammy, all the memories would be unfamiliar so I'd have to sift through each of them. I don't know if I'd survive if I tried to do it all at once. And if I had to stop in the middle, I don't know what would happen."

"You might end up permanently scrambled together with Tammy," Spider said fearfully. "Or lost in the network forever."

A memory-flash of drifting helplessly in interminable data tunnels made my palms go cold and sweaty. "Yeah, that would be bad," I agreed in a voice that didn't sound like my own.

"I don't really think that would happen," Jack disagreed. "You've already experienced Tammy's memories, Aydan, so there's no reason to believe a repeat exposure would make it impossible to extricate yourself. A more likely failure scenario would end with Tammy gaining your classified knowledge by accident."

God, and I'd thought my palms were sweaty before.

"That would be really bad," I croaked.

"Maybe; maybe not," Kane argued. "If you failed the first time you could go back and try again. It wouldn't be a one-shot chance, would it?" At Spider's uncertain headshake, Kane went on, "And if it turned out to be impossible in the end, Tammy would simply go to the secured facility as planned. Your classified knowledge would be safe there."

My voice came out sounding faint. "You don't know what I know."

Kane's jaw hardened as he surveyed me. If my face looked anything like I felt, it probably wasn't a pretty sight.

"Oh," he said. "That's bad, then."

I swallowed the papery dryness in my throat. "Hell, yeah."

"But if you took out all her classified memories, what would Tammy have left?" Spider demanded. "Terry Sherman and the brainwave-driven network are all she's known since she was eight years old. He was her whole family; her..."

He hesitated, blushing. My mind squeamishly filled in 'BDSM lover', along with a deluge of Tammy's memories that I'd been trying to suppress.

Bound and helpless. Completely at the mercy of another. The red-hot slash of a whip that came from my own terrifying memories as well as Tammy's...

"...her everything," Spider finished tactfully.

Jack half-rose from the desk, sudden worry creasing her forehead. "Aydan, what's wrong?"

I breathed through the panic attack that had seized me. "Nothing."

They all eyed me dubiously, but I summoned my best reassuring expression and tried to hyperventilate unobtrusively.

"All right..." Kane said slowly, still frowning in my direction. "...so deleting those memories would be a last resort. How about modifying them instead? Give her some happy memories of a great childhood and a satisfying job and..."

I was already shaking my head. "I wouldn't know how."

"It would be a gigantic task to assemble all the sensory inputs to create even one simple memory," Spider put in. "Touch, taste, smell..."

"...and I'd get them wrong anyway because Tammy's blind," I finished. "So her memories don't have a visual component but all the other senses are amplified."

A gloomy silence descended.

"Maybe we're going about this the wrong way," Jack said at last. "Aydan, would you be able to delete only a piece of a memory? For example, if one of Tammy's day-to-day memories includes sixteen hours of interaction between her and Terry Sherman, there would likely only be a few minutes that referenced classified information. So the editing task may not be as impossible as you think."

Kane sat up straighter. "And I know you said it would be a huge job, but Aydan, do you think you could remove her memories and store them externally? That way you could work with them at your own pace and just restore them to Tammy as you went along. We could tell her she fell and hit her head, and that she's experiencing temporary amnesia but all her memories should come back eventually."

A glance at Spider's miserable countenance assured me that the idea was a non-starter from his perspective, and I didn't like it either.

"I don't know," I said slowly. "Theoretically I might be able to, but it's such a huge job to sort out the memories in the first place, I doubt if I'd have any brainpower left over to pick out specific data and ferry it to an external server."

"All right, what about a medically-induced coma?" Kane asked. "What if you just took away all of Tammy's memories and stored them, leaving her essentially a blank slate-"

"That's sick!" Spider looked as though he was going to either cry or throw up. Or maybe both at the same time. "How can you even..." He trailed off, looking as though he'd just caught Kane eating kittens for breakfast.

Kane held up a calming hand. "I'm not saying it's a good idea; I'm just playing devil's advocate, remember? These are the kinds of possibilities the chain of command will consider. You don't want to get blindsided by something like this at the last minute, do you?"

Spider blinked and swallowed, his Adam's apple jerking convulsively. "No." His voice came out choked but not accusing anymore.

"And anyway," Kane went on, "It would only be for a short time. Aydan could probably get through the bulk of Tammy's memories in a day and restore all the innocuous ones right off the bat. Then Tammy would be free to live as she pleased, and she could just return here under the guise of therapy sessions with Dr. Rawling while Aydan gradually restored the rest of her edited memories."

"But it's *wrong!*" Spider's voice quavered on the edge of breaking. "I won't-"

He snapped his mouth shut as Brock appeared in the doorway.

Brock's beady eyes sharpened and I could just imagine his muckraking little mind eagerly gathering ammunition to use against Spider. The thought of him 'mentioning' to Linda that Spider might be involved in something unethical at work made my hands itch to wrap around his scrawny neck.

"You told me to let you know as soon as Tammy and I were out of the network," Brock said with a show of deference that was clearly intended to be sarcastic. "I texted you but you didn't answer."

Spider glanced at his phone, colour rising in his cheeks. "You texted me thirty seconds ago," he snapped. "I have more important things to do than stare at my phone all day long." He stuffed the phone back in his pocket. "We'll be using the network until two o'clock. Keep Tammy out of it until then."

"Would that be two on the dot, oh mighty leader?" Brock inquired nastily. "Or should I make it two-oh-five just in case you're doing something so *important* that you don't remember to check the time?"

Spider's blush deepened, but he met Brock's sneer with a level gaze. "Make it two-thirty just to be safe. I wouldn't want to take a chance on you accidentally meeting Aydan in the network." His hazel eyes narrowed. "Because I'm sure you remember what happened to the last guy who met her there."

"There, see?" Brock cried, appealing to Kane and Jack. "That was definitely a threat! They're ganging up on me like some incestuous inbred mother-son tag team!" Receiving nothing but stony-faced stares, he turned a sneer on Spider.

"Just remember, hotshot, if you get on my bad side your days are numbered..."

His words dribbled to a halt as Kane rose. I watched in admiration as he seemed to get taller and broader while the room shrank around him. I really needed to learn how to project that kind of sheer intimidating presence. Then again, it probably helped to be six-foot-four with shoulders like the Rocky Mountains.

Kane took a couple of unhurried steps toward Brock, who shrank back into the doorway. "I don't think Webb was threatening you. It sounded more like a warning to me," Kane said mildly.

"Yes," Jack piped up from behind him. "You're very lucky to work under someone as safety-conscious as Spider."

"And I'm sure Stemp would be interested to hear that you just threatened Spider," I put in helpfully.

"You're all a bunch of *losers*," Brock spat, and scuttled away.

Kane extended his arms in a leisurely stretch, muscles bulging and rippling across his back and shoulders. "Well," he said. "That certainly put me in my place."

The tension shattered as we all burst out laughing. The thought of Brock stewing in his own venom at the sound of the uproar behind him made me laugh even harder. When I doubled over hugging my stomach, Spider glanced over and let out a whoop of fresh merriment.

The grinding stress of the past several days spent itself in a gale of laughter that left us all sprawled in our chairs, feebly wiping away tears while the last of the giggles subsided.

"Oh my heavens," Jack said at last. She drew a deep

breath and let it out in a whoosh. "I needed that."

"Me, too," I seconded, and murmurs of agreement came from the men as well.

Spider sobered. "Well, I guess Kane's right." He grimaced. "Let's see if you can even store a memory on our servers. If you can..." He trailed off as if not even wanting to consider the possibility.

I reached over to pat his arm. "You're right, Spider, we need to know. And if I can't do it, the option's off the table and we can tell the chain of command we tried."

He brightened just a bit at that. "Okay. Let's try it. Whenever you're ready, Aydan."

CHAPTER 23

Several frustrating hours and a too-short lunch later, I slumped on the couch rubbing my pounding head.

"It still didn't work." Spider's face was filled with cautious hope. "None of your memories are on the server."

Despite my pain and exhaustion, I smiled. At least my failure had made somebody happy. "Doesn't look promising, does it?"

"Nope." His optimistic expression dissolved into concern. "You look like you need a break."

I squinted at my watch. "I'm about to take one. I have an appointment with Dr. Rawling." Dragging myself to my feet, I offered the group a listless wave. "See you later."

My aching brain sluggishly turned over possibilities while I plodded down the hall to the doctor's office. What would he want to talk about today? Surely I should have gained some brownie points this morning for not throttling Brock.

I tapped on Dr. Rawling's open door and he looked up from his computer with a smile. "Hello, Aydan. Come in and sit down." He rose and came around the desk to take his usual seat in the grouping of soft chairs.

"Hi." I dropped into the chair across from him,

marshalling my mental defenses.

Open. Calm. Cooperative. Sane. Normal...

"Is there anything you'd like to talk about today?" he asked.

"Not really." I gave him a sane, normal smile. "Is there anything you'd like to talk about?"

"Nothing specific." He smiled. "So how was your weekend?"

"Fine, thanks." After a moment I decided I should volunteer something more just to sound cooperative. "I got my exterior doors replaced, so that was nice. And I started some construction in the basement."

Shit, was it abnormally paranoid to construct a secret room in my basement?

"Just a minor renovation," I added.

"Oh, that's nice. Did you have any visitors?"

"None with shotguns," I joked.

Something about his intent gaze set off my alarm bells. Dammit, Brock had watched my surveillance records. Had he blabbed about Kane's visit just to see if he could get me in trouble? If he had, Rawling would know Kane had been over. And that he'd stomped out later.

Shit.

"John dropped over to help me with my doors," I added after a slightly-too-long pause. "It was nice to have the help."

"How nice," Rawling said agreeably. "I understand Kane transferred off your project at the beginning of the year, citing personal involvement. How are you handling that now that you're working together again?"

My defensive hackles sprang to attention. "Fine."

Damn, if he'd watched the surveillance footage, he'd know something sure as hell hadn't been fine when Kane had left my place on Saturday night.

Fighting back the burning desire to tell him it was none of his business, I rearranged my nice, open, relaxed posture and added, "We had a bit of a disagreement over the weekend, but we're good enough friends that it wasn't a big deal. We enjoy working together when we're on desk jobs here at Sirius; it's just that John didn't feel comfortable being placed in an active-duty scenario with me."

"And how do you feel about that?"

I feel like it's none of your damn business, buddy.

I smiled. "I think it was a good decision."

Rawling nodded his agreeable little nod and smiled his agreeable little smile. "It's nice when you can feel in accord like that. So you don't foresee any difficulties now that Kane is on administrative duty and you'll be working together regularly?"

"No, I don't. I'm glad he'll be here and that you'll be available to help him," I said in a burst of honesty that surprised me. "I'm worried about him."

"That's understandable, but try not to upset yourself. I'm sure he'll make a complete recovery." His kind gaze made me suppress an urge to squirm. "And certainly if you have any concerns or if you want to talk about what you're going through, separately or together, my door is always open."

"Thanks," I muttered.

"And speaking of what you're going through, how did you sleep this weekend?" he inquired solicitously.

Shit, was that a dig? Had Brock said something about me sleeping at Eddy's? Or, no, dammit, if Rawling had watched the surveillance footage he'd know I hadn't been sleeping in my house.

I cranked on a self-deprecating smile and lied my ass off. "Actually, pretty well. It's a little silly, but I love my garage so much I often sleep out there, particularly in the summer when it's hot in the house. I was doing some work out there this weekend, and I just lay down on the bed for a minute and when I woke up it was morning."

"Oh, that's nice to hear. I'm glad you're sleeping well and enjoying your hobbies."

He did look glad. He seemed like such a nice man. It was really too bad I hated him just now.

"Did you do anything else on the weekend?" he added.

"Uh... not really..."

What the hell was he fishing for?

Realization dawned. Brock again. The fictitious drinking problem.

With a supreme effort I managed not to roll my eyes back far enough to inspect my own brain.

"Jill and I went out for drinks Friday night," I offered, holding onto my sane, normal smile for all I was worth. "I really enjoyed the chance to get to know her. It's great to spend time with co-workers outside the office."

Jesus, I was going to gag on my own sweetness.

"Yes, it was nice to see you two getting along so well," he agreed.

Wait, what?

Oh shit, now I remembered. He'd been in Blue Eddy's Friday night. Goddamn small towns. Now that he mentioned it, I did vaguely recall giving him a cheery-beery wave across the bar where he'd been sipping a glass of white wine.

When had he left? How much had he seen?

Dammit, I couldn't remember.

"Yes, it was nice to see you there, too," I said, holding onto my smile for all I was worth. "I love Eddy's. He's such a nice guy, and the food and music are always so good."

"Yes, that's true." Dr. Rawling gave me one of his kind smiles. "You looked as though you were enjoying yourself."

Okay, fine. He was going to get to it sooner or later anyway, so I might as well take the offensive.

"I was." I twisted my lips in what I hoped was a disarmingly rueful smile. "A little too much, actually. The evening kind of got away on me."

He nodded understandingly. "How do you feel about that?"

I managed not to snap, 'I feel like I really hate that question'.

"A little silly," I said instead. "I usually don't have more than a drink or two." I tried not to look as though I was making a point in my defense. "In fact, I think other than Friday night I've only had two beers in the last four months. But it was fun with Jill, even though it's not something I'd do often."

"Well, that's good to hear." Dr. Rawling awarded me a benevolent smile. "Self-medicating with alcohol isn't a good habit to get into."

"No, I wouldn't do that," I lied, trying not to think about how much I really, really wanted a fucking beer right now.

My desire for a drink increased exponentially over the next forty minutes while Dr. Rawling prodded me obliquely about everything from Brock's sabotage to my sleeping habits.

At last I stumbled out, holding onto my smile with the

last of my willpower and managing to conceal my relief at our arrangement for another session in a week's time.

A whole week. Thank God. Maybe by then we'd have found out who was behind Drake Mallard's attack, and the threat of the safe house would be eliminated.

Or I'd be dead.

I sighed and trudged back to my office.

After another fruitless brainstorming session with the team, I slumped on the couch and surveyed the dispirited expressions that surrounded me.

Jack sighed and rose, tucking her instrument case under her arm. "I can't believe it's four-thirty already." She patted Spider's shoulder on her way to the door. "Don't worry, Spider, tomorrow's another day."

"Yeah," he mumbled. "Thanks. Have a good evening." He stood slowly as though the weight of the world rested on his skinny shoulders.

Well, maybe not the world. One woman's life. More weight than anyone should have to bear.

"See you tomorrow," he said, and shuffled out.

Kane rose, too. "I'm going to spend a half-hour skimming the current administrative caseload to see where I can do the most good when I'm not needed on Tammy's project, and then I'm going to get supper at Blue Eddy's. Do you want to come?"

"Sure," I said absently, still trying to figure out a third alternative for Tammy in what ultimately came down to an either/or decision.

"I'll come and get you at five, then," Kane said.

"Mm-hmm."

After he left, I sat staring at the ceiling for another quarter of an hour. It offered no useful options, and at last I sighed and trailed over to my desk to check my email.

Most of it was ordinary internal correspondence and I dealt with it with half my attention, but a meeting request summoned me to an interview with an Ursula Ritter on Wednesday at ten AM. Subject: Peer review of Charles Stemp. I had just accepted it with my fingers crossed for luck when Kane leaned into the doorway.

"Are you ready to go?" he asked.

"Uh?" I blinked stupidly at him.

"Go. For supper. To Blue Eddy's. It's five o'clock."

"Oh. Uh..."

Shit, what had I been thinking, accepting his invitation? Dinner at Fiorenza's last night, lunch together today, then dinner again tonight? Bad idea. That's how expectations get created.

Brock drifted by in the corridor behind Kane, his gaze darting between Kane and me while his eyes narrowed in speculation. Then he flashed a nasty smile, curling his left hand into a tunnel and plunging his right forefinger repeatedly into it in a lewd gesture that left no doubt about his meaning.

I smiled pleasantly and flipped him my middle finger.

Kane's brows snapped together, but his mouth quirked at the corner. "If you don't want to go for dinner, just say so. Flipping me off seems a little over the top."

Brock smirked and hurried away, and I laughed. "Sorry, that was for Brock, not you."

Kane spun to survey the empty hallway before turning back to me, grinning. "Oh, sure, that's what they all say." He sobered. "Do you need a bit more time? If you're in the middle of something we can go later."

"Uh, no. That's okay..."

Damn Brock. This would be just more grist for his sordid rumour mill.

But, hell, Kane and I both had to eat. I was starving, I didn't feel like cooking, and I especially didn't feel like cooking while keeping one hand on my gun. It had been such a relief to drink with Jill on Friday night, knowing she was armed and capable of taking care of both of us if necessary. I'd feel even safer with Kane.

And there had been too damn little safety in my life lately.

I smiled and stood. "I'm ready. Let's go."

CHAPTER 24

Somehow, leaving the building at the end of the day seemed more dangerous than leaving it at lunch. The parking lot was almost deserted, and only a few pedestrians strolled by.

I slid hurriedly into the driver's seat of my car, wishing I had accepted Kane's offer to drive us both over to Blue Eddy's in his vehicle.

It did make more sense for us to go to the bar separately, though. He'd go home to his house afterward; I'd go to mine. No need to double back here first.

But it would have been so easy to get in his passenger seat and hand my worries over to him...

"Don't start," I muttered, and put the car in gear.

The short drive to Blue Eddy's seemed longer than usual. Following Kane's shiny black SUV, I checked my rear-view mirror frequently but saw nothing I could identify as a tail. Then again, I couldn't say for sure we *didn't* have a tail. Ninety percent of the small-town traffic travelled the main streets between Sirius and Blue Eddy's. I grimaced and checked my mirror again.

When Kane drove around the block before pulling into Eddy's parking lot I followed, surveying rooftops and alleyways and feeling relieved that I wasn't the only paranoid freak.

We met at the door and I relaxed as I stepped into the comforting familiarity of the bar with Kane's reassuring presence behind me.

My relaxation was short-lived.

"Aydan! Big John!" Lola's larger-than-life voice boomed out from several tables pulled together to accommodate a group I identified with a sinking heart as the Silverside and Area Chamber of Commerce members.

"Aw, shit," I muttered.

Lola stood and hurried toward us, her small figure barely visible until she emerged from behind the seated group. When she did, I hid a smile.

Obviously playing the role of upstanding citizen and committee member, she was attired in a conservative-for-her magenta leather sheath dress with a daring slit up the front of the skirt and a plunging neckline. Matching magenta ankle boots adorned with glittering chains finished the outfit, and her silver hair was razor-cut in a dramatic asymmetrical 'do accented with a shocking pink streak.

"Perfect timing!" she exclaimed, latching onto Kane's arm with one hand and mine with the other. "Come and join us!"

Kane looked momentarily taken aback, then smiled. "Right, the Spring Thing. I need to participate for Kane Consulting. Come on, Aydan, let's sign up to help with the Little Clowns Bicycle Rally. They always need extra volunteers for that."

I started to say 'are you nuts', but a glance at Kane's smile made me choke back the words. The shadows had momentarily lifted from his eyes, and I suddenly realized how healing it would be for him to be surrounded by happy children.

I put on a smile of my own and made the only excuse I could. "You go ahead, John. I promised Lola I'd ride on the Up & Coming float."

"Right on, honey!" Lola crowed. "It'll be a blast, you'll see!"

"That's what I'm afraid of," I mumbled, but not too loudly.

At the communal table we duly committed to our roles and excused ourselves as soon as we could.

Later, tucked behind the shield of my favourite table with my back to the wall, I swallowed the last bite of my Caesar salad and leaned back. Beside me, Kane finished off his burger before doing the same, rocking his chair onto its back legs. Our conversation had revolved around the Spring Thing, but now Kane turned to me with a serious expression that made my belly tighten.

"So tell me about this thing with Brock," he said.

Safe topic. I let out the breath I'd been holding.

"It's probably my fault," I said gloomily. "He startled me with some loud music and I told him next time I'd turn off his stereo with a sledgehammer. He got snippy so I grabbed him by his big scarf and suggested I'd gotten into the habit of killing guys lately so I'd be happy to oblige if he wanted to be next. It escalated from there."

"Escalated how, exactly?" Kane inquired cautiously.

"He ran and tattled to Stemp, Stemp ripped a strip off both of us, and now it's Brock's mission to make my life as miserable as he's making everybody else's."

"Ah." A smile tugged at the corner of Kane's mouth,

activating the delicious laugh lines around his eyes. "So you didn't 'try' to kill him like he said."

"Oh, trust me, if I'd tried, Sirius would have one less analyst right now."

Kane's smile turned into a laugh. "No doubt. You know, there's something about Brock that gets on my last nerve. I had to walk away this morning or I would have wiped that smirk off his face onto the carpet."

I laughed, too. "I think we need to start a Tyler Brock anti-fan club. Even Spider is ready to throttle him."

"Yes." Kane's smile faded. "But you probably shouldn't antagonize him any more than necessary. I didn't like the sound of those threats he made."

"Pshaw." I waved a contemptuous hand. "He's just an insecure little worm with entitlement issues."

"Maybe so, but with his security clearance he could do a lot of damage if he was so inclined."

I blew out a sigh. "Yeah, I know. You're right. I shouldn't let him get to me but he's just... on top of everything else right now, he's like the straw that broke the camel's back." I sipped some of my water, not looking at him. "I think we're all kind of clinging to the ragged edge. Spider's really wound up about Tammy, Jack is beside herself worrying that Dermott will take over from Stemp..."

"Yes, and you're dodging assassins. There's a lot of stress..." Kane hesitated and I turned to face him. "Aydan..." he began.

Something in his expression set off all my alarm bells. Stomach knotting, I clutched my water glass as if it could save me.

"I wanted to talk to you about last Saturday night," Kane said.

"You promised we wouldn't have to talk about it again." I'd intended the words to sound teasing but they came out fearful and defensive instead.

Hurt flashed across his face, but his voice stayed even. "I didn't mean it to be an ultimatum that closed off any chance for discussion. I'll always be ready to listen, especially if we have a misunderstanding as fundamental as this obviously was. As I said, I didn't realize our physical relationship was that important to you."

I nearly blurted, 'It's the only thing I want from you'. Some benevolent deity must have been hovering nearby to intervene, though, because the words never left my lips.

Instead, I stared at Kane, shocked and sickened by what I'd almost said.

Cold, selfish bitch.

But, dammit, I'd told him that from the start. His friendship meant more to me than I cared to admit, but we had agreed friendship was all it would be. Well, okay, friendship with benefits, but that was all. Hellhound was right. It wasn't my fault if Kane changed his mind.

That didn't make me feel any better.

For God's sake, set the poor man free so he can go and find the love he deserves.

Resolve steadied my voice, and I reached over to squeeze his hand. "It's okay, John, it really isn't that big a deal. Like I said, I'm on edge right now and I overreacted. I'm glad you're going for what you truly want. You're doing the right thing."

His troubled grey gaze searched my face. "So you're not hurt?"

"Of course not. I want what's best for you. Always will."

I rose. "I need to get going. I've got a couple of projects calling my name at home. Dinner's on me tonight; I'll pay for it at the bar on my way out."

He stood, too, frowning down at me. "You're upset."

Drawing on long years of miserable practice, I smoothed my face and voice into neutrality and gave him a smile. "No, of course not. I just have to get going."

"At least let me get the bill."

"Are you kidding? After that fabulous meal you cooked the other night? I owe you big time. This is my treat." I reached up to kiss him on the cheek and turned away.

He didn't follow me.

At the bar, I proffered my credit card and leaned on the counter while Eddy rang the transaction through. Glancing around to be sure I wouldn't be overheard, I leaned closer.

"Hey, Eddy, I need to give you the heads-up on something."

He looked up, his gaze sharpening. "What is it?"

"I just wanted to warn you about a rumour that might be floating around about, um..." I hesitated, heat rising in my face. "You know the guy you thought was my nephew?"

Eddy nodded and I went on, "He's got a bit of a hate on for me at the moment and he threatened to tell your girlfriend that you and I are having an affair. You should mention it to her so she doesn't get blindsided if she hears it."

Eddy frowned. "What girlfriend? I'm not seeing anybody right now."

I gaped stupidly at him. "You're not?"

"No." He chuckled and indicated the bar with a wave of his hand. "You were right on Sunday. This is pretty much my life."

"Oh." My flush of embarrassment heated into anger. "That little shit."

Eddy patted my hand. "Don't worry about it. And if I hear any other ugly rumours about you I'll nip them in the bud."

"Oh." My embarrassment came back in a rush. "No, Eddy, I didn't mean it was an ugly rumour... I mean, I wouldn't be ashamed if people thought we were... um. I just didn't want to spoil anything for you."

"Don't worry," Eddy repeated, smiling as he handed back my credit card. "I knew you didn't mean it that way. Don't give it another thought."

"Thanks, Eddy," I said with feeling, and made for the door.

The parking lot seemed ten times more dangerous without Kane beside me. Plastering my back to the wall of the bar, I scanned for any suspicious figures and saw none. A quick once-over of my car revealed no unusual wires, and I slid into the driver's seat and turned the ignition key holding my breath.

When nothing exploded I steered for home, nervously checking my mirrors until I turned off the highway and nobody followed me.

Then again, why would they follow me? They knew where I lived.

Shaking my head at my own idiocy, I switched from checking my mirrors to surveying the woods, fields, and my yard as I drove up. Nothing unusual caught my eye, and I hurried to let myself through the gate and lock it behind me.

Inside my house with the blinds drawn, I couldn't seem to settle. Every noise grew to threatening proportions, and I patrolled the entire house twice with my trank pistol before forbidding myself to do it for a third time.

Sinking into my most comfortable chair, I switched to slow yoga breaths and tried to read, but the book didn't hold my interest and my heart still thumped too rapidly in my chest.

I sighed and abandoned the book for my computer. Placing an online order for my basement room's concealed hinges used up a good ten minutes.

"Whoop-de-doo. Ten minutes down, twelve hours to go," I muttered, and turned resolutely to my bookkeeping.

Familiarizing myself with the substitute bookkeeper's work wasn't nearly as absorbing as I'd hoped. Twitching and squirming in my chair, I managed to stick with it for half an hour before rocketing to my feet.

"Fine," I growled.

I was putting on my boots at the front door when the phone rang.

A surge of adrenaline burned my veins and I sprang to snatch up the handset, trank pistol clenched in a white-knuckled grip.

"Hello!" I barked.

"Hey, darlin'." Hellhound's gravelly voice held a questioning note. "Did I catch ya in the middle a' somethin'?"

"Oh." The syllable came out on a rush of released breath as I sagged against the wall. "No. Sorry." I took another breath, willing my pulse rate down from heart-attack levels. "It's just that the analysts phone me if they spot anything on the surveillance cameras, so I've been jumping every time the phone rings."

"Shit, sorry, Aydan. Didn't mean to freak ya out. Should

I call ya on your cell next time instead?"

"Yeah, thanks, that would be great." Succumbing to the trembling of my knees, I slid down the wall to sit on the floor. "So how are you?"

"Fine, darlin'. Just been talkin' to Weasel."

"And...?" I held my breath all over again.

"An' he says, word is there was some guy offerin' cash for a job a few days ago. I guess there was a bit a' talk 'cause everybody thought it was funny as hell."

"*Funny?*" My voice squeaked on the word. "Murder is funny? Who the hell is Weasel hanging around with, anyway? I thought you said he was small-time and basically harmless."

"He is. But I guess this guy was so pathetic, they were takin' bets on who'd just take his money an' split without ever doin' the job at all."

"So who was the guy? And why was he so pathetic?"

"Didn't get a name, but he was a skinny little fuck with a beard an' a buncha piercin's in his face. Light in his loafers an' scared shitless."

My heart gave a hard thump.

Brock.

CHAPTER 25

My mind whirled, the phone sagging away from my ear. Why the hell would Brock have wanted me dead last week? I hadn't tangled with him until after Mallard showed up, so if he'd hired Mallard it wouldn't have been in revenge for my attack on him and his stereo.

"Aydan? Ya still there?" Hellhound's question prodded me back to the present and I raised the handset again.

"Uh... yeah... When was this?"

"Sorry, darlin', I dunno for sure. Weasel didn't wanna attract attention by askin' too many questions. It might not have even been the guy who's gunnin' for ya."

"Can you get him to dig some more?"

"Nah. Already tried but he said he ain't gettin' involved if it's a hit, even when I offered him twice my normal rate. But you could probl'y get him to do it."

I squeezed my eyes shut. "Do I even want to know what you mean by that?"

"Nah, probl'y not."

"Shit." I drew a deep breath and braced myself. "Okay. What does he want?"

Hellhound's tone was wry. "What d'ya think? He wants ya to beat him up while he beats off."

"Gah." I gave a whole-body shudder. "He is such a disgusting little..."

"...Weasel," we finished together. "But Aydan," Hellhound added, "He says ya already owe him one. An' from the way he had his hand down his pants when he said it, I'm figurin' he wasn't talkin' about a coffee."

"Yeech. I did promise to beat him up that time I needed him for a lookout at the Hogback Tavern, but I sure as hell didn't say he could whack off while I did it."

Hellhound snorted. "Good luck tryin' to keep Weasel from whackin' off. He's pretty much gonna have his hand on his dick the whole time you're whalin' on him 'less ya break both his arms."

"God, this is such a gross conversation!" Shuddering again at the thought of actually touching Weasel, I scrubbed my palm against my jeans. "So you're saying he won't ask around any more unless I promise to come down there and beat the hell out of him."

"Sorry, darlin', it's a little worse than that," Hellhound said regretfully. "He ain't takin' any more promises. If ya don't deliver a beatin' up front, he won't go lookin' for any more info."

"Urgh! Bleah!" I scrubbed my palm even harder. "Now I need brain bleach and hand sanitizer and about ten hot showers with antiseptic soap. And that's just from thinking about it."

"Wish I had better news, but he's a stubborn little fuck. I could lean on him a bit..."

"No, Arnie. Thanks, but don't. I know you need him as an informant for your P.I. jobs, so don't take a chance on pissing him off. I have an idea about who the guy might be anyway, so I'll investigate here. If I can't find out anything more on my own, I'll... I'll think about beating Weasel." I shuddered again. "Bleah. That sounds like a euphemism for masturbation. 'Beating the weasel'."

Hellhound laughed. "Better than 'chokin' the chicken 'til it pukes'."

"Eeuw!" A giggle bubbled up. "How about 'doing the five-knuckle shuffle'?"

"Beatin' the meat; slammin' the ham; yankin' the crank; floggin' the log; ticklin' the pickle..."

By now I was giggling helplessly.

"...polishin' the flagpole; spankin' the monkey; burpin' the worm; wrestlin' with Cyclops; makin' the bald man cry..."

"Stop, you're killing me!" Laughing and gasping for air, I toppled over to sprawl on the floor.

"...an' don't forget 'shakin' hands with your best friend'," Hellhound finished gravely before his laughter joined mine.

At last I managed to stop laughing and dragged myself upright again. "What would I do without you?"

"Hell, darlin', I dunno. Prob'ly just dry up an' blow away."

"I would, and that's a fact."

"Well, lucky I'm comin' up Thursday, then." He hesitated. "If that's okay."

"It's more than okay." Reality intruded on my happy glow and I heaved a sigh. "I might have to sneak around to see you, but I'll see you for sure."

"Sounds good, darlin'. See ya then. Unless you're comin' down here to beat Weasel."

"I really hope not. The only weasel I want to beat is yours."

His laughter warmed me. "Darlin', you're a silver-tongued charmer. Be safe. Love ya."

He hung up before I could reciprocate, but I knew he didn't need to hear me say it.

Smiling, I hauled myself to my feet and replaced the telephone handset in its cradle.

My smile faded as my thoughts returned to the problem at hand. Frowning at the telephone, I considered my new knowledge.

Brock was the only person I knew who fit the description, but I couldn't believe he'd want to kill me. Well, he might now; but probably not last Thursday. I was pretty sure nothing in our brief exchange four months ago would have inspired him to homicide.

But he'd uttered those threats...

Kane's warning took on a whole new level of credibility now.

But what motive could Brock have for killing me? Could he be trying to get rid of me so that he and Tammy would be left as Canada's only option for clandestine decryptions?

My heart clutched. If that was the case, Spider was in danger, too. And Brock had already threatened him twice.

Oh, God. Adrenaline flooded my system, but I fought the need to spring into immediate action.

Calm down and think.

It didn't make sense for Brock to murder us. There was more than enough work to keep all of us busy for the rest of our lives, and despite Stemp's threat to replace Brock, we all knew that would be more easily said than done.

I thumped a fist gently and rhythmically into my palm and began to pace.

Could Brock be working for somebody else?

No; it didn't make sense for somebody else to hire him just to hire an assassin.

Unless...

What if Brock was part of the original group of Fuzzy Bunny's agents who had infiltrated Sirius Dynamics?

My fist met my palm with a smack, my heart lurching up into my throat. What if he had been feeding Fuzzy Bunny information all along? With his high security clearance, he had access to almost everything. I fled for the bedroom to grab a secured phone.

Halfway down the hall, I slowed to a halt.

No, that didn't make sense, either.

Brock had been working with Sirius for as long as Spider. If he had been relaying information to Fuzzy Bunny, we never would have been able to catch them by surprise and accomplish all those arrests last winter.

Frowning at the floor, I traced a scratch in the hardwood with my toe. The Department's security had been overhauled less than a year ago. There was no way a double agent could have slipped through their scrutiny.

But what if Brock was a criminal mastermind? What if he'd been biding his time at Sirius and we'd played into his hands by eliminating Nicholas Parr and all the other big players in Fuzzy Bunny, leaving the organization ripe for a takeover? That was exactly the kind of subversion that would appeal to him. And eliminating Spider and me would cement his position both with Fuzzy Bunny and in Sirius.

I hurried down the hall, only to stop myself again in the bedroom clutching a secured phone.

I couldn't call Stemp yet. This was nothing more than a tangle of paranoid speculation. And if I made groundless accusations against Brock I'd just look childishly vindictive.

There were lots of skinny bearded guys with facial piercings, and I didn't even know for sure the guy in question had been negotiating a contract against me. The chances of Weasel pinpointing exactly the right transaction were ridiculously slim. More likely the guy had been trying to buy drugs or something.

I hissed out a breath between my teeth. But what if it was Brock? And what if he sent an assassin after Spider? Spider wouldn't have a chance.

Panic climbed my throat, but I gulped it down.

Think this through. If he wanted Spider dead, he would have already made an attempt. And anyway...

I drew a deep breath. Brock might be a shithead, but he was a smart shithead or he wouldn't have been able to worm his way inside the Department's security. And hiring a guy like Drake Mallard was definitely stupid. It couldn't be Brock.

It just couldn't be.

I needed more information. A better description of the guy. Details of the contract he was trying to negotiate, and whether anybody had noticed who he was negotiating with. If I could confirm it was Drake Mallard, at least there was a better chance that I was chasing the right lead. And I needed to narrow down the timeframe. It would be pretty damn embarrassing to accuse Brock only to find he'd been in his office surrounded by witnesses at the time.

But I needed to know more about Brock, too. Where he lived, who he hung out with, what he did in his spare time. I needed to sneak into Sirius's network to spy on Brock the way he'd been spying on me.

I smacked my fist into my palm again.

But Stemp had forbidden me to go into the network unless it was necessary. If I told him I needed to check up on Brock I'd have to explain why, and that would look like a petty attempt at revenge. And if I wanted to snoop secretly I'd need my network key, which had to be signed in and out of the secured area. So Stemp would find out, and I'd have to explain anyway.

Damn.

I paced some more.

Then I paused, a slow smile spreading across my face. I might not be able to snoop in the network myself, but I knew somebody who could. Now I just needed to contact him without alerting Brock, who was undoubtedly watching my every move with either murderous or malicious intentions.

Pulling out my cell phone, I texted Spider, hoping he'd remember the code we'd used during the Fuzzy Bunny sting. "Mind if I come over for a beer?"

I was rewarded in only a few seconds. "Come on over. See u soon."

When I pulled up in front of Spider's small bungalow twenty minutes later, he popped out the front door and hurried down to meet me.

"Is something wrong?" he demanded before I was halfway out of the car.

"No, don't worry. I just need your help with something," I reassured him, and his shoulders slumped with relief.

"Come on in, then," he said. "Linda's just getting ready to leave for the night shift, so if it's not urgent maybe we could wait until she leaves...?" He left the question mark hanging in the air, and I nodded.

"That'll be fine. It's not urgent, and I'm glad I'll get a chance to say hi to Linda. I haven't seen her in ages."

When we stepped through the front door, Linda was just pulling a jacket over her brightly-patterned nurses' scrubs.

"Aydan!" She flipped her glossy brunette ponytail free of her collar and greeted me with a hug. "It's great to see you! How are you?"

"I'm fine, how about you?" I took in her healthy makeup-free glow and sparkling eyes. "You look great!" I nudged Spider with an affectionate elbow. "This long drink of water must be good for you."

"Thanks!" She beamed up at Spider. "He is." Her smile faded. "This isn't a social call, is it?"

"No, I'm afraid not. I'm here to pick Spider's brains for a work thing. Sorry."

Worry clouded her face for a moment before she put on a smile and gave Spider a hug. "Well, I hope you figure it out, whatever it is." She went up on her tiptoes and Spider stooped to meet her in a kiss. "See you tomorrow, Sweetie. Have a good night."

"You, too," Spider replied, and my heart warmed to see the fond look they exchanged before she went out the door.

As soon as it closed behind her, the smile vanished from Spider's face. "What do you need, Aydan?" he asked anxiously, then blinked, pink rising in his cheeks. "Oh... um, sorry, I didn't mean to be rude. Did you actually want a beer? We have some left over from our engagement party." He made a half-hearted move toward the kitchen.

"No, thanks, Spider, I'm driving. I was hoping..." I trailed off, suddenly second-guessing my idea. Would he get into trouble? "Um... what are your rules for accessing the Sirius network from home?" I asked instead.

"I can access it whenever I want. I use extra security if

I'm going to access it remotely, that's all. Why?" His gaze sharpened. "What are you looking for?"

"Um... you've got a really high security clearance, right?" I equivocated.

"Yes..." He eyed me with interest. "And...?"

"Would you, um... hypothetically speaking... get in trouble if Stemp found out you had... hypothetically... gone through some personnel files?"

Spider's uber-hacker alter ego blazed to life in his eyes. "Whose?"

"Brock's."

"Oh." His sparkle dampened and he gave me wry smile. "That's no fun. I don't even have to hack those. I'm his team lead, remember? I have full access to all his records."

"Oh, right." I drew a breath of relief. "Good. You won't get in trouble, then."

Spider grinned. "I guess that would depend on whether I get caught showing them to you. And what you do with the information." The wicked sparkle came back. "I hope it's something evil."

I laughed. "If it is, I won't tell you until afterward so you can claim innocence."

"Oh, no, Aydan, I'll take full responsibility," he began, but I waved him to silence.

"It's nothing evil. Yet." I gave him a brief summation of Weasel's information and my conjectures. When I finished, he stared at me with a troubled expression.

"It can't be Brock," he said slowly. "I mean... that's my gut feeling, but I'm also pretty confident in the new screening processes we put in place last year. After those slimeballs infiltrated Sirius and attacked you..." His face hardened at the memory. "Stemp and I completely revamped the system. Everybody had to requalify under the new guidelines, even him and me. I really don't like Brock but I'm pretty sure he wouldn't kill anybody, and I don't think he's selling intel, either."

I sighed. "My gut agrees with yours. He's an irritating little shit, but not a murderer or a traitor. Either way, though, I'd like to know my enemy."

Spider nodded and beckoned me toward the stairs that led to his basement technological lair. "Good idea. And hey." He brightened. "If we catch Brock doing anything underhanded at all, he'll be out of our hair." He clattered down the stairs and hurried to his array of computer equipment.

CHAPTER 26

About an hour later, Spider leaned back in his chair. "That's everything in the Sirius system. Are you sure you don't want me to print it out for you?"

"No, I got a good enough overview and I don't want any tangible evidence that I was snooping. And anyway, there wasn't really anything too useful there except his home address. If I need to recheck any details I'll let you know."

Spider eyed me eagerly. "Now what are you going to do?"

I dragged myself up from the chair beside him and stretched the kinks out of my back. "I don't know yet. I'd love to put a camera on his house and a bug and a tracer on him, but I don't have any of those things and I can't sign them out of Sirius without an explanation..." I hesitated. "And considering that we're both pretty sure it's not him, I wouldn't want to get caught spying on him. Can you imagine the shitstorm he'd stir up?"

Spots of colour climbed Spider's cheeks. "He's been spying on you! Maybe you should stir up some trouble for him. You should complain to the privacy commissioner. You're not under investigation so it's illegal for him to access your personal data."

"I don't have proof that he's done that, though. It's not illegal for him to follow me to the bar, and he has the clearances to view the surveillance footage from my house." I sighed.

"But, Aydan, you're an agent and this is an investigation," Spider protested. "You had to investigate Stemp four months ago, so I don't see any problem with you investigating Brock."

"Except we had evidence that made it look as though Stemp was up to something," I countered. "All we have is one little shred of circumstantial evidence against Brock. Hell, not even evidence, just hearsay from really questionable witnesses. That's why I haven't taken it to Stemp yet. He'd tear me a new one for jumping to conclusions."

"But how can you find evidence if you're not allowed to look?"

"I-"

"Wait, hang on," Spider interrupted. A smile spread across his face. "I have a way." His smile faltered. "Or... I think I have a way. It just depends on how smart Brock is. And how paranoid."

I flopped back into the chair with a groan. "That's the problem. He's either innocent, or he's scary-smart and really paranoid."

"Mm. I already know he's smart." Spider stared into middle distance, his hacker persona blazing in his eyes. "But I can do this."

"Um..." I studied him worriedly. "What are you talking about, and why do I get the feeling you'll be in a hell of a pile of trouble if you get caught?"

"I probably won't," Spider said absently, and I sensed his agile mind assembling data and computing possibilities with lightning speed. "And even if I do get caught, I'll just say it's a security test."

He fell silent and I sat watching him, unwilling to disturb the flow of his thoughts.

After a few moments he said, "Ha!" and leaned back in his chair, grinning. "Okay, Aydan, you said you wanted a camera and bug and tracer?"

I stared at him in wonder. "You're going to build them from scratch?"

Spider laughed. "No. I can do better than that. I'm going to hack Brock's phone and output all the audio, video, browsing history, and text messages, along with GPS tracking so you'll always know where he is."

My jaw dropped. "You can do that?"

"Oh, that's easy." Spider's smile dimmed. "The hard part is not getting caught. If Brock's as smart as I think he is, I'll have to take a lot of precautions so he doesn't realize what's happening."

"Oh." I eyed him anxiously. "I don't want you to get in trouble with Stemp. And if Brock did hire Drake Mallard, it could be dangerous for you if he figures out you're the one who hacked him."

"He won't." Spider sat up straighter in his chair. "Brock may think he's something special, and maybe he is. But this is my thing. This is what I *do*." His grin widened to something considerably more savage than his boyish features should have been able to achieve. "I'm *so* going to pone him!"

"Um... what exactly does that mean?" I inquired cautiously. "It sounds painful. And possibly x-rated."

Spider flushed. "I said 'pone', not, um..." His blush deepened. "...'bone'..." He hurried on, "People pronounce it different ways; 'pone', 'pwon', 'pun, 'own'; but it's spelled P-W-N. It's geek-speak for totally crushing somebody with your computer skills."

I grinned. "Okay, you're totally gonna pone him. You are the hackmeister!"

"Yes!" Spider returned the high-five that I offered, grinning in return. "Leave it to me, Aydan. I'll hack him tonight and send the files..." He trailed off, frowning. "Hmmm. Where should I send his data?"

"Um... to my cell phone?"

"I could send his texts... and probably his audio..." He hesitated. "Video would be too large. I mean, I'll compress it and set a low sample rate but if the data bursts are too big..."

I held up a restraining hand. "Let me know when you figure it out."

He stared into space for a few more moments. "I'll send you his texts directly," he decided. "And the rest I'll FTP up to the cloud and you can access it there."

"Just tell me what to do."

A short time later my phone was set up to get any text Brock sent or received, and I had access to the FTP site that would contain all the other data.

"I should have everything ready in a couple of hours," Spider said. "I mean, the actual hack will only take me a few minutes, but I want to make sure I've got everything set up so it'll be undetectable unless he specifically looks for it."

"Awesome!" I stood, relief and triumph easing my fatigue.

He gave me a hopeful look. "Do you need anything else?

What are you going to do now?"

"I guess..." I suppressed a shudder. "I guess my next move is to see if I can find out more from Weasel." I didn't bother to mention my information-gathering method, and fortunately Spider didn't ask.

"Okay," he said. "Let me know if you need anything more from me."

"Thanks, Spider, I will."

The trip home seemed longer than usual. When I pulled into my garage at last, I dragged myself out of the car with my eyes half-closed and stumbled directly to my air mattress. Falling onto it, I let the dark dreams take me.

I jerked awake, my heart pounding.

It wasn't a nightmare that had woken me.

It was a sound.

Hand on my trank pistol, I lay still, straining my ears.

The sound came again.

My cell phone vibrating.

I snatched it up with trembling hands. Of course, the analysts hadn't seen me going into my house, so they'd text me if anybody was prowling inside the perimeter of my surveillance cameras.

Squinting at the screen, I whooshed out a breathy giggle of relief. Not the analysts at all. Spider must have finished his hack, because I was looking at the first of Brock's texts.

My screen began to fill up, the phone vibrating again and again.

Inane conversation with his friends, and their banal replies.

Then he started complaining. As I watched the lengthening string of whining and insulting remarks about me, Spider, Stemp, Jack, and apparently nearly everybody he worked with at Sirius, I realized my mistake.

He could go on half the night, and probably would. And every time he sent or received a text, my phone would vibrate.

I groaned and buried my head in the pillow.

My phone continued to vibrate regularly and I dragged myself up again. The poor thing was going to shake itself apart. Not to mention drain my battery.

I didn't dare call or text Spider because none of those channels were secure. And I didn't want to drive all the way back into town at...

A glance at the phone's time display made me wince. God, after midnight. Spider had probably gone to bed. Waking him would be rude, and anyway, by the time I made the round trip it would be the wee hours of the morning and I was already exhausted.

Fuck it.

I hauled myself off the mattress and staggered over to my car, where I plugged the phone into the charger and left it lying on the seat where it could vibrate to its heart's content.

Dragging myself back to my air mattress, I fell onto it only to lie staring wide-eyed into the darkness. I could still hear the phone vibrating faintly.

What if Brock was making arrangements with another assassin? It would make sense for him to do it in the middle of the night. What if I fell asleep and missed the transaction, only to wake up to the news of Spider's murder?

Oh, God, I couldn't even think about that.

Or what if I missed a text from the surveillance analysts, leaving me lying here unaware in the darkness while a murderer prowled outside? My mattress wasn't visible from the windows and surely nobody would think to look for me in the garage in the middle of the night, but...

Shut up.

Brock wasn't a murderer. Spider and I both agreed on that, and the security at Sirius was as close to perfect as the brightest minds in the Department could achieve.

And so what if an assassin prowled outside? Even if he did think to look in the garage, I'd hear him coming. The sound of a window breaking or any of the overhead doors rolling up would wake the dead, and in the profound silence of the country night I'd easily hear the sound of anyone trying to pick the lock on the man-door. With my pistol inches away from my hand, I'd be fine.

Really.

I'd be fine...

After a nightmare-ridden sleep I finally gave up around six A.M. and hurried over to retrieve my phone from my car. At least it was silent now, but it took me nearly half an hour to catch up on all of Brock's texts.

His shitty attitude made me dislike him even more, but at least I didn't find anything that sounded like negotiations with a killer-for-hire.

I replaced the phone in my waist pouch and trudged outdoors, hoping the morning air would drive some of the fogginess from my brain. The pearl-grey sky promised rain to come, and I sucked in deep breaths of the cool humid breeze while keeping a wary eye out for early-morning assassins.

My stomach growled, and I eyed the house longingly. Inside were toast and peanut butter and a hot shower, if I was brave enough to claim them.

I rubbed gritty eyes and combed my fingers through my tangled hair.

Or I could go and use the showers in the changing room at Sirius Dynamics and graze on cereal bars in the lunchroom.

But the changing rooms were underground in the secured area. I'd have to overcome my claustrophobia if I wanted a shower.

And if Brock was my mysterious enemy, not even the secured area was safe. His clearances would easily get him in. And hell, even if he wasn't actually the one trying to kill or capture me, he'd probably find some way to prank me. In my current exhausted and frazzled state, that wouldn't end well for Brock.

I shuffled my feet, weighing the options. Shower at Sirius and possibly kill Brock? Or shower at home and possibly get killed myself?

Neither option appealed, but I needed clean clothes. And I really, really needed the toilet.

I growled and headed for the house.

Inside, I rushed through another awkward Glock-clutching shower before heading for the kitchen. Phone in one hand, pistol in the other, I jittered back and forth while I waited for the toaster.

When it popped up, the sudden noise and movement nearly made me pump a bullet into it.

Jesus, idiot, tranquilize. Don't kill. And especially, don't kill the toaster.

I swore softly and slid my Glock into my ankle holster, leaving the trank pistol in easy grabbing distance at my waist.

Perched on the edge of my chair, I gobbled the first slice of toast without incident but few minutes later my shaking fingers dropped the second one peanut-butter-side-down on the table. By the time I cleaned up the mess and shoved the remains of the sorry-looking slice into my mouth, my nerves were stretched to breaking.

"Lucky nobody phoned," I growled as I slung on my jacket and made for the door. "I'd probably have shit my pants. And great," I added as I locked the door behind me. "Now I'm talking to myself, too."

A moment later I realized that not only was I talking to myself, but the surveillance analysts were also watching me talk to myself.

With a tremendous effort I resisted the urge to beat my head against my nice new steel door, and headed for my car.

CHAPTER 27

When I got to the second floor at Sirius Dynamics, I was surprised to hear the click of computer keys emanating from Spider's office. I went over and tapped on the open door.

He looked up from his computer, his eyes bloodshot in a pale face. "Oh, hi, Aydan. Come on in. You're early this morning."

"Yeah." I frowned. "So are you. Is everything okay?"

"Yeah." He sighed. "Well, kind of okay, I guess. I just couldn't sleep, worrying about Tammy. Linda's still at work so I decided to come in early instead of hanging around the house by myself."

He looked so dejected that I rounded the desk and dropped my arm around his shoulders in a quick hug. "I'm sorry this is so hard on you. I wish we could figure something out."

"Oh, Aydan, we have to!" he said tremulously and flung his arms around me.

A flash of movement at the door made me glance up in time to see Brock's thin features twist into a sardonic smile. "How sweet. The cougar and her cub. I hope Linda won't mind sharing you, Webb. Or doesn't she know?"

Spider jerked to his feet so fast he nearly wrenched my

arm from its socket. Fists clenched, cheeks white with fury, he advanced on Brock with blazing eyes.

I sprang forward to lay a restraining hand on his arm.

"You... sick... filthy-minded..." Spider couldn't seem to find the words, but his intent was clear. "If you even..."

"Take a breath, Spider," I advised, dragging him to a halt and thanking my lucky stars for his toothpick physique.

Spider glared at Brock. "Aydan's my friend. But you wouldn't understand that, would you? You wouldn't know friendship if it bit you in the butt! And you stay away from Linda or I'll-"

"*So*," I interrupted before Spider could complete the threat. I sent a narrow-eyed glare at Brock. "What do you know about the guy who tried to kill me?"

"Huh?"

Either he was an excellent actor, or he didn't have a clue what I was talking about. He stared at me, openmouthed.

"N-Nothing," he stammered. Then his eyes narrowed. "You're just blowing smoke," he said scornfully. "Trying to distract me from the fact that your surveillance cameras showed you coming home early this morning wearing the same clothes you wore yesterday. Who were you banging last night? Eddy again? Or Kane this time?" His malicious gaze darted meaningfully between Spider and me. "Or, wait," he added with poisonous sweetness. "Linda was on night shift last night, wasn't she?"

Spider spluttered something unintelligible and lunged, and I found myself in the ironic position of trying to prevent him from doing something I deeply desired to do myself.

"Spider, stop!" I rapped out in the most commanding tone I could muster while struggling to keep him from charging headlong at Brock.

"What's going on here?" Kane's authoritative baritone made Spider stop fighting for an instant, and I used the opportunity to secure my hold on his arms.

I gave Kane my best smile. "Good morning, John. Could you please escort Brock to his office? He seems to have lost his way."

Kane frowned, assessing the scene at a glance before turning to jerk his chin at Brock. "Let's go."

Brock sniffed and tossed his head. "I'm not going anywhere. I have as much right to be here as anybody else. Just because I walked in on your sordid little affair..."

Spider lunged at him again, nearly dragging me off my feet, and Kane clamped a large hand around Brock's upper arm.

"Move it, Brock," he snapped. "Now."

Brock shot Spider and me a hate-filled look. "You're going to regret this," he snarled and made an unsuccessful attempt to jerk his arm free of Kane's grasp. He rounded on Kane. "And you'll be sorry, too. You think you're God's gift to agents, but you can't-"

"Actually, I can." Kane shifted his grip to Brock's collar, seized the seat of his pants, and carried him down the hall, superbly indifferent to his ineffectual flailing and high-pitched protests.

Spider blinked, his jaw dropping as the tension drained from his body. After a moment of silence he said, "When I grow up I want to be Kane."

I laughed and released my hold on his arms. "Me, too."

A door slammed, followed by thumping and muffled yells.

Spider and I exchanged a wide-eyed glance before

lunging for the door, but we both skidded to a halt when Kane reappeared in the doorway. The muted thumping and shouting continued.

I let out a breath. "I thought you were beating him up," I said to Kane.

"No." A thin smile quirked his mouth and he opened his fist to display a door handle. The shaft was bent and sheared off, the torn metal glinting dangerously in his palm.

"I guess his door latch must have been defective," Kane said innocently. Muscles rippled in his forearm as he turned the ravaged hardware over for inspection. "And now he's trapped in his office. But I'm sure Maintenance will get him out eventually. If he thinks to call them instead of screaming and kicking the door."

The world's largest shit-eating grin stretched my mouth, and I clasped my hands theatrically to my bosom. "You are my hero," I cooed.

Kane inclined his head in a debonair bow. "I live to serve."

Stemp strode up behind him. "What is..." He trailed off at the sight of the dismembered hardware in Kane's hand, and his expression went, if possible, even more bland than usual. One eyebrow rose infinitesimally.

"Brock's office door jammed," Kane said smoothly. "I tried to open it, but the latch broke."

"I see." The two dispassionate words held a world of meaning. "I'll call Maintenance." Stemp turned and headed for his office.

"I'm going to go and get a coffee," Kane said. "Do you want anything?"

"No, I'm fine, thanks," I said, and Spider echoed the sentiment.

Kane withdrew, and I turned to Spider. "I'm sorry about this. I should have known Brock would find a way to make trouble. I'll keep my distance from now on."

"Don't. It's not your fault, Aydan. Thanks for the hug; I needed it." Spider straightened as if pulling himself out of his misery by sheer physical effort. "Is everything okay with you? You look really tired. I mean..." His ears turned pink. "You look great, you always do, but..."

I had to smile in spite of myself. "Spider, seriously; working with you is the only thing that makes my life tolerable. Thanks."

His colour deepened. "You're welcome. I'm proud to be part of your team." His troubled hazel gaze searched my face. "But... is something wrong?"

"No, but I wanted to ask you to reroute that information we talked about last night. There's a little too much of it for me to manage."

"Oh." Spider nodded. "Yeah, I thought that might be a problem. I'll do that as soon as I get a chance."

"Thanks." I gave him a smile. "And I've got another technical problem I was hoping my favourite electronic genius could help me with." When he eyed me uncertainly, I added, "That would be you."

"Oh." He blushed. "Thanks. Of course I'll help if I can. Come on, let's sit down." We sank into chairs and he added, "What's the trouble?"

"I hate having analysts watching my house all the time, and it's not really working anyway. Can you come up with a better surveillance system that would notify me instantly if anybody comes close to my house or garage? Or my gate, or hell; anywhere on my yard? I was thinking about something like a motion-detecting camera that could send a picture to a mobile device that I could carry with me."

"Oh. Sure, that wouldn't be too hard..." he trailed off, frowning. "...but what do you mean, the current system isn't working?"

"If I'm not right on top of my phone I don't always get the call in time." I didn't bother to mention that I'd also developed a phobic reaction to the ring of the phone. "And the cameras only cover my house, not my garage."

"We could install more cameras to cover your garage," Spider offered. "It wouldn't cost much, and it wouldn't really be any extra burden on the analysts. The cameras only activate when there's movement."

I grimaced. "Yeah, but that's solving the wrong problem. I hate having people snooping on me at the best of times, and now that Brock's watching the footage..." I trailed off.

At best, he was a creepy voyeur. At worst, a murderer keeping tabs on his potential victim.

Spider gazed at me with earnest puppy-dog eyes. "I totally get that, but, Aydan, the analysts need to watch so they can send backup if you need it. We can't afford to lose you, and... I don't know what I'd do if something happened to you."

My heart warmed despite my worry. "Thanks, Spider. I'm not crazy about something happening to me, either, and I do like the idea of having backup." I thought for a moment. "How about if my handheld had a panic button on it? I don't know; maybe with a GPS so they'd know exactly where I was...?" I trailed off with a sigh. "I guess that's a pretty expensive bunch of technology, though."

"Hmm... no... not necessarily..." Spider sat up straighter, the familiar gleam of technological inspiration lighting his eyes. "Actually, we could do it really cheaply. Your current cameras are fine; if we add a few more to get the kind of coverage you want..." He trailed off and stared into space for a moment before returning his gaze to me. "I still think it would be a good idea to relay the signal back here as well as to your handheld. That way if something happened and you pressed the panic button, they'd be able to see what was happening."

I was already shaking my head, but he went on, "It wouldn't have to be intrusive. We could set it up so it wouldn't activate unless you pressed the panic button."

"Oh..." I leaned back, considering. "That does sound like a good idea."

"And it would be super-easy," Spider said eagerly. "I could program it so it would send a low-resolution photo to you as soon as the motion sensor was activated; that'd be really quick. Then you could switch to streaming video if you wanted to watch what was happening. But if it was, like, just a deer or something, you could just ignore it."

"Oh, that would be great! It'd be practically instantaneous, and I'd know right away who or what it was..." I trailed off, my excitement fading. "Except it's a huge pain in the butt to haul my phone out and punch in the password. By the time the notification came in and I entered my password and navigated to the picture I'd already be dead."

"Oh." He frowned. "But... we wouldn't send it to your phone anyway. You should have a dedicated device that would instantly display the picture." He rose to rummage through the bins of electronics on his worktable.

A whiff of fresh coffee announced Kane's presence a

moment before he spoke. "So." He strolled in and took the chair beside me. "What was Brock's problem this morning?"

"Oh, he was just being a-"

"Kelly." Stemp's terse voice skewered me like a knife between the shoulderblades. "Webb. Kane. In my office, now."

I sucked in a breath and rose, trying to convince my racing heart that nothing bad was going to happen. I hadn't attacked or threatened Brock. I wasn't in trouble. Stemp wouldn't lock me up...

Spider shot me a fearful glance and I did my best to look reassuring. Considering the dew of perspiration forming on my forehead, it probably wasn't convincing.

When we entered Stemp's office, Brock shot us a gloating look. He stabbed a finger at Spider. "He attacked me." The accusing finger tracked to Kane. "He attacked me, too, and then locked me in my office. If there'd been a fire or something, I could have died." The finger jabbed in my direction, and I couldn't prevent my upper lip from lifting in a silent snarl. Brock's finger wavered, but he recovered fast. "And she put them both up to it," he finished triumphantly.

Spider stepped forward, white and trembling. "It's my fault," he said quietly. "I lost my temper. John and Aydan didn't have anything to do with it."

Kane squared his shoulders, settling into a parade rest that emphasized the sculpted muscles of his arms and chest. "When I arrived, Webb and Brock were exchanging heated words," he rumbled. "But there was no physical altercation. As you know, I'm not at my best just now. Maybe I misjudged, but it seemed prudent to remove Brock from the situation. I tried to convince him to stay in his office, but he resisted. In the struggle, his door handle came off."

Stemp turned his deadly gaze on me. "Kelly?"

I tried for an equivocation that wouldn't throw any of us to the wolves. "Spider didn't attack Brock. Kane didn't, either. He just picked him up and carried him to his office. I asked him to do that."

"She lies!" Brock began, but Stemp's cool voice overrode him.

"Why?"

I barely managed to keep my gaze from skittering away from Stemp's dangerous calm. "I thought it would be the best solution," I said evenly. "Brock had made some extremely offensive remarks, and everybody needed a chance to calm down."

Stemp's reptilian gaze flicked to Brock. "What were the remarks?"

Spider, Brock and I all started to speak but Stemp silenced us with a single gesture that slashed the air to ribbons. "Kelly," he said flatly.

I gulped in spite of myself. When he didn't elaborate I ventured, "Yes?"

"What remarks?" Stemp repeated.

"Oh. Sorry. Um... He accused Spider of cheating on his fiancée. With me." Heat spread up my face despite my best effort to tamp it down. "It's not true, of course."

Stemp fixed us all with a cold gaze. The air temperature in the room dropped like a stone and I held back a shiver.

"There's no place for this kind of childishness here," he said at last, his voice dripping icicles. "You're all suspended for two days without pay. The office is closed for the parade on Thursday morning, and when you return on Thursday at thirteen hundred I expect you to put aside your differences and show some professionalism. Kane and Kelly, you may retain your weapons. Don't make me regret that decision. Dismissed."

He turned to his computer and began to type, ignoring us completely.

CHAPTER 28

"You can't do that!" Brock yelped. "I'm the victim here-"

"I said 'dismissed'," Stemp repeated without raising his gaze from the computer screen.

"That's bull hockey! It's not my fault! They attacked me-"

Stemp picked up the phone. In bored tones, he said, "Please send Security to my office to remove Mr. Brock. Confiscate his security fob and escort him outside."

It was tempting to stick around and watch Brock dig himself in deeper, but I didn't want to take a chance on getting caught in the fallout. Kane and I exchanged a look, and he strode out.

Spider was still standing motionless, chalk-white and staring straight ahead. "Come on, Spider," I said quietly.

He blinked and his lips moved but no sound came out. Or maybe his words were just drowned out by Brock's escalating complaints.

"Come on," I repeated, and tugged gently at his arm. After a moment he blinked again and let me tow him out of the office, shambling along like a marionette operated by a particularly inept puppeteer.

Kane was waiting a few yards down the hall, and he

glanced at Spider before coming over to prop up his other side. Together we piloted him back to his office and lowered him into his chair. I squatted to look into his ashen face while I patted his hand.

"Hey, Earth to Spider," I kidded gently. "Come back to us."

He blinked, his eyes glittering with unshed tears. "How could I be so stupid?" he quavered. "I've never even had a reprimand before and now I'm sus..." He sucked in a ragged breath that sounded like a sob. "Suspended. Linda will be so disappointed in me. And Tammy..." This time there was no mistaking his sob. "I just wasted two days. Two days we could have used to help her!" He sprang up and fled for the men's room.

I started to follow, but Kane put out a restraining hand. "Let him go," he advised. "I'll check on him in a few minutes."

I blew out a breath and flopped into Spider's vacated chair. Two days wasted. How could I save Tammy from jail now? My stomach twisted into a queasy knot.

And I'd dragged Kane into the mess as well.

I groaned. "Shit, I'm sorry, John. I shouldn't have involved you."

"It's all right." Kane lowered himself into the other chair and gave me a grim smile. "I'm not sorry. My only regret is that I didn't give in to the urge to smack Brock while I was at it. If I'd known I was going to get suspended anyway, I'd have made it worthwhile."

"Probably better you didn't know, then."

"Probably."

We fell silent, watching while two security guards frog-marched Brock down the hallway. As they passed the doorway he spotted us and hissed, "I'll get you for this!" The threat segued into a list of creative though physically impossible instructions, but the guards kept moving and his vituperation faded in the distance.

Kane said, "For a brilliant guy, he's not too smart, is he?"

"Nope."

"Still, though, you need to watch your back. Webb should, too."

I sighed. "I know." Keeping my voice down, I related the previous night's activities while Kane listened, his frown deepening.

"That's... interesting," he said when I was finished. "I wouldn't peg Brock for a murderer, either. And as you say, it's only a scrap of hearsay. I think you're smart to keep it under the radar for now, but if anything changes you should tell Stemp..." He broke off, giving me a rueful look. "I'm sorry, of course you know all this. I didn't mean to imply that you need my advice."

"Oh!" I blinked. "No, I didn't feel that way at all. I appreciate your help."

Hell, how often had he held back useful information because he thought I knew what I was doing?

"Any time you have an idea, please tell me," I added. "I always want to hear your input."

He relaxed into a smile. "Thank you. It's so nice to work with an agent of your calibre who doesn't have an ego problem."

I managed not to choke on the irony, and managed a sickly smile in return.

Kane leaned back, linking his hands behind his head to offer me a delicious view of double-barrelled biceps. "So, what do you plan to do with your two days of freedom?"

I tore my gaze away to glance at my watch. Only nine AM.

Ordinarily I'd be thrilled with a chance to spend some time at home. The assassin had taken the fun out of that, though.

I sighed. "I guess I'll call Lola and Eddy and see if I can do their books earlier today. And then I have to go to Calgary, if I can set up the meeting I need." Before I could stop it, my palm scrubbed against my thigh in unconscious distaste.

That didn't escape Kane's keen observation. He frowned. "What's in Calgary?"

I hesitated. Kane probably didn't know about Weasel, and enlightening him seemed like a bad idea. Hellhound's interpretation of the law tended to be considerably more elastic than Kane's, and I didn't want to cost Hellhound his informant.

Hell, I didn't want to cost myself an informant, either, no matter how slimy and repulsive he was. I needed that information.

My silence had stretched too long. Kane's frown deepened. "If you're going down to see Hellhound, you don't need to conceal it from me," he said stiffly.

I bit back the angry urge to tell him I had no intention of asking for or waiting on his permission. "Uh, thanks," I muttered instead, mentally patting myself on the back for my restraint. "But I have other business there."

His gaze searched my face. "Is it dangerous? Do you want backup?"

I sighed. "No, and no. But thanks anyway."

"If you're suspended, you shouldn't be working on any

cases," Kane prodded.

"Personal business," I clarified. "And trust me when I tell you; you really, really don't want to know any more than that."

A muscle jumped in his jaw. "I see."

"Actually, you probably don't see," I said with resignation, and stood. "And if you did, you'd need to bleach your retinas afterward. Are you going to go and check on Spider or should I?"

He looked as though he might not drop the discussion, but after a moment he rose, too. "I'll check on him." He reached for my hand and held it in a gentle grip. "Be careful. Call me if you need help."

"Thanks, but I won't. I'm not doing anything dangerous."

Kane gave me a twisted smile. "Famous last words."

"Don't even joke." I retrieved my hand and made for the door, then paused. "Actually... would you please give Spider a message for me? Just ask him to take over monitoring the data, if he feels up to it. I won't be able to stay on top of it while I'm travelling."

"All right," Kane agreed. "And if he can't do it, I can. I have time."

"Thanks." I gave him a smile and headed for the stairs.

When I signed out at the security wicket, Leo gave me a conspiratorial wink. "So I hear you and your friends are taking a little unscheduled vacation."

I dropped my fob in the turntable and spun it around. "That's some grapevine you've got there."

He offered a modest shrug. "It's my job to watch the surveillance footage. And I get the list of who's approved for fobs." He winked again. "And who's not." He leaned closer. "That Tyler Brock is some piece of work. You should have heard him mouthing off when they threw him out. I'm surprised nobody's offed him yet."

"Does that happen a lot around here?"

Leo laughed. "Not as often as it should. See you Thursday."

"Right. See you." I summoned a smile and trudged over to the door, where I peered out through the glass.

No visible gunmen. Hopefully there wasn't one perched on top of Sirius Dynamics, ready to shoot me in the back as I left.

Suddenly feeling very old and tired, I sidled out the door and hugged the wall of the building until I got to the parking lot. A few moments of fearful exposure to the open space assured me that there were no assassins on the roof, and I turned my attention to inspecting my car for bombs.

Finding none, I crept into the driver's seat and pulled out my cell phone. After a couple of calls, my morning was rearranged to complete my bookkeeping duties by noon if necessary. Reluctantly, I dialled Hellhound's cell number.

He picked up on the second ring. "Hey, darlin'. How's it goin'?"

"Not great. John, Spider, and I just got suspended without pay for two days."

"Shit, what happened?"

"Long story." I heaved a sigh. "I'll tell you about it later, but right now I've got something else on my mind. Can you call Weasel and tell him I can beat him up this afternoon if he promises to try to find some more information?"

"Jesus, darlin', your day just keeps gettin' worse."

"Yeah, if somebody actually managed to kill me, my day

would be perfect. So will you call Weasel?"

"Yeah..." Hellhound hesitated. "But can ya do it tomorrow instead? I got stuff I gotta do today."

"Oh, that's okay, Arnie, I don't need you to come with me." I grimaced. "In fact, it's probably better if you don't."

"I dunno about that, darlin'. I'd rather be there just in case."

"Just in case what?" I demanded. "I thought you said Weasel was harmless."

"He is, but..."

He didn't complete the sentence, and after a moment I said, "Look, if you think something's going to go wrong, tell me. As far as I know I just have to go down there, hit him a few times, and leave. Five minutes, tops. Unless there's something you're not telling me."

"Nah, darlin', I ain't holdin' out on ya. But... I dunno, I just don't feel right about ya goin' there alone."

"I have my Glock and a trank pistol if he gets out of hand. But if he wants this and you're sure he's harmless anyway, I don't see what the problem is." I shuddered. "Other than the fact that the whole thing totally creeps me out."

"Well, yeah. That's why I wanna be there."

"Thanks, Arnie, but I'll be fine. I'll meet you afterward, okay?"

He hesitated again. "Uh, actually, that's the problem. I just shipped outta town on a job. Dunno how long it's gonna take, but prob'ly mosta the night."

I laughed. "Is your 'job' blonde or brunette?"

"Huh? Oh." His gravelly laughter tickled my eardrum. "Hell, darlin', I wish. If it was a chick, it'd be no problem; I'd just set her up for another night. But this's somethin' I can't blow off."

I read between the lines. He had said 'a job', not 'P.I. stuff'. That meant the Special Forces needed a sniper. Someone would die by his bullet tonight.

I dragged my attention back to Hellhound's voice. He was saying, "...well, that ain't exactly right. If I thought ya were in trouble, I'd be there no matter what, but I know ya can take care a' yourself with Weasel. I just... I hate knowin' ya gotta do somethin' ya ain't comfortable with."

I snuggled the phone closer to my cheek, warmed by his concern. "Thanks, Arnie. You're sweet to worry, but there's no need. If you're busy, why don't you just give me his number? I'll call him myself."

"Nah, that ain't happenin'. Far's he knows you're just Jane; no last name an' no phone number. I didn't tell him your real name or your cover names, an' I didn't tell him the hit was anythin' to do with ya. The only way he can get to ya is through me, an' that's how it stays. I'll call him. What d'ya want me to say?"

"Just see if he wants to do it today." I squeezed my eyes shut, trying not to think about what I was negotiating. "I can be down there by three, so any time after that. No later than seven, though. I'm tired and I don't want to drive home in the dark."

My eyes popped open at a sudden thought. "Hang on. If I have to do this, tell him there are ground rules or I walk. I'll hit him, but he doesn't get to touch me. And no nudity. If he's missing any of his clothes when I get there, or if he tries to take them off while I'm there, the deal's off. And if he touches himself at all while I'm hitting him, I'm done and gone."

"Good thinkin', darlin'. Ya might wanna set a limit on the beatin', too. Like maybe you'll only hit him a certain number a' times."

"Ugh." I swallowed nausea. "I don't know if I can just hit him in cold blood."

"He likes it, darlin'. Ya know that. Ya already beat him unconscious once, an' he came back for more."

"Yeah, I know, I just... bleah." I drew a deep breath and let it out slowly. "Okay. Tell him I'll hit him twenty times or until he tells me to stop, whichever comes first."

Hellhound chuckled. "Twenty? That's big of ya."

"I'm trying to build a little goodwill. I really need that information."

"Okay, darlin'. I'll call him an' then call ya back. I'll tell him you'll meet him at his shop."

I sighed. "Thanks."

"An' Aydan?" His normally cheerful rasp was serious. "Rent a car so he can't ID your car or plates. An' don't go home with him. Do it at his shop an' then bug out soon's ya can. An' if anythin' feels off to ya, anythin' at all, shoot first an' ask questions later."

A shiver tracked down my spine, but I kept my voice steady and confident. "Thanks, Arnie. I'll be fine."

"I know ya will. Talk to ya soon."

True to his word, Hellhound called back five minutes later, but he didn't sound happy. "Okay, darlin', it's set up. Go to his shop at six. His safe word is 'banana'."

"Safe word?" A squirmy sensation twisted my stomach. "This isn't sex play. I promised to beat him up and that's all I'm going to do."

Hellhound sounded grim. "It ain't sex play for you, but it

is for him. An' I feel like some kinda fuckin' sick pimp for settin' it up." He paused before bursting out, "Fuck this shit! Listen, Aydan, forget the whole thing. I'll call him back an' tell him it's off. I'll lean on him a little harder an' he'll gimme the information."

"No, Arnie, don't." I took a deep breath and let it out slowly. "It'll be fine. And anyway, I promised him. He's right, I owe him already for looking out for me."

"Bullshit. Ya don't owe him fuck-all. He's just a slimy little car thief an' he wouldn't know honour if it bit him in the ass. I know how much your promise is worth, darlin', but there's times to keep your word an' times to break it. This's a time to break it."

I squared my shoulders and sat up straight. "No, Arnie, I promised, and I'm going to deliver. And that'll get me the information without making him mad at you."

Silence hung on the line until at last I heard the sound of his exhalation. "Okay. I don't like it, but it's your call, darlin'. I told him the rules an' I told him you're gonna call me right after, an' if everythin' ain't peachy when I talk to ya, I'm gonna give him a beatin' he sure as hell won't enjoy an' he won't ever forget." He hesitated. "Problem is, I was bluffin'. I'm gonna be off-grid by then. But call me anyway an' leave me a message so I know you're okay."

"I will. Thanks, Arnie." I hugged the phone closer. "Be careful tonight. Stay safe. And don't freak out, but... I love you."

His rasp softened. "Thanks, Aydan. I love ya, too. But don't say it again for a while, or I'll hafta run for Tijuana."

I laughed. "Okay. How about if I just say I'm looking forward to polishing your flagpole."

"Mm. Love gettin' my flagpole all shined up-" A crackle

that sounded like a radio command interrupted his words, and he added, "Gotta go. Be safe, darlin'."

"You, too," I said, but he had already disconnected.

I sent a heartfelt prayer skyward.

Please keep him safe.

CHAPTER 29

The hours crept by as though they were just as reluctant as I was. I dawdled over Lola's books before dragging my heels over to Eddy's for a late lunch.

I had just finished slurping the last of the hot-wing sauce off my fingers when my phone vibrated. The call display showed Spider's home number, and I punched the Talk button with a blip of worry.

"Hey, Spider, how are you doing?" I asked in lieu of a 'hello'.

"Oh... I'm okay," he mumbled. "I just wanted to let you know that our friend is heading for Calgary."

"Oh." Afraid to ask any more questions on an unsecured line, I said, "Thanks, maybe I'll see him there. But are you really okay? Do you want to meet me at Blue Eddy's? I'll buy you a Coke. And lunch, if you haven't already eaten."

"Thanks, Aydan, but... I'm not feeling very well." He sighed. "I think I'll just stay home."

"Oh." My heart squeezed at the misery in his voice, but I couldn't think of any way to fix things for him. "Well... I hope you feel better soon," I said awkwardly.

"Thanks. 'Bye."

He hung up, and I glumly surveyed the denuded chicken

bones on my plate. Finding no inspiration there, I heaved a sigh and retreated to Eddy's office, where I checked over the past four months of the substitute bookkeeper's work.

At last I trailed out to my car at three o'clock. After another bomb check I hit the highway, promising myself a nice meal in Calgary before I had to do the dirty deed. It wasn't a particularly inspiring promise since my stomach was churning, but it was all I had. Gritting my teeth, I tried to concentrate on the stark beauty of the empty fields slipping by outside my car.

Two hours later I pulled into the outskirts of Calgary, fighting a tension headache and a distinct feeling of nausea.

How and where should I hit him? And how hard? I didn't think I could bring myself to really hurt him, but I was pretty sure he wasn't going to be satisfied if I just socked him on the shoulder and called it a beating.

What if I just hit him so hard the first time that he yelled out his safe word? Then I'd be off the hook.

Should I kick him in the nuts? That would end it for most guys.

My stomach heaved. God, that was just sick.

And besides, Weasel had been turned on even when I drew blood and knocked him unconscious. What if I took my best shot and he didn't use his safe word, just demanded more? And what if I accidentally killed him? I cringed at the thought of having to explain that my latest dead body was the result of sadistic sex play that got out of hand.

Maybe I could just kick him in the ass. I definitely felt like doing that.

But not twenty times. I wouldn't have the heart to hit him in the same place over and over. I shuddered at the thought of the bruises.

What the hell had I been thinking? I should've said five hits, not twenty.

Maybe I could just slap his face. That might work.

But still. Twenty times?

God, I couldn't do this.

But I needed the information. And dammit, I should stop worrying about hurting Weasel. He wanted it. He was the one forcing me to do this.

I pulled to a stop at my favourite Italian restaurant and sat staring at its door. I'd feel better if I ate something.

But I couldn't sit there and eat, pretending everything was fine. And the fine food would be utterly wasted on my queasy stomach.

Letting out a breath of resignation, I put the car back in gear and headed for the nearest fast-food joint. I had to go in to use the washroom after my long drive anyway, but I couldn't bear to stay in the bright noisy restaurant. Clutching my burger and fries, I retreated to my car and forced myself to swallow the food despite my nausea. It sat like a rock in my stomach, but at least my hands stopped trembling.

A small fee at the nearest big-box building-supply store netted me the use of a half-ton truck for ninety minutes, and a short time later I was heading toward the semi-industrial area that housed Weasel's automotive shop.

In the parking lot I turned off the ignition, then closed my eyes and concentrated on my breathing.

In. Out. Slow like ocean waves.

I was not going in there to beat a frightened, helpless victim. I was going to fulfill a man's fantasies. He could tell me to stop anytime. This was what he wanted. I was doing him a favour, dammit.

I opened my eyes and straightened my spine.

Don't let him see weakness. He expected hard and tough; give it to him.

Besides, this was Weasel, not somebody I actually liked. I summoned up the memories of his disgusting stale-cigarette stench, his foul innuendos, his public masturbation, and his incredibly irritating habit of invading my personal space.

And I'd had to drive four hours round trip for this.

That little shit.

I'd kick his ass, all right.

I slammed the truck door behind me and marched across the parking lot.

When I shoved open the door to the front office and strode inside Weasel jumped up from behind the grubby desk, his unattractive face splitting into a grin that displayed nicotine-yellowed teeth. His stringy shoulder-length hair didn't look as though it had been washed since the last time I'd seen him months ago, and the do-rag that covered it was so caked with black grease that its pattern of grinning skulls was barely visible.

"Jane Crazy-Bitch! I didn't think you'd come!" He hurried over to push his face close to my neck, inhaling deeply.

"Back off," I snapped. "If you touch me, I'm out of here."

"Mm, you still smell crazy good!" Weasel withdrew a few inches, but not far enough to make my skin stop crawling. "Goddamn, Jane Crazy! I've been whacking off all day thinking about you and I'm still hard as nails."

His hand drifted toward the conspicuous bulge in his

dirty jeans and I barked a warning. "Touch it and I'm gone!"

"Aw, Jane Crazy..." He thrust his hips at me. "Look how big it is! Let's fuck. I'm good, you'll like it, all the bitches do-"

Without even thinking, my hand flashed out. My palm connected with his cheek with a sound like a rifle shot, and he reeled backward, clutching his face while his eyes rolled back in ecstasy.

"I love you, Jane Crazy!"

"One," I snapped.

That focused his attention. His eyes widened. "Aw, Jane, that didn't count! I didn't even get ready yet!"

"One," I repeated implacably.

His cocky demeanor vanished. "Wait!" he yelped as I advanced on him. "I have to get ready. Wait right here. Don't go away. I'll only be a minute. Or, no, do you want a beer? I'll get you a beer. You can go sit on the couch in the back and have a beer."

"No beer," I growled. "No waiting. We're doing this now."

"Okay. Okay. Come into the back." He beckoned me anxiously toward the filthy door that separated the front office from the automotive bay.

I eyed him suspiciously. "No tricks, or I'll hurt you in ways you can't even imagine."

His eyes drifted half-closed and he groaned. "Goddamn, you're gonna make jizz in my pants before you even hit me." He ground his crotch against the door frame, moaning.

I recoiled. "Cut it out! The deal was 'no masturbating'."

His eyes popped open. "I didn't touch myself! I just... it was an accident, I swear!"

"Get in the back," I ground out.

"Okay. Okay, Mistress Jane, whatever you say."

The sudden change from obnoxious to obsequious was profoundly disturbing. I followed him into the automotive bay with even more distrust than before, but I couldn't see anything threatening.

A half-stripped car occupied one end of the bay and the grungy sofa and chairs looked as though they'd acquired an additional layer of grime since the last time I'd been here, but other than that everything looked the same.

"Please sit," Weasel said, and my jaw dropped at his use of the word 'please'.

I held back a shudder at the state of the chairs. "I'll stand."

"Okay." He nodded vigorously. "That's cool. Whatever you say, Mistress. I brought my favourite whip. I hope you like it." He pointed toward the couch, where a vicious-looking black leather riding crop lay half-camouflaged by the dirty cushions.

A wave of horrible memories crashed over me and I stiffened my knees to keep from staggering back a step.

"I don't do whips." My voice came out half-strangled.

Suddenly Obnoxious Weasel was back. "I want the whip. That was our deal. You promised."

"I promised to beat you up," I gritted through clenched teeth. "I didn't promise anything about whips."

"No, you promised to whip my ass. That's what you said in the Hogback."

I couldn't argue. I couldn't remember exactly what I'd said, but I'd been so terrified I would have agreed to almost anything. It was just sheer luck I hadn't promised him something worse.

Weasel planted his fists on his hips, looking as immovable as a boulder despite his puny stature. "If you don't whip my ass like you promised, the deal's off and you can find somebody else to get your information."

A rush of hot irritation mercifully broke the icy paralysis of the flashback. "Listen, you little shit, if I didn't know you'd enjoy it, I'd kick your ass from here to..." I bit off the words as his eyelids fluttered closed with a beatific gasp.

Since his eyes were closed anyway, I allowed myself the luxury of a whole-body shudder.

"More," he begged, thrusting rhythmically at me. "Please, Mistress."

I averted my gaze from the repulsive sight and gnawed my lower lip. Dammit, I needed that information. And I'd driven all the way down here. It'd be stupid to back out now.

I could do this. I only had to hit him nineteen more times. I could do it fast and get out.

"Fine." My voice came out harsh. "The whip it is, then."

He shivered and his hand dipped toward his crotch, but he quickly aborted the movement when I growled a warning.

"Thank you, Mistress Jane," he babbled. "I'll go and get ready. I have my nipple clamps and..."

My mind mercifully zoned out while he described pain-inducing paraphernalia I didn't even want to imagine.

"I don't care what you do, but you'd better be fully dressed when you get back here," I snapped. "If I see any more skin than I'm seeing right now, the deal's off."

"Yes, Mistress, of course, Mistress." He bobbed his head. "I'll be right back."

He scurried off to the washroom and I succumbed to my trembling knees, sinking down on the nearest chair despite its filth. Hell, it didn't matter anymore. I was going to have to scrub off an entire layer of skin when I was finished here anyway.

In a few minutes Weasel was back, wearing sweatpants instead of jeans. My gaze dropped involuntarily to the stiffly-tented fabric at his crotch while my brain served up an unwanted memory of his voice saying 'barbed leather cock bindings'.

I jerked my attention up to his face, which wore an expression of bliss. "Goddamn, this is so hot," he whispered. "I almost jizzed just putting the bindings on. I'm so hard, my cock-"

"Shut up!"

My bark was a desperate attempt to avoid any more hideous mental images, but Weasel took it as part of the dominance play and let out a happy little moan of acquiescence. Picking up the whip, he knelt in front of me and offered it up with both hands like a medieval knight presenting a sword to his king.

I clenched my teeth and forced myself to take it from him.

"I've been bad, Mistress Jane," he whispered. "I deserve to be punished." He crawled back to the couch and bent over it, eyes closed, knees astride.

The whip handle was smooth and hard in my sweaty hand. I almost gagged at the sight of Weasel's skinny ass quivering with anticipation under the thin knit fabric.

I squeezed my eyes shut.

I didn't need information this badly. I could just wait for the next assassin to show up. Hell, even death would be better than this.

Weasel was making pleading little whimpers, and I

opened my eyes in time to see him squirming as though he was trying to masturbate against the fabric of his sweats.

A deep anger seized me. Goddammit, a year ago I'd been happily escaping the city to live out my dream of country tranquillity. And what did I get? Fresh scars, a whole new crop of horrific flashbacks, and a slimebucket like Weasel sticking his ass in my face.

In a single movement I sprang to my feet, my arm scything out in a savage backhand. The riding crop cracked across Weasel's ass and he yelped, his hips driving forward against the couch.

Bile surged into my throat and I dropped the whip and spun away to gulp frantically.

Don't throw up. Do *not* throw up.

Hunched over with my elbows on my knees, I gulped air.

Absorbed in my internal struggle, it took a few moments before I realized Weasel was whimpering eagerly and crooning, "Yes, Mistress, please, Mistress, yes, Mistress" over and over.

I breathed some more.

Weasel's croons turned to begging. "Please hit me, please whip my ass, oh please Mistress..."

I drew a deep breath and straightened slowly.

Do it. Get it over with.

I reached for the whip again but my hand hovered above it. Wouldn't close around it.

Do it, dammit.

I grabbed the horrible object and managed a few more smart strokes. By now Weasel was moaning and twitching, and with a shock I realized his spasmodic hip movements weren't an attempt to escape the bite of whip as I had first thought.

No, it was something more nefarious altogether.

He was humping the couch.

That did it. I went to town on his ass.

"...seventeen, eighteen, nineteen, *twenty!*" I threw down the whip. "We're square."

"Oh please Mistress don't stop! Please, please, more, please! Please get me off, just one more, *please!*"

The frantic note in his voice tugged unwilling pity from my heart. Slimy and disgusting he might be, but he'd held up his end of the bargain. He was still fully clothed and both white-knuckled hands clenched the cushions of the couch, muscles knotted under the mechanic's perma-grime that soiled his skin. Couch-humping notwithstanding, he hadn't touched himself at all, which for Weasel was unprecedented.

"Oh please Mistress, please, I'll do anything, anything you say, please just whip me again!"

"Our deal was twenty. We're done." I tried to sound hard and cold, but it was a struggle. I couldn't believe I was actually feeling sorry for him.

"*Please!* I'll get any information you need! Any time. Just ask. I'll do anything! Whatever you want! *Please*, Mistress, I'm almost there, I need it so bad..."

I was weakening. In the miserable days of my first marriage, I'd been all too familiar with the desperation of being taken almost to orgasm only to be abandoned. My ex had delighted in refusing me that. In refusing me even the smallest pleasure.

I pitched my voice to a growl. "Anything. Any time I want it. For free. Forever."

"*Yes*, Mistress, oh, yes, please, yes, *anything!*"

"Deal."

The whip cracked and his ecstatic cries rose to the rafters.

It didn't take long. After a couple more strokes he shrieked "*Jesus!*" and went into overdrive, grunting and moaning while he pumped like a spastic rabbit against the filthy cushions.

A moment later he collapsed to the floor and lay panting. "Mistress Jane... I love you...," he gasped. "Can I lick your shoes?"

"No." I dropped the whip on top of him, feeling as though my hands would never be clean again. "Call Hellhound as soon as you have more information."

I turned on my heel and stalked out on trembling legs, but not before his satiated moan reached my ears. "Best Mistress *ever!*"

I barely made it to the parking lot before I vomited, retching over and over until I had nothing left inside me.

CHAPTER 30

Creeping shakily into the truck, I denied myself the luxury of curling into a ball and turning off my brain. Weasel might come out and see me.

Be hard and tough.

I drove back to the store and returned the truck, thankful that the overworked man who returned my deposit didn't seem to notice my white face and quivering hands. Sliding back into my own driver's seat, I left a fake-cheerful message for Hellhound and then hit the road.

Nearly an hour later I finally stopped trembling. Interspersing sips of water with nibbles of peanuts and dried fruit, I slowly recovered enough to pay attention to the darkening countryside around me. Heavy clouds blotted out the last of the daylight, and as I switched to my country-bright headlights the first drops of rain spotted my windshield.

Shivering, I cranked the heater up another notch and marshalled my frazzled wits. That had actually gone better than I could have hoped. Despite its shattering effect on me, I had secured Weasel's absolute loyalty. If there was any more information to be found, he would find it.

Now I only had to wait.

The rain got heavier and I turned up my windshield wipers, growling under my breath.

Some time later I was blinking heavy eyelids and patting my face in an attempt to stay awake when my cell phone vibrated.

Switching to hands-free, I accepted the call.

Hellhound's rasp made me smile. "Hey, darlin', I got your message. So everythin's okay an' you're headed home? How did it go?"

"It went." I grimaced even though he couldn't see me. "Just call me Mistress Jane."

He laughed. "Kinky. Dunno if that's really my flavour, though."

"That's good, because I puked my guts out afterward." I had intended it to sound like a joke, but my voice came out small and tremulous.

The humour vanished from his voice. "Aw, shit, Aydan, I'm sorry. I shoulda been there."

"No, it's okay," I hastened to reassure him. "It wasn't that big a deal, I just... I had a bit of a reaction because he had..." I had to stop and swallow. "A whip..." I tried a light laugh, but it nosedived to its death. "Like you said; not really my flavour."

"Fuck. Where are ya, darlin'? Ya still got your key, right? I'm gonna be back in Calgary in a few hours, so go on over to my place an' I'll be there soon's I can."

"Thanks, Arnie, but I'm okay. And I'm almost home now." I changed the subject. "So you're done? Everything went all right?"

"Yeah."

He didn't elaborate, and I added, "Are you okay?"

"Yeah." He let out a weary breath. "Same old shit."

Maybe he needed me as much as I needed him just now.

"I could turn around and come back to Calgary," I offered. "I don't have to go to work tomorrow."

"Nah, it's okay, darlin'. Sounds like ya had a helluva day an' I don't want ya drivin' all that way in the dark when you're tired. I'll see ya on Thursday, okay?"

"Okay..."

I didn't really want to hang up, but asking him to stay on the line until I got home would just be pathetic. And he probably couldn't anyway. He was probably still on duty, and he'd have to debrief, too.

"Well, thanks for calling," I said. "Good night."

"G'night, darlin'."

The night seemed even darker when he hung up.

By the time I let myself through my gate, the rain was coming down so hard that I was soaked and shivering in the short time it took to get it locked behind me. When the overhead door rolled down behind my car at last, I let out a long breath and let my head sink back against the headrest.

I should go into the house and have a shower and a hot drink. Plus I should make an appearance on the surveillance cameras so when Brock returned to work and snooped in my footage he wouldn't be able to say I hadn't been home.

But shit, that wouldn't help because I still wasn't planning to sleep in the house. He'd see me coming out again, and he'd make some snide remark about me only coming home long enough to change clothes before I got in somebody else's bed.

Forget it. Fuck him.

In fact, come to think of it, fuck the world.

I got out of the car and trudged over to fall face-first onto my air mattress.

Despite my fatigue, I couldn't sleep. The sound of whip-cracks echoed in my mind and I fought the flashbacks of pain and terror.

After tossing and turning for a while, I swore and sat up. At least I knew what would help. I hauled myself out of bed and went over to flip on the overhead lights. Nothing like a little recreational wrenching to settle the nerves.

Turning to my '53 Chevy, I smiled. Perfect time to get some work done on the new wiring system. Switching the original six-volt system over to twelve volts had seemed like a good idea when I made the decision, but I was no electronic genius. Painstakingly consulting the diagrams, I began tracing wires.

Draped over the front fender with my head and arms swallowed by the cavernous engine bay, I was securing a ground wire when a little gust of rain-drenched spring air reached my nose. Inhaling appreciatively, I made a single twist of the screwdriver before realization struck me.

The doors were all closed.

I was already in motion when a rough hand clamped onto my ponytail and an unfamiliar male voice growled, "Do what I say and you won't get-"

Jerking upright, I whirled, my screwdriver slashing a lethal up-and-back arc.

His sentence finished in a shriek as the long bit ripped a deep red gouge up his cheekbone to slam into the corner of his eye. He reeled back clutching his face, blood already leaking between his fingers. I snatched my trank pistol out of its holster.

Too late. His foot dropped over the edge of the concrete slab.

He fell backward onto the plastic pail I'd used to cover the ends of the reinforcing steel.

The pail shattered.

He kept falling.

A scream tore the air as a blood-slicked spear of rebar punched up through his belly. His body arched in the horrible spasm of agony I remembered all too well, his arms flinging out, his knife falling from fingers contorted like blood-streaked talons.

Screams filled the garage, throat-ripping inhuman sounds that went on and on. My finger convulsed on the trigger and the tranquilizer dart found its mark, but the screams wouldn't stop.

Again and again I fired, all control lost while I frantically jerked the trigger, pushing the pistol in front of me as if to ward off the horror.

Just as I realized the screams were coming from my own throat, everything went black.

CHAPTER 31

Consciousness returned slowly. I fought it, clinging to the dark safety of oblivion.

Something bad had happened.

I didn't want to know.

Inexorably, sensation returned to my body. Throbbing ache at the back of my skull. Hard surface under me. Smells.

Safe happy aromas of rubber and warm engine oil.

And the pungent blood-and-shit reek of ruptured intestines.

Whimpering, I dragged my uncooperative body into a ball without opening my eyes.

At last my brain ground into motion despite my best efforts. I'd fired the entire trank magazine at close range and gassed myself with the aerosolized tranquilizer. Must've hit my head on the way down. Lucky I hadn't killed myself.

The concrete floor was hard, but I didn't want to move or open my eyes. At least it was warm. I'd just stay here...

I couldn't stay here forever. Somebody would find me. If it was a civilian, I'd be in deep trouble with Stemp. If it was another assassin, I'd be dead.

I slowly uncurled and opened my eyes.

The impaled body was only a few feet from my face.

Screams ripped from my throat again, my body starfishing involuntarily in the attempt to escape. My frantic flailing resolved into a panicked backward scoot on hands and heels until my back slammed into the side of the Chevy, slapping some sense into me.

Fighting the terror of the flashback and the gruesome sight in front of me, I throttled my screams down to hysterical whimpers. My heart tried to hammer its way out through my backbone.

Unable to look away, I stared wide-eyed. Waiting for his screams to begin again. Waiting for the limply-dangling hands to contort into claws and strain upward in desperate supplication. Waiting for the broken body to writhe...

Nothing happened.

Breathe.

I clamped down on my shrill panting, slowing it to deep ragged gasps of air. My head throbbed with the thudding of my pulse and a fiery path burned from my throat to my chest, searing with every breath. My eyes stung. Finally I had to blink, realizing as I did that my cheeks were wet with tears.

"Okay," I whispered. "I'm okay. Just a flashback. I'm okay. Just breathe..."

Slowly my muscles began to cooperate, releasing from their rigor to dissolve into quivering blobs of mush.

This ugly thing was in my beloved garage.

My safe haven violated; the last of my bright dreams defiled.

My heart crumbled to dark powder, my guts twisting with pain sharper than barbed wire. Utterly bereft, I curled into a ball and cried the great wrenching sobs of a lost child.

At last my tears stopped. Dry sobs still shook me, but I stifled them to silence.

The cold emptiness expanding inside my chest made thinking easier. Trembling in every limb, I dragged myself to my feet and stood staring at the corpse.

And he was definitely a corpse. No breath moved his chest around the gory steel spear and his body hung limp, hands slack at the end of stiffly-outflung arms. The gravel beneath him was dark with blood and less attractive things.

Nine tranquilizer darts bristled in his neck and upper body. I couldn't believe I'd only missed with one. The way I'd been flinging that pistol around, I shouldn't have been able to hit the broadside of a barn.

Then again, it had been point-blank range. And it wasn't like he could go anywhere.

A bark of humourless laughter startled me and made my throat hurt more. Drawing a deep breath, I stepped carefully down onto the gravel of the excavation, the short drop feeling precarious on my shaking legs.

As a formality I checked for a pulse in the body's neck. There was none.

I considered searching him but my box of nitrile gloves was on my workbench, which seemed miles away. Screw it. Stemp's team would do a better job anyway. I plucked the darts out of the body and stowed them in my pocket.

Lurching up out of the excavation again, I stumbled over to lock the garage door. Had I locked it earlier? I couldn't remember. Maybe my intruder had picked the lock.

It didn't matter.

After a moment of thought I turned out the lights. From the darkness outside, the bright interior would show up through the windows like a horror-show stage if anybody glanced in. Shuffling cautiously back by the dim illumination of the trouble-light half swallowed by the Chevy's engine bay, I navigated to where my waist pouch lay beside my air mattress. I extracted my phone and called for a cleanup crew, then sat staring numbly into the darkness.

After a few minutes I roused myself and swapped the empty trank magazine for the full spare I'd tucked in my holster. Then I busied myself covering the windows with a couple of small tarps and some cardboard I scavenged from the lift's packing crates.

Once that was done I huddled into the corner of my mattress, but after a moment I evicted myself from there, too. I couldn't sleep there tonight. Probably never again.

I had just finished deflating the air mattress and trussing my pillow and sleeping bag into a neat bedroll when the sound of tires on gravel made me stiffen and reach for my Glock.

Screw the trank pistol. Blowing out a kneecap would immobilize somebody just as effectively, and probably provide an incentive for some confessions, too.

My cell phone vibrated and I whisked it out. The text message's words made me ease out a slow breath.

"Clean-up crew outside."

I texted back, "Thanks, be right there", and went over to unlock the door. When I opened it the same two techs stood outside, their dark van fading into the blackness at the edge of my yardlight. Beyond my gate I caught a glint of chrome through the silver-black sheets of rain. Must be the assassin's vehicle. I hadn't even heard the crunch of tires on gravel over the pounding of the rain.

"Hi again," I said, my voice rasping painfully over my raw vocal cords.

"This is getting to be a bad habit," the spokesman quipped. He glanced around. "Lights?"

"Yeah." I flipped the switch and we stood blinking in the sudden brilliance. "I just turned them off until I could get the windows covered up."

"Good thinking. Where's the body?"

I led them past my vehicles, slightly surprised that neither of them oohed or aahed over the Corvette. Either they were extremely focused, or they weren't car guys.

"Ooh," the strong-but-silent Elmer Fudd said as he rounded the corner and caught sight of the body.

"Aah," the spokesman contributed. "Nasty."

I couldn't help smirking at the thought that I'd gotten my oohs and aahs after all. Unfortunately, Elmer caught the expression on my face. He glanced from me to the body, looking disturbed.

I considered trying to explain the inappropriate humour, but mentally filed the effort under 'probably doomed to failure' and kept my mouth shut.

After a moment he turned back to the job at hand, and they unrolled the body bag and got to work. When they began to pry the body off the rebar I buried myself under the Chevy's hood, where I stayed until they carried the bag away.

In a surprisingly short time, they were finished.

"Easier cleanup this time," the spokesman said with approval. "Too bad you weren't getting your floor poured tomorrow. Then we wouldn't have had to do much at all."

"Well, I'll try to plan better next time," I promised with perhaps a touch of sarcasm.

He grunted amusement and they left.

Bone-weary, I followed them to the door and locked it behind them, then stood staring at nothing while I tried to figure out a plan. Or at least a place to sleep.

Maybe I should just sleep in the house. I was probably pretty safe at the moment. It would likely take at least a day for this guy's employer to figure out that another assassin had vanished with his deposit. Assuming there had been a deposit. Probably should've checked his wallet.

"Fuck it," I said aloud. Stemp's team would let me know.

Another thought occurred to me and I sagged against the truck to consider it. This guy hadn't been an assassin. He'd started to say 'Do as I say and you won't get hurt'. Or that's what it had sounded like, anyway.

So if he was just a kidnapper, whoever was expecting me to be delivered to them tonight already knew something was wrong.

And several hours had already passed. They might even be coming to see what had happened.

"Shit!"

I had thought I'd used up every ounce of adrenaline, but apparently I'd been wrong. Trembling, I lurched upright and hurried to the trunk of my Legacy to collect the night vision gear I had originally planned to return to Sirius before all this started.

My heart drumming an anxious tattoo against my ribs, I grabbed my winter survival backpack out of the trunk as well, then stuck the night vision goggles on my forehead and scooped up my sleeping bag before vacating the garage at a trot.

The rain sluiced over me again and I slowed to a halt halfway to the house, shivering. Where could I go?

A top agent like Kane would prepare an ambush inside the house and coolly wait for the kidnapper's boss to show up, but I was fresh out of courage. The thought of being cornered inside the house or garage weakened my knees and made my stomach churn.

My exhausted mind crept sluggishly from one possibility to the next.

I couldn't go to the hotel because I'd scream my stupid head off as soon as I fell asleep, and that was far more humiliation than I needed. Not to mention it would require a lot of explanations I wasn't prepared to give.

Going over to Tom's was out of the question for the same reasons, plus it would endanger him.

Same with Spider, or any of my friends. Too dangerous.

I could call Kane and ask to stay with him...

No.

He was battling his own demons. He didn't need the additional stress of protecting me, and anyway, it was time I learned to live without him. No more using him for sex and protection. He deserved to have the life he wanted, unspoiled by my bullshit.

I could drive back to Calgary. Hellhound would keep me safe and give me multiple orgasms to boot.

The dark rain faded around me as I pictured the cozy warmth of his shabby but clean apartment. The sound of his guitar, the sexy rasp of his singing, Hooker purring on my lap...

I swayed on my feet and forced my eyes open.

Shit. Too tired. Phasing out standing here in the rain.

I stumbled forward aimlessly. I couldn't make it to Calgary. I'd either fall asleep at the wheel and kill myself, or pull over for a nap and get captured while I was fast asleep by the side of the road.

Belatedly remembering my night vision goggles, I pulled them over my eyes and scanned around me, flipping between thermal-only and combined vision. No heat signatures showed, and I drew a breath of relief. Safe for the moment.

Okay, think.

I could sleep in my shed.

But it was windowless with only one door. Nobody could see me or shoot me through a window, but if they opened the door I'd be cornered like a rat in a barrel.

A shudder shook me. No fucking way.

At last an idea seeped into my aching brain.

Stashing my gear outside the visual range of my cameras, I headed for the house. At the back door, I straightened out of my tired slouch and waved at the hidden camera for the benefit of the surveillance analysts.

Inside, I peeled out of my sodden jacket and swapped it for a waterproof one. I was still shivering in my wet clothes, but the thought of getting caught in mid-strip while I put on dry ones negated any thought of changing. Instead, I jogged to the bedroom and rolled a T-shirt and underwear up in a clean pair of jeans. Stuffing the roll into the inside pocket of my jacket, I trotted for the stairs.

A trip to the basement unearthed my fishing tackle, and I detached the reel and stowed it in my jacket pocket. I hesitated. Did I need anything else?

My exhausted brain refused to disgorge any useful ideas, overwhelmed by my adrenal system's relentless demands.

Get out. Get out fast. Get out *now*.

I hurried upstairs and was on my way to the back door when the blinking light of my answering machine caught my eye. Fighting down nervousness, I scurried over and pressed the button.

Spider's anxious voice emanated from the machine, obviously trying to sound casual and failing. "Hi, Aydan. I just wanted to let you know I found something really cool on that website I was telling you about last night. Check it out when you get a chance, okay? Look for timestamp three-forty-five, I hope..." His voice cracked and he swallowed audibly. "...um, I hope you like it. Take care... 'bye..."

Uh-oh.

I hesitated, torn between fleeing the confinement of the house and finding out what new threat Spider had discovered.

My need for information won and I hurried for the bedroom, Glock in hand.

Finding the data seemed to take forever, though I knew it was only a few seconds. When I opened the file Spider had tagged, the blast of discordant music from my speakers made me yelp and flinch.

Snatches of conversation were barely audible in the din, and I forced myself to listen closely despite my urge to turn the volume down.

Crash-bang-guitar-scream. "...job for you..."

Drum solo that sounded like a twenty-car pileup in progress. "...hate that bitch..."

More discordant screaming guitars. Then the garbled voice that might have been Brock spoke again. "...kill her..."

After a few more moments of musical mayhem, the clip ended.

I stood staring at my computer screen. Three forty-five this afternoon. Was that enough time to hire someone to come and attack me tonight?

Theoretically, yes.

But I could have sworn my attacker had only been trying to abduct me.

I wiped my clammy palms on my jeans. Who knew; maybe he'd been planning to take me somewhere more convenient before killing me. It didn't really matter at this point. I was alive and he wasn't, and I intended to keep it that way.

I made for the back door. Locking it behind me, I did my best decisive stride until I was out of camera range. Fatigue dragged at every limb, and I stifled a whimper.

Move your ass. Almost there.

Plodding back to where I'd left my gear, I let numb detachment take over. When I scanned around me with the night-vision headset, a long breath leaked out.

Nothing.

Thank God.

I dragged my backpack and sleeping bag onto my shoulders before trudging for the trees.

Just keep moving. One foot in front of the other.

It was only a short walk to my favourite fallen log but the rain was still pouring down and I was shivering violently by the time I got there.

Should've taken a chance and changed in the house.

Too late now. Too tired. And soon I'd have my shelter up anyway.

This particular clearing held hot memories of Kane but they seemed distant, as though it had been someone else wrapping her legs around him and screaming her climax into his iron shoulder.

Anyway, that was all over now. That ship had sailed.

I let the memories fade into the pale icy bubble of detachment expanding around me.

Forcing myself into motion, I set up a rudimentary shelter with the mylar blankets from my survival kit. The rain rattled against it, but I hoped it wouldn't be audible more than a few paces away.

Apathy weighted my shoulders. Who cared? It was all I had. It would have to do. Stooping against the stiffness of cold overworked muscles, I unrolled my sleeping bag under the mylar.

My eyelids drooped and I fought the urge to just fall into my sleeping bag and hope for oblivion.

One more thing to do.

I extracted the reel from my pocket and paced several yards out from the clearing. Fixing a trail of fishing line a couple of feet off the ground, I made a complete circuit, pushing through the sodden undergrowth and barely flinching when the water-laden leaves tipped their icy burden onto my soggy jeans. What the hell, I wasn't going to get any wetter now.

I made wraps at knee, hip, chest, and throat height. It wouldn't stop anybody, but it'd give me some advance warning when they walked into it. Even in my night vision the transparent glint was barely visible. No two-legged or even four-legged intruder would see it.

Dragging myself back to my shelter, I gritted my teeth against their chattering and stripped as fast as possible. Wrestling the dry clothes over my damp icy skin took the last of my strength, and I fell into my sleeping bag. My eyes closed and I slipped straight into hell.

A hunched form rose from the black abyss. Straightening slowly, the figure turned to face me, grinning with Weasel's yellowed teeth. A bloodstained stake protruded from his belly, but below it his giant erect penis was sheathed in glittering spikes. His grin widened as he uncoiled the black whip in his hand and cracked it with a hissing report.

I tried to flee but my arms and legs were bound. Silent screams tore my throat, futile whispers of sound. Weasel advanced, laughter rolling from his bloody lips like thunder. Thrashing frantically in my bonds, I screamed and screamed...

Another thunderbolt jerked me awake. Rain mixed with snow pelted my face. My struggles had pulled my shelter down and my sleeping bag was soaked, clinging to my body and increasing the horrible trapped sensation.

Hysterical whimpers fell from my lips while I flailed free of my soggy cocoon to sprawl gasping on the ground. Thunder rolled again, but in the silence that followed it I felt rather than heard a new nightmare approaching.

The fast rhythmic thud of rapidly-approaching footsteps.

CHAPTER 32

I jerked into a crouch, night-vision goggles in place and Glock at the ready. Now that I wasn't pressed to the ground anymore, I couldn't hear the footsteps over the wind and rain and thunder. Flipping to thermal-only, I scanned a fast three-sixty.

There.

A flicker of heat signature moving between the trees.

Man-sized.

Coming fast.

I fumbled the goggles back to night-vision. Even my tournament-shooting reflexes couldn't overcome the violent shivering of adrenaline and bone-deep cold. I trained my shaking Glock approximately where the centre of body mass would be.

Any second now...

A large figure burst out of the undergrowth.

My finger convulsed on the trigger at the same time as recognition jerked my aim off-target.

Kane hit the ground and rolled, his Sig jerking up to point at my muzzle flash.

"Don't shoot!" My ravaged vocal cords barely overcame the din of the storm. "It's me, Aydan!"

"Aydan, what's happening?" He was wearing night vision goggles, thank God. If I could see him, he could see me. He stayed down, his gun steady.

I holstered my Glock and waved, the gesture taking the last of my strength.

"I'm sorry I fired. I didn't know it was you. It's safe." My voice shook, a thin thread of sound against nature's fury. A livid flare of lightning made me flinch even though my goggles compensated for the brightness. The clap of thunder followed it almost instantly. The storm was right on top of us.

I tried to stand but my trembling legs wouldn't hold me. The rain and sleet bucketed down and I groped for the waterproof jacket I'd taken off when I'd changed earlier. It wouldn't do much good now that I was soaked to the skin all over again, but at least it was another layer. I was shaking so hard I could barely stuff my arms into the sleeves.

Holstering his gun, Kane rose to his feet and moved forward only to jerk to a halt, his arms flailing in some complicated martial-arts move.

"It's okay, it's just fishing line," I croaked, my voice all but gone.

"I noticed," he said as he came toward me, and I realized he had a knife in his hand and the 'martial arts moves' had actually been him slashing his way through my makeshift fence.

My brain slowed to a crawl. How could he be holding a knife? He'd just been holding a gun...

"How many hands do you have, anyway?" I muttered.

"Aydan?" He crouched in front of me, his head swivelling to take in the disarray of my erstwhile campsite.

"What are you doing out here?"

Explaining was too much work. My thoughts faded to garbled static behind one simple truth.

Kane was here.

I was safe.

I slumped, my muscles melting like sugar in the rain.

I was finally starting to warm up. And I was tired as hell. Maybe I could catch a few zees...

"Aydan!" Kane's sharp voice made me drag open eyelids that felt like they weighed two pounds apiece. His hand cupped my cheek, so hot that I giggled sleepily at the thought of the rain sizzling and evaporating under it.

"Aydan! Talk to me." The hot hand patted my cheek firmly and annoyingly.   "Aydan, come on.   You're hypothermic. Talk to me. Why are you out here?"

I leaned into the hot hand. "Safe."

"What? Did you say we're safe?"

I nodded dreamily, letting my eyelids slip closed.

"Come on, then." An arm around my shoulders roused me again. "Let's go back to the house."

"No." I shook my head, fighting the warm sleepiness. What had he said?

Hypothermia.

That was bad.

Stay awake.

House. He'd said 'go back to the house'.

He was lifting me, and I struggled free to balance precariously on rubber legs. "No. Not the house."

"Why not?"

I shook my head again. My thoughts crept forward, stalled, lurched into motion again, bumping into each other like drunken caterpillars.

Too hard to explain.

"Not safe," I mumbled.

He was stripping. That was nice.

I watched with remote appreciation while he peeled off his waterproof jacket. In seconds his T-shirt was soaked and plastered to his massive chest and shoulders.

Nice indeed.

He wrapped the jacket around me, the last vestiges of his body heat making me shiver.

"We'll go to my place then," he said. "Can you walk?"

"Uh-huh."

I wasn't really sure if I could, but what the hell. I put one foot in front of the other, slithering precariously on the snowy ground while his arm supported me.

The snow had stopped, but rain still fell mercilessly and a cold mist rose from the ground. Staggering through the woods and ducking involuntarily each time the lightning flashed, I could feel him shivering against me.

That was probably bad.

I hugged him tighter, but that didn't seem to help either of us. My steps slowed.

"C-come on, Aydan," he said through chattering teeth. "Almost there."

I nodded and concentrated. One foot in front of the other.

When his SUV loomed up out of the darkness I blinked at it without comprehension. He bundled me into the passenger's seat and buckled me in before hurrying around to the driver's side.

Then we were moving, the heater fan roaring and blasting too-hot air on me. It rushed by my skin without warming me, and the shivers came back.

"Stay awake, Aydan," Kane commanded.

"'M awake," I mumbled.

"Talk to me. Why were you out in the rain?"

I sighed. Talking was so much work.

"Come on, talk to me. Why were you out there?"

I fought off the lethargy. "Long story."

"I've got time."

I glanced over to see the muscles bulging in his jaw, but he didn't look angry. More likely he was trying to keep his teeth from chattering. His hair and clothes were soaked, water trickling down his neck.

I fumbled guiltily at his jacket, still wrapped around me.

"What are you doing? Keep that on."

"You n-need it. You look f-frozen."

Kane let out a breath, the hard lines easing from his face. "You're back. Thank God."

"Y-Yeah." Violent shivers shook me. "W-warming up. Sh-shivering like hell now."

"That's a good sign. When the shivering stops you're in trouble."

"Y-yeah." I clamped my chattering teeth together for a moment before prying them apart to add, "S-sorry I shot at you. I d-didn't expect you out there."

He shot me a worried look. "I can't believe you missed. I've never seen you miss a target."

"I realized it w-was you at the last s-second." I clamped my arms around myself as a particularly fierce shivering fit seized me. "T-too late to stop f-firing, b-but I p-pulled the shot. Wh-wh..." I stopped and shivered some more. "Wh-what the h-hell were you d-doing out there?"

"Hellhound called me." Kane turned onto the highway

and accelerated toward Silverside. "He'd been trying to call you but couldn't get an answer on either of your phones. He was afraid something had happened. I called Sirius but..." He grimaced. "They wouldn't tell me if they'd seen anything on your surveillance cameras because I'm suspended. So I drove out to see if your car was home, but all the windows were covered in your garage. I was just getting ready to pick the lock when I heard screaming. I thought you were being attacked. I got to you as fast as I could."

He glanced over, his frown accusing. "What were you doing out there? Why were you screaming? And why didn't you answer your phone?"

I sighed. "L-Like I said; long s-story." I drew a long breath and fought my chattering teeth to a standstill. "May I borrow your phone? I'll call Hellhound and you can listen in. That way I'll only have to tell it once."

Kane nodded and punched in his passcode one-handed before handing me the phone. When I dialled Hellhound's number he answered on the first ring.

"Did ya find her?"

"Hi, Arnie, it's me."

"Aydan! Jesus Christ, ya scared the shit outta me! Are ya okay? Where were ya? How come ya didn't answer your phones?"

"I'm sorry you were worried, Arnie. I'm okay." I slumped in the seat, certain I should be feeling guilty but too tired to feel anything. My ears still pulsed with the din of gunshots and thunder, and everything felt distant. "Another guy tried to abduct me from my garage tonight. I... He... d-died." I drew a breath. "I had to wait for the cleanup crew. I'd taken off my waist pouch so I didn't have my phone on

me. And then I... d-decided to sleep in the woods... but..."
My voice faded.

Words were so cumbersome. And I was so damn tired.

"Aydan?" Hellhound still sounded worried. "Come on, darlin', talk to me."

"Sorry," I mumbled. "I'm just cold and tired. Be okay tomorrow."

"Okay." His rasp softened to a gentle rumble. "That's okay, Aydan, don't worry about it. Is Kane there with ya?"

"Uh-huh."

"Put him on, would ya, darlin'? An' just take it easy. Everythin's gonna be okay."

I slumped deeper in the seat, my eyelids drooping. "Thanks, Arnie. 'Bye." I held the phone in Kane's direction without looking up. "He wants to talk to you."

Kane appropriated the phone. "Hello?" He listened for a moment, then replied, "No, nothing more than what she just told you." A pause. "I think she will be. She was borderline hypothermic when I found her but she's warming up now... Yes, out in the woods. She had a shelter but it was in tatters and her sleeping bag was soaked..." His voice was beginning to fade as sleep overcame me.

"Aydan!"

I jerked upright. "Christ! What?"

"Don't go to sleep," Kane warned.

"Not sleeping." I patted my racing heart, and the momentary adrenaline jolt dissipated quickly. Kane's voice faded again as my eyelids drooped. I fought slumber, his words blurring together until his 'goodbye' roused me.

A moment later the drumming of the rain on the vehicle cut off as we rolled into Kane's garage. I drew a breath of relief, the sound loud in the sudden silence. Or maybe that was just my hearing coming back.

"Can you make it to the house?" Kane asked.

"Yeah. I'm okay." I unbuckled the seat belt with cold clumsy hands and dragged myself out of the SUV to balance on legs that felt too weak to hold my weight.

Tottering out into the rain again felt even worse after fifteen minutes of comparative warmth, and Kane's arm around me did nothing to ease my shivering.

Inside, I stooped to remove my boots and nearly toppled over.

"Come on," Kane urged, half carrying me down the hall.

"W-wait, I'm d-dripping all over-"

"Don't worry about it." He propelled me around the corner into the bathroom and turned on the shower. "Take off your weapons," he commanded, and after a moment of dull incomprehension I fumbled my Glock and trank pistol out and laid them on the vanity. Kane did the same with his Sig while I stood shivering dumbly. Then he dipped his hand under the spray and gave a satisfied nod. Wrapping his arms around me, he stepped us both under the hot spray and swung the door shut behind us.

I yelped and tried to jump out of range as the water seared my scalp, but Kane held me fast.

"It's not that hot," he comforted. "You're just that cold."

He pulled me closer, tucking his head down beside mine so the water ran over both of us. He was still shivering, too, and I tightened my arms around him.

"I'm sorry," I mumbled into his soggy T-shirt. "Thanks for finding me."

"You're welcome. Now," he said against my cheek, "Do you want to tell me what really happened?"

Defensive caution levelled my voice. "Just what I told you. Some guy attacked me. By the time it was all cleaned up I was exhausted and I didn't want to sleep with one ear open so I moved out to where I knew nobody would look." I grimaced into his shoulder. "It would have been a better hiding place if I hadn't had a screaming nightmare. And it would have been a lot more comfortable if the weather gods hadn't decided to take a shit on me."

Kane pulled away far enough to give me a searching look while he worked the jackets off my shoulders to drop with a splat to the floor of the shower. "Why didn't you call me if you were afraid to be alone?" he asked. "You could have stayed here, or I would have come out to stay with you."

I was saved from an immediate reply when he lifted the hem of my sweatshirt and pulled it over my head. Sputtering, I emerged from its sodden confines and back into the spray from the shower head.

"I thought..." I began, but my brain short-circuited when he pulled off his T-shirt, revealing that spectacular upper body. I was fighting the urge to lick the water droplets off his bulging pecs and work my way down to the corrugated abs below when he reached for the hem of my T-shirt and lifted it off.

"... uh..." I added not-too-usefully as I emerged from the dripping fabric.

His gaze stayed above my shoulders. "You thought what?"

Sweet Jesus, he was undoing his jeans.

"...uh..." I repeated. "I thought, um..."

He peeled off the jeans and stepped out of them, pushing them into the corner of the shower with one foot.

Nothing left but those hip-hugging black briefs.

His hips weren't the only thing they were hugging. I wrenched my gaze back up to his face, but not before noting that he was packing some serious hardware. Ready for immediate use, according to my hasty but gratifying assessment.

"You were saying?" he inquired as he reached for the button on my jeans.

"Uh..."

He knelt in front of me, working the wet clinging fabric down my legs. The spray blasted off the broad expanse of his back, water running in rivulets down the muscled groove of his backbone. The medium-grade sandpaper of his five o'clock shadow brushed my thigh, and my breath short-circuited right along with my brain.

Suddenly it seemed extra hot and steamy in the shower. I shivered for a different reason.

Kane stood again, holding eye contact, but I was pretty sure he'd noticed my leopard-print bra and thong. He seemed to be breathing pretty rapidly for a guy in top physical condition.

Exerting every ounce of my willpower, I managed not to turn around and bend over to pick up some non-existent soap.

I cleared my throat. "Uh, I didn't want to bother you."

He made a gesture of frustration, his hand clenching on air before dropping to his side. "Dammit, Aydan, we're friends! At least trust me enough to ask for help when you need it!"

Fighting the memory of how safe I'd felt with his hand on my cheek while the storm roared around us, I snapped, "I didn't *need* help. I'd have made it on my own."

He stared down at me for a moment. "Well, let me know if you ever *want* it," he said quietly. "Help yourself to the soap and shampoo. I'll leave clean towels outside the door."

He stepped out of the shower, wrapped a towel around his waist, and closed the bathroom door behind him, leaving me alone with mounds of soggy clothing and a large helping of regret.

CHAPTER 33

By the time I emerged from Kane's shower I was barely functional. Somewhere between the soap and the shampoo my arousal had dissolved and gurgled down the drain, leaving nothing but an empty husk. If I had still been capable of feeling anything at all, I would have been grateful for the absence of emotion.

Wringing out the sodden clothes was more effort than I could muster, so I heaped them in the shower and trod all over them to squeeze out as much water as possible.

A couple of folded towels lay on the floor outside the door as promised, and I dried off and wrapped my hair and body in them before padding barefoot down the hall.

Kane stepped out of his den fully dressed, still keeping his gaze on my face. "Better?" he inquired.

"Yes. Thanks."

Talking was so much work. I just wanted to sink into the silence inside my soul.

I forced myself to make the effort. "I squeezed out our clothes as much as I could, but they're still in the shower stall, soaking wet."

"I'll put them in the dryer." He made no move toward the bathroom. "I made you a cup of hot chocolate. It's on the island in the kitchen."

"Thanks." Even the thought of hot chocolate didn't appeal. I pushed more words out of my mouth. "Do you have sweats and a T-shirt I can borrow? If you'll just drop me at home, I'll wash your clothes and bring them back tomorrow."

"No."

I blinked stupidly. "What do you mean, no? I know you have sweats."

Kane frowned down at me. "I meant, no; I'm not going to take you home. If you're afraid to sleep in your house and your campsite is wrecked, what are you planning to do?"

"I... I don't know. I'll figure something out..."

"Aydan, for God's sake!" His sudden bark startled me despite my lethargy. "Why won't you just let me protect you? Just once? Why do you have to be so goddamn bull-headed?"

His raised voice did it.

I had always imagined that when I finally broke, it would be a violent shattering.

It wasn't.

It was small and quiet, the barely audible ping of a single glass filament snapping. I reached for my usual anger and found nothing. Only the sound of distant screams fading into oblivion.

I stood frozen for a long moment while everything crumbled to dust inside me.

Nothing left.

Empty.

I spoke in the voice of a stranger.

"Okay."

Kane was getting ready to speak again, and my single

quiet word obviously threw him. He blinked. "What?"

"Okay. You win."

"Wh...?" He blinked again, visibly shifting gears. "All right. Good. You'll stay here tonight then?"

"Yes."

"All right..." He sounded tentative, thrown off-balance by my lack of resistance. "Uh... you can have the bed, and I'll sleep on the couch..."

Too tired to fight the inevitable. Just give in.

My voice came out steady but still not quite my own. "I'd rather share the bed with you."

His eyes dilated, his hot gaze sweeping up my legs and lingering on my towel.

"Aydan..." He jerked his gaze up to my face again. "No, I'm sorry. For my own sanity I can't. I need to get my head straight, and the only way I can do that is to keep things platonic between us until you're ready to discuss commitment."

Give him what he wants. Don't be a cold selfish bitch.

"I'm ready."

My words hung in the heavy silence. Kane's jaw-dangling stare would have been comical if I'd been capable of feeling anything.

The terrified screaming started again in the back of my brain. *No-no-no-no...*

Shut up. Too late for that.

After a long silence, Kane cleared his throat. "Aydan, I don't want you to rush into this. You've been through a lot lately..."

Now or later; it didn't matter. It would end the same.

I smothered the screamer. Shoved a pillow over her face

until she choked into silence, then jammed her corpse down into the cold abyss that held the last shards of my heart.

"I've decided." My voice was firm and emotionless. "I'll commit to you. We can get married if you want. Or not, it's up to you."

"Uh..."

I'd never seen Kane at a loss for words before. Too bad I couldn't enjoy it.

He squared his shoulders, a cautious smile lighting his face. "All right. But we should talk about this."

Please, no more talking. Just let the silence take me.

"In the morning." I dropped my towel.

"Aydan..."

I stepped against him and silenced his protest with my mouth. His arms closed around me, tight and possessive, and I nearly jerked away in claustrophobic terror.

No. Too late for that.

I let my body melt against his hard contours.

He broke the kiss to run hot hands down my back, pulling me closer still as if to merge our bodies into one.

"Aydan," he said hoarsely. "I love you."

"I love you, too," the stranger replied with my mouth, and it was true.

But not the truth.

Kane's lips met mine again, and I turned off all thoughts and fell into the safe mindlessness of sensation.

His hands were gentle on my body, his kisses slow and tender. After a while he drew back to look down into my eyes. "I want you, Aydan," he whispered. "God help me, I want you tonight, but I know you must be exhausted. You can just go to sleep if you want." He smiled. "We have all the time in the world."

My heart twisted, one final feeble protest.

I pulled him down so he couldn't look into my eyes and whispered against his lips, "I want you, too. Take me to bed."

Hand in hand, we turned for the bedroom. Inside, he pulled me to him again, weaving his fingers through my hair while he kissed me softly and slowly. His grip tightened and I let him position my mouth where he wanted it, opening for his tongue and trying to lose myself in his skillful touch.

He drew away a fraction, and I glimpsed a flicker of uncertainty in his eyes.

Of course, dammit, he was used to me ripping his clothes off and flinging myself at him.

Give him what he wants.

I summoned the last of the strength in my aching body and sprang, pushing him onto the bed. When he landed on his back, grinning up at me, I swung astride and leaned down to kiss him with as much hunger as I could fake.

He growled and flipped us over, pinning me to the bed with his weight. Smiling down at me, he rumbled, "Well, Ms. Kelly, I seem to have gained the upper hand here."

"You always do," I said quietly. The uncertainty flickered in his eyes again, and I pushed a smile onto my face and bounced my hips playfully under him. "But that doesn't mean you're the boss. Strip for me, big fella."

A wicked grin lit his face. "Yes, ma'am."

He rose slowly, trailing his fingertips lightly down my body. I squirmed up in the bed to prop myself against the pillows, watching his eyes ignite when I tucked my arms behind my head and wriggled my hips into a more comfortable position.

His gaze burning on mine, he ran a hand down his chest, bumping over his abs to find the hem of his T-shirt. His hips circled slowly and sensuously, raw power schooled into savage grace.

Despite my exhaustion, slow heat kindled in my belly. I mirrored his gesture, gliding my hands over my breasts and down my thighs.

His lips parted, his breath coming faster.

He peeled off his T-shirt and tossed it into the corner of the bedroom, his gaze still devouring me.

Licking my lips, I took in every perfectly-sculpted contour of his arms and torso. His washboard abs rippled with the movement of his hips, more forceful now; suggestion giving way to promise.

His hands moved down to pop the button of his jeans, then to the zipper. Unhurriedly easing it down, he let his jeans fall open as he stretched toward the ceiling, a slow sexy flex and release of each muscle. The jeans rode lower on his circling hips and my breath caught at the first glimpse of black briefs.

Grinning, he pushed the jeans down and stepped out of them in a move so swift and graceful I gasped all over again.

As he straightened, my gaze snagged and held on the giant erection barely contained by thin black fabric.

My heart gave a hard contraction and other muscles lower down followed suit.

When I dragged my attention back up to Kane's face, he was smiling, his eyes blazing hunger. "Ms. Kelly," he rumbled. "The help wants to know... what do you want me to do next?"

"Take them off," I croaked.

His hands slid down to his hips.

His thumbs hooked under the elastic.

My heart stopped beating as he teased down first one side, then the other.

Then the briefs gave up the struggle and all that premium hardware sprang free. After a single light-headed moment I remembered to breathe again.

He was magnificent. Even in the soft light of the bedside lamp, every muscle was chiseled to perfection. But the muscles faded to a pleasing backdrop as my gaze locked onto his most outstanding feature.

Realizing I'd been goggling open-mouthed, I dragged my gaze back up to his face. The raw desire in his eyes stole my breath all over again, but he stood as though carved from stone, his only movement the rapid beat of the pulse in his throat.

His intensity sent a shiver through me, and I fluttered my eyelashes at him and clasped my hands to my chest. "For me?" I quipped, trying to lighten the mood.

"All for you." His voice was deep and hoarse. "Always."

The word jabbed sudden terror through me.

No-no-no...

Stop. It's too late.

I detached the terrified screamer and pushed her away to float in the corner of the room.

"What do you want me to do now?" Kane growled.

From the corner of the room I watched my naked body quiver with need as the rough bass notes vibrated along my nerve endings.

"Come here," I/she said.

Kane pounced, landing on top of me with the fluid grace of a hunting jungle cat. His body hovered a fraction of an inch above mine, his weight balanced on elbows and knees. Heat rolled off his skin in searing waves and his erection jammed against my thigh.

Still maintaining his plank position above me, he cupped my face in his palms. "Aydan," he whispered, his lips almost on mine. "Are you sure?"

I ignored the screaming from the corner of the room. "Yes."

When he hesitated, I reached up to kiss him. "John, I promise. And you know I keep my promises."

"Yes." He lowered his forehead to rest on mine. "Aydan." My name came out on a breath, and he gathered me close to him and kissed me as though his life depended on it.

I watched/felt his hands move over my body, the sensations somehow both distant and intensely immediate. He kissed his way down my neck, moving lower and cupping my breasts. A feather-light stroke of his tongue made my nipple tighten almost painfully. The little nip he delivered immediately afterward made me cry out and arch up to him, begging for more.

Kissing, licking, nibbling, he moved lower, then lower still, setting me afire with his heat. The distant me watched my body arch and writhe under his touch and listened to my moans and intakes of breath, slowly warming with arousal of its own.

Kane bestowed a kiss and a flick of his tongue in a place that left me gasping, then raised his head to meet my gaze with dilated eyes.

"Are you ready for me?" The breathless roughness in his voice left no doubt about how he was holding back.

A surge of pure need overcame me. "God, yes!"

He reached over to fumble in the bedside table for a condom. His gaze never left me while he rolled it on, his erection stretching it to its limits. Then he was pressing my legs apart and lowering himself to me.

He filled me slowly, pushing deeper and deeper until my body spasmed around him and I cried out in ecstasy edged with a tiny shiver of pain.

He gasped. Held still.

"More. Please." My voice was almost as hoarse as his.

His breath hissed between his teeth as he moved slowly again, the muscles in his arms quivering with tension.

A blaze of heat consumed me and I rocked my hips up to meet him, burying him to the hilt. A groan wrenched out of him and he dropped onto his elbows to pull me against his chest. His entire body was vibrating, iron muscles strained to their limits.

"Aydan?" he gasped, and I understood the question.

"Yes, fuck me," I whispered. "Please fuck me now."

With a groan that was almost a sob he rocked into motion, gently at first but then with more force as my body responded to him.

Watching/feeling my fingernails dig into his back and my legs lift to clamp around his hips, I surrendered to the rising wave. The heat blazed higher, every nerve electrified. His face was buried in my neck, his five o'clock shadow stimulating the sensitive flesh. His teeth closed on my skin in a jolt of sensation that wasn't quite pain and I cried out, clutching him closer and moaning.

He slowed and changed to a deeper stroke, sliding almost all the way out before driving home, and I whimpered approval and mindlessly matched his rhythm.

The expanding ripples of pleasure rocked me higher and higher until I teetered on the pinnacle, breathlessly close to orgasm. Rising moans escaped me, my body tightening as the slow waves advanced. Almost...

"Aydan..." Kane's voice was the harsh rasp of a man holding himself barely in check. "Can't... wait..."

"Now!" I raked my nails across his back, jerking my hips up to meet him. "Now! Hard! Now!"

A groan burst from his lips and he slammed into me.

A tiny ascending, "Please?" drifted up from someone who might have been me. The word floated off into space as my orgasm claimed me, rocking my body with such force I couldn't tell whether the spasms were my own or Kane's powerful thrusts.

A few moments later he went rigid with a raw-throated cry that seemed ripped from his very soul. Straining me against him, he buried his face in my neck, his breath hissing between his teeth.

Locked together, we rode the final waves, my cries mingling with his harsh panting. Gradually the spasms eased and our muscles softened against each other, our bodies slippery with sweat.

At last Kane drew a long breath and raised his head to sprinkle kisses on my lips and cheeks. Then he released me and rolled over, and we sprawled bonelessly hand in hand.

CHAPTER 34

Kane sat up and removed the condom before rolling back to gather me into his arms. Butterfly kisses brushed my collarbone, my neck, my lips.

"That was..." he began, then shook his head and pressed another kiss to my lips. "That was mind-blowing."

"Mmhmm," I mumbled, utterly spent.

My conscience prodded me. I should say something else, something to make him feel loved and wanted. Distant screams echoed in my mind but I smothered them ruthlessly. He was happy. I was doing the right thing.

I forced myself to utter more words. "I had an out-of-body experience."

He laughed, and the joy in it made me smile despite the cold emptiness inside my chest. "The first of many," he promised, his arms tightening around me.

My body twitched involuntarily with the need to escape, and Kane leaned up on one elbow to look down at me with concern. "Are you all right?" he asked anxiously. "I didn't hurt you, did I?"

I laid a finger softly on his lips. "You didn't hurt me. That was just the last of the head-banging orgasm."

"Oh." His grin returned. "Good." Another kiss. "You

must be exhausted," he added. "Here..." He tugged at the rumpled blankets and we synchronized a lift-and-squirm to pull them out from under us and over top.

"Which side do you want?" Kane asked. "I usually sleep on the left but I can change..."

"Right is fine," I mumbled, fatigue dragging my eyelids down.

"All right." He tucked me close to his heart. "Good night, Aydan." He kissed me lingeringly. "I love you," he whispered against my lips.

"I love you, too."

I kept my eyes closed, unable to look at him while I said it. As he settled on the pillow beside me, I made a silent promise to do better tomorrow.

He was a good man and he loved me. Tomorrow would be easier. And the tomorrow after that, and the next and the next...

My body went rigid at the thought, but I fought my muscles into submission.

Get some sleep. Perfectly safe tonight. Just sleep...

Trapped. I was trapped. My arms and legs were bound. A heavy weight crushed me. Something terrible was approaching. It was invisible but I sensed its darkness; the horrible *thing* that would consume me utterly. I fought its bonds, whimpering and struggling.

I couldn't escape. My whimpers turned to screams. The thing was upon me, its grip tightening, pinning me helplessly-

"Aydan! Aydan, wake up! You're dreaming, wake up!"

Kane's voice. Kane's arms pinning me, holding me

against my will in a waking nightmare...

The screams tore my throat, my body thrashing against his grip.

"Aydan, you're safe! Wake up!"

At last I managed to tear free. A frantic roll off the bed landed me on my feet, my back pressed against the closet door, my fists clenched in a fighter's stance. My breath rasped in my throat.

"Aydan," Kane said gently. "Wake up." I could barely make out the dark shadow of his shape sitting up in bed. "It's all right," he went on in soothing tones. "It's just me. John Kane. You're here at my house and you're safe. You had a bad dream, but you're safe. Do you understand?"

I understood.

The weight of my promise crushed me.

My arms dropped to my sides and I shuffled back to the bed. "I'm sorry, John. Are you okay? I didn't hurt you, did I?"

"No, I'm fine. Come here." He reached out his arms and I forced myself to sink into them. Holding me close, he kissed me before settling us back on the pillows. His hand stroked gently over my hair. "Go back to sleep, Aydan. You're safe here."

"Thanks." I pressed my face into the pillow.

After a few minutes his stroking hand faltered, then fell away as his breathing slowed and deepened. Wide-eyed, I lay in his arms staring into the blackness.

It was a long night. Twice more I woke screaming and struggling, and the second time I landed a vicious kick on Kane's thigh before I knew what I was doing. He teased me with gentle humour over my near-miss of his family jewels and cuddled me close again, but after that I lay awake staring into the darkness and listening to his even breathing.

Too dangerous to fall asleep. What if I grabbed my gun and shot him during a half-awake terror? God, I'd never forgive myself.

By the time the darkness lightened to gray I was vibrating with tension and fatigue, my eyes burning from holding them open.

Kane stirred and released me at last, easing his arm away as though trying not to wake me. I feigned deep sleep while he moved noiselessly around the room collecting clothes.

The quiet click of the door closing behind him wrenched a silent sob of relief from me. Burying my face in the pillow, I flung out my arms and legs in the mercifully empty bed. The released tension left my muscles weak and trembling, and I fought ragged breathing that wanted to turn into tears.

Stop. Suck it up.

I shook myself and extracted my face from the pillow to check the bedside clock.

Only five-thirty AM.

Thank God he was an early riser.

Limbs still splayed to occupy all the heavenly space and solitude, I gave in to sleep.

It didn't go well.

Twice Kane rushed in at the sound of my screams to hold me while I fought the nightmare. Both times I managed to convince him not to stay, and at last I fell into a deeper sleep.

A familiar insistent sound roused me, but I had barely dragged my eyelids open when it stopped. Letting out a breath of relief, I fell back into slumber.

When it penetrated my sleep again I groaned and pulled the pillow over my head, but this time there was no reprieve.

"Aydan." Kane's voice was soft from the doorway. "Aydan?"

"Grmmgrfff."

Gentle hands pried the pillow away from my face. "Aydan."

"Wha'...?" I tried to retrieve the pillow but he held it out of reach.

"I'm sorry to wake you, but Stemp is on the phone. He needs you to come in this morning."

My voice came out in a sleep-slurred growl. "Fuck'im. Suspended. Don' hafta go in." I grabbed the other pillow and flopped over to bury my face in it.

The mattress dipped as Kane sat beside me. His hand made warm circles on my back. "I'm sorry, Aydan, but you really need to talk to him. I'll bring you the phone."

"No."

Either he didn't hear my muffled refusal, or he ignored it. The mattress sprang up again and a few seconds later I felt a gentle grip on my wrist. Kane pried my hand free of the pillow and pressed a hard cool object into it, and I let out a groan of resignation and flopped over to lie on my back.

Eyes still closed, I brought the handset to my face and croaked, "What."

"Kelly. Your presence is required this morning." Stemp's dispassionate voice was offensively wide-awake. "Please be here by zero nine thirty to go over the autopsy results from your latest attacker. Also, Ms. Ritter is still expecting you at ten hundred for your peer review meeting."

I dragged my eyes open to squint at the bedside clock.

Nine AM.

I held back a spate of profanity and focused as hard as I

could on the positive.

Could've been worse. At least I'd gotten nearly three hours of sleep. I was already in Silverside so I didn't have the fifteen-minute drive from my place. I did want to know what they'd found out about my attacker, and I really didn't want to miss that interview with Ursula Ritter to put in my vote of support for Stemp. As annoyed as I was by his crisp voice, a morning call from Dermott would have been infinitely worse.

"Kelly?" Stemp inquired, and I realized I hadn't replied yet.

"Uh. Sorry. Okay. See you at nine-thirty," I mumbled.

"I'll collect you from the lobby," he said, and hung up.

"I'll collect you from the lobby," I mouthed, grimacing, before adding aloud, "You can stick that right up your lobby and rotate on it, you-" I broke off at the sight of Kane's alarmed expression. "He already hung up," I explained, and passed the handset back.

"Oh." Kane accepted the phone with visible relief. Then his gaze dipped to travel over the twisted sheets that revealed a good bit of skin I hadn't bothered to cover. "Good morning," he said, grinning. "Waking up next to you was great, but this is almost as good."

I grunted, then realized that probably wasn't the response he was looking for.

Do better. You made the commitment; now deliver.

My old habits slid back into place with an almost-audible click and the familiar numbness descended like a curtain of mercy.

"Sorry it has to be short-lived," I added as I swung my legs wearily over the edge of the bed. "I've got exactly..." I paused to glance at the alarm clock. "...Twenty-five minutes to get my shit together and get to Sirius..." I trailed off and sank my head into my hands with a groan. "Shit, I'll have to go wearing your clothes. I don't have anything dry."

"No, it's all right," Kane countered. "I washed and dried your clothes this morning while you were sleeping. And I cleaned your Glock and the trank pistol and dried your holsters, too."

"Thanks!" I rose and linked my arms around his neck for a kiss. "I love you!" The words came out smoothly, and I even managed to smile and look him in the eyes.

Kane chuckled and kissed me back. "But wait, there's more. I have bread and peanut butter."

"I really, really love you," I declared.

Our kiss was longer this time.

Kane ran his hands down my back, giving the bed a meaningful look. "It's too bad you're so rushed this morning."

"Yeah," I agreed, silently thanking Stemp for the intervention before giving myself a mental slap to the head.

I had promised myself I'd give Kane what he wanted, and that included the kind of passionate sex he expected from me. And anyway, I'd be crazy to avoid it. He was amazing in bed.

But if he pinned me under him again I'd lose it completely and fight my way free screaming and scratching.

I slammed the brakes on that thought. No. I could do this. I pressed my hips against him and gave a little shimmy. "Next time I get to ride on top, though."

"Is that so?" Kane grinned down at me.

"Uh-huh. But not until I get back, unfortunately." I pulled away. "Now, where are my clothes?"

"In the bathroom." Kane followed as I headed down the hall. "Hellhound phoned earlier, too. He said he has some more information for you."

My heart soared, then stuttered to a halt, tumbling down my ribs to clatter into my stomach.

Arnie.

Oh, God.

"I'll call him when I get back," I choked, and hurried into the bathroom to lock the door behind me.

Fifteen minutes later I kissed Kane goodbye at the door and headed for his garage, the keys to his SUV clutched in my fist. The merciful numbness had spread. My hands were steady despite the fatigue that gripped me, and my emotions were completely frozen over.

I let out a breath as I slid behind the steering wheel. Numbness was so much better. No danger of losing my temper, no fear of suddenly bursting into tears.

No chance of joy, either, a small sad voice reminded me, but I dismissed it.

I could fake joy.

CHAPTER 35

Stemp was waiting in the lobby when I arrived at Sirius. Appreciating my newfound composure, I greeted him civilly and even managed to banter with Leo while Stemp signed me in at the security booth.

At the door to his office, Stemp stepped aside and gestured me ahead of him. Then he closed the door and took a seat behind his desk, waving me into the opposite chair.

"So." He pressed two fingers to the bridge of his nose, closing his eyes. "Norman Perkins, thirty-one years old, multiple weapons and assault convictions. Carrying another photo of Arlene Widdenback with your particulars, but the only fingerprints on it were his own. Another crisp twenty-five hundred dollars cash in his wallet; nylon zip ties in his pocket. So far neither my analysts nor the Calgary police have been able to identify any connection between Mallard and Perkins. The autopsy showed Perkins died of massive internal bleeding from a torn abdominal aorta."

He opened his eyes again to transfix me with his unnerving reptilian stare. "The examiner also noted a deep facial wound and nine punctures consistent with tranquilizer darts. Potentially enough to kill him, if he hadn't bled to death." He eyed me unblinkingly. "What happened?"

I sighed and slouched in the chair, aching to the very marrow of my bones. "I was working on my car when I realized he'd sneaked up behind me. He grabbed me but I was already coming up with a screwdriver in my hand and I nailed him in the face. He staggered back and I pulled my pistol to trank him, but..." I had to stop and swallow. "...he tripped over the edge of my concrete slab and fell onto a steel reinforcing rod."

Stemp's expression never changed. "And...?"

I swallowed again. "I... had... a flashback." Stemp's silence compelled me to keep talking. "Another impalement... from years ago. I thought he was screaming. Struggling. Like the other guy."

The horror threatened to overtake me and I huddled into my old emotionless shell.

It still fit me perfectly. My voice came out dead level. "Maybe he was, I don't know for sure. I tranked him but I could still hear screaming. That would have been part of the flashback, because the other guy never lost consciousness..." I bit off the explanation and met Stemp's gaze steadily. "Anyway, I lost control. I kept firing until I passed out from the aerosolized trank. When I woke up he was dead."

I drew a breath and let it out into the thick silence. "But you said he didn't die from the trank overdose."

"Correct." The single emotionless word gave away nothing.

"But..." I licked dry lips, not wanting to talk but unable to stop. "It was only a little piece of half-inch rebar. How could it have killed him? The other guy... it was a three-inch fence post. Punched through his ass and out his belly and took half his guts with it. And he never even passed out. He screamed..." My throat closed and my voice came out in a dry whisper despite my best attempt to control it. "He was still screaming... when they cut the post and took him away..."

The horrific spectre rose in front of my eyes again, and I clung to my shield of detachment with everything I had.

Stemp's shoulder lifted in a fractional shrug. "At the angle you describe, it likely missed his aorta. And a smooth object the size of a fence post would jam into the body cavity so tightly that virtually no blood leakage could occur. Since it was below the level of his heart, his circulatory system would continue to supply blood to the brain without causing a sufficient drop in blood pressure to render him unconscious. Conversely, the rebar was small with a ribbed texture that effectively acted as blood vents. It tore the aorta and allowed massive bleeding into the abdominal cavity."

He sounded as though he was discussing the weather, and I envied his detachment with every fibre in my body. I also wondered briefly why he was so familiar with the location of major blood vessels, but I decided I didn't really want to know.

"So you didn't fire your weapon until after he was impaled?" Stemp added.

"No."

"Are you certain? Could you have fired before he fell?"

I frowned. "No. I'm positive I didn't."

"Because it wouldn't be surprising if you were a little quicker to shoot than you normally are," Stemp went on as if I hadn't spoken. "That would certainly be understandable-"

"What are you trying to say?" I demanded. "Are you calling me a liar?"

"No, of course not." He steepled his fingers and

regarded me over top of them. "Dr. Rawling simply expressed concern that you might have... overreacted."

Yesterday I might have been irritated. Now the comment didn't even chip the ice of my composure.

"I didn't." I hesitated, then added, "Well, until the flashback, anyway. But if he was bleeding out as fast as you say, he was nearly dead by the time the first dart hit him. You can tell Dr. Rawling my overreaction was strictly due to the flashback, and I don't think there's much danger that I'll have another."

"How can you be sure?"

I held his gaze. "How many impalements have you seen in your life?"

A taut silence vibrated between us. "None that were accidental," he said quietly.

Oh, God, I shouldn't have asked.

"Two intentional ones," he finished.

I swallowed hard. "I'm sorry. I didn't mean to..." He waved away my apology and I went on, "What I meant was, it's not exactly a common occurrence so the chance of triggers is relatively slim. And I'd had a really bad day with some other, um..."

I didn't even want to go there.

"...stuff," I finished carefully. "But I've dealt with it."

Suddenly I was looking into the barrel of his trank pistol.

"Nobody deals with trauma overnight," Stemp said. "Particularly not long-standing post-traumatic reactions. You overreacted. I think it's best if you go to a safe house and stay there until this situation is resolved."

Staring into the soulless black eye of the muzzle, I fought back bitter laughter. A safe house. Ha. Maybe yesterday I could have been saved. Not now. Compared to the life sentence I'd just imposed on myself, short-term captivity in a safe house was nothing.

I leaned back in the chair with a sigh. "Whatever."

Despite Stemp's deadpan façade, I could have sworn I saw an infinitesimal raise of his eyebrow. "That's all you have to say?"

"Yeah. Go ahead and lock me up if you want. That won't help you figure out who's behind this, though." Inspiration struck, and I added, "If you don't believe I shot Perkins after he fell, get the medical examiner to test the blood that leaked into his abdominal cavity. If he bled out that fast, he'd only have the fast-acting inhaled trank in that blood. The tranquilizer from the darts might be in the rest of his body, but not in the blood that escaped first."

Stemp holstered his pistol, his lips curving into a slow smile. "The blood was already tested. With exactly the results you described."

I gaped at him in silence for a moment. "So what the hell...?"

He lifted a shoulder in a fractional shrug. "Dr. Rawling believed the multiple shots were a stress reaction to your current situation. He also believed you would experience an intense anxiety reaction to the prospect of being restrained in a safe house."

Yesterday I would have. Not now.

I gave Stemp a dose of his own medicine, eyeing him in silence.

"So I tested you," he said amiably. "I'm pleased to say that you passed with flying colours. So what is your next step in this case?"

For a moment I just stared at him. No apology, not even

a hint of discomfort over the fact that he'd just pulled a gun on me and threatened to have me incarcerated. Bastard.

Well, fine. I shouldn't have expected anything different.

I sighed. "My informant tells me that the contract might have been initiated by a skinny little guy with piercings who looks like Tyler Brock. I'll know more after I talk to the informant again this morning. Meanwhile, I'll check the databases for Norman Perkins..." I trailed off, then added, "No, I guess I won't. Not until Thursday. Unless you're reinstating me."

"No." Stemp's gaze bored into me. "But the suspect looks like Brock?"

"Yeah." I hesitated. Did I have enough evidence to voice my suspicions about Brock without being dismissed as petty and vindictive?

But, hell. If Brock was the mastermind behind the assassins, Spider might be in danger. I'd never forgive myself if something happened to him.

Stemp was still waiting and watching, and I pushed away the uncomfortable conviction that he was reading my mind.

I sighed and laid it all out, finishing, "I don't have any solid evidence and I know it seems really unlikely that it's him, but at this point I don't dare ignore the possibility. I'm hoping to find out from my informant when the original contract was negotiated, to see if Brock has an alibi."

"Ah." Stemp eyed me narrowly. "And this informant? Who is he or she?"

I hesitated. Shit, this might not turn out well for Hellhound.

I put on my best poker face. "I'm not at liberty to say."

Stemp regarded me with unblinking intensity. "But you'll document the identity in your classified reports."

For once, his subtle reptilian menace failed to intimidate me. I met his gaze squarely. "Unfortunately, I'm suspended. So I can't file any reports."

After an instant of silence, Stemp let out a bark of laughter. "Checkmate. Well played, Kelly." He sobered. "Nevertheless, I will require the identity of your informant."

"Sorry, you can't have it." When he began to speak again, I held up a restraining hand and talked over him. "This informant owes me some personal favours. He only knows me as Jane and I only contact him through an intermediary so there's no way he can trace me. He poses no risk to national security or to me, but in the unlikely event that anything happens to me, the intermediary will contact you directly. I can't give you anything else."

Stemp gave me the silent-treatment stare, but it didn't even dent my composure. After a long silence, he said, "You mean you *won't* give me anything else."

I shrugged and said nothing.

Stemp's voice dropped to an icy quiet that cut like a scalpel. "I could have you arrested and imprisoned for withholding information in a case."

Weary beyond words, I slid lower in the chair and let my head fall against the chair back. "Yeah."

This time he was definitely disconcerted. His hand twitched up to adjust his tie and his gaze flicked sideways for a bare instant.

"What's the matter?" I inquired. "Your favourite manipulation tactics not working the way they should?"

He surprised me with honesty. "No, they're not. I wonder why."

"I told you, I dealt with my shit."

"So it would seem." Stemp's eyes narrowed as if trying to hone his gaze sharp enough to slice open my skull and expose my secrets. When that didn't work, he leaned back in his chair with a sigh and massaged the bridge of his nose.

"Very well. For now, I'll trust your judgement on this. Keep me apprised of any new information you receive."

"Okay. Um... Sorry, I know this sounds really paranoid, but... I have to ask..." I gave him a pleading look. "I'm worried about Spider. He's unarmed and vulnerable. Is there any way we can protect him? Just in case? Brock's threatened him a couple of times."

Stemp frowned. "That seems prudent. In the short term, at least." He glanced at his wristwatch. "Germain is debriefing from his last mission right now. I'd prefer not to reassign him until he completes his post-mission psych evaluation, but with Kane and Holt both relieved of duty..." He let out a breath. "Since I know Germain's mission went well, I don't foresee any problems with his psych evaluation." He hesitated only a moment. "Very well. I'll assign Germain to protect Webb."

"Oh, thank you!" I sagged with relief. "And that will keep Linda safe, too." At Stemp's quizzical look, I clarified, "I think Brock might have been harassing her."

Stemp nodded. "Then this will be the optimum solution, at least for the short term. I'll keep the analysts working on finding connections between Norman Perkins and Drake Mallard and let you know if anything surfaces. I'll also get Brock to provide a timeline of his activities so we can check it against your informant's information." He raised a deadly eyebrow. "I presume I can reach you at Kane's house if you don't answer your phones."

What the hell, he'd obviously guessed where to find me

this morning. I met his gaze without flinching. "Yep."

He rose. "I'll escort you to the conference room and wait with you until Ms. Ritter arrives. She will escort you out after your interview."

I hauled myself to my feet, too. "It's only a few doors down. You don't need to bother."

"On the contrary, while you are under suspension I'm required to treat you the same as I would any other visitor who doesn't possess a valid security clearance."

I sighed and headed for the door. "Fine. Knock yourself out."

A few paces down the hall, I stepped into the conference room with Stemp right behind me. Sinking into a chair, I stretched out my legs and stared at the wall. Stemp propped a shoulder against the doorframe and stood regarding me expressionlessly.

When he spoke, I had to suppress a twitch.

"Where is your waist pouch?"

I studied the wall intently. No way I was going to admit I'd been so messed up I'd run away and left it in my garage.

"Didn't bring it today."

"I can see that. Why?"

God, I was so sick of questions. Just make him shut up.

My evil twin took over my mouth. "Because I was so busy fucking Kane's brains out this morning, I forgot it at his place."

Stemp didn't react at all.

Ursula Ritter, however, jerked to a halt as though she'd run into an invisible force field in the doorway, her mouth dropping open to form a lipsticked 'O'.

Perfect. Absolutely fucking perfect.

CHAPTER 36

Stemp's legendary composure didn't even flicker. "Ms. Ritter," he said, courteously inclining his head. "This is Agent Aydan Kelly. If you would be so kind as to escort her from the building when you're finished your interview...?"

Ursula Ritter gave a jerky nod, colour darkening her cheeks even under the powdery layer of makeup she wore. After a moment of expectant silence from Stemp, she blinked and stepped through the doorway into the conference room. He offered us a nod and withdrew, leaving Ritter and me staring at each other.

I was pretty sure I was blushing hotter than she was. Any second my eyebrows were going to catch fire...

"Sorry," I croaked. "I know that sounded really inappropriate, but he'd just irritated me and I was trying to shock him. It's not what it sounded like..."

I trailed off. Hell, it was exactly what it sounded like. With a supreme effort I prevented myself from beating my forehead against the tabletop until I lost consciousness.

Instead, I rose and extended my hand. "I'm sorry. Can we start over? I'm Aydan Kelly."

Her mouth snapped shut, her lipstick thinning into a straight red slash.

Aw, shit. I could read my doom in the severe cut of her navy blue suit and the bun scraping her artificially dark hair away from her face so tightly that the corners of her eyes looked tilted.

She gave me a stiff nod and regarded my hand as though I'd offered her a rotting fish. "Please sit, Agent Kelly."

I sat.

She inspected the chair across from me with a disapproving frown before lowering herself into it with fastidious reluctance.

God, she looked so tight-assed it was a miracle she could even move. I imagined clenched buttocks squeaking as she bent to sit, and almost snickered aloud. Hellhound would laugh his ass off when I told him.

Sick misery punched me in the gut.

Could we still be friends now that I'd committed to Kane? Sex was so much a part of our relationship; the bawdy jokes, the teasing touches, the easy intimacy...

"Agent Kelly!"

"Uh?" I jerked up from my despairing slouch. "I'm sorry, what?"

"I *said*..." She paused for emphasis and made a disapproving moue, tight lines forming a starburst around her puckered lips.

Hellhound would say it looked like she had a bright-red asshole on her face.

My heart clenched again. God, what if I lost him?

"...what is your relationship to Charles Stemp?"

I blinked, dragging my attention back up to her slitty eyes. Focus, dipshit. Just because your personal life is a disaster, there's no need to sabotage your work life.

"We don't have a relationship," I said weakly. "Like I said, what you heard-"

An impatient sigh hissed out between her pursed lips. "Your *professional* relationship," she snapped. "This is the first question on the interview sheet." Her conservatively-manicured fingertip stabbed at the top of her sheaf of papers.

"Oh. Sorry. Um... well, he's the director of clandestine operations and I'm an agent. I report directly to him." I frowned. "I thought you knew that already."

Another huff of impatience escaped her. "Of course I know that. I'm simply following the standard interview format. Consistency is very important. Now, if we may continue?"

Her last sentence came loaded with a substantial dose of snark, but I bit my tongue and nodded.

Do *not* sabotage this.

We worked through a series of pointless questions and I kept a pleasant expression on my face and answered like a good little robot. At last Ritter gathered up the papers she'd been marking off and tapped the stack into alignment before laying them aside, their rectangle perfectly parallel with the table edge.

The routine seemed to have settled her composure, and she spoke with crisp dispassionate tones. "These next questions deal with your personal relationship with Charles Stemp." She hesitated and for an instant I thought she'd make a crack, but thank God she didn't go there. Instead, she finished, "This will help identify any biases or personality conflicts that might colour your perception of his effectiveness as director. Have you ever had any conflicts or differences of opinion with Charles Stemp?"

A snort of laughter escaped me before I could stop it.

Her brows snapped together and I hurriedly got my face and voice under control. "Um, yes," I said meekly.

"Please describe them."

My evil twin took over again. "You don't have enough paper there to hold it all."

The slitty eyes and thin lips were back. "Then please describe the top three conflicts you've experienced."

My God, the woman had less sense of humour than a dyspeptic wolverine.

I drew a deep breath, my mind racing. It seemed like a bad idea to relate the time I'd shoved my gun under Stemp's chin and threatened to kill him. And probably all those times I'd called him a dickhead weren't ideal interview fodder, either.

But, hell, if she'd done any research at all she probably knew about those times already and she was just trying to catch me in a lie.

Fatigue dragged at me, jumbling my thoughts into a paranoid mess.

To hell with it.

I told her the truth.

Ritter's only reaction was a tightening around her eyes. I had a momentary flash of the overstressed skin splitting, pulling apart into gory crevices like the trail of a screwdriver tearing through flesh...

"Agent Kelly!"

I started violently, my heart hammering. "Sorry." My voice came out in a weak quaver and I cleared my throat. "What did you say?"

"I *said*..."

The pissy emphasis was back, and I huddled thankfully

around the rush of irritation that warmed the chill at my heart.

"...please describe any personal feelings you may have for Charles Stemp."

"What exactly does that mean?" I inquired warily.

She glared across the table. "Are you enemies?"

I was pretty sure that wasn't one of the standard questions on her list, but I answered as civilly as I could manage. "No, of course not."

Her eyes narrowed. "Are you lovers?"

I recoiled. "Christ, no! We're co-workers, nothing more. Sometimes we butt heads, but there's nobody I'd trust more as a director. Stemp is excellent at his job."

"So you would like him to continue as director?"

"Absolutely." I leaned forward, willing her to understand. "He's brilliant. He's a manipulative sonofa-" I bit off the end of that and substituted, "He knows how to convince people to do things his way, and sometimes that causes conflict. But he's always thinking ahead, always on top of things. Even if I call him at three o'clock in the morning in the middle of a fucked-up mission..."

She twitched at the f-bomb and I added, "...sorry, a messed-up mission, he always answers on the first ring, and he always knows exactly what's going on. I don't even want to think about what it would be like trying to do my job without him."

"But yet you threatened to kill him."

I managed not to grind my teeth. "I just explained to you that there were mitigating factors."

Ritter gave me another glare. "Perhaps he's always available for your calls because he gives you preferential treatment."

"Fuck, he just suspended me for something that wasn't even my fault. How the hell is that preferential treatment?" The words sprang out before I could stop them.

Dammit, I was too tired. Losing it.

Her eyes narrowed again, and I wondered how she could even see out of those tiny slits. "Everyone knows you're the only agent with 24/7 surveillance on her personal dwelling," she said icily. "That smacks of favouritism."

I held onto my temper for all I was worth. "No," I ground out. "That's not favouritism. That's protecting an asset. Up until a few months ago..." I stopped before I could spill any details. She probably didn't have the security clearance. "...I was the only option for one of our highly-classified projects. If Stemp hadn't protected me adequately, his chain of command would have handed him his head."

"But you say that changed a few months ago," she repeated silkily. "And yet, you're still consuming valuable hours of our analysts' surveillance time."

"I haven't consumed any of their time," I said shortly. "I've been away on a mission for the past four months. And the surveillance program is being discontinued this week."

I'd managed to surprise her. Her eyebrows rose, stretching her face into a tight mask. "Stemp didn't mention that to me," she said.

"He had no reason to," I snapped. "He doesn't care about popularity contests and he doesn't have to justify his decisions to every little pissant who questions him. He's too busy doing his job the best he can, and that's a hell of a lot better than anybody else could do it."

I rose. "We're done. I need to talk to Stemp again. Are you going to escort me to his office or do you want to stay here and watch while I walk the ten feet?"

She flushed and stood. A loud squeak emanated from behind her and I nearly choked myself trying not to laugh.

It was the chair, not her ass. I knew it was the chair. Dammit, don't laugh. Don't... laugh...

"Go," she snapped, her face turning dusky purple under the makeup.

I fled before I could guffaw and make things worse.

Tapping on Stemp's open door, I could feel Ritter's glower burning holes in my back. When Stemp called, "Come in", I couldn't help turning to give her a silly little finger-wave and a sugary-sweet smile before walking into Stemp's office.

He frowned. "Kelly?"

"Hi again." I swung the door shut behind me and reached automatically for my absent waist pouch. "Shit."

Stemp's frown deepened, and I gestured around the room before cupping a hand behind my ear.

His gaze sharpened and he withdrew a bug detector from his desk. At the sight of its steady green light, I let out a breath and walked over to stand in front of his desk.

"That wasn't the best interview ever," I said quietly. "I told her exactly how important you were to the program, but she took a major dislike to me so I'm not sure how valuable my reference will be."

Stemp's shoulder rose and fell in a tiny shrug. "Thank you for your recommendation, nonetheless. But why the precautions?"

"You're welcome. And the precautions are because I told a truth that isn't quite true yet. I wanted to make sure you knew about it before anybody asked you."

"A truth that isn't quite true yet." Stemp's lips quirked.

"Do tell."

"I told her you're cancelling the surveillance on my house."

He frowned. "I'm not, nor do I intend to. That surveillance is crucial."

"Actually, it hasn't been working too well, and Spider and I have a better and cheaper solution." I took his raised eyebrow as an invitation to continue, and laid out our plan in a few sentences.

By the time I finished, he was nodding. "You're right, that will be superior to the current system."

I let out a breath of relief. "Good. So plug it to your chain of command as a cost-cutting measure, or whatever makes you look good. And that'll spoil Ritter's accusations of favouritism, too."

Stemp's expression froze over. "She accused me of playing favourites?"

"Not... really..." I grimaced. "I think she was just trying to rattle my cage."

"I see." His immobility reminded me of a snake about to strike, and I hid a sudden shiver. "Perhaps..." he said in clinical tones, "Perhaps it's time to do a little cage-rattling of my own."

"Well, then, I guess I'll leave you to it," I chirped in a falsely cheerful voice. "I can find my own way out."

I scuttled for the door, abjectly grateful that I wasn't Ursula Ritter. Having Stemp as an ally was scary enough. I didn't even want to think about what he'd be like as an enemy.

"No, I'll escort you, of course," Stemp said pleasantly, and followed me out.

We strode down the hall and navigated the stairs in silence. As we emerged into the lobby Jack glanced over from the security wicket, pen in hand.

"Aydan!" she exclaimed. Her gaze darted from me to Stemp and back again. "Just the person I wanted to see! Do you want to go for an early lunch?"

Anything that kept me far away from the impending clash between Stemp and Ritter.

"Sure!" I pulled on a grin. "That sounds great!" One last glance at Stemp's composed face and cold snake eyes sent a shiver down my spine. "I'll just wait for you outside," I added, and fled for the sidewalk.

CHAPTER 37

As I shot out the front door of Sirius Dynamics a skinny hoodie-clad figure spun to hurry away across the parking lot, but not before I glimpsed a straggly beard and facial piercings.

Adrenaline exploded into my veins. My hand dove for my holster and I nearly dislocated my neck whipping my head around to be sure I wasn't in anybody's sights.

Nothing.

No bullets thudded into the building beside me. No knife-wielding thugs tried to grab me. In fact, the street was deserted except for the rapidly-receding Tyler Brock lookalike and an elderly pedestrian who was eyeing me askance while she toddled nearer.

I offered her a reassuring smile and tried to pretend I hadn't just jumped as though somebody had jammed a cattle prod up my ass. Apparently I wasn't as reassuring as I'd hoped, because she crossed the street and continued on her way, sneaking wary glances over her shoulder at me.

"All set?"

I yelped and my feet left the sidewalk entirely as I corkscrewed around to face Jack's alarmed expression.

She threw a fearful look around us, falling back a step as

her hand flew to her lips. "What's wrong?"

"Shit. Sorry. Nothing." I sagged against the handrail, trying to convince my trembling knees to hold my weight. "I just... I forgot... I went out the door without looking and there was this guy..."

My flustered babbling wasn't helping. Jack went even paler.

I sucked in a breath and let it out slowly. "Everything's fine. I'm just an idiot. Let's go get lunch."

"There was a *guy*?" she quavered. "Should I call security?"

"No!" I thudded the heel of my hand against my forehead. "No, I just meant I came out the door too fast and got startled by this guy, that's all. And then you scared me again when you came up behind me. Everything's fine."

At least I hoped it was.

"Oh." Her pallor eased. "I'm sorry, I didn't mean to startle you."

I waved away her apology and we fell into step toward the Melted Spoon.

"I guess you must be a little on edge these days," she said tentatively. "Have you found out anything more about the man who attacked you?"

"No, there hasn't been enough time, but Stemp put some analysts on it this morning."

Jack frowned. "That was last Thursday. Today is Wednesday. Why is Charles only getting around to assigning analysts now?"

"Oh." I hesitated. "I thought you meant the guy who attacked me last night."

"*What?*" Jack stopped dead in the middle of the sidewalk, staring wide-eyed. "Another man attacked you last night?"

"Shhh." I shot a worried look around us, but fortunately the only other pedestrians were a block away. "Yeah."

A sudden thought occurred to me, kicking my heart rate into overdrive all over again. If I was a target, Jack could be in danger just standing beside me. Shit, shit, shit!

I kept my tone calm as I backed away. "Jack, why don't you tell me what you want for lunch? I'll go and pick it up, and then we can eat at Sirius."

She obviously wasn't fooled. Her cheeks blanched again. "Do you think..." She cast a frightened glance around us. "...somebody might...?"

"I doubt it." I summoned my most reassuring tone. "They've been targeting me when I'm isolated. This is just a precaution. What can I get you- Aw, shit." Embarrassment heated my cheeks. "Jack, I'm sorry, we'll have to do it another time. I forgot my waist pouch today and I don't have-"

"Oh, no problem, I'll buy," Jack interrupted.

"No, that's-"

"No, really, I insist." Jack pushed a couple of bills into my hand, glancing nervously around us while she stammered out an order. She retreated hurriedly into the building, and I squared my shoulders and did my best confident stride down the sidewalk.

They wouldn't attack me in broad daylight in public.

Surely not...

When a panel van pulled to a stop at the curb beside me, I sprang to the far side of the sidewalk.

The skinny bearded driver swung out, giving me a quizzical glance from under pierced eyebrows as he strode into the building beside me, parcel under one arm and clipboard under the other.

Just a courier. Jeez, I was getting paranoid.

Easing out a shaky breath, I headed for the Melted Spoon.

Inside, the skinny bearded barista took my order, a silver ring gleaming in his nose. Two thin young men with beards and facial piercings slouched at a table in the corner, engrossed in their phones.

"Okay, now you're just messing with me," I muttered to the gods of paranoia.

The barista was familiar, but I kept a wary eye on the pair in the corner while I waited for my order. Maybe they were Brock's buddies from Blue Eddy's Friday night. They looked the same to me, but who knew? My attention had been so drawn to their piercings that I hadn't really noticed their facial features earlier. Perfect disguise, dammit.

They made no move to follow me when I left, but that didn't prevent me from hurrying along trying to watch in all directions at once.

I made it back to Sirius Dynamics unscathed, but when I stepped into the lobby with my burden of sandwiches I came face-to-face with Tyler Brock himself.

"Fuck, *really?*" I snapped before I could stop myself. I almost apologized, but gave up the effort before I began. Explaining that I'd been talking aloud to nonexistent gods probably wasn't going to make the situation any better.

"What are you doing here, Kelly?" Brock sneered.

"Stemp called me in. What are you doing here?"

"So you're buying Stemp lunch?" He twisted his face into a suggestive leer. "Isn't that... *thoughtful?*"

"Fuck off, you little prick," I growled. "It's not for

Stemp." I pushed past, accidentally-on-purpose jostling him and striding over to where Jack stood watching us anxiously.

"Let's have lunch in my office," she suggested with a glance at Brock. "Come on, I'll sign you in."

We headed for the security wicket, but Leo was already shaking his head when we arrived. "Sorry," he said with an apologetic look. "If you're suspended, only someone in your chain of command can..."

He trailed off and I followed the direction of his gaze. Stemp strode across the lobby, giving Brock a nod in passing. He took in the situation at a glance.

"Dr. Travers, you will recall that Agent Kelly is suspended," he said.

I slid between them. "She knows. But..." I lowered my voice so only he could hear. "We were going for lunch and as long as I'm a target I thought it would be safer for her if we stayed in the building."

He hesitated, and Jack spoke up.

"Director, I need to consult with Aydan on a... personal matter. If you would allow her to have lunch with me in my office, I'd be very grateful."

With her sultry voice and stunning blonde beauty, she could have infused her words with a suggestive note that would bring any man to his knees in a puddle of drool. But she didn't. She said the words with simple dignity, her chin high and her blue gaze direct.

Stemp glanced at his watch with the tight-lipped expression of a man late for a meeting. Then he met my eyes with his flat emotionless stare. "Kelly, I require your word that you won't access any data or in any way violate the conditions of your suspension."

"You have my word," I agreed. "We're just going to eat lunch."

"See that you do." His usual cool tone chilled into something considerably frostier. "I don't play favourites. If you violate your suspension both you and Dr. Travers will be disciplined."

Even though I had no intention of breaking my word, I gulped anyway. Jeez, the man could make me feel guilty even when I was completely innocent. Jack paled, too.

"Understood," I croaked.

"Very well." Stemp turned to Leo. "Sign her in on my authority. Half an hour." He turned back to me. "You're authorized to travel between here and Dr. Travers's office in the upper building only. Not her office in the secured area." His reptilian gaze slid to Jack. "Dr. Travers, Agent Kelly is not to leave your direct visual supervision at any time, for any reason. Understood?"

We both nodded silently and he turned away, striding over to collect Brock. As they moved toward the security wicket, Jack and I hurried toward the stairs.

"He certainly seems to have a bee in his bonnet today," Jack whispered.

"Yeah," I muttered. "Ursula Ritter accused him of playing favourites and giving me special treatment. And she implied that Stemp and I were..." I trailed off, not even wanting to say the words. Instead, I fisted both hands and bumped the knuckles together a couple of times.

Jack's brow furrowed. "Butting heads?"

"Screwing," I hissed.

"Ew!" Jack recoiled. Then her expression of revulsion faded into uncertainty. "I mean, not that I... Um, I mean... I have a great deal of respect for both of you, and certainly you're entitled to..." She gave me a beseeching look. "You're not, are you?"

"Hell, no!"

She let out a breath, her shoulders relaxing. "Well, that's a relief." We turned the corner into her office and she swung the door shut behind us before asking, "Do you think she'll make trouble for Charles?"

"She'd be incredibly stupid to try. He'd eat her alive." I sank into a chair with a sigh. "Unfortunately, she didn't strike me as particularly bright. But to be honest, that could just be my bad attitude. We started off on the wrong foot and things went downhill from there."

"Oh." Jack perched on the edge of her chair, frowning and toying with her sandwich wrapper. "Brock complained to Charles's chain of command that Charles is treating him unfairly." Her fingers clenched on the wrapper, crushing it into a ball. "He's such a troublemaker! Everywhere he goes, he stirs up new problems. Did you know he's bullied the social committee into letting his band play on the Sirius Dynamics float? The Ballistic Rutabagas; what kind of name is that? And have you heard their so-called songs? They're horrible. Brendan and Ivy are riding in the Little Clowns Bicycle Rally right behind our float and I don't want my children hearing that misogynistic filth!"

She took a savage bite of her sandwich.

"Mm," I mumbled around a mouthful of my own. "Can you ask him to do a clean version? Even the big-time rappers do that."

She gulped her mouthful. "I already did, but it's not just the four-letter words. It's the whole attitude. Calling women whores and bitches and promoting the rape culture as if it's cool and desirable. But he refused anyway, and spouted some... some... *crap* about artistic integrity and censorship. Artistic, my Aunt Fanny! He's a talentless little... little *turd!*" Her face flushed and red blotches marred the ivory skin of her throat. "I'm sorry for my language, Aydan, but I'm so angry right now I could just spit! And if he gets Charles fired and I lose my research budget, I'll, I'll... I don't know what I'll do!"

I eyed her worriedly. She looked more than capable of murder with her blue eyes blazing above flaming cheeks. A very small part of me hoped she'd snap and use one of the weapons from the classified lab to end Tyler Brock and all our problems with him, but this time I managed to wrestle my evil twin into submission.

"Don't do anything rash," I soothed. "Stemp can take care of himself, and he was really pissed off about that favouritism thing. I wouldn't want to be Ursula Ritter right now. It'd be safer to play Russian Roulette with a semi-auto than to get on Stemp's bad side."

Confusion crinkled her forehead, and I explained, "Russian Roulette only works with a revolver. You load a cartridge into one chamber and spin the cylinder before you put the gun to your head and pull the trigger. So there's a five-out-of-six chance that the chamber will be empty and you won't die. But a semi-automatic will always load a cartridge into the chamber, even if there's only one left in the magazine."

"Oh." Jack blinked. "So death would be certain." A smile tugged at her lips. "Russian Roulette with a semi-auto. I get it. Spy humour."

"Yeah. Not so funny when it's explained, sorry." I moved on. "Anyway, my point is, don't worry about Stemp.

We've done all we can. And I gave him a cost-cutting measure to make him look good with his chain of command, so maybe that'll help." I added, "Was that what you wanted to talk to me about?" before taking another bite of my sandwich.

"Partly." Jack chewed and swallowed. "I'm very concerned about Spider. He was despondent before, but since he's been suspended, he seems..." She made a helpless gesture. "Hopeless, I guess. I telephoned him but he just said he wasn't feeling well, thanked me for my concern, and hung up."

Guilt squeezed my heart. "I'll call him," I promised. "I don't know what I can do to help, but maybe I can go over to his place and get him to talk it out."

"That would be good," Jack agreed. "He looks up to you. And you always seem to be able to make things better."

My guts twisted with bitter irony. I could make things better for everybody but myself.

I jerked myself out of my self-pity. Stop whining. You can make things better for yourself if you just try a little harder, so suck it up.

I managed a smile. "Thanks for the vote of confidence, Jack." I popped the last bite of my sandwich into my mouth and gulped without tasting it before rising. "I'll give Spider a call right away. And don't worry, everything will work out."

Jack flushed. "Aydan, I'm ashamed of myself. I just realized I've been crying on your shoulder all this time, and you're dealing with somebody trying to kill you. I'm sorry. Do you want to talk? Is there anything I can do to help?"

"No, thanks, Jack. There's nothing you can do, and it's been good for me to think about something else for a change." I headed for the door before she could ask any more questions. "Will you escort me out?"

"Of course."

She abandoned the remains of her sandwich and stood. While we walked back to the security wicket I diverted her with questions about her kids, and when she gave me a final wave and went back to her office I breathed a sigh of relief.

Flopping into one of the reception chairs, I pulled the public phone over and dialled Spider's number. It rang four times before going to voicemail, and I left him a message to call me. Letting the receiver sag into my lap, I stared into space.

Should I drive over to his house? Maybe he was in such a funk that he wasn't answering his phone. Or what if an assassin was stalking him even now?

I hissed out a breath. If he wasn't answering his phone, he likely wouldn't answer his door, either. What was I going to do? Break in?

But maybe I should break in. Maybe his lifeblood was draining away while I stood here deliberating.

Oh, God, don't even think about that.

But if everything was fine and Linda was home sleeping off her night shift, how could I explain it when I came crashing through their door?

Inspiration finally glimmered through my fog of exhaustion, and I punched in Germain's number.

He picked up on the second ring with a cheerful, "Germain speaking."

Feeling better already, I imagined his powerful square build and keen brown eyes under crisp black curls. "Hi, Carl, it's Aydan," I began.

"Hi, Aydan. Sounds like you're in the thick of things as

usual."

I let out a breath. "You've been briefed?"

"Yes, I'm over at Webb's place now. Linda is asleep, and Webb just went to lie down, too. He's exhausted."

"Oh, thank God. I'm so glad you're there." I hesitated. "What, um... what are you going to tell Linda? To explain why you're there all the time?"

He chuckled. "She knows I don't have a place up here. The story is that Webb invited me to stay with them instead of at the hotel until I ship out on my next mission."

"Perfect." Relief eased the tension in my muscles, leaving me limp. "Thanks, Carl, and welcome back. I'll drop by and see you pretty soon."

"Great. You take care of yourself, you hear? Watch your back."

I sighed. "It's all I ever do. Talk to you later."

Sidling out the front doors, I scanned for any skinny bearded young men, but apparently I'd seen my quota for the day. No threatening figures lurked on the roofs of the surrounding buildings, and none of the pedestrians paid me any attention.

I plodded to the parking lot, then trailed to halt. My pulse accelerated to a rapid thudding.

My car was gone.

I shook my head vigorously. Take a breath. Double-check. You're tired, maybe you didn't park in the usual spot...

I scanned the rows of vehicles. No blue Legacy.

My gaze lit on the shiny black Expedition two rows over and I let out a grunt of chagrin. "Moron," I mumbled, and fished Kane's keys out of my jacket pocket.

I had almost made it to the safety of the SUV when a low venomous voice spoke from close behind me.

"You're going to pay!"

CHAPTER 38

I spun, my trank pistol already in my hand before I recognized Brock's scowling face.

He paled and took a rapid step backward.

Hoping he thought it was my Glock, I slid it into my jacket pocket in case of passersby and pointed the pocket theatrically at him. Getting any kind of decent shot off even with the Glock would have been damn near impossible, but I was hoping he didn't know that.

"What the hell is your problem?" I snapped.

His lips twisted in an ugly grimace. "You. You're my problem. Spreading lies about me."

An incredulous laugh burst from my lips. "You've got to be kidding me. *Me* spreading lies about *you*? You got that backward, you little turd-burglar."

"You must have told Stemp I was trying to kill you," he hissed. "He just finished interrogating me about my movements for the past week. You'll be sorry for that!"

He'd never know how lucky he was that my emotions were currently encased in several layers of ice. Instead of violent rage, I achieved only intense irritation.

I grabbed his scarf and twisted hard. "Bring it, dickbreath," I barked in his face. "I've had enough of your bullshit. Any time you want to dance, little man, you just name the time and place." He was making gurgling noises and clutching my wrist, so I released him with a shove that sent him staggering.

"Now get lost," I growled. "And if you threaten me again, I'll put a bullet in your brain and pretend it was an accident."

It probably wasn't the brightest thing I ever did, but I turned my back on him. I got in the SUV and drove away, leaving him practically dancing with rage in the parking lot.

When Kane's garage door rolled down behind me I drew a long breath.

Put on the game face.

I could do this.

At the back door of his house, I hesitated. Should I ring the doorbell?

No, that was silly. If we were going to get m...

Terror seized me and I breathed through it. Okay, too soon for the m-word.

If we were *together* now...

Breathe, breathe...

...then I should probably walk right in...

The door swung open and I yelped and sprang back.

Kane twitched, too. Then he smiled. "I'm sorry, I didn't mean to startle you. I thought I heard the garage door." He stepped out on the back porch and pulled me into his arms for a lingering kiss.

I managed not to tense up, and he drew me into the house with his arm around my shoulders. The door closed behind me with a quiet thump of finality, making me suck in a shaky breath.

Kane dropped another light kiss on my lips before taking my hand to tow me toward the kitchen. "You must be starving," he said. "You hardly ate anything for breakfast."

"No, I'm fine. Jack and I had an early lunch..."

In the nick of time my exhausted brain identified the aromas that filled the air. Bacon. Coffee. A caramelized-sugar scent that reminded me of...

We turned the corner into the kitchen.

Waffles. Oh, shit.

The disappointment in Kane's eyes made me hurriedly add, "...but I just sat there and watched her eat because I wasn't that hungry. But it smells so good in here, now I'm starving! Are those homemade Belgian waffles? Yum!"

His smile returned. "I have fresh strawberries and whipped cream for them in the fridge. And I'm just going to make the hollandaise sauce for our Eggs Benedict. It'll only take a few minutes, but I didn't want to start it until you got home."

"Oh, wow!" I hugged him and planted a kiss on his lips. "This is fabulous! Thank you!"

Kane squeezed me in return and I couldn't prevent a little squeak of panic, but fortunately he didn't notice. "Enjoy it while it lasts," he said with a smile. "When we're both working again I'll only have time to make brunch on weekends."

He released me and headed for the fridge, and I swallowed hard to get my voice back in working order. "Well, gee," I teased. "Brunch only on weekends? I don't know; I might have to rethink this deal. I was expecting gourmet treats for every meal."

He laughed and got busy with his saucepan and whisk.

The cozy domestic scene closed around me like a straitjacket and I backed away. "I'd better call Arnie about his new information," I croaked. "I'll just use the phone in the other room."

Without waiting for his reply, I fled to the relative freedom of the living room. Clutching the phone, I perched on the edge of the leather sofa and concentrated on my breathing.

In. Out. Slow like ocean waves.

No more eating meals whenever and however I chose. I had to consider Kane now.

The screaming started again in the back of my brain, but I banished it to silence.

Shut up. Kane was a fabulous cook and I was incredibly lucky to be with him. It was just a bit of an adjustment. I'd just have to get in the habit of checking with him before I ate.

Before I ate anything ever again...

For the rest of my life...

My pulse hammered in my temples and I fought back the incipient panic attack.

Settle down.

Breathe.

I eased out a long breath, my heart still pounding. Just get over it, for chrissake.

I wouldn't go back on my promise to Kane, and fighting constant panic attacks was stupid. It was long past time I dealt with my shit. If I wasn't doing better in a couple of days I'd talk to Dr. Rawling.

The thought of admitting my weakness to him nearly choked me with renewed panic.

I clenched my fists and breathed.

Calm down...

I took yoga breaths until I thought I could fake a normal voice, and then dialled Hellhound's cell phone.

He picked up on the second ring with a gruff, "Yeah."

"Uh... hi, Arnie. Did I catch you at a bad time?"

The gruffness vanished. "Oh, hey, darlin', how ya doin'? Nah, now's fine. I just saw Kane's number on the call display an' thought it was him."

"No..."

I tried to tell him about Kane and me but the words wouldn't come.

"I'm, um... still here," I said instead. "He wouldn't take me home last night."

"Prob'ly a good thing. Ya didn't sound so good last night. Did ya get warmed up? How ya feelin' today?"

"Fine," I said with determination, and changed the subject. "John said you called this morning?"

"Yeah, Weasel got some more details. Nothin' more on the buyer. Nobody's seen him around before so maybe he's new in town. But he was definitely talkin' to Drake Mallard last Wednesday evenin' around eight. An' word is that Mallard stiffed the guy and took off with the deposit so everybody was laughin' behind his back when he hired another guy yesterday afternoon. Guy's name was Norman Perkins. Ring a bell?"

My heart gave a thump. "Yesterday afternoon? What time?"

"Weasel didn't say exactly, just afternoon."

Around three-forty-five, maybe?

"Um, where did the transaction take place?"

"Tony's Bar. It's a dive close to downtown."

"Do they have live music there?"

Hellhound hesitated, and I imagined his frown. "Hell, darlin', I dunno. Is it important?"

I sighed. "Maybe. I'll have to check the timeframe for the first transaction before I know for sure. And Stemp gave me the ID on the dead guy this morning. Norman Perkins, ta-da. Has our guy hired anybody else?"

"Not that Weasel knew. All he heard was laughin' about how Perkins probl'y fucked off with the guy's deposit just like Mallard did."

"Oh, he fucked off all right," I said grimly. "Permanently." I shuddered involuntarily, making my voice waver on the last word.

Hellhound's voice softened. "Sounds like it was pretty bad. Wanna talk about it?"

I drew an unsteady breath. "No, I'm fine."

"Ya don't sound fine. Come on, darlin', talk to me."

The previous night already seemed fuzzy and distant, the trauma of the flashback diminished by the sheer panic I was fighting at the moment. But I couldn't say that to Arnie.

I'd be better by tomorrow. A bit more sleep, and then I'd be ready to face him.

"Aydan? Come on, darlin'," he coaxed.

Dammit, he knew I was covering up. I'd have to tell him something.

I took a deep breath. "I... It was pretty bad. He fell onto some rebar in my garage and..." I sucked in another breath. "It went right through him like a... a bug on a specimen board. I..."

I had to stop and swallow before continuing, "I had a flashback and completely lost it. Shot him with nine darts and the only reason it wasn't all ten was because I was waving the damn gun around like I was fighting off a swarm of bees. And then the aerosolized trank knocked me out."

I explored the tender spot on the back of my head with my fingertips and added, "Stemp got the autopsy report this morning. When he found out how many times I shot Perkins he just about locked me up, but I talked him out of it."

"Aw, shit, darlin'." Hellhound's soft rasp wrapped around me like a hug and I squeezed my eyes closed and huddled into its comfort. "Aydan," he said gently. "Maybe ya oughta think about goin' to the safe house for a little while. Two flashbacks in a day, that ain't good. I know you're tough as nails, darlin', but ya can't keep this up. You're gonna break if ya try."

A single despairing sob escaped me before I clamped my lips shut.

Too late for that.

Get over it.

I used my best fake-normal voice. "I'm okay, Arnie. It was a tough day yesterday, but neither of those things are likely to happen again, so there shouldn't be any more triggers for me. And..." I hesitated, not capable of lying to him but not quite able to tell the truth yet. "...John's going to stay with me tonight..."

And forever more...

I fought my way through the incipient panic attack and finished levelly, "...so that'll be just as good as going to a safe house."

Hellhound let out a breath. "I'm glad he's gonna be lookin' out for ya 'til I get there. Are ya sure you're okay?"

"Positive," I lied. I even sounded convincing.

"Good. Listen, darlin', I gotta go; I'm meetin' one a' my clients. See ya tomorrow mornin'. I'll get to your place around ten so we can be at the parade grounds by ten-thirty. Get some rest, okay? Ya still sound pretty rough."

"Thanks, Arnie, I will. See you tomorrow."

I clicked off the handset and folded over my aching chest to rest my forehead on my knees.

No-no-no-no...

"Aydan? What's wrong?" Kane's voice was quick with concern as he hurried over to crouch beside me. "Are you sick?"

I twitched and jerked upright, rearranging my face into a sheepish smile. "No, I'm fine. I guess I just dropped off for a minute. I'm still really tired."

"Oh." His worried expression eased. "Well, brunch is ready. You can go back to bed afterward if you want."

"I might just do that. But I can hardly wait to taste all the goodies you made! Mmm, it smells so fabulous in here!" I plastered an eager expression on my face. "First I have to make a quick call to Stemp, though." I grimaced. "I'm going nuts without my waist pouch. Do you have a secured phone handy?"

Kane handed me one from his pocket and withdrew to the kitchen, and I punched the speed dial reflecting that at least this part of our relationship was going to be convenient. A backup supply of secured phones, and no need to sneak away to use them.

When I reported Hellhound's new information to Stemp, he asked, "Is your source certain about the meeting times?"

I shrugged even though he couldn't see me. "That's the best information I can get."

"Hm. According to Brock, he was practicing with his band yesterday afternoon at one of the band members' homes. He says he was at home alone on Wednesday evening. The analysts are attempting to verify that by checking his cell phone records. They're also doing full background checks on all of Brock's band members and their known associates."

"So nothing conclusive one way or the other."

"Not yet," he agreed. "But unless Perkins was a band member or was visiting during the practice, it seems unlikely that what you overheard was a negotiation for a contract on your life. In any case, it shouldn't be difficult to verify. I'll notify you of any developments."

I thanked him and hung up, then padded into the kitchen.

"How was Hellhound?" Kane asked as I dug into a waffle piled high with whipped cream and strawberries. My already-full stomach whimpered a complaint but I ignored it.

"Ohmigod, this is amazing," I mumbled, and went for another big forkful while I composed my reply.

Kane was still watching me, so I gulped my mouthful and added, "He's fine. He confirmed that the Brock lookalike was negotiating with both Mallard and Perkins-"

"Perkins was the name of last night's attacker?" Kane interrupted.

"Yeah. Norman Perkins. Stemp confirmed that this morning. He's putting an analyst onto the case, and the police will still be investigating, too. And he's assigned Germain to protect Spider, just in case."

"Good." Kane hesitated. "Aydan, I'll do everything I can to protect you, too, but have you considered going to a safe house? At least until we can gather some more data?"

Slicing into the perfect Benny on my plate, I avoided his gaze. "Stemp and I talked about it this morning. I might end up doing that, but not just yet. But..." I glanced up. "Remember, you might be at risk, too. Brock was pretty pissed off at you. If he's behind all this he might decide to send an assassin your way."

"I'll deal with it if it happens." Kane shrugged easily, but his hand clenched into a momentary fist and his gaze flashed around the kitchen as if verifying its safety. He covered his reaction with a grin. "Maybe you and I should go to a safe house together. That would make it far more fun."

I managed a chuckle, and he hesitated before adding, "Did you tell Hellhound about... us?"

I busied myself with my cutlery. "No, he was in a hurry so we didn't really talk. We can tell him together when he gets here tomorrow morning."

"Aydan." Kane reached over to still the clattering of my knife and fork. When I met his gaze reluctantly, he looked into my eyes. "Are you avoiding telling him? Are you afraid he'll be upset?"

"Oh, hell, no." My smile was as genuine as I could make it. "He's been trying to push you and me together practically since the day I met him. He's always telling me what a good guy you are and how I should settle down with you. He'll be happy for us."

"Oh." Kane relaxed into a smile. "I didn't know that. He really is the best friend we could ask for, isn't he?"

I ignored the stab of pain in my gut. "Yes, he is."

Somehow I managed to stuff in a respectable amount of Kane's delicious brunch. Singing the praises of his cooking, I pled exhaustion and retreated to the bedroom, where I curled into a ball with both arms cradling my overstuffed belly.

My gastric distress held sleep at bay, and after an hour I

gave up. When I padded sock-footed back to the kitchen, it was pristine and Kane was absent. He wasn't in his office, either, and I hovered uncertainly in the hallway of the silent house.

A faint clank from the basement made my adrenal glands leap to attention, but a moment later I recognized the rhythmic sounds of weightlifting. Drawing a breath of relief, I headed for the basement stairs.

When I got downstairs and rounded the corner into the weight room, Kane jerked violently, the dumbbells in his hands crashing to the floor as he grabbed for his holster.

Adrenaline punched into my veins and I spun and slammed my back against the wall to face whatever threat he'd spotted behind me.

CHAPTER 39

A moment later Kane and I both let out a burst of shaky laughter.

"Sorry," we apologized simultaneously.

"I'm not used to having somebody else in the house," Kane said sheepishly. "I'm still a little on edge."

"It's okay," I assured him. "I get it, believe me."

"Did you get some sleep?" he asked as he retrieved the dumbbells and replaced them in the rack.

"No, I guess I ate too much." I shrugged. "And it's an unfamiliar bed. You know."

He nodded. "Would you like to go home?"

"If you wouldn't mind. I feel naked without my waist pouch."

A spark kindled in his eyes. "Naked is a good look for you."

I summoned a grin and gave him an appreciative up-and-down look. "Ditto. But don't even think about getting me naked for at least an hour or two. I'm still so stuffed that if you squeeze me I'll explode."

True in more ways than one.

He slung a towel around his neck and moved closer, studying me. His shoulders loomed over me, and I gave in to my claustrophobia with a quick sidestep into the doorway so he couldn't pin me against the wall.

"Aydan..." Kane's fingertips lifted my chin so he could look down into my eyes. "You didn't eat that much brunch. You fibbed to me, didn't you? You really did eat a full lunch with Jack."

I couldn't quite prevent my gaze from slipping sideways, and he made a sound that was half-groan, half-chuckle. "Aydan, for heaven's sake! You didn't have to hurt yourself just because I cooked for you."

"It was so good I couldn't resist," I mumbled.

"Well, next time tell me the truth. Trust me, I won't be hurt."

I was pretty sure he was fibbing a bit himself, so I reached up to kiss him. "Next time I'll call you before I eat anything."

"Deal." He dropped a kiss on the end of my nose. "Ready to go?"

"I'm not in a hurry. Finish your workout."

He put his hands on my shoulders and turned me toward the door. "I'm finished. I wasn't really working out; just killing time until you got up."

At my farm, I handed him the key and waved him toward the house with the best smile I could muster. "I guess we should've gotten a key cut for you while we were in town. Let yourself in; I just have to get my waist pouch from the garage. I'll be there in a minute."

He nodded and headed for the house, and I strode toward the garage. My steps slowed as I approached it.

At the door, my hand hovered reluctantly above the doorknob. The windows were still covered with tarps and cardboard. I couldn't see in. What if somebody was waiting for me inside?

Or what if...

The hair rose on the back of my neck, cold sweat turning my skin clammy.

What if the tortured soul of Norman Perkins still lurked inside? Some half-seen phantasmal form struggling eternally against the implacable steel, broken body arched in agony, hands clawing the air...

"Cut it out!" My voice came out thin and shrill and I backed away, panting as if I'd run a mile. I swallowed hard and pitched my voice down to a menacing growl. "Get it together, chickenshit."

Not giving myself time to think, I strode around to the nearest overhead door and punched the combination into the remote opener. Gun drawn, I spun to press my back against the outer wall as the door began to roll up.

No earthly or unearthly intruders greeted me. I ducked around the corner, snapping a glance around.

Everything was as it had been the previous night. My vehicles were all in their accustomed places. The drawer of my big floor-standing tool chest was still pulled out, awaiting the return of the screwdriver that had been cleaned and laid on the floor beside my Chevy.

I drew a deep breath and let it out slowly. Then another.

Then I holstered my gun and started removing the window coverings, averting my gaze from the rebar.

When everything was folded and stowed away, I clenched my teeth and turned slowly.

Look at it.

Just look at it.

Nothing to fear. Just ordinary reinforcing steel, waiting for a concrete pad.

When I finally managed to force my gaze toward it, the memory drove me back a couple of paces, my knees turning to jelly.

"It's just rebar," I ground out. "*My* rebar."

I stooped and picked up the screwdriver, my fingers clenching on it so tightly my knuckles glowed phosphorescent.

"*My* screwdriver." I carried it to the tool chest and pried my fingers loose with difficulty to lay it in the drawer. "*My* tools. *My* garage." My voice rose to a shout. "My *life!* My *dream,* dammit, and I'm not letting you take it!"

"Aydan?"

I wish I could say I yelped or swore, but the truth is I spun around with a scream that would have made a slasher-movie actress proud, and damn near shit my pants.

Kane slammed his back to the wall, hand on holster and head snapping around in an attempt to identify the threat.

I slumped against the fender of the Chevy, clutching my chest with one hand and flapping a feeble calm-down gesture with the other. "Sorry," I quavered. "Everything's okay. You just scared the hell out of me."

"Oh." He let out a breath and came over to hug me. Under my ear, his heart thudded almost as rapidly as mine. "I'm sorry I scared you. I was coming out to see what was taking you so long and I thought I heard yelling."

"That was just me." I grimaced up at him. "You didn't realize what a nutjob I am, did you? If you want to call it off, I'll understand."

My faint hope was dashed when he stared down at me, frowning. "Aydan, I hope you're not serious. I love you. And I understand better than anyone what you're going through right now. For better or worse; that's the deal."

I pressed my face into his chest so he couldn't see my expression, and his arms tightened around me.

I fought the panicky smothering sensation for as long as I could before pulling away. When I did, I detected that tiny flash of disappointment in his eyes again.

Shit. I should have reciprocated.

I pushed a smile onto my face. "I love you, too. And I'm in it for the long haul, just like I promised." I turned away. "There's my waist pouch." I hurried over to retrieve it and then turned back to him, trying not to look as though I was barricading myself behind my workbench.

The trapped sensation gnawed at me, and I forced another smile onto my aching face. "I'm feeling so gross, I think I need to go for a run. Why don't you make yourself comfortable in the house? Or if you've got things to do today, you can head back into town and I'll meet you later."

"No, I'll run with you. I don't want you unprotected."

"Oh." I tried not to look as though I was gritting my teeth. "Thanks."

The waist pouch vibrated in my hands and I yelped and flung it away as if it had bitten me. The instant after it left my hand I realized what had happened. Growling obscenities, I chased after it to retrieve my phone, which was fortunately still vibrating.

At the sight of Spider's home number I hurriedly pressed the Talk button. When I said hello, Linda's worried voice made my heart clutch.

"Hi, Aydan, it's Linda..."

"What's wrong?" I demanded.

"Oh..." She attempted a laugh, but it trembled into silence. "It's that obvious?"

I pushed back my fear. If it was an emergency she would have just blurted it out.

"Well, you do sound upset. What is it, Linda?" I asked in a gentler tone.

"I'm calling because..." She hesitated and lowered her voice as though afraid to be overheard. "I'm worried about Spider. He's so down, and all he can tell me is that it's a work thing. I was hoping he'd cheer up now that Carl's staying with us, but if anything he seems more worried. I can hardly believe he got suspended but he won't tell me why, and... I just... I know you can't tell me, either, but Tyler has been making it sound as though Spider got caught doing something really bad."

"Don't listen to Brock," I comforted. "He's the one who caused the problem in the first place. Spider hasn't done anything wrong and the only reason he got suspended was because he got caught in the crossfire between Brock and me."

"Oh." The word came out on a breath, and she added, "Oh, thank goodness! I just couldn't imagine him doing anything bad enough to get suspended."

"Don't worry, Linda, he hasn't done anything wrong and I'm going to figure out a way to fix things at work so this doesn't happen again."

The already-taut muscles in my neck and shoulders tightened up even more at the thought of yet another problem, and I kneaded them fruitlessly with my free hand.

"I'll come over and talk to Spider," I promised. "Is it

okay if I come in about half an hour?"

"Oh. Um, thanks, Aydan, but we have plans. We're going down to Calgary to see a sci-fi movie at the IMAX this evening. I'm hoping that will cheer him up."

"Good idea," I agreed. "What movie are you going to see? And is Carl going with you?"

"Yes, he's the one who suggested it."

I drew a silent breath of relief. Thank God for Germain. They'd be safer away from their house.

"And, um..." Linda giggled. "Actually, I don't remember the name of the movie. I'm not really into sci-fi. It's Galaxy Something... or no, um... Something-Something Universe..."

I laughed. "It's okay, Linda, I'm sure Spider will tell me all about it the next time I see him. And you're right; a new movie will definitely cheer him up. Don't worry; and tell him not to worry, either. Everything will work out."

"Thanks, Aydan. At least I know nothing really bad is happening. That helps a lot. Talk to you later!"

As I hung up the phone, Kane gave me an inquiring look.

"Linda," I explained. "She's worried about Spider." I drew a deep breath and rolled my shoulders, trying to ease the heavy weight of my promises. "Let's go for that run."

The afternoon dragged on. After our run I retreated under the hood of the Chevy, and Kane insisted on helping.

With a couple of beers and some therapeutic wrenching I finally eased into the soothing rhythm of automotive work. We lapsed into a comfortable silence broken only by the clink of wrenches, the quiet slosh-fizz of our communion with the beer bottles, and an occasional muffled expletive when one of us sacrificed some knuckle-skin to the god of backyard mechanics.

When the crunch of wheels on gravel drifted from the lane, we jerked upright and exchanged a single wide-eyed glance.

I hadn't heard an engine, and we'd closed and locked the gate.

CHAPTER 40

Hands hovering over our holsters, Kane and I sprang to press our backs against the wall next to the man-door. My heart banged hard enough to shake my entire body while the sound of crunching wheels drew closer, interspersed with muffled thumping.

"Aydan! Hello! Anybody home?"

"Shit," I growled to Kane. "It's Tom."

We let out a simultaneous breath and I shook the tension out of my hands before opening the door to emerge blinking into the sunlight. Kane stepped out behind me, and we both stopped short.

A matched pair of gigantic brown horses stood patiently side by side, swishing long white tails and occasionally shifting hooves the size of dinner plates. Behind them, an old-fashioned wagon was crisply painted in red and black and piled with bales of golden straw.

But it was Tom's sudden grab for the shotgun that made us freeze.

He didn't quite point it at Kane. But he didn't lower it, either.

"Hi, Tom," I chirped with frantic gaiety. "Wow, what a beautiful team and wagon! And are these your grandkids?"

Apparently realizing that two sets of round eyes were watching his every move from the wagon, Tom gave me a thin smile and replaced the shotgun in the bracket beside the driver's seat.

"Hi, Aydan," he said. His voice hardened. "Kane."

Kane nodded, his body tense beside me.

"Aydan, this is my son, Cory." Tom gestured to the driver beside him with visible pride. "Cory, Aydan Kelly." A younger version of Tom transferred the reins to one hand and tipped his cowboy hat with a smile. "And this is my daughter-in-law, Charlene," Tom went on, indicating the plump smiling young woman sitting on the bales. "...and my grandkids, Jackson and Emily."

"Hi!" Jackson swung tiny cowboy boots over the edge of the bales and jumped down. Straightening his small cowboy hat with dignity, he marched over and offered us each a manly handshake.

Tom swung down off the driver's seat to hover protectively behind him, casting a hard look at Kane.

Kane ignored Tom, stooping to accept Jackson's handshake with gravity. "It's a pleasure to meet you," Kane said. "I can tell you're the man of the house."

"Wight." Jackson planted his feet apart, hands on hips. "Daddy and me takes caew of Mommy and Emmy."

Kane nodded seriously and straightened, and Jackson's gaze travelled up and up to track Kane's full height and the breadth of his shoulders.

"Wow," he said. "Aw you Soopooman?"

Kane chuckled. "No, I'm not Superman."

"You Soopooman," Jackson insisted. "My jammies gots Soopooman on them and you look like Soopooman." His face split into a grin and he jumped up and down. "Yay! Soopooman! Soopooman!" Jackson seized Kane's hand and tugged. "Soopooman, say hi to Blaze and Wocket!"

Letting go of Kane's hand, he darted toward the horses and I tensed, half-reaching to restrain him.

Tom smiled. "It's all right. Those two are as gentle as lambs." He turned his smile toward the two placid horses snuffling companionably at Jackson while he leaned against their massive legs, reaching as high as he could to pat them. Their ears flicked in response to Jackson's happy cries, and they stood like statues while he wove between their hooves and under the gleaming barrels of their bellies.

Tom stepped forward to corral the boy. "Hey, Sport. Remember what we talked about. Stay where they can see you and use your quiet voice."

"Okay, Gwampa." Jackson turned a solemn face toward Kane. "Come say hi but you haffa use you quiet voice."

Kane and I exchanged a smile and he stepped forward to run his hand cautiously down one of the white-blazed faces. "Are you Blaze or Rocket?" he inquired.

An ear twitched and wise eyes regarded him while a velvety nose snuffled his hand as if searching for a treat.

"They can't talk, silly!" Jackson danced to the front of the team. "That's Blaze and this's Wocket. He's a boy and she's a girl." His lisp made 'girl' sound like 'ghoul', and Kane smiled.

Taking that as encouragement, Jackson dragged Kane back to point a tiny finger at the gigantic protuberance jutting from the horse's underbelly. "Boy hoses have pee-pees," he informed us earnestly. "Ghoul hoses don't."

I knew he was trying to say 'horse' not 'hose', but damn if 'hose' wasn't appropriate. Kane took a rapid step back as the animal unleashed a cataract of piss.

Trying to hide my amusement, I turned back to Tom. "They're beautiful. Are they Percherons?"

"Belgians." Tom patted the huge arching neck and tugged affectionately at an ear as Blaze nuzzled the front of his denim jacket. "I like the Belgian temperament. They're so quiet and good with kids."

He stooped to extract Jackson from under the horse's belly again. "Speaking of kids, it's time to get back on the wagon, Sport."

"Not yet, wanna play wif Soopooman!" Jackson seized Kane's hand again and dragged him toward the front lawn. "Let's play aiwplanes! You be Soopooman and I'll be a aiwplane!"

He flung out his arms and ran in circles around Kane, making airplane noises interspersed with jubilant cries of "Soo-poo-man!"

His parents watched the action with smiles. Emily bounced up and down on chubby legs within her mother's watchful reach, squealing and giggling while Kane spread his arms and swooped around Jackson making airplane noises of his own and grinning from ear to ear.

Tom guided me a few paces away from the wagon. "What's going on here, Aydan?" he muttered. "I thought you said you'd dumped him."

I sighed. "Long story. The short version is we've worked through our disagreements."

"Really? You don't look very happy about it."

I wasn't sure whether he was seeing what he wanted to see or if my acting skills weren't as good as I'd thought. I forced a smile. "I'm just tired. I didn't sleep well last night."

"Neither did I." Tom frowned at me. "Were you up tracking that cougar, too?"

"Uh." I blinked. "Cougar?"

"Yes, I heard it screaming down by the creek again late last night. It must have made a kill. I got up and rode my side of the creek, but I couldn't see any sign of it. Would you like me to ride your side, too?"

"Um, no, that's okay," I said hurriedly. "I'll take care of it."

God, that was all I needed, for Tom to come across my wrecked campsite and freak out because he thought some vagrant was living there.

"Okay..." Tom shot a suspicious glance at Kane and Jackson romping on the lawn. "Is he... Do you trust him around kids?"

"Absolutely," I assured him, but I didn't have much hope he'd be convinced. In his hard blue gaze I could see that the only way he'd trust Kane around his grandkids was if he had his shotgun within arm's reach.

I changed the subject. "So what brings you here this afternoon?"

"Oh." Tom reluctantly returned his attention to me. "We're just getting the wagon ready for the parade tomorrow, but since we were going by your place I thought I'd drop in and let you know about the cougar. And I wanted to tell you I saw that same bearded guy going by your place yesterday afternoon. He was driving a black half-ton this time, but as soon as he saw me he peeled out of here."

My heart kicked my ribs, and I swallowed hard. "You're sure it was him?"

"Pretty sure. I didn't get a good look at him, but I could see he had a beard and he was wearing a ball cap just like before. I left a message on your machine, but I guess you didn't get it...?" He accompanied the question with another narrow-eyed glance at Kane.

"Um, no. I forgot to check my machine. Sorry," I said absently, my mind racing. Who the hell was this guy? Perkins had been clean-shaven so it couldn't have been him.

I shook myself back to the present, realizing Tom was watching me again. "Thanks," I added belatedly. "I'll keep an eye out for him."

"Have you thought about calling the police?"

"Not yet." At his frown, I continued, "There's no law against driving on a public road. But if he keeps hanging around I might file a police report just in case."

"You should anyway-"

A whoop from the lawn made us both glance over in time to see Kane lift Jackson above his head. Jackson spread out his arms to fly in true Superman fashion while Kane jogged toward us accompanied by Jackson's squeals of "Doo doo-doo-dooooo! Soo-poo-man!"

Tom took two fast steps forward, his eyes blazing. "Put him down," he ground out.

Kane swooped Jackson down and placed him carefully on his feet before backing away. "That was fun, Jackson," he said quietly. "But it looks as though you have to go now."

"No! Gwampa, come play wif me and Soopooman!" Jackson tugged Tom's hand.

Tom gave Kane one last deadly look before scooping Jackson up to blow a fat raspberry on his belly. "Sorry, Sport, it's time to go." He carried the boy over and lifted him onto the wagon before swinging up onto the seat beside Cory.

"See you later, Aydan," he said with a courteous tip of his

hat, but his gaze was locked on Kane and his hand touched the shotgun meaningfully.

"Uh, yeah... Thanks for letting me know about, um..." I let the sentence trail off and waved instead. "Nice to meet you, Cory and Charlene." Jackson jumped up and down in the wagon, and I added, "And Jackson and Emily."

"Bye-bye," Jackson called, waving vigorously while the wagon followed my turnaround circle and headed out the lane. "Bye-bye, Soopooman!"

"Goodbye, Jackson," Kane called back. The smile lingered on his lips while he watched the wagon turn onto the road and disappear behind the trees. "He's quite the little man, isn't he?" he added.

"Yeah. But I don't think you'd better play with him again."

Kane sighed. "I know. But I don't blame Rossburn for being twitchy with that shotgun. If those were my kids I'd do the same."

The sudden recollection of Kane's desire to have a family paralyzed me where I stood.

Oh God. What if he wanted to adopt? I couldn't deal with the demands and responsibilities of young children.

"Aydan?" Kane took hold of my shoulders, staring worriedly down into my face. "What's wrong? Are you sick?"

His grip nearly sent me over the edge. Panic spiked into my veins and it took every ounce of my willpower not to claw his hands and run screaming.

"Aydan? What's wrong? Are you having pain anywhere? Talk to me!"

"I'm fine," I gasped. "Just a panic attack."

"Oh." He face softened and he pulled me into a hug.

"It's okay, you're safe. You can get through it. Just breathe with me. Nice and slow."

I wrenched free and backed away panting and trembling. Hurt flashed across his face and my guts twisted.

"Sorry." I gasped. "Just... couldn't get my breath... that way."

"Oh. I'm sorry, I didn't realize." He approached me slowly. "Would you like me to hold your hand or rub your back?"

If he held me in any way I'd lose it completely.

"Rub my back," I croaked. "Please."

"Of course." He stepped behind me and his broad palm made slow warm circles on my back. "Just breathe. It'll pass soon."

I nodded and concentrated on slowing my breath.

Settle down, stupid. You can do this.

I breathed.

Of course I could do this. I'd be fine. I just needed to get used to the idea of kids...

My pulse red-lined all over again and I diverted my thoughts. He wouldn't expect everything right away. Just settle down. Lots of time to talk it over, and he wouldn't force me into anything.

He wouldn't.

He was still rubbing my back gently, murmuring reassurances.

No, he wouldn't force me. He'd manipulate me.

"Stop it!" I barked aloud, and Kane started and snatched his hand away from my back.

That was enough to break the terrifying spiral of my thoughts. A high-pitched giggle escaped me and I turned to face his worried expression.

"Sorry, not you. I was talking to myself again."

"Oh." He relaxed into a smile. "That's going to take some getting-used-to."

"I'm sorry, I'm not usually so messed up. I just..."

"It's all right," he interrupted. "I understand. After what you've been through in the past week, I'd be more worried if it was business as usual."

I managed a weak chuckle. "Yeah, I guess."

"Are you feeling better now?"

"I'm fine," I lied.

CHAPTER 41

Kane frowned down at me, but fortunately he didn't argue. "What was Rossburn talking about, 'letting you know'?" he asked instead.

"Oh. Um, I guess he heard me screaming last night and thought it was a cougar, so he was warning me about that. And he saw the guy who's been spying on me. Looks as though he's snooping around again, but in a black half-ton instead of a silver crossover."

"What guy who's been spying on you?" Kane snapped. His hand hovered over his holster and he glared around us as if challenging an invisible opponent.

"Oh." I gulped. "I guess I didn't tell you about that part."

Kane drew a deep breath. "Get in the house," he said tightly, and practically glued himself to my back to cover us for the short walk.

Inside, he guided me into a kitchen chair with firm hands before lowering the blinds. That accomplished, he pulled up the chair across from me and pinned me with a hard gaze.

"Now," he said. "Tell me *everything*."

"Sorry." I drew a few circles on the tabletop with my

fingertip. "That's all there is. I just forgot to mention that part."

"Start at the very beginning and tell me everything," Kane repeated with exaggerated patience.

I blew out a breath and complied.

"...so that's it," I finished. "Except I need to go and get my sleeping bag and stuff out of the woods in case Tom decides to do the good-neighbour thing and ride my side of the creek looking for the non-existent cougar. Plus my sleeping bag will be wrecked if I don't get it dried out."

"I'll get it. You stay in the house." Kane rose. "What's Rossburn got against cougars, anyway? What's with these rednecks who want to shoot anything that moves?"

"He has livestock to protect," I snapped. "And young grandchildren that look like yummy snacks to a cougar. And I'm not staying in the house."

"Aydan..." Kane began with exasperation.

"I'm safer in the woods," I interrupted. "In case you've already forgotten the part about Mallard and his shotgun coming through my door."

"No, I haven't forgotten, I'm just looking for the most defensible position-"

"I have to get *out!*" My raised voice startled both of us.

Kane's surprised expression softened into understanding. "All right. Let's go and get your gear. Then we're going back to my place."

"I don't want to-"

"No arguments," he interrupted. "I'm protecting you and that's the best way to do it."

Too exhausted to fight about it, I followed him out the door.

A few minutes later Kane ushered me to his SUV, soggy

sleeping bag in hand, but I balked at the passenger door.

"I need my car."

"They know your vehicle," Kane demurred. "And anyway, I know you don't drive if you've had a drink. We'll take the Expedition."

Desperation flared. "It was only a couple of beers, and it was over an hour ago. We need two vehicles. I'm not going to be completely at your mercy."

Kane frowned. "At my mercy? You make it sound as though I'm abducting you. I'm trying to protect you."

Mentally cursing my slip of the tongue, I tried again. "I know; I just meant it's not safe for us to only have one vehicle. We might need to go to separate places at the same time. We can't be together twenty-four-seven."

"Of course we can. Now, please, get in the vehicle. It's not safe standing out here where anybody can take a shot."

I knew it was irrational, but the claustrophobic terror rose again and I backed away. "Either I take my car or I stay here."

"Aydan, for heaven's sake, be reasonable!"

There was that word again.

"No." My pulse thundered in my ears and I kept backing away. One step. Then another.

"What?" Water squished from my sleeping bag as Kane's fist clenched on it.

"No. I said no." My voice quavered on the last word as my back bumped against the garage.

"Aydan, calm down." Kane's voice slowed and deepened to his 'everybody-stay-calm' cop voice. "Just take a breath."

"I'm calm." My back pressed against the garage wall so hard my vertebrae protested the painful ridges of the vinyl siding.

"All right, that's good," Kane agreed soothingly. "Take your car if you feel that strongly about it. I didn't mean to second-guess you; I was just surprised that you'd drive after drinking all that beer."

I breathed, fighting my way back to rationality.

What if I had an accident and someone was injured or killed? I couldn't live with that guilt.

And anyway, this was all in my mind. I could get over it.

No-no-no-no...

I shook the screamer out of my head with determination and pried myself away from the garage. Forcing myself to walk over to Kane, I reached up to give him a kiss. "I'm sorry. You're right, it would be stupid for me to drive. Thanks for pointing that out."

He reached as if to hug me, but stopped himself as though remembering my last freak-out. Instead, he smiled and squeezed my hand. "You're welcome. Ready to go?"

I hid my need to hyperventilate with a smile. "Sure."

Inside Kane's house, I couldn't settle. The walls seemed to close in, and the evening limped along while we circled each other and made stilted conversation.

At last I faked a yawn, the tense muscles in my jaw crackling. "Well, I'm beat. I'm going to bed."

Kane smiled, his voice warming and deepening. "That's a good idea."

Claustrophobia seized me again but I hid it in a fake smile and a sultry tone. "Remember, I get to ride on top this time."

"Hmm." Kane paced toward me, grinning. "I like

assertive women."

"That's good," I purred as I forced myself not to back away. "Then it's time for you to take those clothes off."

Later, lying wide-eyed in the darkness, I held back the need to pull away from the loose clasp of his arms and tried to let his slow deep breathing soothe me.

I was okay. I'd get used to this. It would get better.

I didn't sleep.

As dawn lightened the room, Kane stirred at last. I lay still, keeping my breathing slow and deep until the door closed behind him.

Then I turned my face into the pillow, but my heart hammered with the need to escape and sleep wouldn't come. Finally at nine o'clock I dragged my aching body out of bed and staggered to the bathroom.

A few seconds after I'd flushed the toilet, a tap at the door made me twitch.

"Good morning," Kane called. "What would you like for breakfast?"

My stomach rolled at the thought of more rich food. "Uh, just toast and peanut butter, thanks."

"I could make you a proper breakfast."

Today I'd do better. Today I'd make him feel as appreciated as he deserved to be.

I opened the door and reached up to kiss him. "Good morning! And thanks, but toast and peanut butter is a proper breakfast."

He grinned and eyed my tousled hair and nakedness. "You look like a proper breakfast. One I could eat every morning."

"Mmm," I purred. "Promises, promises."

His grin widened. "Did I mention I always keep my promises?" He linked his hands under my hips and boosted me up to sit on the vanity before slowly kissing his way down my body.

Some time later, Kane reached past me to turn off the shower. Clinging to him to prevent my rubber legs from dropping me to the shower floor, I breathed slowly in the steamy air. Sometime in the past fifteen minutes, squashed between his hot hard body and the cold tile wall, I had passed beyond panic to exhausted numbness.

"Now that's a *good* morning," Kane growled into the hollow of my neck before helping me out of the shower stall.

I slumped onto the toilet seat and sat staring blankly while he disposed of the condom and then wiped the condensation off the mirror, twisting to inspect the fresh scratches on his back.

He chuckled. "Good grief. Maybe I should wear my bike jacket next time."

My face smiled without me and my voice came out low and sexy. "Mmm, I love a man in leather." I straightened as realization struck. "Oh, shit, I forgot to tell Arnie I'm here. He's going to be at my place at ten o'clock."

Kane smiled, but uncertainty lurked in his eyes. "I'm not sure if I like the way you made that connection."

Laughter rolled out of me, deep and convincing and utterly fake. "Don't worry. I'm with you now. I told Arnie quite a while ago that if I made a commitment to you, it would be exclusive and permanent."

His smile widened. "I like the sound of that."

"Well, then, I'll just have to keep saying it." I dragged myself upright. "Could you call him, please? I'm going to dry my hair, and then I need to go and find some clothes."

He nodded and kissed me lingeringly before he withdrew, and I turned to face my reflection in the mirror, trying not to look it in the eye. With my hair more or less dried, I tottered back to the bedroom and managed to haul myself into my clothes. I emerged dressed just as the doorbell rang.

Thank God I couldn't feel a thing. Now I just had to get through telling Arnie that the 'benefits' part of our friendship was over.

The rumble of male voices drifted down the hall and I squared my shoulders and padded toward them, rounding the corner into the living room.

Hellhound's face lit up at the sight of me but as I neared him his smile fled, leaving worry in its place.

"Jesus, Aydan," he rasped. "What the hell's wrong?"

CHAPTER 42

"Nothing's wrong." I gave Hellhound my most convincing smile.

He frowned. "Bullshit."

"No, really. I'm just a bit tired, that's all."

Hellhound gave me a worried look before turning to Kane. "Cap? What's goin' on?"

"Nothing." Kane slipped an arm around me. "Everything's fine. Great, in fact."

Hellhound cast a suspicious glance around the room before pantomiming 'are we bugged?' with a hand to his ear and a sweeping gesture.

"No, we're not bugged." Kane frowned at him. "Everything's fine."

"Fuck, Cap, everythin' sure as hell ain't fine." Hellhound gestured toward my face. "Look at her. I ain't seen eyes like that since that hellhole prison camp... in..." His words trailed off, his gaze flicking to Kane's arm around me. "Aydan?" he asked softly. "What happened, darlin'?"

My face smiled easily and my words came out warm and happy. "You'll be glad to know I finally brained up and took your advice." I turned my smile up to Kane. "John and I are together now. Permanently." I didn't even choke on the last word. If I'd been capable of feeling anything, I would have been proud of myself.

Kane smiled down at me and dropped a kiss on my lips before turning to Hellhound, his arm tightening around me. "Thank you," he said. "Aydan told me how you've been helping her get over her fear."

"Aw, fuck," Hellhound whispered. Stepping closer, he cupped my chin with a feather-light touch and gazed down into my eyes.

I gave him my best smile and he recoiled.

His hands dropped away, clenching into fists by his sides as he glared at Kane. "What the hell did ya do to her?" he ground out.

Kane stiffened. "What are you implying?"

"I ain't *implyin'*," Hellhound growled. "I'm sayin' flat out." He turned back to me and his voice softened. "Darlin', what happened?"

Anxiety crept through my protective layer of numbness. Oh God, he wasn't going to cause problems, was he?

"I took your advice." I tried to keep the plaintive note out of my voice, but I didn't quite succeed. "This is what you wanted. This is what he wanted."

"An' what d'*you* want, Aydan?" His voice was dangerously quiet.

I avoided the question. "Arnie, I'm with John now. I told you; when that happened, nothing you could say or do would change it. Please, just be happy for us."

Kane's arm tightened around me. "Look, Arnie, we've been friends... *family*... for decades. Don't spoil it with jealousy."

"Jealousy?" Hellhound scowled. "I ain't fuckin' jealous.

I'm sayin' ya mind-fucked her. Now tell me, *what the hell did ya do?*"

"It looks like jealousy to me," Kane said coldly. "You can't commit to anyone, you endanger Aydan's health by screwing around on her whenever you get the chance, but yet you're begrudging me happiness with her. Why? Because I've stolen one of your harem?"

Hellhound flushed, his eyes narrowing. "I ain't ever endangered her health. I always use protection. *Always*. An' look who's talkin', ya fuckin' hypocrite. I ain't been with anybody but Aydan since last fall. How many has it been for you?"

Oh, no. This can't be happening.

Kane didn't reply, and Hellhound went on, "Yeah, ya don't wanna answer that, do ya? 'Cause I know for sure you've had at least two; prob'ly more. An' I bet ya weren't too fuckin' careful with the condoms, were ya?"

It was Kane's turn to redden. "I was undercover. I didn't always have a choice. And I got tested right after-"

"Oh, that's fuckin' great! Don't gimme your fuckin' bullshit excuses-"

"Guys," I interrupted. "Please don't do this."

"I'm not making excuses," Kane snapped. "I had to do my duty whether I liked it or not, but that's over now. And you can just be happy for me and my fiancée." His arm jerked tighter around me and a squeak slipped from my lips before I could prevent it.

Hellhound's eyes blazed. "'Your fiancée'. So she ain't even got a name anymore. She's just your fuckin' property now, is that it? Let her go!"

Kane flung his arm open. "There. I let her go. Do you see her running? Are you happy now?"

"No, I *ain't* fuckin' happy-"

I drew a breath, my pulse kicking higher at the sight of Hellhound's glare even though it wasn't directed at me.

"Arnie, don't," I pleaded. "Please, just-"

"You see?" Kane demanded. "You always say Aydan won't lie to you. So ask her. Ask her what she wants."

Hellhound gave me a long look, his hand rising as if to touch my cheek before dropping to his side. "Aydan ain't in there anymore," he said quietly. "Look in her eyes. All that's left is somethin' that looks like her. She'll say whatever ya wanna hear."

"That's ridiculous-" Kane began.

"Oh, yeah?" Hellhound interrupted. "I don't fuckin' think so. I think ya broke her. I think ya saw your chance an' ya took it."

I tried again. "Arnie, please, let it go."

"When was it, darlin'?" he asked gently. "I'm guessin' two nights ago, right? When ya said he wouldn't take ya home."

I swallowed hard. He'd see through any lie I told, but I had to protect Kane's feelings...

Kane barked, "You're crossing the line, Helmand."

"Don't gimme that fuckin' bullshit!" Hellhound's fists bunched, the last trace of his usual easygoing humour vanishing in a menacing scowl. "You're the one that's 'way fuckin' outta line here!"

I had never seen him truly angry before. I fell back an involuntary step.

Only an inch shorter than Kane, he made up the difference in bulk and bulging muscle. His bearded battle-scarred face and tattoos made him intimidating at the best of times, but with the habitual twinkle gone from his eyes he looked exactly like what he was: six feet three inches of stone-cold killer.

"Lemme guess how it went down," he grated. "Ya found her out in the woods soakin' wet an' half dead from hypothermia so ya brought her back here. Ya knew she'd had the day from hell. Fightin' flashbacks, pukin' her guts out-"

"What? No, I didn't know about any of that," Kane protested, throwing a frown in my direction.

"Did ya ask?" Hellhound barked. "No, ya fuckin' didn't, did ya?"

Kane tried to speak but Hellhound talked over him. "So ya dragged her back here knowin' she was completely fucked up. Did ya at least let her warm up before ya made your move? Give her somethin' to eat?"

"Of course I put her in a hot shower. And I made her a hot chocolate but she didn't drink it." Kane gave me another look.

"Arnie, please let it go," I begged. "I've made my promise to John and nothing's going to change that."

"Your promise doesn't count if it was coerced, darlin'," Hellhound rasped.

"For God's sake, I didn't coerce her!" Kane shouted. "Goddammit, what is your-"

Hellhound ignored him and went on relentlessly, "An' why didn't she drink the hot chocolate? 'Cause she was tryin' to get ya to take her home, wasn't she? An' ya wouldn't."

They were glaring at each other from close range now, fists clenched and faces reddening.

The last of my ability to care slipped away.

They'd work it out.

Or they wouldn't.

I couldn't change it, and if I stayed I'd only make things worse. I sidestepped toward the back door.

"So she asked ya to take her home," Hellhound ground out. "An' ya said no. So she was trapped. An' then what? Did ya at least give her a hug?"

"Of course I..." Kane trailed off as if remembering he hadn't.

"Oh, that's nice! That's real fuckin' nice!"

I was almost at the door.

"An' I bet she asked ya for comfort, didn't she? Just a bit a' comfort in bed after a fuckin' hellish day. An' I bet ya wouldn't give it to her." Hellhound's tone changed to a mocking imitation of Kane. "'No, Aydan, I'm such a sorry bastard I can't think 'cept with my fuckin' dick so I ain't gonna give ya even a fuckin' *speck* a' comfort unless ya gimme your whole fuckin' *life* in return...' Didn't ya?" His voice rose to a full-throated bellow. "*Didn't ya?* Ya froze her, kidnapped her, starved her, mind-fucked her; did ya fuckin' waterboard her, too, just to make sure she'd break? Ya fuckin' asshole!"

Kane's fisted knuckles turned white. "*Goddammit!* You have no right..."

I scooped up my jacket and shoes and slipped out the door, closing it quietly behind me. As I stooped to tie the laces I could hear their voices booming through the wall, louder and louder as if to vanquish each other through volume alone.

Please don't let them hurt each other.

Blinking at the tears that blurred my eyes, I stumbled down the steps and slipped out the back gate. With no clear idea of where I was going, I started to walk.

"Arlene?"

Adrenaline punched into my veins at the sound of my alias and I snapped my head up, my hand going for my waist holster before I identified the speaker stumbling up the back alley.

Eleanor Parr.

She was a mess. Thin and haggard, her eyes were desperate under unkempt blonde hair. Her expensive clothes were rumpled and the cool composure I remembered was long gone.

"Wha...?" I began.

A sharp hot crackle burned the middle of my back and everything tumbled into chaos.

CHAPTER 43

Through the jumble of misfiring nerves I vaguely registered a hard impact on my side before everything went dark with a thump.

Trunk.

They'd shut me in the trunk of a car.

A male voice growled, "Do it or else."

The only response was a whimper from Eleanor Parr before the suspension dipped as though someone had gotten into the driver's seat. A moment later the engine fired up and we were moving.

Every nerve zapped and fizzed, my body twitching and shivering uncontrollably. My heart hammered and my breath came in sobbing gasps, whether from the effect of the Taser or my own terror, I couldn't tell.

We rounded several corners and my body flopped helplessly with the motion of the car. The too-familiar bite of nylon ties told me my hands were bound behind my back. My twitching diaphragm strangled my screams to breathy whimpers.

Maybe there was an emergency trunk release. But folded into the confines of the trunk with my hands tied and my muscles alternating between uselessly limp and spasming in painful jerks, I couldn't find it.

We made one last turn before the car accelerated smoothly.

On the highway. But headed where?

Panic clawed my chest. Were Kane and Hellhound still fighting? Had they even noticed me leaving?

But even if they had, they'd have seen me walking away alone. They'd assume I'd gone off in a huff. They likely wouldn't come after me; they'd just wait for me to cool down and come back.

And worse, my waist pouch was still in Kane's house. No knife to free myself even if I could have controlled my muscles enough to wield it.

Shallow hysterical panting seized me and I fought my bonds with what little muscle control I could summon.

Flopping and twitching uselessly, I realized the trank pistol was gone from my waist holster. They must have seen my aborted grab for it and disarmed me before they put me in the trunk. I'd missed that part while my brain was short-circuiting.

And now they had a classified weapon.

I groaned aloud. If I somehow managed to survive this, Stemp was going to have my hide.

The car slowed, then turned. The crunch of gravel under the tires told me we'd left the highway. That probably meant we'd be arriving at our destination soon.

I forced down panic.

Think.

We hadn't been on the highway for more than ten or fifteen minutes. I had no idea which direction we'd been travelling, but it couldn't have been much farther than the drive to my farm. So where were they taking me?

And what was the 'it' that Eleanor Parr was supposed to do?

My muscles were finally coming back under my control, and I clamped down on my panting and forced myself to draw a slow deep breath. Then another.

Stay calm. Figure it out.

What did Eleanor have to do with this? If not for the man threatening her I would have assumed she was part of the plot, but it seemed she was a victim. So who would force an influential woman like Eleanor Parr to do their bidding? And how?

And how the hell did they find me at Kane's house?

My breathing accelerated again as a terrifying thought occurred. Oh, God. Brock knew Kane and I were together. He'd seen us leaving the office, and the next day he'd seen me driving Kane's SUV.

And worse, my abductor had used a Taser instead of killing me outright. That meant they wanted something from me before I died.

Oh, God, no.

Brock had sold me out to Fuzzy Bunny. They'd torture me until I gave up everything. And nobody was coming to save me.

The car slowed and jounced over several large bumps.

With all my will I fought the debilitating fear.

Think.

My legs finally cooperated enough to move with some degree of control. Not bound. Thank God. I could kick, and run. Maybe. If the nerves weren't too scrambled to relay instructions from my brain, and if the muscles weren't too fatigued after their violent spasms.

I eased my leg up and down. Come on, you can do it...

My heart leaped as my shoe caught on a hard object strapped to my ankle. Unbelievable. They hadn't taken my Glock. They must have assumed the trank pistol was my only weapon.

Some more squirming made my momentary elation fade. Despite contortions that made my muscles scream, I couldn't reach my gun. I was wedged too tightly in the trunk.

Fighting residual spasms, I twisted and thrashed, the ties cutting into my wrists. Had to get... that... gun...

My breath came in hard gasps and sweat poured off me, stinging my eyes and burning the abraded skin on my wrists.

The car stopped.

The doors opened and thumped closed. A moment later a heavy pounding above my head made me flinch.

"Hey in there!" The man's voice again. "I've got a gun. Make one wrong move when I open the trunk, and you're dead. Got it?"

My frantic efforts to retrieve my Glock changed to frantic efforts to work my pant leg down over top of it again. If they found it, I was doomed.

If I could have gotten my legs under me I might have been able to launch myself at him when the trunk opened, but my back was to the opening. And my movements were still uncoordinated...

The trunk latch popped, and in a last-minute decision I lay motionless and silent.

Well, almost motionless. A spasm rippled down my leg and another twitched my hand.

"Still out of it," the man grunted. "Fine."

Nothing happened.

What the hell? I hadn't heard him walk away. Surely I

should have heard footsteps, or at least the rustle of cloth. I strained my ears, but couldn't hear any movement. A whiff of Eleanor's perfume wafted on the breeze, but if she was there she didn't say anything.

If they weren't concerned about being spotted with an unconscious woman in their trunk, where the hell were we?

"Maybe she's dead." Eleanor spoke at last. "If you've killed her..."

"She's not dead, Blondie. I can see her breathing."

Damn, they couldn't be more than a few feet away. Just standing there watching me in silence. That was almost creepier than being shut in the trunk.

I forced myself to lie still, fighting to keep my breathing slow and even. Stall, stall...

I heard a small clink followed by something dragging across cloth. Like the sound of...

Oh, shit.

A belt being removed.

The man spoke. "Hit her."

A sharp blow across my ass wrenched a cry of shock and pain out of me. The memory of a whip slashing red-hot paths across my skin sent helpless shudders through my body.

"Awright, Red, I know you're awake. Get up, or Blondie here'll tan your hide."

I squeezed my eyes shut in a futile attempt to make it all go away. My breath came in jerky gasps while I fought the panic.

Should I play dead a little longer?

But he knew I was conscious. I'd have to move sooner or later, and choosing 'later' would only net me a beating.

I groaned and lurched awkwardly onto my knees, my head hanging to avoid the trunk lid. Let them think I was still completely out of it.

Peering through the curtain of my hair, I took stock. Now I knew why they weren't worried about getting caught. I recognized the abandoned Wright farmyard from the time I'd brought a spy here to coerce information from him.

Back then I'd chosen this place because there was nothing around for miles, and the tumbledown house hid us from the road even on the off-chance that someone drove by on the way to nowhere.

Karma's such a heartless bitch.

I groaned again.

"Get out." The man's voice jerked my attention back to him.

Head still hanging, I memorized his features. No idea who he was. And I'd definitely recognize that bulbous nose if I'd ever seen him before. Christ, the thing looked like a potato in the middle of his face. Beside him, Eleanor Parr still clutched his belt, her face almost as white as her knuckles.

"Now, bitch! Move it!" Potato-nose jerked his chin from Eleanor to me. "Hit her again."

I hunched my shoulders against the blow. "Gettin' out," I mumbled, my mouth not quite cooperating. "Jus' gimme a minnit."

Shit, if I squirmed around and stuck my legs over the edge of the trunk to slide out, they'd see my Glock for sure when my pant leg rode up.

Kneeling like this, I could reach it. But I couldn't shoot them with my hands tied behind my back. I'd probably end up shooting myself in the ass.

"Hit her."

I did the only thing I could think of. Tucking my head under, I toppled forward out of the trunk, twisting as I fell.

The impact slammed the breath out of me. The long dead grass prickled my cheek, and when I managed to get my lungs working the winter's accumulation of dust and mildew made me cough and sneeze.

But I had succeeded. I'd landed on my side with my legs bent away from my captors. Please let my pant leg conceal my gun...

"On your feet, Red. Let's go for a walk."

I drew in another breath and went into a paroxysm of coughing that left my eyes and nose streaming. Tears and snot trickled down but with my hands tied behind my back I couldn't even twist my face around to wipe it on my shoulder.

"Get her up, Blondie." Potato-nose let out an evil chuckle. "Or hell, pull her pants down and give her a good spanking with that belt. I like me a little girl-on-girl action."

"You're disgusting." Eleanor's cultured voice trembled, whether with fear or revulsion, I couldn't tell. "You can carry her in. You're certainly being paid well enough to do a little manual labour."

He guffawed. "Blondie, the only manual labour I'm gonna do is jacking off while you get it on with Red here. She can walk on her own. She's too damn heavy to carry. Besides, when they find her body the only DNA evidence they're gonna find on it is yours." He raised his voice. "Hey, lardass, move it! You ever think about going on a diet?"

"Fuck you. It's muscle," I mumbled through the snot and residual Taser reaction.

"Hit her."

"No." Eleanor's voice was faint but defiant.

"What was that, Blondie?" His voice turned ugly. "Did I hear you say 'go ahead and blow my kid into a million pieces'?"

"*No!*" Her shriek of sheer terror froze my blood. "No-don't-I'll-do-anything-you-say-*please!*"

His chuckle turned my stomach. "That's better. Now hit her. And make it a good one."

The belt whistled and cracked across my hip and I didn't even try to suppress my cry of pain and fear. If I made it look good, maybe she wouldn't hit me so hard next time.

"Now get moving, Red, or I'm gonna make Blondie here get real funky with you." The revolting chuckle came again. "'Course maybe you'd like that."

I almost told him to fuck himself again, but managed to keep my mouth shut. Instead I squirmed to draw my knees under me, then lurched precariously to my feet.

"Bring her." Potato-nose jabbed a finger at the caved-in porch of the house, and Eleanor took my arm.

Up close she looked even worse, her pallor accentuated by dark circles under her eyes and her formerly-manicured nails bitten down to nothing.

My grand plans to kick and run were completely unattainable. It was all I could do to stay upright.

We navigated erratically toward the house, staggering and stumbling while my still-uncooperative legs negotiated the uneven ground. Eleanor clung to my arm with skeletal white fingers, and I wasn't sure which of us was holding the other up.

Inside the dubious shelter of the porch, Potato-nose gave me a shove that sent me sprawling across torn linoleum, shards of broken glass, and other things I preferred not to identify.

"Tie her legs." He tossed a nylon tie on the floor and Eleanor picked it up from the filth with the tips of two fingers before advancing on me, white-faced.

My heart lurched. If she tied my ankles she'd find my gun.

As she crouched and reached for my ankle I kicked. My foot thudded into her arm and she cried out and toppled to the floor, whimpering.

"Hit her."

As Eleanor staggered to her feet I met her eyes, pushing a psychic message at her with every fibre of my being.

Don't tell him about my gun...

Apparently she got 'psychic' and 'psycho' mixed up. Her face contorted, her eyes blazing.

"I *hate* you, you *bitch!*" she hissed, and laid into me with the belt.

The blows fell thick and fast. I tried to spin and kick, to catch the belt with my legs and yank it away from her, but she gripped it with both hands and slashed at me again and again with berserk strength.

Nowhere to go. Couldn't even protect my head and face with my hands tied. Panting and wheezing, my heart slamming against my ribs, I kicked and flailed frantically.

At last I got a solid hit on her knee and she crashed to the floor with a scream.

Potato-nose chuckled. "Awright. Playtime's over, girls."

The sizzle and burn of the Taser reduced me to scrambled brains and twitching muscles.

CHAPTER 44

When I recovered enough to comprehend my surroundings again, my ankles were tightly bound and my Glock was gone. Eleanor Parr crouched in one corner of the dilapidated room, looking barely human with filthy clothes and dishevelled hair and savage hatred gleaming in her eyes.

Potato-nose lounged in the opposite corner, idly turning my trank pistol around and around its trigger guard. "Hey, Red," he said. "You ready to talk now?"

I spared a moment of thankfulness for the aftereffects of the Taser. He couldn't know that my violent shivering and tears were sheer terror, not electrical overload.

I said nothing, mainly because I wasn't capable of speaking.

Potato-nose gave an exaggerated yawn. "This is boring as shit. I should just kill her now."

"Don't you dare!" Eleanor's voice was a venomous hiss. "I paid you well for this. You'll leave her alive until I have my answers or you'll never get another dime out of me."

Wait, what? *She* paid *him*?

My still-foggy mind attempted gymnastics far beyond its current ability and I groaned.

He glared at Eleanor. "Hey, Blondie, if you get snotty

with me I'll blow up your kid." He extracted what looked like a television remote from his jacket pocket and hovered a finger threateningly over one of the buttons.

"NO!" Eleanor rocketed to her feet. "I told you, I'll do anything you want, but I want my answers first!" Tears tracked through the grime on her cheeks. "I need my answers! That was our deal! That's what I *paid* you for!"

Potato-nose snorted. "Honey, I don't think you're getting the picture here. I've got a gun. Hell, two guns." He laid down my trank pistol and drew a Glock from behind his back.

Not mine. Too big. So where was mine?

"And I've got your kid," he went on. He gestured with the remote. "You rich bitches are all alike, you think the whole world should lick your fancy shoes just because you throw some money around. Well, I got news for you, Blondie. I *own* you now." His gaze travelled over her from top to toe. "Hell, maybe I should take you for a little test-drive. Like a new car. Make sure the ride's good." His face twisted in a leer.

Eleanor went stock-still, her face blanching to bone. After a moment her mouth opened, looking horribly like a reanimated corpse. "I told you," she said in a bloodless voice. "I'll do anything you want. But I'll have my answers first."

"Well, hell, Blondie, if it means that much to you." Potato-nose made a magnanimous gesture with the Glock before pointing it at me and miming pulling the trigger. "Shoot."

Eleanor advanced on me, her eyes glittering in the half-light. "You're Arlene Widdenback," she said. "The arms dealer."

It wasn't a question. And it was safer than admitting my real name.

I nodded.

"Bitch!" she hissed, and her foot flashed out.

I reared back, but apparently she wasn't trying to kick me. Her foot scuffed the dirty floor, sending a shower of filth and broken glass into my face.

I jerked my chin to my chest, squeezing my eyes shut. Something stung my cheek, followed by the warm tickle of blood.

"Why did you frame my husband?"

The question was so unexpected that my eyes popped open to goggle up at her. "I didn't."

"Do you know what you took from me?" she snarled. "My husband. My friends. My good name. My *life*!" Her voice rose to a shriek. "*My son thinks his father was a criminal! Don't you lie to me, you bitch!*"

This time she did kick me, but she wasn't very strong and I rolled with the blow as best I could. Still, it was enough to make me curl up and suck air.

"Not... lying," I gasped, flinching away from the belt that was already whistling down. It cracked across my thigh and suddenly I was furious.

I couldn't prevent my cry of pain, but before she could hit me again I yelled, "Fuck off with the belt! Why would I lie to you?"

"To stay out of prison," she snapped.

I surprised myself with a bark of laughter. "That's really not a big worry for me right now, is it? I don't see any cops around here."

"Oh..." The belt wavered and her brows drew together.

"No, I suppose not..." Her spine stiffened. "My husband was not a criminal!"

I said nothing, since it didn't seem wise to piss her off all over again.

"He wasn't!" she insisted. "Was he?"

She had probably meant the question to be challenging, but it came out more like a plea.

I looked up at the ravaged shell of what had once been a poised and beautiful woman. White and trembling, she stared down at me, the belt hanging as if forgotten in her grimy nail-bitten hand.

I could only imagine the loss of social status and the desertion of all but her truest friends. Her husband dead. Her marriage a lie. Her child endangered by the casual cruelty of scum like Potato-nose.

Pushed beyond her limits.

I understood.

Sympathy welled up despite the knowledge that these were probably my last moments on earth. Or maybe because of it.

"Eleanor," I said gently. "I'm sorry. All the charges laid against him were accurate. I'm pretty sure he loved you, but Nick really was a criminal."

"You *lie!*" Her voice broke like a shattering heart. Tears rolled down her face. "You... lie..."

She collapsed to sit on the floor, legs splayed in front of her like a broken doll. Staring blindly at the wall, she whispered, "He never loved me. I'm such a fool."

"No, Eleanor, that's not true."

She said nothing, just stared at the wall with tears sliding down her cheeks.

"Eleanor. Eleanor, look at me!"

Her empty gaze turned to mine.

"Eleanor, he loved you," I repeated. "I could see it in his eyes, there on the plane when we were talking. He might have taken advantage of your family connections, but first and always he loved you. If he hadn't, he'd have used you. Framed you for his crimes and let you go to jail in his place."

She straightened just a bit. "He never took a penny of my money. Any time I tried to invest in his business, he just..." Her voice choked to a whisper. "...he'd always say, 'That's your money, Dearest... save it...'" Her chest heaved, strangling her words. "...for a... rainy... day..." She curled into herself, weeping great racking sobs.

My heart breaking for her, I could only lie there helplessly watching her cry.

Potato-nose rose, jerking my attention back to him. "I'm so touched," he mocked. "Let me get a tissue, boo-hoo. Got your answers, Blondie?"

Eleanor gave no indication she'd heard; just rocked back and forth shaking with sobs.

He leaned against the wall, turning the trank pistol around and around. "My turn, then." His piggy little eyes narrowed. "So, Miss Arms Dealer. This something new on the market?"

He hefted the pistol. "Tell me. Or else."

When I didn't reply, he said, "Hit her."

Eleanor ignored him, or more likely never heard him. Lost in her grief, she rocked and cried as though she was utterly alone.

Potato-nose's lips tightened. Ejecting the magazine, he held it up. "Little darts instead of bullets. These poison darts?"

I clenched my teeth and stared up at him in silence, my heart hammering.

Completely at his mercy. No rescuers coming.

I was no hero. I wouldn't last long under torture, but I wouldn't quit without trying.

He growled and slapped the magazine back into place, working the slide. "Hell with it. Gonna kill you anyway, so let's see what this thing really does. Say goodnight, Red."

He pointed the pistol at me and pulled the trigger.

CHAPTER 45

I swam slowly up through murky depths. Afraid to breach the surface. Afraid not to.

Terrifying reality lurked above, but urgency drove me toward it. Had to do something. Something important...

I dragged my eyelids open.

Face pressed to the filthy floor. Entire body aching.

I managed not to groan.

Stay awake.

Take stock.

A tiny movement of my head took a gargantuan effort, but I managed it.

No sign of Potato-nose.

Eleanor Parr crouched facing the doorway with her back to me, holding my Glock. She must've taken it off me without telling Potato-nose when she tied my ankles.

She obviously didn't know anything about firearms. Clutching the gun two-handed, she had both forefingers wrapped over the trigger. Her right hand was so high on the grip that if she fired, the slide recoil would shred her thumb.

My heart leaped at the opportunity, then plummeted. I might be able to knock her over if I could get my body to cooperate, but I'd never get the gun away from her with my hands and feet tied. And even if she'd never fired a gun before, she could hardly miss me at this range.

Considering the level of hatred she'd shown, throwing myself on her mercy would be a waste of time. But maybe I had some leverage.

"Eleanor," I whispered, mildly surprised that my mouth seemed to be working. A cautious wriggle proved that the rest of my muscles were more or less under my control again, too. Nothing like a nice drug-induced nap to shake off the Taser reaction.

She squeaked and spun to face me, the gun shaking wildly as she pointed it at me. "I thought you were dead."

I managed not to flinch. "Nope. Eleanor, let me help you. Cut me loose and give me my gun, and I'll take care of Potato-nose for you."

"Potato...?" She gulped, half-laugh and half-sob. "How stupid do you think I am? If I let you go, you'll kill me."

"No, I won't. But I'll kill him."

Her eyes blazed with momentary hope before dulling to despair again. "You lie. You're a criminal just like him."

"I'm not lying."

I almost said 'trust me', but thought better of it. Adrenaline pounded in my veins. How long did we have before he came back?

I went on rapidly, "Eleanor, think about it. Killing you would be stupid. A high-profile woman like you? The investigation would never end. I don't need that kind of trouble."

She turned away to train the gun on the doorway again. "I don't need your help. I'll k... kill him myself."

The hesitation on the word 'kill' told me everything I

needed to know.

"Eleanor." I kept my tone soft and unhurried despite the panic constricting my lungs. Making it hard to breathe. Trapped...

Don't blow this one chance.

I forced a deep breath into my wooden lungs.

"Eleanor, you're not a killer. Don't make your son think you are."

She stiffened. "Leave my son out of this. When I k-kill... Potato-nose..." She hesitated. "He calls himself Harold Jones. When I kill him my troubles will be over."

"No, they won't. Eleanor, listen to me. If you kill him, then what? What are you going to do with the body? The car? Me? Your fingerprints and DNA evidence are all over his belt, all over the car, all over that gun, all over me. You have motive and opportunity. You'll go to jail for life and someone else will raise your son-"

"*No!*" Her voice was a hiss. "I'm smart. I'll figure something out."

"Maybe you will. But Eleanor..." I drew another breath, fighting the terror that wanted to strangle me. "You have to kill him with your first shot. If you don't, he'll blow up your son just for spite. And I can tell you right now, the way you're holding that gun you'll hurt yourself worse than you'll hurt him."

A whimper escaped her and her shoulders slumped. "Promise me," she whispered. "Promise you won't kill me. I'll do anything you ask. I'll pay you. I would have paid him anyway. I would have let him bleed me dry. Let him rape me. Anything. I just have to be there to raise my son. That's all I ask."

My heart thumped so loudly I was afraid she'd hear it,

but I kept my voice firm and calm. "I promise, Eleanor. Now please cut me loose and give me the gun."

She turned and crept closer, trembling. "I don't have a knife," she whispered. I was beginning to speak when she added, "Why don't you just break the ties?"

I jerked my wrists fruitlessly, pain and fear turning to anger. "Do I look like Arnold-Fucking-Schwarzenegger to you? Cut the damn ties! Use some broken glass!"

"No, that would cut both of us," she argued. "You don't have to be that strong. Just get on your knees and then smack your wrists hard against your back. The tie will break."

She obviously wasn't going to cooperate until I proved her wrong.

Frantically cursing her stupidity under my breath, I dragged myself to my knees. A couple of whacks of my bound hands against my butt sent pain slicing through my wrists.

"It doesn't fucking work," I hissed. "Now will you *please-*"

"Harder! You have to hit them harder."

"Fuck *you!*" I reared back and slammed my hands against my ass, too furious to even feel the pain.

The tie snapped, smacking my knuckles against the floor on either side of me.

"*Ow! Fuck!*" Realization dawned and I straightened slowly, flexing my freed hands and wrists. "Well, fuck me," I added mildly.

"I told you it would work," Eleanor said. "I saw it on an episode of 'Castle'."

I gaped at her for an instant, caught between the urge to

laugh and the burning desire to beat the living shit out of her.

But she still had the gun. With both fingers wrapped around the trigger.

"Okay," I said in the most soothing tone I could manage. "Now I want you to take your fingers away from the trigger. Nice and slow. Make sure you don't-"

My sentence ended in a yelp and a flinch as her hands jerked convulsively. The Glock somersaulted through the air, landing with a thud in front of me.

I scooped it up, my heart battering my chest, my panting whistling loud in the country silence.

"I hate guns!" Eleanor covered her face with both dirty hands, shivering violently. "I hate them!"

"It's okay," I comforted, trying to calm my breath.

Slow and easy. In. Out. Ocean waves. I'd only get one chance at this. If I missed and he blew up Eleanor's son...

I shuddered the thought away and concentrated on my breathing. "Where did Jones go?" I asked, holding my voice steady with all my might. "How long has he been gone?"

"I don't know. I must have fainted when he shot you. When I came to, he was gone. But I thought I heard something just before you woke up. That's why I was watching the door."

Of course. She'd been right next to me. I got the dart, but she'd been caught in the aerosolized tranquilizer.

"Maybe he thought we were both dead and left," she added hopefully.

"Yeah, maybe."

But if I were him, I'd be back.

When Eleanor collapsed he might have feared a release of poison gas and fled, but he'd check on his handiwork after he was sure the gas had dissipated.

Because he'd want to advertise the full capabilities of the classified weapon that he was about to sell on the black market.

My teeth clenched. Shit, how long should I wait here? What if he'd just jumped in his vehicle and driven away? What if he was negotiating with a buyer right now?

Shit, shit, shit!

The sound of approaching footsteps swishing through the dead grass made my heart punch my chest.

I hissed, "Distract him!" and shoved Eleanor to the other side of the room.

Crouching, I aimed at the doorway but the Glock wouldn't steady in my hands. Low blood sugar, dammit.

Footsteps on the broken porch.

Thump, thump...

Breathe in. Half out...

Thump...

Eleanor screamed.

The shock of the sudden screech jerked my already-shaking gun off target as Jones stepped into the room, his gaze snapping toward Eleanor. The Glock kicked in my hands.

One. Two.

Missed the heart-shot high and to the left. The bullet slammed into his shoulder.

Missed the head-shot entirely.

No, not entirely. A thin crease of red bloomed on his temple as he staggered back against the wall.

Thank God the remote was falling from his useless left hand.

He grabbed for his gun, his face twisting in fury and pain.

I fired again. He fell.

Eleanor was screaming in earnest, a high chilling note that pierced the din of gunshots like an icy needle.

Now Potato-nose didn't have a nose at all, just a shattered bleeding hole. The remains of his head thudded against the gore-spattered wall over and over, matching the rhythm of my trigger finger.

I sucked in a breath and stopped firing. Lowered the gun slowly.

Violent shudders rocked me. A sound seeped through my ringing deafness. Eleanor vomiting.

I let her get on with it.

Crawling over to the body felt like traversing the continent. I inchwormed my way painfully over dirt and broken glass, fighting tremors that threatened to drop me on my face. Beside the corpse, I reached out a shaking hand, holding my breath while I nudged the remote away from the fallen hand. Then I flopped onto my butt and brought my bound ankles down hard across his splayed-out leg.

Nothing.

Again.

Then once more. My trembling muscles could barely lift my own legs.

When the tie snapped at last I sprawled on my back panting, heedless of the debris under me.

God, just let me lie here. Fall asleep and never wake up.

My eyelids dipped and I shook my head vigorously. What kind of fucked-up sicko murders a man and then falls asleep with her feet propped on his bullet-ridden corpse?

A sleep-deprived one, the remains of my rational mind

reminded me.

I shook my head again and rolled over to creep onto my knees, still clutching my Glock. A rapid search of the body netted the trank pistol as well as his Glock. Juggling the guns awkwardly, I ejected the trank gun's magazine and let out a sigh of relief. Still only one dart missing. I replaced the magazine and holstered the pistol at my waist, then dragged myself unsteadily to my feet.

Eleanor pushed herself back from the mess of vomit in front of her, both hands braced on the floor. She looked up slowly and went still when her gaze settled on the pistols still in each of my hands.

"I suppose you'll kill me now," she said in a bleak voice.

"No." The word came out in a croak. I pushed my Glock into my ankle holster and the other into the back of my jeans, and cleared my throat. "Get the remote. Let's go save your son."

CHAPTER 46

Eleanor let out a whimper and scrambled over to snatch up the remote from the filthy floor.

I flung out a restraining hand, my pulse accelerating all over again. "Be careful! Don't touch any buttons."

"How stupid do you think I am?" she snarled, and carefully picked the device up.

I chose not to answer that question; just jerked my head toward the door. "Have you got a phone?" I asked instead.

"No. It's in my purse in my car." She made for the door.

I fell to my knees again beside the corpse and rifled its pockets. A set of car keys in his jacket pocket. Nothing but loose change in his front jeans pockets. Dammit, he had to have a phone!

I hauled him over onto what remained of his face, my abused body protesting the exertion with creaks and crackles.

Thank God, a big tablet-type phone in his back pocket.

My heart sank when I pulled it out. The screen was shattered. He must have fallen on it.

Clinging to hope, I pressed the power button but nothing happened.

Too exhausted to even swear, I dragged myself to my feet

and headed for the door. When I stumbled outside, blinking in the brightness, my trembling knees nearly dropped me down the dilapidated stairs.

Get it together.

I straightened my shoulders, every bruised muscle screaming its protest. I managed a more-or-less straight path to the car, where Eleanor was ransacking the glove compartment.

"Get your phone," I snapped.

"This is his vehicle. My car is in Silverside," she snapped back without ceasing her frantic search. "Dammit, dammit, where are his keys?"

"Here." I held them up and slid into the driver's seat.

Eleanor let out a cry that might have been fear or triumph and dove into the passenger seat.

I stepped on the gas. "Where is he holding your son?" I demanded.

"Nowhere. He just p-pushed him out of the car in Silverside. He c-could be anywhere." She gulped. "Some horrid p-pedophile might have him by now! What if-"

"No, he'll be fine; it's a small town and people look out for each other," I comforted. It didn't seem tactful to mention that a pedophile would get a hell of a surprise if he abducted a kid with a bomb strapped to him.

As we neared my farm I braked.

Eleanor tensed, easing her two-handed grip on the remote to clutch it in her left hand instead. Her right dropped down beside her. "What are you doing?" she demanded.

"Going in to my place to phone the police-" The words strangled in my throat as she lunged to press a wickedly-glittering shard of glass against my cheek. "Keep driving," she growled.

I drew a shallow breath. "Eleanor, I know you're not a killer-"

"No, but I'll cut you. I'll stab your eye out..." The threat ended in a sob, but her hand didn't waver.

A sidelong glance at her set face convinced me she meant it. I cautiously got back on the gas.

Trying for my calmest voice, I said, "Eleanor, if your son has a bomb attached to him, we need the police and a bomb squad. They'll be able to disarm the bomb safely. You and I can't do that."

"No police. Jones told my son he'd kill me if he went to the police. If Logan sees a police officer he'll run away. And if he runs he might set off the bomb." She gulped back a sob. "You just keep driving. I have to find him myself. He won't come to anybody else."

"But, Eleanor, the town needs to be evacuated. The parade's on this morning and there will be a huge crowd-"

"Nobody matters but Logan!" The glass pressed harder, a thin slash of pain. "You remember that! Nobody!"

Christ, she was 'way over the edge.

Then again, I didn't know what it was like to have a bomb strapped to my child.

But I knew what it was like to have my dearest friends threatened. They'd all be down at the parade. Lola, Eddy, Kane and Hellhound, too, if they decided to fulfill their commitments to the parade while they waited for me to return. My heart thudded harder. Tom. Oh God, and Cory and Charlene and Jackson and Emily. And Jack and her kids, too.

I fought panic.

Keep a calm front. She'd react to my fear.

"Okay. Okay, we'll find Logan," I agreed, holding my voice level. "Tell me what he looks like. And what do you know about the bomb?"

"No tricks." The glass quivered against my cheek. "No tricks or I'll cut you."

"I promise I won't try to trick you." When she didn't ease up the pressure, I added, "Eleanor, if I didn't want to help you I would have shot you dead and walked away. You need to believe I'm trying to help you and Logan. Tell me about him."

"You don't get to know about him!" The glass pressed even more fiercely. "He's none of your concern! You stay away from him, leave him alone!"

My pulse pounded in my temples and I slowed the car, afraid I'd hit a bump in the road and get blinded by accident.

"Eleanor." My calm tone was badly ravelled at the edges. "You're not thinking this through. Two of us can find him faster than you can alone. You think you're protecting him, but you might end up causing his death if we can't find him fast enough."

In the silence that followed I barely breathed.

Then she said matter-of-factly, "You're right. Keep your hands on the steering wheel where I can see them. And remember I can reach over and slash you faster than you can draw your gun." She took the glass away from my face and perched on the edge of her seat, staring out the windshield as if it would make us go faster. "He's seven years old, about four feet tall, short blond hair and blue eyes. He's wearing blue jeans and a blue jacket and..." Her voice wavered. "...carrying a Spiderman backpack. That's where the bomb is."

"It's just in a backpack?" Relief washed over me. "It's not attached to him?"

"No." Eleanor hunched her shoulders miserably. "But it's his favourite backpack. He even sleeps with it. He'd never put it down, even for an instant. And he doesn't know there's a bomb in it."

I braked and turned onto the highway, accelerating considerably past the speed limit.

"What do you know about the bomb?"

"N-nothing." Silent tears tracked down her cheeks. "It's a gray lump about the size of a baseball..."

Shit. Plastic explosive. More than enough to kill Logan. But at least there wouldn't be any shrapnel ripping through the crowd.

"...with a timer on it. And it's in a box full of nails and screws," Eleanor finished.

Oh, God.

And a seven-year-old boy would naturally be attracted to a parade.

Sick horror crawled up the back of my throat, and I gulped and stepped harder on the accelerator.

"How much time was on the timer?" I demanded.

"I d-don't *know*!"

Terror gripped me. It could explode any minute and there was nothing I could do. I should have stopped the car and called it in from my house. Even if she cut me. I could live with only one eye, but if my friends were torn apart in a bomb blast because I was a coward, I'd...

Stop it.

I couldn't change it now. Just drive as fast as possible and don't get in an accident. Stay focused.

"How did this happen?" I asked, trying to keep my voice steady and gentle.

"It's all my f-fault. I was so n-naïve." Her shoulders shook with quiet sobs. "I..." She threw me a glance, white lines of strain around her mouth. "I h-hated you. I thought N-Nick..." She choked on the name but recovered.

She stiffened her spine and spoke calmly even though tears still rolled down her cheeks. "I thought Nick was innocent and that you had caused all this. While he was still alive I did everything I could within the legal system. When he d..." She swallowed. "When he was killed, I..."

Her head drooped. "I was obsessed," she went on quietly. "I found the photo of you between the pages of one of his paperback books, months after the police had finished searching everything. I knew I should turn it in as evidence, but instead I put on gloves so my fingerprints wouldn't be on it, and made copies..."

She straightened suddenly and turned to me with an imploring expression. "Don't you see? I had to know. I *had* to." Her momentary burst of energy vanished and she slumped back into the seat. Her voice came out in a monotone. "I hired a private investigator to find you. He couldn't for weeks. Then, finally, he reported you had returned home."

"The bearded guy in the silver SUV," I interjected.

She gave me a startled glance. "Yes. You noticed him? He was supposed to be discreet. I paid him a great deal of money."

"Maybe you should ask for a refund."

She slumped again. "It doesn't matter. Anyway, one of the charities I support is for troubled youth. I asked one of the young men to set up a meeting for me. I disguised myself with a beard and fake piercings..."

I nearly drove off the road. "The skinny bearded guy with the piercings was *you*?"

"Yes." Her shoulders rose and fell. "I suppose you saw me at that dreadful bar Saturday morning, and again outside your office yesterday. I thought I was so smart."

I nearly protested that Eddy's was a far cry from dreadful, but I managed to bite my tongue as she continued, "So in my new male persona I hired a cocky young man-"

"Drake Mallard," I put in.

This time she didn't look surprised. "I didn't know his name. But he swore he could easily do what I asked. He would kidnap you and I would question you in that abandoned house, hidden in the darkness while wearing my disguise. I had recorded my questions and altered my voice so it couldn't be recognized. Nobody was supposed to get hurt."

I successfully resisted the urge to pound my forehead against the steering wheel. "Surely your P.I. found my phone number. Why didn't you just call me and ask your questions?"

Eleanor shot me a contemptuous look. "You would have lied to me. I had to have you at my mercy. To know you were telling the truth..." Her voice wavered and I thought she'd break down again, but instead she swallowed and went on, "But I waited in that horrid house for hours and the kidnapper never came. Instead, he absconded with the deposit I'd given him. So I hired another."

"Norman Perkins."

She sighed. "I feel like such a fool. You knew everything all along." I didn't enlighten her with the truth, and she added, "Of course he took my money and ran, too. So I tried again. That's when I discovered how truly foolish I had been."

We were only a couple of miles out of town.

Keep her talking. As long as she was talking, she wasn't threatening to blind me with broken glass, and I wasn't thinking about explosions and blood and death.

"Jones turned on you," I prompted.

"Yes. He seemed so much more... professional than the others. He promised to do the job and took my deposit. I told him everything I knew about you. We fixed a date and time, and he said we should meet in Silverside beforehand to work out the last details." Her bitter laugh twisted my heart. "Little did I know that he'd beaten my young friend until he divulged my true identity." She gulped, fresh tears tracking down her cheeks. "He's in the hospital. Profoundly brain-damaged and not expected to live. I'll never forgive myself for that."

I murmured sympathetically and she went on, "I had left Logan with the nanny. English is not her first language, and she tends to be fearful of authorities. Jones disguised himself as a police officer and told the nanny he needed to take Logan downtown to answer more questions." She made a helpless gesture. "You can imagine what our lives were like after Nick's arrest. Questions after questions after questions. She suspected nothing."

"So Jones had Logan," I encouraged, only half-listening.

Just another mile. Maybe a police cruiser would catch me speeding and I could report the bomb.

"Yes, he had Logan, with the bomb in his backpack," Eleanor confirmed bitterly. "With that leverage he revealed his true intentions, to involve me in your murder. Then he planned to take over your arms empire and blackmail me with threats to reveal my complicity. When I saw you yesterday at your office, I noted the license number of that black SUV you were driving. My private investigator traced it to the house where you were staying, so we knew where to find you this morning."

She sighed. "Jones abandoned Logan in Silverside and forced me to act as a decoy to draw you out. I would have knocked on the door and pretended some emergency in the alley if you hadn't come outside on your own. The rest you know."

And their plan wouldn't have worked if I hadn't been so caught up in my stupid commitment phobia.

Dammit, none of this had to happen. Kane and Hellhound could have easily dealt with both her and Jones if she'd knocked at the door. But no; I had to wander off down the alley like a fucking idiot, and now everybody I cared about might get blown to pieces.

All my fault.

I swallowed sickening guilt and slowed at the edge of town, heart hammering. Where were all the damn police? Never a goddamn radar trap handy when you need one.

"Take me to my car," Eleanor demanded. "It's in the next alley over from where yours was. Then we can both look for Logan."

I nodded and didn't add that the instant I was free of her damn glass dagger I'd break into Kane's house and use his phone to report the bomb. Evacuate the parade route. If there were no crowds Logan would be easier to spot, and fewer people would be maimed or killed if the unthinkable happened.

I clenched my teeth and cornered hard, tires squealing.

A few moments later I skidded to halt in a shower of gravel next to Eleanor's sleek silver Mercedes. She sprang from the passenger seat, but as she straightened a thunderous blast from the direction of downtown froze her in her tracks.

Cold horror paralyzed me, staring up at her bone-white face.

A chorus of sirens wailed.

"*NO!*" The scream ripped from Eleanor's throat. Her face contorted with berserk rage. "*This is all your fault!*" She dove at me swinging the piece of broken glass like a sabre.

I shot her.

CHAPTER 47

Holding my breath, I lurched out of the car to stand a safe distance away from the aerosolized trank. Gasping and trembling, I stared at Eleanor Parr's unconscious body sprawled in the car. The glass had cut her palm and a thread of bright blood trickled onto the driver's seat cover, slow in the endless moment.

The sirens fell silent.

Deathly silent.

Oh, God.

Giving thanks for the brisk spring breeze and the open doors of the car, I lunged back toward it. Wasted precious moments stuffing Eleanor's legs inside and yanking her roughly upright in the passenger seat. Slammed the passenger door and dashed for the driver's side.

Peeling out of the alley, I negotiated the turns at breakneck speed, the tires squealing protest.

What was I going to do when I got there? I only knew basic first aid. Logan was almost certainly dead.

How many others with him? Oh God, could I face the massacre?

But I had to know.

Which of my friends had I lost?

The tiny downtown was clogged with vehicles double-parked on both sides of the street and people milling around. Abandoning the car and Eleanor, I sprang out and accosted the first person I reached.

Young, skinny, and bearded with facial piercings. I didn't stop to consider the irony, just seized his shoulder and shouted, "Where was the explosion?" in his face.

He blinked stupidly at me. Shock.

I shook him. "*Which way?* Where was the explosion?"

His mouth dropped open, emitting a solid jolt of alcoholic breath but no voice. He pointed wordlessly toward a knot of people and I began to shove in that direction.

When I finally pushed to the front a chaotic scene confronted me. Screams rose on the air, and shrieking children dressed as clowns zipped everywhere on their bicycles.

After a paralyzed moment I realized the screaming came from the Sirius Dynamics float right in front of me. Tyler Brock was screeching at a microphone, backed by a quartet of skinny bearded-and-pierced young men belabouring guitars and drums. Just ahead of them, Tom sat on the driver's seat of a wagonload of bales and children. Reins held loosely, he was leaning forward as if to murmur reassurance to his team. They shifted their giant hooves patiently, ears flicking. Farther up, I glimpsed colourful elongated balloons attached to a brown-paper-wrapped pickup truck.

No terror. No blood. No emergency vehicles or grim-faced first responders.

Just the usual disorder of a parade about to start.

Panting and confused, I scanned the crowd. Nobody

seemed upset.

With a gasp of relief, I spotted Spider, Linda, and Germain standing with Jill at the edge of the crowd near Tom's wagon. Shoving toward them, I spared a moment to wonder why the hell Germain would take a chance on exposing Spider and Linda to the uncontrolled environment of a parade. Thank God it didn't matter anymore, but still...

A glance at Linda told the story. She clasped Spider's hand in both of hers, cheeks rosy and eyes sparkling while she bounced on her toes like an excited little girl.

Of course. Germain wouldn't have been able to manufacture any excuse to prevent them from attending the parade.

That explained Jill's presence, too. As I neared them, Germain bent to kiss her and murmur in her ear, but I recognized their hyper-vigilance as they scanned the crowd before parting again to subtly take up guard on either side of Spider and Linda.

I pushed through the last of the crowd, and four sets of eyes widened at the sight of me. "What's wrong?" they demanded in unison.

"Was that a bomb earlier?" I barked.

"No, what-"

No. Thank God.

I interrupted before Jill could complete the sentence. "Spider, Linda, get inside a building *now*. Stay there." Spider's eyes widened and he hustled Linda away without hesitation. Germain began to follow, but I grabbed his sleeve. "It's okay, they're safe." I snagged Jill's jacket, too, and pulled them both close to mutter, "There's a bomb. In a backpack. Seven-year-old boy, blond with blue eyes, jeans and a blue jacket, Spiderman backpack-"

"Aydan, thank God!" Kane's voice interrupted me and I wheeled to see him punch a button on his cell phone as he hurried toward us. "She's here at the start of the parade route by the Little Clowns..." he began before I interrupted.

"Bomb!" I hissed. "Seven-year-old-"

"There!" Jill's arm swung out to point at a small boy staring up with fascination at Tom's horses.

"He's scared and he might run," I panted as the four of us surged forward. "It's in the Spiderman backpack."

Germain was already on his phone and I caught the words 'bomb squad'.

"Surround him," Kane rapped out. "Get him out of here."

As we swooped down, Logan's eyes widened and he turned to run.

"Logan!" I yelled. "It's okay, we're..."

He shrieked as Kane leaped forward and seized him by the shoulder. Kane immediately went down on one knee, making calming gestures and trying to convince Logan to give up the backpack. The child shook his head, crying and clinging stubbornly to it.

Jill was next to arrive, placing herself on the other side of the backpack and reaching out a soothing hand.

I tried to push forward, but Germain pulled me back. "You'll only scare him worse," he muttered. "You look like hell. What happened?"

"Long story," I began, but fell silent as Jill managed to get Logan calmed enough to loosen his hold on the backpack. Kane seized the opportunity, snatching the pack away and turning to push for the edge of the crowd.

Logan set up a piercing wail and Jill shushed him

fruitlessly, rubbing his shoulder and subtly preventing him from pursuing.

Kane was beside the wagonload of children when a small jubilant voice filled me with sick dismay.

"Soo-poo-man!"　Jackson launched himself off the wagon directly at Kane.

And at the backpack.

It happened too fast. I could only stand frozen, my brain calculating trajectories at lightning speed and computing the inevitable collision.

Time slowed.

Kane spun, his eyes widening at the sight of the beaming child hurtling toward him. One muscular arm hugged the backpack to his chest. The other darted out, snatching Jackson out of the air by the waistband of his jeans.

The momentum swung him around, his arm swooping lower as though he'd put Jackson down, only to realize he was going too fast.

His arm jerked up again and Kane let go, shouting, "Germain!"

Jackson soared, squealing with delight, to be snagged in Germain's sure grip. He carried the child back to the wagon and the arms of his mother, who was clutching Emily open-mouthed. She managed a faint nod of thanks, and Germain withdrew with a pleasant smile that belied the adrenaline that must have been pumping through his veins.

Hell, if it wasn't, I was pumping enough for both of us.

Jackson was babbling, "I flew, Mommy, I flew like Soopooman! Did you see me, Mommy? Soopooman flew me!"

Tom cast a murderous glare at Kane from the wagon seat, but with the reins in his hands and the children in his wagon, he couldn't do anything, thank God.

Oblivious to Tom's rage, Kane resumed his slow progress toward the edge of the crowd, hugging the backpack. Every time someone jostled him he froze, turning this way and that to protect his dangerous burden. I wondered why he didn't use his height advantage to hold it overhead, but then realized he was trying to minimize injuries to the crowd by blocking the potential explosion with his body.

Logan was still screaming despite Jill's murmuring and shushing, and she jerked a 'take-over-here' gesture at Germain with her chin before hurrying after Kane. A moment later she slid in front of him and stepped backward, reaching behind her to lock her fingers in his belt loops and sandwich the backpack between them. Kane gripped her hip with his free hand and they wove slowly through the crowd, both wearing nonchalant smiles. Just a loving couple trying not to get separated in the bustle.

And if the bomb exploded it would rip them both in half.

Frozen, I stared, willing them safe with all my might. Another shriek from Logan jolted me into action and I trotted over, turning apologetically to the crowd to say, "Sorry, he's just overtired."

"That guy stole his backpack!" An indignant woman planted her hands on ample hips and glared.

"No, that was just his father," I soothed. "He just-"

"That's not my daddy!" Logan's voice was far too audible.

"Divorced and remarried," I offered with a sickly smile. "He's having trouble getting used to-"

"You're not my mommy! I want my mommy!" Logan was still in full cry and suspicious murmurs were beginning around us.

Germain wove toward us, making reassuring noises at the crowd. I knelt beside Logan and his wails grew louder.

"Hey, Logan," I said over his cries. "Do you want to go to your mommy? She's okay, the bad man's gone and I brought her back."

Germain's face softened in relief. "Oh, good. I'll get her and bring her here..." He trailed off at my headshake, looking worried again.

"Let's go to her, okay, Logan?" I cajoled. "She's just resting now, but..."

"Mommy said not to go with strangers." Tears still puddled in his eyes, but his little chin was firm with determination. Logan wasn't going anywhere without enough kicking and screaming to get us labelled kidnappers or worse.

I gave Germain a desperate glance, and he crouched down to Logan's level. "Your mommy's a smart lady," he said. "And you're a smart boy to do as she said. But she's worried about you so we need to take you to her now. How about..." He leaned over to whisper in Logan's ear.

Logan turned a wide-eyed gaze on him, forgotten tears still glistening on his cheeks. "Really?"

"Really," Germain said gravely, but humour twinkled in his brown eyes. "So what do you say, Logan? It's up to you."

Logan took his hand without hesitation. "Let's go to Mommy."

Relief whooshed out of me. Thank God Germain had kids of his own. He must have used some magic inducement known only to dads.

As I rose to lead the way Hellhound shoved through the crowd, scanning anxiously until his gaze locked onto me. His brow creased in worry.

I was giving him my best reassuring smile when an explosion rocked the street.

It came from the direction Kane and Jill had gone.

A cacophony of sirens screamed.

CHAPTER 48

All my blood drained away, the aftershocks of the explosion ringing in my abused ears. Unable to move, I stood rooted to the spot as the crowd surged forward. Germain's face was carved with deep lines, his eyes anguished.

Then Hellhound's solid bulk was beside me. I clutched his hand, gazing up at him as if he could make everything better. "John took the bomb," I quavered.

His face twisted as if in pain. Then his expression smoothed to a grim mask, but his hand was steady when he touched my cheek. "Ya can't help him, darlin'," he murmured in my ear. "Let's get ya outta here." The crowd jostled us, and he said, "Which way d'ya wanna go?"

I pointed mutely in the direction I'd come and he stepped in front of me. Before his threatening presence the crowd parted, flowing around us like lumpy water. Germain swung Logan up onto his shoulders and I hooked my hand in the back of Hellhound's jeans, letting him tow me along.

The crowd thinned rapidly and by the time we approached the car only a few stragglers remained. Eleanor was still slumped in the passenger's seat, but I couldn't tell whether she was conscious. Her face was immobile and pale as death, and a terrible thought penetrated my fear for Kane and Jill.

What if she'd had a reaction to the trank and died?

"Mommy!" Logan shrieked.

She didn't move.

"Shit-shit-shit!" I relinquished my grip on Hellhound and hurried forward as fast as my shaking legs would carry me, but Germain had swung Logan down from his shoulders and he rushed ahead of me.

"Mommy! Mommy!"

She twitched.

Vacant eyes turned toward us in a tear-streaked face.

"Mommy!" Logan catapulted into her lap, clinging and burrowing against her.

The white mask shattered and Eleanor's eyes kindled with fierce joy. Arms crushing the squirming bundle in her lap, she buried her face in Logan's tousled blond hair.

I turned away.

Empty.

Tottering back to Hellhound and Germain, I murmured, "I have to talk to her for a bit. Go check on J..." My throat closed.

"I'm stayin' with ya," Hellhound said flatly.

"I'll call you as soon as I find out anything," Germain promised, and hurried away.

Hellhound's arms closed gently around me and I leaned into him, pressing my face into his chest and letting the steady beat of his heart block out everything else.

After a year or possibly a few minutes I realized Hellhound was talking to me.

"Aydan. Come on, darlin'. Ya said ya needed to talk to

her, an' she's askin' for ya." When I gazed up at him without comprehension, he added, "You can do this. Go on."

I shook my head, trying to jar my brain back into motion. It responded sluggishly, the effort almost more than I could muster.

When I turned, Eleanor was beckoning from the passenger seat of the car. Logan was still in her lap, both arms wrapped around her while she rocked him.

Taking a deep breath, I squared my shoulders and trudged over.

"You did it!" Her smile was radiant even under the dirt and tear tracks. "How...?"

I shook my head, too tired to explain.

She turned her smile down to Logan. "Logan, sweetheart, I need to talk to this lady for a few minutes. Will you please sit here in the car and be good?"

Logan pulled away far enough to look up with trembling lips. "That man took my backpack," he sniffled. "I want my backpack."

"We'll get it, sweetheart, I promise." Eleanor met my gaze over his head but I said nothing. Couldn't speak.

"You just sit here for a few minutes," Eleanor coaxed, prying her son loose. "Just a few minutes and then we'll go home."

After some more whimpering and sniffling, Logan obeyed.

Eleanor cast a nervous glance at Hellhound, towering like Mount Doom a few yards away. Then she inclined her head in the opposite direction and we walked several paces.

"What do you want?" she asked abruptly.

I stared dumbly at her.

"What do you want from me?" she repeated. "I know

how you people work. What will this cost me?"

"Nothing."

Her eyes narrowed. "So it's to be blackmail, is it?"

"Huh?" I blinked, slowly processing her words. "No. I don't have anything to blackmail you with."

"Except that I abducted and attacked you. And my fingerprints are on the gun that killed Jones."

Glancing around, I realized the crowd had moved on and we were alone. I drew my Glock. Eleanor caught her breath, going white and backing away, but I held the muzzle in a safe direction and mumbled, "No, calm down. Stand closer." When she reluctantly edged nearer, I used our bodies to conceal the gun while I wiped it down with the tail of my T-shirt and returned it to my holster.

"There. No evidence," I said. Belatedly remembering I was supposed to be Arlene Widdenback the ruthless arms dealer, I added, "My people will clean up the mess at the house and get rid of Jones's body and car. I don't have any proof that you did anything. Nobody ever saw us fight. The only witnesses saw me reunite you with your son a few minutes ago and now we're chatting quietly. Nobody would ever believe a prominent and upstanding citizen like you would attack me."

"Except the first two men I hired," she said caustically. "I'm sure they'll be back with their hands out as soon as they finish spending the cash I gave them."

"They're dead. Permanently vanished just like Jones."

She staggered back a step, her hand flying to her lips. "You k... killed them, too?" When I didn't reply, she hesitated, then stiffened her shoulders. "All right. But I know you want something. Nothing's free in your world."

Weariness overcame me. "You're right," I said, dragging the words up with the last of my strength. "I do want something from you."

The white mask froze her face again and she stared at me with haunted eyes.

"Here's what I want." I met her gaze to make sure she was listening. "I want you and your son to get psychological help. You both need it. I want you to go back to your life and pick up the pieces and hold onto any friends who were good enough to stick with you through all this. I want you to continue your charity work and raise your son right and treasure every minute. And I never want to see your face again."

"And...?" The word came out faint and breathless.

"And that's it. I told you, you're more trouble than I need. I don't do blackmail and I don't give a shit about revenge. I won't bother you if you don't bother me."

Too soft. Be a ruthless arms dealer.

I leaned forward, letting the chill around my heart pour into the coldest emptiest tone I could summon. "To compensate me for my trouble I'm keeping the cash you gave your stupid little amateurs. And if you ever say a word to anybody; or if you cause even the tiniest bit of trouble for me ever again..."

I let the threat trail off as she blanched.

"I won't," she quavered.

"Good. Get in. I'll drive you back to your car." I turned back to Jones's car.

"Wait... what about... Logan's backpack?"

Pain paralyzed me for a moment. I didn't turn, and when I spoke my voice was emotionless. "Buy him another."

I beckoned to Hellhound and he ambled over, obviously

attempting to look non-threatening and failing utterly.

Eleanor took a step backward. "Logan, sweetheart," she said in a voice slightly too high-pitched. "We're just going to sit in the back while these people drive us back to our car. And then we're going home."

A few minutes later Hellhound and I sat in Jones's car, watching the tail end of Eleanor's Mercedes vanish around the corner.

He turned to me, cupping my chin with his light touch and turning my cheek gently toward him. "This your blood, darlin'?"

I craned my neck to look in the rear-view mirror and would have recoiled if I'd had the energy. "God, I look like shit. No wonder Logan freaked out." I inspected the small trail of dried blood on my cheek, squinting to focus at close range. "Yeah, that's probably mine. She kicked some broken glass in my face. It's just a tiny nick, though."

"Ya look like ya can barely move." Hellhound frowned worriedly at me. "D'ya need to go to the hospital?"

"No."

He didn't look reassured. "What happened, Aydan?" he demanded. "Weasel called an' said your guy hired out another contract, an' K..." He cleared his throat. "...John an' I've been lookin' all over for ya. Searched the whole damn town an' even drove out to your place. Where the hell did ya go? An' who was kickin' glass in your face? Was it that blonde with the kid?"

Too many questions.

I slumped back in the seat, closing my eyes. "The last assassin showed up. I found out who was behind it all and solved the problem. It's over."

"The last... shit, Aydan, ya went somewhere with him?"

I grunted sour amusement. "Not intentionally. I've got a couple of Taser burns to show for that little adventure."

"Aw, shit, darlin'." He took my hand. "I'm sorry. This was my fault."

"Of course it's not your fault." I dragged my eyes open and squeezed his hand. "Thanks for getting me out of the crowd and back here."

He studied me, brow furrowed. "Ya sure you're safe? An' ya sure ya don't wanna go get checked over at the hospital?"

"Yes."

Bless him, he didn't ask any more questions, just leaned over so I could rest my head on his shoulder while he stroked my hair.

Exhaustion and grinding fear for Kane and Jill dragged at me, but I forced myself to straighten. Keep it together. Maybe they weren't holding the bomb when it went off.

With all my remaining will I pushed away the thoughts of torn flesh and spattered blood. Stay focused. Finish off the mission.

"May I borrow your phone?" I asked.

Hellhound passed it over and I dialled Stemp's number. His crisp 'yes' was all but drowned out by crowd noise and I wondered if he'd been watching the parade before the bomb went off. It seemed such an oddly ordinary, human thing for him to do.

"Yes?" he repeated with a rising inflection. "Who is this?"

"Oh. Sorry. It's me. Aydan." With a great effort I marshalled my wits. "It's over. I need a cleanup crew at the old Wright homestead, four miles north and a mile east of my farm. And we'll need to get rid of a car, too. I'll leave it at Kane's house."

"Very well. Debrief at the office in half an hour, and then you can complete your work with Ms. Mellor this afternoon."

He hung up and I slowly lowered the phone to stare blankly at it.

That was it. No 'are you okay'; nothing. Just a command to debrief and get onto the next problem.

And, God, I had completely forgotten about Tammy's plight. In the next couple of hours I had to come up with some way to protect her freedom.

Could I even care about that? What if Kane and Jill...

Don't think about it.

Surely Stemp would have said something if he knew.

I passed the phone back to Hellhound and took slow breaths, trying to blank my mind.

His phone rang.

We both tensed and he punched the button. "Yeah?"

I couldn't decipher the faint crackle from the speaker, but after only a few moments Hellhound let out a breath and slumped in the seat, closing his eyes.

No. Oh, no.

I closed my eyes, too, sinking into the numbness of despair.

A shout of laughter made them pop open again, and I gaped at Hellhound while he roared with mirth beside me.

"They're fine, darlin'," he crowed. "The bomb was a fake. Modellin' clay wrapped around a little digital clock. An' the explosions were the fuckin' cannon over by the library. They fire it off fifteen minutes before the parade an' then again when the first marchers start. Scared the fuckin' shit outta me!"

I sucked in a breath that didn't seem to fill my lungs. "And the sirens?" I managed.

"Police, fire, an' ambulance whoopin' it up. They're at the head a' the parade."

I went limp. "So... they're really okay?"

"They're fine, darlin'. Kane's gonna meet us at his place in a few minutes."

"Oh." My relief drained away into emptiness. "Good." The word came out without inflection and Hellhound glanced over worriedly.

"It's gonna be okay, Aydan," he said softly.

I pushed a smile onto my face. "It's already okay. But I have to be at Sirius to debrief in half an hour, so..." I held out a violently trembling hand. "Do you still have your key to John's place?" I let my hand fall, too weak to hold it up any longer. "I didn't get breakfast this morning and I'm ready to drop."

"Shit!" Hellhound eyed me with concern. "Yeah, I got my key. Ya want me to drive?"

"It's only a block. And I'm too tired to swap places."

Moments later I pulled to a stop in front of Kane's house.

"Stay here, darlin'," Hellhound said, unbuckling his seatbelt. "I'll go grab ya some juice."

"I'm okay." I hauled myself out of the car. "If I had to run I'd fall flat on my face, but I can make it to the house."

With Hellhound's strong arm around me I managed to totter up the walk and inside. He lowered me onto the sofa and vanished into the kitchen to clatter around, returning a few moments later with a tall glass of orange juice.

While I sipped gratefully he withdrew again, and soon the comforting smell of toast wafted to my nose.

"Here ya go, darlin'," he said a few minutes later as he handed me a giant plate of toast slathered with peanut butter.

"Omigod, I love you!" I exclaimed just as Kane stepped through the door.

CHAPTER 49

I froze, but Kane and Hellhound only exchanged a nod. The air felt brittle.

Keeping my gaze glued to my plate, I inhaled the toast in record time. Barely preventing myself from licking my fingers, I laid the crusts on the plate.

"Hands are too dirty," I said in response to Kane's raised eyebrow. "I didn't want to eat anything I'd touched." I turned my grubby palms toward him and he grimaced.

"Your other jeans and T-shirt are in the bedroom along with your waist pouch," he said.

"Thanks." I hauled myself upright. "I'm supposed to be at Sirius to debrief in fifteen minutes. Could you please call Stemp and tell him I'm going to be late? I need a shower."

In the bathroom, I winced and turned away from the mirror. My skin, hair, and clothes were caked with grime. Under the dirt my face was chalk-white and baggy black circles hollowed my eyes. Dead grass and cobwebs festooned my hair, and the small trickle of dried blood on my cheek completed my fresh-from-the-crypt look. An angry pink welt stood out on my chin, and when I shed my filthy clothes more welts crisscrossed my legs and body.

"Whatever," I mumbled, and staggered into the shower.

I intentionally stayed there a full fifteen minutes to avoid the tension in the living room. Letting the hot water cascade over my head and ease my aches and bruises, I still couldn't relax. I kept expecting Kane to come in the door, encroaching on my space and privacy.

When he didn't, I drew a shaky breath at last and turned off the water. Then I dragged on my clean clothes, blasted the hair dryer at my scalp long enough to dry the roots of my hair, and pasted on a confident expression. Snapping on my waist pouch, I drew a deep breath and persuaded my aching body to straighten out of its exhausted slouch.

Okay. Do it.

I cruised through the living room and shoved my feet into my shoes. "Gotta go; I'm late," I chirped with my best attempt at a smile. "John, may I borrow the Expedition?"

To my relief, he tossed me the keys without comment and I hurried out the door before he or Hellhound could get started on me.

It was only a two-minute drive to Sirius Dynamics, but I fought sleep all the way. In the parking lot, I sagged in the driver's seat, my eyelids dropping closed.

A sharp blow to my forehead made me jerk upright, heart hammering and hand on my gun, but then I realized I'd fallen asleep and cracked my head on the steering wheel when I slumped over.

Muttering, I dragged myself out of the SUV. Habit made me glance warily around, searching for potential threats, but I drew a deep breath and let it out slowly.

It's over. No more assassins. Stemp was right; it was time to concentrate on the next thing. Tammy's life depended on it.

Despite my mental pep-talk, my back prickled with the expectation of an attack while I strode across the parking lot.

Leo wasn't on duty but his counterpart signed me in without fuss, so Stemp must have lifted my suspension half an hour early. Clipping my security fob onto my sweatshirt, I plodded upstairs to his office.

There, I handed over Jones's Glock before slumping into the guest chair to reel off my report, thankful that at least the act of talking would keep me awake.

When I was finished, Stemp studied me in silence for a moment before saying, "So you don't intend to press charges against Eleanor Parr?"

"No." At his raised eyebrow, I elaborated, "I don't want to take a chance on blowing my cover by going through the court system, and I think I've created enough goodwill that she won't cause me any more problems."

When he eyed me in silence, I added, "And I felt sorry for her and her son. If they get psychological help, Logan might grow up okay. Sending Eleanor to jail would just screw him up even more."

Stemp nodded slowly. "Very well. Is that all?"

I nodded, too tired to speak, and he glanced at my hands quivering on the armrests of the chair before adding, "I'm removing you from active duty effective immediately. Despite your apparent ability to suppress your emotions, don't forget..." His gaze bored into me. "...I've been where you are. It's impossible to perform at peak efficiency after experiencing as much trauma as you have lately. You'll have administrative duties only, and see Dr. Rawling as frequently as he considers optimal."

I managed a lopsided smile. "No argument."

He leaned back in his chair, his shoulders relaxing.

"Good." He glanced at his watch, then added, "You and your team have less than an hour left to put together your recommendations for Ms. Mellor, so I'll meet you in the conference room at fourteen hundred hours. Dismissed."

As I trudged down the hallway Spider emerged from the stairwell, looking tired and miserable. "Aydan, thank God!" he cried, hurrying toward me. "Where have you been? Why did you tell us to hide? And what happened? You look terrible-" Before I could answer he blushed scarlet and stuttered, "I m-mean, you never look terrible, I just-"

"It's okay, Spider," I interrupted. "Considering how I look right now, 'terrible' is a tactful understatement. And I'm sorry I scared you. There was a bomb threat at the parade, but it turned out to be a fake."

He paled. "Oh, no! How did you find out..." He trailed off, propping a hand under my elbow and adding, "Come on, let's go and sit down in your office."

I smiled. "Christ, I must really look like hell if you're treating me like a feeble little old lady."

"Oh, no, of course not!" He flushed again, his eyes widening in consternation. "I didn't mean to insult you, it's just... you're shaking, and I thought-"

"I'm pulling your leg." I gave him a one-armed hug as we navigated toward my office. "Thanks for looking out for me."

"Oh... you're welcome, Aydan, but... what happened?"

I sighed. "I solved the mystery of the assassins today. It got a little hairy."

"A little h...?" Spider trailed off as Stemp strode toward us.

"Webb, welcome back," Stemp greeted him. "Kelly, the clean-up crew just reported they've finished at the Wright place."

As he spoke a siren wailed outside the building, followed by another, then another. They faded into the distance and Stemp continued, "Apparently you left too much of a mess for them to clean effectively without it looking suspicious in such a derelict building." He inclined his head in the direction the sirens had faded. "The volunteer fire department will get some practice today."

"Oh." I spared a worried moment for Tom and the rest of the volunteers. "I hope nobody gets hurt."

Stemp shook his head. "By the time they get there the fire will be too advanced for them to do anything but contain it. The danger to personnel should be minimal."

"Okay. Thanks."

He nodded and kept on walking, and I turned to face Spider's wide eyes.

"C-cleanup crew?" he quavered. "You had to...?" He broke off as one of the civilian researchers passed in the hallway, then towed me into my office and lowered his voice. "Aydan, what happened? Are you okay?"

"I'm fine. Just sore and tired. Another assassin showed up this morning and kidnapped me."

He went white and I added hurriedly, "But don't worry, Brock wasn't involved. I found out who was behind the attacks and solved the problem."

"S-solved...?" Spider glanced in the direction the sirens had gone, looking sick. Then he swallowed hard and squared his shoulders. "I'm glad you're okay," he said firmly. "Who was behind it?"

I patted him on the shoulder. "Can't tell you; sorry. But it's over, and now we need to concentrate on Tammy."

"Oh, Aydan!" He dropped into my chair, burying his

head in his hands. "I've been worrying about it day and night and I just can't think of anything! I don't want to lose my job but..." He dragged his head up his bloodshot gaze steady even though his lips trembled. "I won't compromise on this."

"I know, Spider." I flopped onto the sofa opposite him. "I wouldn't expect you to."

Little did he know that if Stemp's review didn't go well this afternoon, he probably wouldn't have a job anyway.

I didn't bother to mention that.

"Let's go over this one more time," I said instead.

A few minutes later Jack arrived, her cheeks flushed pink but her eyes worried. "Sorry I'm late," she said breathlessly. "The parade went a little longer than I expected and then I had to get the children off to their day home. I didn't even take time to get them out of their clown costumes." She smiled. "But it was okay; I didn't feel quite so inadequate when I got to the day home and half the children there were still wearing their costumes, too."

"Oh, that's good," I said mechanically, then hesitated. "Um, so, they had fun?"

"Oh, yes!" Her eyes sparkled. "Despite Tyler's dreadful music. Fortunately his enunciation is so poor that his lyrics were completely unintelligible."

"Good. You didn't notice anything... unusual?"

"No..." She frowned. "Should I have? I thought I glimpsed you beside the horses before the parade, but when I turned back you were gone. And John was helping with the Little Clowns, but then he disappeared."

"Yeah, he got called away on an emergency," I said, giving Spider a warning look. No need to upset Jack.

Spider changed the subject. "Have you had a chance to think about Tammy while we've been gone?"

Jack's brow furrowed. "I've thought of little else..." She hesitated. "Well, except Charles's review. I'm worried about that, too. Their meeting is at three o'clock."

"Well, there's nothing we can do about that," Spider said. "Did you come up with anything for Tammy?"

Jack sighed. "No. I'm afraid we're searching for a solution that doesn't exist. Did you have any luck?" She glanced at us each in turn.

Our dispirited 'no's plunged the room into gloomy silence.

A moment later the silence was broken by Brock's spiteful voice as he poked his head in the door. "Well, if it isn't the Three Stooges; Fairy, Surly, and Slow." He nodded to Spider, me, and Jack in turn. "Why so glum? Did you just find out your precious Director is going to get shit-canned in an hour?"

Too drained to work up any amount of anger, I said, "Fuck off, Brock" without expression before adding, "At least now I see why you call your band The Flying Turnips. People must throw vegetables at you all the time."

"It's The Ballistic Rutabagas," he hissed. "And I can hardly wait 'til Dermott takes over. He'll cut you down to size, bitch."

I fixed him with a fishy eyeball. "I doubt it. He likes me. I make him laugh. You might want to keep that in mind the next time you're tongueing his asshole."

Jack's hand flew to her lips with a small cry of revulsion, and Spider snickered.

I stood slowly, trying to emulate Kane's threatening coefficient of expansion. "Now get lost. I've been called a bitch one too many times today and it's starting to affect my sweet nature."

"The truth hurts," Brock needled, but at least he left.

I stood staring at the empty doorway, my fingers flexing by my side.

"Aydan...?" Spider inquired cautiously.

"He'll never know how lucky he is that I'm too goddamn tired to rip his head off," I muttered, and sat.

Spider sank his head into his hands again. "I should just quit right now. If I do, I won't be facing disciplinary action and I might still get a good reference for a civilian job. And then I'd never have to see Brock again."

I reached over to pat him on the shoulder. "No; buck up, Spider. We'll figure something out. Now that I don't have to be looking over my shoulder for assassins all the time I won't be so messed up and tired..."

Oh, God. I'd only get an hour or two of sleep a night, after Kane got up in the mornings.

"...and I'll be ready to deal with him," I finished with determination.

Spider raised a hopeless countenance. "But it's too late for Tammy." He turned his wristwatch toward us. "It's time to go to the meeting."

CHAPTER 50

As Spider, Jack and I filed out of my office like a procession to the gallows, Jill and Tammy emerged from the elevator at the end of the hall. As usual, Tammy was hugging Jill's arm and chattering nonstop.

Jill waved and smiled. "Hey, Aydan, you're looking a lot better."

"Thanks." I gave her a grin, relieved all over again at the knowledge that she was unharmed. "Good job at the parade today."

She shrugged. "All in a day's work."

"Not quite-" I began, but Tammy broke in.

"Hi, Aydan, how *are* you? I'm so *glad* we ran into you, it's been *ages* and I've been *so* looking forward to working with you, but what does Jill mean, 'you look *better*'? Were you *sick*? Oh, I hope not, being sick is just *awful*, isn't it?"

For once she actually paused and waited for a reply. Her childlike eagerness wrenched my heart.

"Thanks, Tammy. No, I haven't been sick," I said. "But I was pretty funny-looking when Jill saw me earlier. I, um... got caught in a dust-devil and I was completely covered with dirt."

She giggled. "Oh, that must have been *funny*! Are there

many dust-devils around here?"

"Hardly any, thank goodness..." I began, but she was off and babbling again.

"Dust-devil is such a *funny* word, don't you think? There are so many funny words, like *brouhaha*, isn't that a funny word? And nincompoop and hoosegow, and flabby, and blubber and skedaddle and-"

"Ms. Mellor." Stemp's dry tone cut across her recitation. "Please excuse us, we're just going into a meeting."

I twitched violently. I hadn't heard him coming up behind me.

Tammy beamed. "Oh, *hello*, Charles! I *thought* that sounded like your step. Of course I won't hold you up, but I was just about to say how *nice* it is to have everybody here; I know Dr. Travers is here because her perfume is so *beautiful* and of course I'd know Spider *anywhere*; his shampoo smells like limes and ginger and it's absolutely *yummy*, don't *ever* change your shampoo, Spider-"

"Come on, Tammy," Jill interrupted gently. "Let's go and get started with Tyler."

"Oh, *yes!*" Tammy gushed, turning her smile back to Jill. "I've been listening and *listening* to his Ballistic Rutabagas CD and do you know, I think I'm starting to *like* it just a little bit. And isn't *rutabaga* a funny word, too?" Her voice faded as Jill walked her farther down the hall. "Did you know rutabaga is another name for *turnip*?" Tammy went on. "So Tyler's band is like the Flying Turnips..."

"You should tell him that, Tammy," my evil twin called down the hallway. "He'll get a laugh out of it for sure!"

She turned, beaming. "Oh, do you *think* so? I'd *love* to make him laugh, he's been so *grumpy* lately."

"Um, no, maybe you'd better not," I muttered guiltily. "It might hurt his feelings."

"Oh." Tammy looked downcast. "Well, then I won't. But *I* thought it was funny, didn't *you*?"

"Kelly." Stemp's dry tone saved me from replying.

I called, "See you later", and slunk into the conference room, closing the door behind me. "Sorry," I added as I took a seat. "I guess I'm overtired."

Stemp made no comment, just leaned back in his chair and raked us with his flat gaze. "So. Recommendations regarding Ms. Mellor?"

Jack, Spider and I exchanged an unhappy glance. Spider perched at the edge of his chair, his bony fingers tangling in his lap.

Jack spoke up. "Well, Director, we've considered several options..."

While she laid out our thought processes and conclusions to date, I blessed her penchant for presenting everything as a scientific analysis.

Stall, Jack, stall...

Come on, brain, get with the program. There had to be something we'd missed; some simple solution.

"...so really," Jack was concluding, "...our only remaining option is for Aydan to try to extract the relevant memories from Tammy's mind."

"And I refuse to do that without her consent," Spider said tremulously.

A great light dawned in my brain.

"So we have a suggestion," I took over smoothly from Spider. "We'd like to ask Tammy's opinion and let her decide. Up to now we haven't been able to do that because we know she'll blab anything we tell her, but if she chooses to let me edit her memories I can take away the memories of us explaining this to her, too."

Spider and Jack stared at me open-mouthed. Stemp's eyes narrowed. "And if she refuses?"

I sighed. "Then it'll be one more piece of classified information she'll take to the secured facility when she goes. We'll just have to explain it to her so she understands she's really got no alternative other than being imprisoned."

"But, Aydan," Jack said gently, "You don't know if you can even edit her memories successfully. And in your current condition..." She paused, measuring my frazzled state with a clinical gaze before continuing, "I would strongly recommend against you attempting this."

I pushed myself straighter in the chair. "If I have to do it, I'll find a way."

"Or you'll destroy yourself trying," Stemp said softly.

"Aydan, you can't! Not when you're so tired!" Spider's hazel eyes were dark with worry. "Remember how awful it was last time; Kane had to drag you out of the sim and you were all torn up and bleeding!"

"That won't happen," I said, trying to convince myself as well as them. "And anyway..." I straightened, remembering Kane's earlier suggestion. "...it doesn't have to be all-or-nothing. I could do it a bit at a time. It wouldn't be too bad if she just had to be in the secured facility for a little while, until I could be sure I'd gotten all the memories."

"But with her full consent," Spider put in, looking more hopeful than I'd seen him all week.

"Right." I gave him a smile.

The three of us turned toward Stemp.

Stemp leaned back in his chair and eyed us, his

expression unreadable as always.

"Very well," he said at last. He picked up the phone and dialled. "Francis? Please bring Ms. Mellor to the conference room."

In the silence after he hung up the phone, my mind raced. I should be able to delete the memories. Or better still, only the parts that referenced any classified information. She'd have a few gaps, but it might not be too bad.

But would Stemp make me start today?

It was all I could do to drag my own thoughts into some semblance of order. It would be criminally irresponsible to mess with Tammy's mind right now.

And I hadn't needed Spider to remind me of the last time I'd fought this battle in cyberspace. In my current condition, there was a pretty good chance it would kill me.

A tap on the door heralded Tammy's arrival. Jill guided her in, then hesitated. Stemp nodded at a chair. "Please have a seat, Francis; Ms. Mellor."

Jill smiled and sat next to Tammy.

Stemp turned to Spider. "Webb, please lay out your proposal to Ms. Mellor."

Tammy sat forward in her seat, her head turning as though scanning the room. "Who's here?" she asked. "Charles, and Spider..."

"I'm sorry," Stemp apologized graciously. "Dr. Travers and Aydan Kelly are here, too. And Jill Francis, of course."

"Oh, of *course*!" Tammy turned a beaming face toward Jill. "I can *always* count on my Jilly-bean!" She turned to face slightly to Spider's left, apparently identifying him by scent but not certain exactly where he was. "What's your proposal, Spider? Since you're getting married in a few months, I'm *sure* it's not a marriage proposal." She giggled. "Isn't that *funny*? I always think proposal is such a *funny* word because whenever you hear somebody say they're going to *propose* it means *marriage*, but-"

"Let's hear what Spider has to say," Jill interrupted gently.

"Okey-dokey, Jilly-bean! My lips are zipped!" Tammy mimed zipping her lips.

Spider hesitated as if mistrusting her ability to actually stay silent, but after a moment he spoke. "Tammy, we've been thinking. It seems like we're always bugging you to not tell certain things to people, and you must be tired of it. But it's really important for you not to tell." He darted an unhappy glance at Stemp's impassive features. "In fact, it's so important that..." Spider hesitated and swallowed. "...that you're not going to be able to work here anymore unless we change some things. You'd have to go to live and work in a different building, one where it's safe for you to say whatever you want."

"Oh!" Tammy clutched Jill's hand. "Not work here anymore? But I *love* it here! I *love* working with you and Tyler and Aydan and my Jilly-bean!"

"We like working with you, too, Tammy," Spider said. "That's why we want to try something different, if it's okay with you. But we'll need your permission."

"Oh..." Tammy relaxed into a smile. "I'm *sure* it'll be fine. Whatever you want me to do, just tell me."

Her naive trust made my stomach curdle with guilt.

Spider looked as sick as I felt. "This decision isn't up to us," he said gently. "It'll be up to you. I'll tell you what we have in mind, and you can say yes or no."

"Okey-dokey!" She turned her radiant smile toward him. "Shoot, Spider."

"We..." He glanced at me as if for moral support. "If it's okay with you, we'd like to remove the memories that are classified. Take them out of your mind. That way you'd never have to worry about accidentally saying the wrong thing."

"Remove..." Her smile dissolved into uncertainty and she reached for Jill's hand again. "You mean... I wouldn't *remember* anymore?"

"You'd still remember everything that's not classified," Spider reassured her. "We'd only take out the bits about the network and the work you've done here and some things Terry Sherman told you."

She seemed to shrink in her chair, her arms tucking tight to her body. "You'd take away my Terry?" she quavered.

Spider looked nearly as traumatized as she did. "No, you'd still remember him. But there would just be some memories that-"

"No! Oh, no, I *couldn't* let you take away my *Terry*," Tammy cried. "I *love* working here and I *love* working with all of you, but I can't let you take away even the *tiniest* memory of my Terry! He was my one and only, and I never, never, *never* want to forget him!"

Spider looked utterly miserable, and Stemp spoke into the expanding silence. "The only alternative is for you to be transferred to the secure facility."

"What..." Tammy looked very small and vulnerable huddled in her chair. "What would that be like?" Her voice came out in a whisper.

"You'd have an apartment of your own," Stemp said. "It would be quite a bit smaller than the one you have now, and it wouldn't have a kitchen, just a bed and bathroom and a small sitting room. You'd eat your meals in a cafeteria and you'd go to work the same as you do here. You wouldn't have to worry about saying the wrong thing to anybody, but you wouldn't be able to leave the building without an escort."

"And..." Her grip tightened on Jill's hand. "What about my Jilly-bean? And Spider and Aydan?"

My heart twisted. Poor Tammy. Forced to choose between losing precious memories of the man who had been everything to her, or leaving behind the only people she knew in the world.

"Their work is here." Stemp sounded sympathetic but firm. "You would have to leave them behind, but they could still come and visit you."

"They could *visit*?" Hope dawned on Tammy's face and she sat up. "And I'd live in a safe building where I didn't have to go *out*? And I'd *never* have to worry about saying the wrong thing?"

"That's correct," Stemp confirmed.

"Oh!" Tammy's smile reappeared. "Oh, that would be *wonderful*!" She squeezed Jill's hand. "Don't get me wrong, Jilly-bean, I'll miss you like *crazy* and I so *appreciate* how you've been looking after me, but it's so *scary* to have to go around to all these places and never know who I can *talk* to and have so much *space* around me in the apartment, and Charles, you know how *thankful* I am for everything you've done for me, but I'd so *love* to go and live in your safe building instead!"

Everyone gaped open-mouthed at her except Stemp, who maintained his expressionless façade as always.

"And..." Tammy leaned forward, then hesitated. "What

about... would I still work with Tyler?"

"Yes," Stemp replied. "He would go with you."

"*Really*?" Tammy's smile lit up the room. "That's super-duper-*perfect*! I just love-love-*love* my Tyler! When do we leave?"

Spider and I exchanged a cautious look while my shock faded into slowly-swelling elation.

Stemp said, "Immediately, if you wish."

"Oh, *yes*!" Tammy turned to Jill, who looked like a woman glimpsing daylight for the first time after months in a dark dungeon. "Jilly-bean, you don't *mind*, do you?" Tammy asked worriedly. "I don't want to hurt your feelings 'cause I *love* working with you, too, but-"

"Tammy, it's fine with me," Jill interrupted, and hugged her. "If you'll be happy there, I'll be happy, too."

Well, shit.

It had never occurred to me how overwhelming a normal existence would seem to someone who had spent her entire life sequestered. I'd been fighting the wrong battle all along.

Tammy was going to be safe and happy. And Tyler Brock's irritating presence would be gone forever, incarcerated along with Tammy.

In the back of my exhausted mind a triumphal chorus began belting out hallelujahs.

"Very well." Stemp's dispassionate voice brought me back to the conference room. "Webb, please inform Brock of the change. Francis, please make the arrangements to transfer Ms. Mellor's belongings." He rose. "Ms. Mellor, thank you for your service and cooperation. I wish you well in your new position."

He took her hand and shook it, then transferred it back to Jill's arm. We all rose, Spider's eyes gleaming with gleeful anticipation. "Come on, Tammy," he said. "Let's go tell Tyler. He'll be just..." The gleam in his eye took on a wicked glint. "...speechless," he finished, grinning. "Oh, and..." he turned to me. "Aydan, I've finished your new, um..." He glanced at Tammy. "...handheld. Come and see me later and we'll get it set up."

I nodded, too tired to form words, and Jill, Tammy, and Spider hurried out. I was beginning to follow them when Jack's quiet voice made me stop and turn.

"Director," she said. "Do you have any inkling..." She hesitated. "Of course I understand you won't know for sure until after your meeting. But please let us know how your review goes. We're all hoping you'll stay."

"Thank you, Dr. Travers." Stemp gave her a level look. "It appears I'll be remaining in the director's position."

Guarded hope lit Jack's eyes. "But... I thought your meeting wasn't until three."

Stemp's shoulder rose and fell in a fractional shrug. "True. But there was only one remaining bone of contention that might have tipped the balance toward Dermott. Now that Ms. Mellor is to be transferred to the secure facility, all issues of concern to my chain of command have been resolved."

My tired brain slowly ground through the implications. "Wait..." I frowned, putting the pieces together. "You mean if we'd persuaded Tammy to let me try to alter her memories, you'd have been fired?"

"Very probably. Ms. Mellor's continued freedom has been a major source of friction between my chain of command and myself."

"But..." I stared at his impassive face. "Why didn't you

tell us?"

He met my gaze without expression. "I gave you my word that you'd be allowed to try. I know how important it was to all of you. And I refuse to ask anyone to compromise their principles. Now, if you'll excuse me, I need to make arrangements for Ms. Mellor's transfer."

He moved toward the door and without thinking I reached to halt him with a hand on his arm.

He stopped, giving me an unreadable look, and I suddenly realized it was the only time I'd ever touched him without violent intent.

"Thank you," I whispered, and took my hand off him.

"You're welcome." For a moment his eyes softened to warm amber and the corner of his mouth turned up. "Take the rest of the day off and get some rest over the long weekend," he added. "See you Monday."

His stone-faced façade descended again and he turned and strode out.

CHAPTER 51

I trailed out of the conference room in a daze, feeling as though a great weight had been lifted from my shoulders. Tammy safe and happy. Stemp in his rightful position as director. Spider's and Jack's jobs secure. Tyler Brock gone.

It seemed too good to be true.

My bemused euphoria lasted all the way down the stairs, but when I stepped into the main-floor reception area my heart plummeted at the sight of Kane and Hellhound leaning against the wall.

They both straightened, their gazes boring into me, and I used every shred of my self-control to keep from bolting back up the stairs and barricading myself in my office.

Instead I forced a smile and strolled over. "Hi, guys. What's up?"

"We came to take you home," Kane said. "We didn't want to risk losing you again."

I fought off the feeling of being under arrest. "Thanks, but everything's okay now. There won't be any more attacks." They both looked unconvinced, and I added, "Oh, and you'll be glad to know it looks as though Stemp will be staying on as director. They still have to have the official meeting but it looks as though it's only a formality. And

Tyler Brock is being transferred, effective today."

"That's good news," Kane agreed, but his scrutiny was still uncomfortably intense. As if he was trying to see all my private thoughts...

I shivered.

Trying to hide it in a yawn and stretch, I said, "I'm just going to go and sign out, and then I've got the rest of the day off."

"Good. Me, too," Kane said.

"That's good, darlin'," Hellhound seconded and gave me a smile, but his gaze searched me as well.

When I turned away from signing out a few moments later, Kane and Hellhound fell in beside me, one on each side. They didn't actually grip my arms, but the sense of being a prisoner intensified.

I was trying to be unobtrusive about drawing deep breaths when Lola bustled into the lobby clutching a small gift bag and a handful of the brightly-coloured inflated condoms on strings. She stopped short at the sight of me.

"There you are!" she exclaimed. She studied my face for a moment before hurrying over to give me a hug. "Honey, you look like death warmed over! What happened?"

Oh, hell.

My worn-out brain punted my bullshit factory into emergency production. "Lola! I'm so sorry, I've been trying to call you but my calls weren't going through. Isn't your phone working?"

She frowned. "I think it is. I thought your phone was the problem. I've been trying to call you, but I just kept getting your voicemail. I finally called Spider and he said you were here. I was so worried about you when you didn't show up for the parade, honey. Where were you? Is everything okay?"

"Everything's fine, and I'm so, so sorry! I did show up for the parade, but when I got out of my car I got caught in the dust-devil from hell. I was dirt from head to toe and something hit me in the face so it was bleeding..." I touched the tender nick on my cheek for corroboration. "...so I ran home for a shower and a change of clothes and I thought I'd still make it back in time but then I had a flat tire. And I couldn't get you on your phone. I'm so sorry. Did the parade go okay?"

Lola reached up to trace the welt on my chin. "It looks like something nailed you here, too. And on your neck."

"I think that was a chunk of cardboard," I lied glibly. "There was all kinds of crap swirling around."

"Oh, honey, you've had the day from hell." Lola gave me another hug. "And don't worry, I went with the trench coat and bathing suit and threw the candy myself. It was a hoot! You should have seen people's faces!"

"Oh, that's great. I'm glad it went well," I said absently. "Well, I guess-"

"Here he is!" Lola interrupted, glancing behind me. "The winner of the coveted Up & Coming prize package!"

I turned to see Tyler Brock approaching like a petulant thundercloud.

Lola hurried over to meet him, smiling so widely that I was instantly suspicious. "Young man, congratulations!" she exclaimed, pitching her voice loud enough to make it clear that everyone in the lobby was expected to pay attention. "Your performance in the parade was worthy of my extra-special prize package!" She thrust the bouquet of inflated condoms and the gift bag into his hands. "I love alternative music, and after hearing you play, I just had to give you this!"

Brock held the 'balloons' away from his body and glanced into the gift bag, then gave Lola a sour look. "Condoms?"

"Yes, dear!" Lola patted his hand, doing a startlingly convincing sweet-little-old-lady act. "I hope you'll put them to good use."

Brock's mouth opened and closed a couple of times, but apparently even he wasn't nasty enough to insult a sweet little old lady. He settled for a jerky nod and we all watched in silence while he signed out at the security wicket and hurried out the door.

As soon as the doors closed behind him, Lola's deep infectious laugh boomed out. "And good riddance," she called after him.

I turned a skeptical gaze on her. "Since when are you an alternative music fan?"

"I do like some alternative music," Lola protested.

"And?" I prodded.

She grinned, pure evil in an angelic-looking wrinkled package. "And the kindest thing I can do for alternative music is to make sure that boy never reproduces."

A shout of laughter rose to the ceiling, and Lola wiggled her fingers in a coquettish goodbye. "See you later, boys," she said to Kane and Hellhound, then leaned in to give me a hug. "Thanks for trying so hard to get to the parade, honey," she said. "Go home and get some rest, and I hope your day gets better."

I blinked away sudden tears. "Thanks, Lola," I whispered. "I hope it does, too."

But that didn't seem likely.

Kane and Hellhound closed in and we all stepped out

onto the sidewalk together.

"We're takin' ya home," Hellhound said. "You'll ride with me, an' Kane'll follow."

I sagged in defeat, too tired to argue. Handing Kane's keys back to him, I trudged in silence to Hellhound's SUV and fell into the passenger seat.

Kane left us with a nod and a significant look at Hellhound, and I stifled a groan. Nearly twenty minutes alone with Arnie. He'd grill me for sure. But maybe if I feigned sleep he'd have mercy.

Only moments later his soft rasp roused me. "Hey, darlin'. Time to wake up. You're home."

"Uh?" I swam up out of slumber, blinking stupidly at my house. "We're...? Oh. I guess I fell asleep."

"Yeah." He caressed the hair away from my cheek. "How long since ya slept last, darlin'?"

When I didn't reply, he added, "I bet ya ain't slept since ya been at Kane's."

I turned away from his worried scrutiny. "Arnie, please don't start."

"It's gonna be okay, darlin'. Come on, let's get ya inside."

As we walked to the house he put his arm around me, but I could feel the tension in his body. Kane got out of his Expedition, and the three of us went into the house in silence.

I summoned a smile and turned to them. "Well, thanks for the escort. I'm wiped out, so I'm going to bed."

"Not so fast, darlin'." Hellhound shed his boots and jacket and Kane followed suit. "I know you're bagged," Hellhound added. "But we got some unfinished business an' it can't wait."

I backed away, desperation driving my voice up to a squeak. "No, please..."

Stop begging, dammit.

I dragged my aching body straighter, trying to hide my trembling and forcing my voice louder and stronger. "No. I'm not doing this with you. Not now; not ever."

Kane and Hellhound exchanged a glance. Then Kane said, "Aydan, I'm sorry, but we are going to do this. The only way out is to shoot us both."

I squeezed my eyes shut. "Or I could just shoot myself," I muttered, and stooped.

Hard hands seized me, making me yelp with shock. Hellhound barked, "Get her weapons!" and pinned my arms by my sides while Kane frisked me rapidly, confiscating my waist pouch, Glock, and trank pistol.

"Christ, you guys, I was joking!" I protested. "I was just going to untie my boots!"

"Oh." Hellhound released me. "Sorry, darlin'. But after what ya said earlier I was afraid to take the chance."

Kane frowned at both of us. "What did she say earlier?"

Hellhound gave him a poker face almost as good as Stemp's. "My fault. Just a misunderstandin'."

"Aydan?" Kane's gaze bored into me.

"Never mind..." I began, but he raised his voice to talk over me.

"Were you talking about harming yourself?"

"No, of course not."

Hellhound cleared his throat and gave me a look, but I gave him the stink-eye in return and backed away, keeping my voice light. "Hey, do you guys want a beer?"

Kane's voice rose to a near-shout. "No, goddammit, I don't want a beer and I don't want evasions! Why are you keeping secrets from me?"

Cornered, I lashed out. "Because it's none of your goddamn business, that's why!"

"SHUT UP!" Hellhound's bellow was so loud and sudden that we jerked in unison and turned to gape at him. He grinned, but the smile didn't reach his eyes. "Now that I got your attention..." he said in normal tones, "...let's get back on track. I ain't gonna stand here an' watch the two a' ya hurt each other anymore. Move it. Into the livin' room, sit down, an' shut up."

Kane looked ready to explode, but to my surprise he gave a short nod and marched into the living room, his shoulders stiff.

"Come on, darlin'. You, too," Hellhound said gently.

Groaning, I took off my boots and trudged into the living room, where I threw myself into a chair and closed my eyes in despair.

"Okay," Hellhound rasped. "Now we're gonna have it out. I'm goin' first. I ain't sorry for what I said earlier, but I'm sorry for how I said it." I opened my eyes to see him perched on the edge of the sofa, leaning forward with elbows on knees. "Aydan; Cap; I'm sorry I lost my temper. It was fuckin' stupid, an' it coulda killed Aydan. Cap, I know ya been through hell lately an' I shoulda cut ya some slack." His voice softened. "An' Aydan, darlin', I never want ya to feel like ya gotta run away from me. I never wanna be like my fuckin' ol' man."

His voice was steady but I could read the anguish in his eyes.

My heart clenched. "Oh, Arnie, you could never be like him! And I wasn't running away from you, I was..."

I bit off the hurtful truth, 'running away from John', and substituted, "...I just couldn't bear to watch the two of you fight. And anyway..." I reached over to squeeze his hand. "...that sounded like a pretty tough mission you had on Tuesday. Don't be hard on yourself. You're still recovering, too."

"What mission?" Kane demanded.

Hellhound shrugged. "Had a job. Same old, same old."

Kane looked stricken. "I'm sorry. I didn't know."

"Hell, it ain't your job to know. Ya ain't my mother."

"No," Kane said. "I'm your brother. I should have asked, and I'm sorry."

Hellhound shifted uncomfortably. "No sweat, Cap. Shit happens." His jaw firmed. "An' that ain't what I wanna talk about. Aydan..." His gaze searched my face. "D'ya still trust me?"

"Of course." I reached to squeeze his hand again. "You haven't given me any reason to stop."

He smiled, his eyes softening. "Thanks, darlin'." He turned to Kane. "How 'bout you, Cap? Ya still trust me?"

Kane's gaze flicked to our clasped hands and a muscle rippled in his jaw, but his cop face and cop voice were neutral. "You've had my back for over forty years. We're brothers."

Hellhound gently disengaged my hand and sat up straighter to lock eyes with Kane. "That ain't what I asked. I wanna know if ya trust me enough to listen to what I got to say."

Kane met his gaze levelly. "I trust you enough to listen."

A flicker of pain chased itself across Hellhound's face, but his voice was steady. "Good. Then listen up, the two a' ya. I ain't a shrink, but I know ya both pretty well an' I got a helluva good bullshit detector. Ya ain't bein' straight with each other, an' it's time ya were or you're just gonna end up hurtin' each other worse." He gave us a ferocious scowl. "An' nobody hurts my friends. So I'm gonna sit here an' referee, an' you're gonna start tellin' the truth."

CHAPTER 52

"I'm not doing this," I said at the same time as Kane snapped, "This is ridiculous."

Hellhound leaned back on the couch, eyeing us both shrewdly. "Huh. Well, if neither of ya is lyin', what've ya got against hearin' the truth?"

We began to spout denials and objections, but he silenced us with an outflung palm. "Shut up," he said mildly. "Here's the truth. You're both fucked up right now. Cap, if you're smart enough to take yourself off active duty, be smart enough to know how dumb it is to make a commitment when ya can't even get your head straight. I know ya love Aydan, but now ain't the time to jump into anythin'."

He turned to me, his voice softening. "An' Aydan, I know ya made a promise when ya were feelin' weak. That ain't anythin' to be ashamed of; Christ knows anybody'd break after what ya been through. But now you're forcin' yourself to keep that promise even if it kills ya. An' darlin'..." He leaned forward to touch my cheek and look into my eyes. "It's killin' ya. Ya gotta sleep sometime."

"She has been sleeping," Kane objected. "She had a few nightmares the first night but then she settled down, and she didn't have any nightmares at all last night."

He looked to me for corroboration, but as I nodded Hellhound said softly, "That's 'cause she ain't been sleepin' at all. Ain't that right, darlin'?"

I studied my toes and said nothing.

"Aydan?" Kane sounded anxious. "Is that true?"

Driven to answer, I gave him a bright smile while simultaneously sending 'shut up' vibes in Hellhound's direction. "You're right, I didn't have any nightmares last night."

Kane frowned, obviously seeing through my misdirection. "So you haven't been sleeping. Why not?"

"I... I didn't want to hurt you. After those couple of times I kicked you and jumped out of bed, I was afraid that if I had a really bad nightmare I might accidentally shoot you before I woke up completely, so I didn't dare go to sleep."

"The whole truth, darlin'," Hellhound growled softly. "Why were ya havin' such bad nightmares an' fightin' to get outta bed?"

I copped an attitude, tilting my head and pressing my forefinger into my cheek while I did a breathless ditzy voice. "Well, jeepers creepers, I just don't know. It couldn't have been all the guys breaking into my house and trying to kill me, could it?"

Hellhound remained unmoved by my sarcasm. "Nope, you're right, darlin', it couldn'ta been that. 'Cause I know when ya wake up from those kinda nightmares, ya need a hug. Ya don't fight to get outta bed."

"What are you saying?" Kane rumbled ominously.

"I'm sayin' she's doin' her level best to pretend everythin's fine and make ya happy. Ya oughta be glad she loves ya enough to do that. An' ya oughta set her free, 'cause it's killin' her."

Kane and I both began to protest, but Hellhound snapped his penetrating gaze to Kane. "An' gettin' married ain't what ya really want right now, either. Is it?"

Kane stopped in mid-argument, his mouth hanging open. Then he shook his head as if trying to restart his brain and snapped, "Don't be ridiculous."

But his words lacked conviction. And he hadn't denied it.

I stared at him, my own jaw dropping. "John?" I asked softly. "I thought you said you wanted commitment. A wife and family."

"I do." His reply came too fast.

Hellhound growled, "Truth, Cap."

The muscles bunched in Kane's jaw. "I... just..." The words grated out between his teeth as if they were being extracted with pliers. "Didn't expect it... quite so soon."

Kane sprang up and came over to crouch beside my chair, taking my hand. "I do want that with you, Aydan. Never believe that I don't; I just..." He made a frustrated gesture. "I'm sorry. But when you said you were ready, how could I say I wasn't? After my big speech about commitment, and when you were so angry..." He gave me an imploring look. "I didn't want to hurt you. But why did you pretend it was what you wanted?"

It was my turn to stammer. "I, um... I just... You said that was what you wanted. And I was so worn down and so sick of hurting you and I know you're going through a horrible time right now, and..."

"*I'm going through a hard time?*" Kane gave me an incredulous glare. "You were going to base our marriage on *pity*?"

A whimper escaped me and Hellhound said, "Ease off, Cap. It ain't pity, it's love. An' if you're too much of a dumbfuck to see that, ya don't deserve her."

Kane eyed him for a moment. Then he drew a breath, the hard lines in his face softening as he turned back to me and took both my hands in his. "Arnie's right. As usual, but don't tell him I said that."

Hellhound snorted amusement.

Kane ignored him, raising my hands to his lips and kissing each knuckle in a way that felt like a solemn ritual. "Aydan, can we agree to release each other from our promises?"

I swallowed hard. "Wh... what does that really mean?"

"It means we go back to the way we were before. No expectations. You..." He hesitated, then squared his shoulders. "...you sleep with whomever you please. I'll do the same. And I won't bring up commitment until I'm ready for it. But, Aydan..." He caressed my cheek, avoiding the small painful nick from the glass. "Please don't lie to me like this again. I know your heart was in the right place, but if we end up together I want to know that you're with me because it's what you truly want. Not because you're feeling sorry for me or because you feel pressured into it."

"Okay... but you have to promise me the same." I hesitated, fighting an internal battle before blurting, "Were you really feeling as trapped as I was? Why didn't you just say something, for chrissake?"

"I..." His jaw muscles rippled again. "I'd have gotten used to it. With time."

"You..." My mouth opened and closed a couple of times, words failing me utterly. At last I managed a strangled,

"You'd get *used* to it?"

Kane gave me an apologetic grimace and half-shrug, and sudden frantic laughter seized me.

"Used to... it..." I choked between fits of hysterical giggles. "What, like an annoying rash?"

"Well..." Kane went completely deadpan. "I was pretty sure it would grow on me."

"Aaaagh!" I managed a single shriek of outrage at the pun before I lost it completely. Laughing helplessly, I smacked his shoulder while Hellhound guffawed.

Kane managed to hold his serious mien only a moment longer before he dissolved into laughter, too. He rocked backward to sit on the floor and we all laughed until we were limp and wiping away tears.

At last Kane sobered and drew a deep breath. Taking my hand again, he glanced at Hellhound before returning his attention to me. "Aydan, you and Arnie have... something special together. I want that kind of trust and honesty with you, but I know I haven't earned it." He gave me an intense look. "Yet. But I'll be working toward it with all I've got. In the meantime..."

He brushed his lips over my knuckles, then placed my hand in Hellhound's and turned to his lifelong best friend. "I'm going to keep watch outside just to make sure we don't get any more surprises. Will you please take my ex-fiancée to bed and hold her while she sleeps?" He gave me a long look. "I don't think she's quite ready for me to do that."

Blinking renewed moisture away from my eyes, I hauled myself to my feet and both men stood, too. Gently releasing Hellhound's hand, I linked my arms around Kane's neck.

"No, I'm not ready for that," I murmured. "Maybe I never will be. But now I know you'll let me go, and that...

helps." I kissed him softly. "You do know I love you, don't you? That part wasn't a lie."

"I know." Kane kissed me back, holding me as if I was made of eggshells. "I love you, too."

I touched his cheek. "I know."

We parted, smiling, and Hellhound rasped, "Now that's the kinda truth I wanted to hear. Come on, darlin', let's get ya to bed."

Kane headed for the door and Hellhound and I turned toward the bedroom, his arm warm around my shoulders.

Inside, he swung the door shut behind us and guided me toward the bed. Every exhausted cell of my body yearned toward it. Sleep. Sweet oblivion...

I pulled away from Hellhound's arm to face him.

"Arnie..." I hesitated, my pulse ticking up a notch. Did I really want to know? Or were some things better left alone?

"What, darlin'?" he asked.

I had to know. Otherwise his embrace would give me nightmares to rival the ones I'd had in Kane's bed.

Looking him square in the eyes, I said, "I need you to tell me the truth."

"I never lied to ya before, darlin', an' I ain't gonna start now. Ask me anythin' ya want."

"Did you... You said you hadn't slept with anybody but me since last fall. That sounds a lot like m-monogamy to me." I swallowed hard. "Commitment."

He flinched. "Shit, stop usin' dirty words! You're givin' me the cold sweats."

"The feeling's mutual," I agreed. "So explain."

"I told ya, darlin', I just been gettin' lazy about findin' new prospects." He shrugged. "I been busy so I ain't been jammin' much, an' ya know I ain't ever gonna get laid unless I sing chicks into my bed. They sure as hell ain't gonna do a guy like me otherwise."

When I made a small sound of protest he added, "Hell, darlin', ya know it's true. An' anyway, I get sick a' havin' to give 'em the 'no commitment' speech an' the 'no STD' speech, an' then wonderin' if they been lyin' to me about havin' herpes or HPV or HIV or some-fuckin'-thing. Condoms ain't a hundred-percent guarantee." He caressed my cheek. "An' Kane's right, I don't like feelin' like I might be riskin' your health as well as mine, and I was fuckin' tired of gettin' tested all the time."

"But..." I took a step backward, my pulse accelerating.

"But nothin', darlin', an' stop freakin' out. I told ya, that's just the way it's worked out lately. Some hot chick gives me a smile an' I'll be ballin' her so fast it'll make your head spin. Promise."

I chuckled in spite of my worry. "That'd be a first. I've never known you to ball fast. Slow and easy is more your style."

Hellhound leered. "Guess ya better do some more research." I laughed out loud, but he sobered and took my hand. "Aydan, I promise, ya got nothin' to worry about. I'll never want anythin' from ya 'cept what we got right now."

"So..." I hesitated. "If you hadn't known John and I were both ambivalent-"

My question was cut off by his snort. "Ambivalent?" he repeated incredulously. "Hell, darlin', try 'scared fuckin' shitless'."

"Okay, John was ambivalent; I was scared shitless," I agreed. "But if you hadn't known that..."

His face softened. "You're askin', would I have tried to

break the two a' ya up just to keep ya in my bed?"

I gave him an uncertain half-nod, half-shrug.

"Aydan, if I'd thought ya were both happy, I'd 'a been the one plannin' the party."

I looked into his eyes and saw it was the truth.

I sagged into his arms. "Thank you."

He planted a gentle whiskery kiss on my forehead. "You're welcome, darlin'. But now it's my turn to ask ya somethin'."

I couldn't help stiffening. "What is it?"

"Don't worry, I ain't gonna make any demands. I'm just askin'."

"Okay..." I studied his serious expression anxiously.

He caressed the hair away from cheek, looking down into my eyes. "Aydan, will ya think about talkin' to Doc Rawling?"

The tension fell away from my body and I couldn't prevent a breath of relief. "I'm already going to do that. Stemp told me I had to, but I didn't need any convincing."

"I ain't talkin' about post-mission stuff." Hellhound held me with his gaze. "I'm talkin' about your personal shit."

When I looked away, he added, "Now don't freak out. The doc ain't gonna make ya do anythin' ya don't wanna do. If ya really don't wanna be with anybody, he'll help ya feel okay about tellin' Kane that. An' if it turns out you're just avoidin' it 'cause you're scared, he can help ya with that, too. But I don't ever wanna see ya go through this shit again."

I let out a breath. "You're right. None of it had to happen, and it could have turned out..." Thinking of what my retreat to the alley might have cost, I shuddered. "...so badly."

Meeting Hellhound's eyes, I made a promise to myself as well as to him. "I'm not going to let my past rule me anymore. I'll get help. But not from Doctor Rawling. I'll find a psychologist who's not connected to work." I rested my forehead against his chest. "Thanks, Arnie. But you know I'm getting spoiled, knowing you'll always come to my rescue."

He chuckled. "That's a chance I'm willin' to take. Now come on over here."

My muscles already slackening with the glorious anticipation of sleep, I let him guide me to the bed. Through my yawns I soothed his concern over the welts and bruises on my body while he removed my clothes.

Then I was blessedly horizontal in the harbour of his arms. My mind drifted, casting off the moorings of consciousness as my last thoughts floated away into fluffy clouds of drowsiness.

Home...

Safe...

I slept.

Book 11 is available!

Visit my Books page at dianehenders.com/books for progress updates and announcements.

A Request

Thanks for reading!

If you enjoyed this book, I'd really appreciate it if you'd take a moment to review it online.

Here are some suggestions for the "star" ratings:
Five stars: Loved the book and can hardly wait for the next one.
Four stars: Liked the book and plan to read the next one.
Three stars: The book was okay. Might read the next one.
Two stars: Didn't like the book. Probably won't read the next one.
One star: Hated the book. Would never read another in the series.

You can help prospective readers by writing a few sentences about what you liked or disliked about the book.

Thanks for taking the time to do a review!

About Me

Before I started writing fiction, I had a checkered career: technical writer, computer geek, and interior designer. I'm good at two out of three of those. Fortunately, I had the sense to quit the one I sucked at (interior design).

When my mid-life crisis hit, I took up muay thai and started writing thrillers featuring a middle-aged female protagonist. ('Walter Mitty', you say? Nope, never heard of him.)

Writing and kicking the hell out of stuff seemed more productive than more typical mid-life-crisis activities like getting a divorce, buying a Harley Crossbones, and cruising across the country picking up men in sleazy bars; especially since it's winter most months of the year here in Canada.

It's much more comfortable to sit at my computer. And Harleys are expensive. Come to think of it, so are beer and gasoline.

Oh, and I still love my husband. There's that. So I stuck with the writing.

Diane Henders

And here's my "professional" bio, in case you need something more suitable for mixed company:

Diane Henders is the Kindle best-selling author of the NEVER SAY SPY series: Sexy thrillers packed with tension, laughs, profanity, and sometimes warm fuzzies.

The first book in the series, NEVER SAY SPY, has had over 450,000 downloads to date, and stayed on Kindle's 'Women Sleuths' Top 100 list for 60 consecutive months.

Diane enjoys target shooting, gardening, auto mechanics, painting (art, not walls), music, and martial arts; and loves food and drink almost as much as she loves her husband. They live in the wilds of British Columbia, Canada, where they get all the adrenaline rush they could ever want by growing fruit trees in bear country.

Want to know what else is roiling around in the cesspit of my mind? Drop by my blog and website at dianehenders.com, check out the extras, and don't forget to leave a comment in the guest book to say hi – I love hearing from you! Or you can connect with me on Facebook at:
https://www.facebook.com/authordianehenders.
See you there!